TWICE
THE
TROUBLE

TWICE
THE
TROUBLE

A NOVEL

ASH CLIFTON

CROOKED
LANE

NEW YORK

Copyright © 2024 by Ashley Clifton

Published in the United States by Crooked Lane Books, an imprint of The Quick Brown Fox & Company LLC.

Crooked Lane Books and its logo are trademarks of The Quick Brown Fox & Company LLC.

Library of Congress Catalog-in-Publication data available upon request.

ISBN (hardcover): 978-1-63910-697-4
ISBN (ebook): 978-1-63910-698-1

Cover design by Nebojsa Zoric

Printed in the United States.

www.crookedlanebooks.com

Crooked Lane Books
34 West 27th St., 10th Floor
New York, NY 10001

First Edition: March 2024

10 9 8 7 6 5 4 3 2 1

For Cathy

Let the lamp affix its beam.
The only emperor is the emperor of ice-cream.

—Wallace Stevens

CHAPTER

1

NOLAND DIDN'T KNOW the cop working the entrance to the courthouse that day, but the cop knew him. He could tell from the way the guy squinted at him, ruffling his pale brow in that manner of a person trying to put a name to a face. Noland wasn't nervous, but he wasn't happy either. Especially when the cop waved him over to the rubber mat beside the metal detector.

"Could you state your business, sir?" the cop asked, passing the electronic wand up and down Noland's sides.

"I'm meeting a client."

The cop gave him a different look. This one said: *You don't look like no lawyer.* He wasn't wrong. Noland didn't look like a lawyer. Rather, in his faded jeans and loose, linen shirt, two sizes too big, Noland looked like a defendant.

"I'm a private investigator," he added.

The cop nodded. He took Noland's JanSport off the conveyor belt and searched it, poking his fat fingers through each pocket. Now Noland was pissed. He could understand the cop pulling him aside, especially if the guy was having trouble placing him—an unsettling effect Noland often had on people, and one he was used to. But giving the pack the full CSI treatment? After it had just gone through the machine? That was uncalled for. Rude.

But the cop kept at it. Next he was palpating the seams of the pack with his fingers, looking for hidden weapons.

"There's nothing in there but some papers and a water bottle," Noland said.

The cop ignored him. Noland kept his cool. He was telling the truth about the pack. There was nothing untoward in it: not his lock rake, not his stiletto blade, and certainly not his gun.

And yet, after a few more moments of searching, the cop unzipped one of the little side pockets that Noland never used—the cell phone holder, with its little rubberized X for the earphone cord to snake through—and put his hand inside as far as it would go. When he pulled it out, his fingertips held a little red pocket knife. Noland caught his breath. It was the Swiss Army knife his father, Zeb, had given him for Christmas when he was ten years old.

Noland thought to himself: *How the fuck did that get in there?* But all he said was: "Wow."

The cop unfolded the knife and seemed to admire the tiny silver blade. He even touched it with his thumb.

"Nothing but paper, huh?"

"Come on, man," Noland said. "The blade is two inches long. Who am I gonna stab? Mickey Mouse?"

The cop didn't laugh, just sniffed and looked at the knife again.

"You can go put it in your car," the cop said.

"I'm parked eight blocks away. Can't I stow it behind the flowers or something? Get it when I come out?"

The cop shook his head. As he did so, Noland looked at the soft tissue beneath the man's jaw and above his Adam's apple. One *Fak Sau* strike to that location on his neck and the big man would go down like a dead mule. Noland's hand tingled at the thought of it.

And yet, even as he contemplated killing the cop, Noland found himself hoping that someone else in the line—some better, smarter, kinder citizen—would recognize him and call out "*Twice! Hey, you're Noland Twice!*" and jar the stupid cop's memory. He wished it because he knew the real reason for the cop's vague recollection of him. It came not from any recent encounter—not from his many visits to the courthouse as a P.I. over the past years, nor from his rarer visits as a sheriff's deputy in the years before that. No, the cop recognized him from his days playing football. That long-ago autumn when Noland, at nineteen, had played strong safety for the Gators and done some things on the field that people found amazing, at least for a while. So amazing that he'd been famous, briefly. Not movie-star famous, or even rich-guy famous, but famous enough to be remembered, thirteen years later by a bored cop with nothing better to do.

The cop waited. He had closed the knife but still held it between his thumb and forefinger. Noland knew there was only one way this could end that didn't result in death and/or incarceration. With one swift motion, he snatched the knife from the cop's hand and, before the man could react, tossed it into the garbage can behind the scanner, where it landed with a sharp, metallic pop.

"Are we good now?" Noland asked.

The cop narrowed his eyes.

Noland waited.

"Yeah," the cop said at last, and handed him the pack. He hadn't bothered to zip the flaps up.

Noland slung the JanSport over his shoulder and walked off toward Courtroom C.

As expected, it was nearly empty, with just a few principals at the front. Faith stood at the defendant's table, dressed in her usual sleek business suit. Her client sat beside her, perched on the straight-backed chair, too small for him, a big, blond man in a much nicer suit. Across the aisle, Assistant State Attorney Sydney Cross sat at his table, tapping on a MacBook, his chestnut brown hair sculpted up into a perfect, postmodern ducktail. And above all of them, looming on the bench like a bald Moses, was Judge Matthew R.

Abercrombie. The judge must have been having as bad a day as Noland because he looked pissed too.

"Are you serious?" he boomed, addressing Faith. Of course. Only Faith could inspire such biblical wrath. He punctuated his next question by jabbing a finger into the smooth pine surface of the bench. "You really have the nerve to ask for two more weeks, Miss Carlton?"

Faith didn't flinch. "I don't know about my nerve, Your Honor. But yes, I am asking for two more weeks. We have another witness to depose. Mr. Valkenburg."

The judge's eyebrows climbed his forehead like enraged caterpillars, fighting each other. "Yes, yes. Valkenburg." He bit his lower lip. "Gone missing, has he? A month ago?"

"That's true, Judge. We've been unsuccessful in locating him."

"Well, what makes you think you'll have any more success in the next two weeks?"

"We have added some resources," Faith said.

"Oh, well, that changes everything," he sneered.

Noland sneaked into the back row of the gallery and sat down, keeping his eye on the judge. He knew exactly what Abercrombie was thinking at that moment because he, Noland, had thought the same thing himself many times. Namely, that Faith, at five foot two and one hundred and six pounds, was too slight and delicate to be such a colossal pain in the ass. Even her good looks were of a disconcerting type—not beautiful, exactly, with her pointy cheekbones and slit of a mouth, but striking, especially her eyes, which shone a clear blue even in the harsh, artificial light of Courtroom C. To Abercrombie, she must have stood out a mile from the sea of bland faces he confronted each day, the drab government men and women who found themselves before his bench, cowed by his reputation. Faith wasn't cowed. She might look like a flamingo, but she was really an alligator.

Abercrombie shook his head. He seemed about to scoff. But then, by chance, he raised his eyes to the gallery. He spotted Noland for the first time, squinted, and smiled.

"Good Lord. Is that you, Nole?"

Noland stood up. He felt all eyes wheel toward him.

"It is, Your Honor."

Abercrombie nodded portentously and looked back at Faith.

"I see your point, Miss Carlton. Your *additional resources* are noted." He cocked a bulging eye at Sydney. "Any objection to another two weeks, Mr. Cross?"

Without looking up from his laptop, Sydney shook his head. Noland smiled. A cold fish, that Sydney. But smart. Knew how to pick his battles. The judge conferred with the clerk to set a new court date. As he did so, Noland took a long look at Faith's client, whose disinterested expression hadn't changed. Bisby—that was the name she'd mentioned in the email. Frank Bisby. CEO of Selberis Constructors, one of the biggest firms in the state. Even from across the courtroom, Noland was impressed by the force field of entitlement that emanated from the man. Slumped forward in the chair, he looked not only bored but annoyed. His hands rested lightly on the table, occupying the one narrow patch of surface not covered with the flotsam of Faith's legal briefs. If Sydney Cross was a cold fish, then Bisby was a block of ice.

"All right, Miss Carlton," the judge intoned at last. A disgusted grin spread across his face, even as his tongue lodged itself in his cheek like a vicious little mole, gone to ground. "You have your two weeks. Discovery will commence on Monday, the twenty-seventh of June."

With that, he gaveled the hearing to an end. Everyone rose as he was cried out by his favorite bailiff, Bruce Sutherland, a wiry, freckle-faced ex-deputy whose sole claim to fame was having once broken the shaft of his nightstick across the skull of an accused wife beater. At the last moment, Abercrombie glanced out over the gallery and called to Noland again.

"How's your mama?"

"Still minding the hip, Your Honor."

"Well, give her my best." Then he pointed a thick finger at Noland. "And you stay the hell out of trouble, Nole. I don't want to see you in the dock again."

"Yes, sir."

Bruce the bailiff followed the judge through the big oak door, and when it closed the room felt suddenly empty. Noland walked to the front just as Sydney Cross folded up the MacBook. He smiled. "Back on the job, Nole?"

Noland tilted his head at Faith. "Ask her."

Sydney chuckled and shook his head in sympathy, as if he knew something that Noland didn't. Faith was gathering her briefs as Bisby leaned over and whispered something in her ear. He had one of those broad, bland, Protestant faces that were a prerequisite to doing business in that part of the South, a good-old-boy businessman, handsome but not overly so, aging well in the way prosperous men do. Noland wondered what he had done to get himself here, in Courtroom C, facing a criminal trial and maybe a prison sentence. Whatever it was, the man's apparent indifference could only mean one of two things: he was either a hopeless fool or an ice-cold sociopath.

Faith nodded as Bisby finished his whispering. Then the man rose and strode down the aisle. As he passed, his clear, gray eyes fixed on Noland for a fraction of a second, then moved on. Noland's nostrils itched—Bisby had left an acrid, biting odor of cologne in his wake, one of those top-shelf, citrusy brands that came in crystal bottles thick as cobblestones, two hundred dollars apiece. Noland watched as Bisby left the courtroom, swinging his arms easily, free from any burdens.

"Hey," he said to Faith. "Why am I here?"

"I wanted you to see him. What did you think?"

"He's an asshole."

She gathered the rest of her papers and stuffed them into her fat, satchel-style briefcase. Only then did she allow herself a moment of repose, running a fingertip from her temple to the back of her ear, restoring a tendril of ash-blond hair that had pulled loose from the tight bun she wore high on the back of her head, school-marm style. She regarded Noland with her gimlet eyes. "Want lunch?"

"On the firm?"

"Naturally."

They left the courthouse and walked toward Lake Eola as the first rays of afternoon sun began skating off the choppy water with a hard, silvery glint. The air was hot and he regretted wearing the white linen shirt, already damp and cleaving to his torso, revealing the massive chest and shoulder muscles that he normally kept hidden under loose clothes. His muscles were his first and best tool, and he kept them big and powerful. But they also made him stand out. He felt a little self-conscious as she led him into Nino's, a pizza joint that did a good business in courthouse staffers and juries. They took a booth near the front and looked out the window.

"What's the gig?" he said. "Another tax thing?"

She stirred her glass of iced tea with her straw. Clearly, she wasn't ready to fill him in yet, and in the pause that followed Noland studied her. She looked even thinner than usual, and her skin—ordinarily the color of fresh milk—was almost translucent. If someone were to place a strong light behind her, it would shine through like an X-ray, revealing her slender, exquisite bones.

"You look like shit," he said. "What you been eating? Carrots and water?"

She moved her shoulders up and down.

"Still running every morning?"

Again, she didn't answer. After a long while, she took a breath and leaned forward, clearly not wanting to think about the matter at hand, but having no choice.

"We need to lay our hands on a guy," she said.

"No shit."

She glared at him. "Bisby's partner."

"The dude that Mutt was bitching about? Valkenstein?"

"Valken*burg*. Arthur."

"Sounds like an Ivy League jerk-off."

Her eyes hardened. "So? Noland Twice sounds like a working-class jerk-off. What kind of name is Twice, anyway?"

"Dutch. But never mind. When did this Valkenburg fade?"

"Two days before the charges against Bisby came down. And he didn't just fade. He stole. Embezzled."

Noland sucked his teeth. "How much?"

"Cleaned out Selberis's offshore account."

"You didn't answer my question."

"That's the only answer you're gonna get."

He decided to fall back. "How do you know he stole it?"

"The others say so."

"What others?"

"The other partners. Of the firm."

"Have they told the cops?"

She blinked at him.

Noland's skin turned cold. The air conditioning vent had been blowing down on him all this time, and his skin felt clammy. A voice in his head asked: *How did you end up here?* But of course, he knew the answer to that, as he knew the meaning of Faith's silence now.

"The usual complications?" he asked.

She nodded. "The usual complications."

He sighed. His optimism from earlier in the morning had evaporated and been replaced by a vague, unfocused dread. So this was how it was going to be. A black op. Of course, he had no right to be surprised; much of his work was dark. That was why Faith hired him instead of one of the big, generic P.I. firms. He was used to taking extraordinary—and often illegal—measures to unfuck a client's case. But even so, he didn't like to rush into things. He had already been to prison once, and he was never going back.

"I'm assuming we have to keep the cops completely out of the picture?"

"Completely," she said. "And if we do our job properly, that won't be a problem. Correct?"

"Oh, sure." He blew a raspberry in disgust. "Don't suppose you have any idea where Mr. Valkenburg lit off to?"

"We know he likes to hike on the Appalachian Trail."

Noland laughed. "Wonderful. And what if he's still on it, somewhere?"

She opened her hands over the Formica tabletop. Her way of saying: *Your problem.*

Their food came. He had ordered a small pizza. Faith got a salad. Noland had skipped breakfast, and he took a greedy bite of his first slice, which was nuclear hot, searing the roof of his mouth. He gulped some ice water and thought: *What a lunk.* He had just turned thirty-two a week before, and yet he couldn't get through a meal with a woman—not even Faith—without acting like a buffoon. As he swished the water around his mouth, the number echoed in his head. *Thirty-two.* Thirteen autumns since he'd played his last quarter. He took some solace in the knowledge that, in those thirteen years, he had lived the equivalent of several lifetimes. His agonizing months in P.T. His years as a deputy. His arrest and brief stint in Raiford. And now, his new life as a P.I. Even so, he sometimes wanted to weep at the thought of it—the gulf of time that had opened up between himself and that long-ago boy on that long-ago field, reveling in the cheers: *Twice! Twice! Twice!* How could he not feel old? His life had peaked at nineteen.

"Where should I start?" he asked.

Fortunately, the question did not annoy her. "I did some preliminary snooping. Went by his apartment. The landlady says he's paid up three months in advance."

"Does he have a girlfriend?"

"Not that we know of. But he has an ex-wife. She lives in town. Does that help?"

"It might." He ran the tip of his tongue across the roof of his mouth. It felt numb, like wax. "Okay. Let's say I find him. Then what?"

She gave him a baleful look, even harder than before.

"We need the money back, obviously. That's priority one."

"I thought *he* was priority one. Don't you need his testimony?"

She took a sip of her tea.

Noland felt his face sag. Another veil of her deception had been lifted. He understood, at last, that his role in this case would lie not so much in finding Valkenburg himself as in recovering whatever items—cash, presumably—Valkenburg had taken with him. As he realized this, Noland felt a little bit frightened. Sad too, not so much for himself as for Faith, without really knowing why. He had known the truth about Faith, and the kinds of things she had to do, for a long time now. Ever since their first case, when she had sent him to find the runaway daughter of a wealthy doctor named Edwards. Edwards turned out to be a pill doctor, and the "daughter" turned out to be his mistress, who had stolen 15,000 oxyco-done tablets from his personal stash. So, yeah, Noland knew what Faith was about, the breed of clients she took. Still, he felt sad.

"What's my pretext?"

"You're trying to serve him. I've got the subpoena."

She dug around in her briefcase. It was an old, butter-col-ored leather case, heavily creased but still shiny. It must have been very expensive once—a graduation present, lovingly chosen by her mom or dad or some other proud relation. But her years as a public defender had left innumerable marks in the leather, every DUI a fold, every coke dealer a wrinkle. Of course, as the junior partner of Reynolds, Adams, and Scruggs, she was making some serious jing now. She could ditch the old case just as she had the rest of her old life, and replace it with something appropriately sexy and laser sharp, Prada or Donna Karan. But she hadn't, and Noland liked that she hadn't.

"Here it is." She produced a thin manila envelope bearing the state seal. She set it on the table between them. Noland hesitated. The top of the envelope read VALKENBURG ARTHUR M.

At that moment, an unexpected but seductive thought flashed into his mind: *Walk away.* His two years in Raiford had made him a believer in premonitions, and he was getting a big one now. This Valkenburg dude was trouble. Noland should pass on him, the whole case. He imagined himself standing up and leaving the restaurant, emerging into the bright sunlight beyond.

Faith watched him. "My firm will pay you twenty-five K if you recover the assets. And the usual per diem, of course."

"I love it when you talk Latin. Makes me wish I'd met you in law school."

She rolled her eyes. Then she got out a company checkbook, wrote out a check, and set it on top of the subpoena. "Here's a five K advance."

He stared at the check. If it had come six months earlier, when he'd been flush, he could've turned it down easily. But once again fate had conspired against him. His last big case, which had involved digging up dirt for a lawsuit, ended badly. The client had ended up suing Noland instead, and Noland had settled with him for ten K. Then Noland's mom had needed a hip replacement, and her cut-rate insurance wouldn't cover the operation unless she used some quack in the sticks. So Noland paid for a surgeon in Orlando. Another twenty K gone. He hadn't paid his mortgage in two months. His property tax was overdue. As things stood, he would probably have to declare bankruptcy in the next month, losing both his house and his business.

So, yeah, he needed the work. Bad.

And yet he continued staring at the check. "I dunno."

She clenched her jaw. "What?"

"I'm getting a bad vibe."

"You *are* a bad vibe. That's why we pay you."

"No, I'm serious."

Instead of replying, she reached back into the briefcase and came up with a glossy 5×7 photograph. She placed it on top of the check and the subpoena, the stack of papers growing rather thick now. Noland reached out and took the photo. It was a shot of two men wading into a river whose dark surface was ruffled with whitecaps. Each man held a fishing rod cocked at the same angle over the water. The first man was Bisby, dressed in some dorky, Eddie Bauer gear, but totally recognizable, his grin unexpectedly real, involving both his eyes and his mouth, as if he had just won the lottery. The other man was a stranger. While Bisby had seemed to embrace the camera, this other guy seemed to turn instinctively from it, his broad, flat face reflecting the sunlight like a sheet of metal. A brutish face, really, but good-looking in a coarse, Eastern European kind of way. Back at Raiford, Noland had befriended a trio of Serbs doing a nickel each for aggravated assault. This guy looked like them: pale skin, black hair, black eyes. The hair was wet and combed straight back from his thick forehead, which gave him a look of cultivated dissipation.

"He's younger than I expected," Noland said.

"Not so young. Late forties."

Noland held the photo in his hands. As he looked at the two men, standing in the fast water, smiling, some vast, tectonic plate in his mind slid silently into place. Valkenburg was a smug son of a bitch. It would be fun to catch him. Running down rich guys like him was what Noland liked most about his job.

"Okay, I'll find him."

"And the money?"

"And the money."

She took another sip of tea. He stood and gathered the pile, shoving it all into the backpack. The top of his mouth was starting to throb from the pizza burn.

"I'll email you," she said. "Everything we know about him."

"Start with the ex-wife."

"I can tell you that now. Her name's Cassandra Raines. Couldn't be too many of those in Orange County."

"Yeah, that's a hit."

There was nothing more to say, but he found himself frozen. Once again, he heard it, the little voice inside his head, saying: *Don't do it.* The voice was very faint now, almost lost in the jet-engine roar of the blood coursing through his temples. But it was there, insistent, even in its dying moments. Faith seemed to hear it, too, giving him a sudden concerned look. For a moment, he thought she might give him some last word of encouragement, some final assurance that the case would work out. He had never failed her before, after all. He had this.

"Noland," she said.

"Yeah?"

"Don't fuck this up. Okay?"

"Sure."

He slung the pack over his shoulder and left.

2

WHEN HE GOT home, his pit bulls, Quick and Silver, went berserk, mauling him with their huge paws. The mauling hurt, of course, but not nearly as bad as the pang of guilt Noland felt. Even before Deirdre had moved out, the dogs had been left alone too often, sometimes for days. But there was nothing he could do—it was the very strangeness of his work that necessitated the dogs in the first place. Each time he came home, he knew with absolute certainty that no one had entered. Otherwise, someone—either the intruder or the dogs or perhaps all three—would be dead on the floor.

He fed them and took them for a long walk, still feeling guilty. Not only was he a shitty dog owner, he was a shitty son, too. He hadn't called his mom in over two weeks, and hadn't visited Zeb in almost two months. Of these two filial lapses, his neglect of his mother was far less forgivable, considering all he had to do was pick up the phone, while visiting Zeb at Hanford Correctional, fifty miles away, involved a much greater effort. Still, they were both sins, of a sort. Two more overdue bills.

When he got back to the house, he shooed the dogs into the big fenced yard, where they knew better than to bother him again. Finally, unable to put off work any longer, he sat down with his laptop and ran a credit check on Valkenburg. It showed the same address Faith had given him, in Longwood, where he had apparently lived for two years, with no recent suspicious debts or other activity. A cursory web search came up empty, too. Valkenburg had no online presence, no blogs or Facebook pages or tweets. Noland was unsurprised. He was obviously smart, and smart crooks hated social media.

Noland closed the laptop. It didn't matter that he'd come up empty. He would find Valkenburg. It would just take a bit longer.

The first order of business was to fuel up the van, which meant a trip to his favorite gas station, a mom-and-pop place called Beaumont's. Tucked between two giant oak trees a mile off I-4, Beaumont's was always fifty cents pricier than anywhere else in Orange County, which made Noland wonder how the old man stayed in business. Maybe there were enough odd people like himself who dug the vibe of the place, with the previous set of antique gas pumps still standing off to the side, and the vintage Coca-Cola signs nailed to the walls. But there were other reasons to visit Beaumont's. For one thing, the old man knew everybody in central Florida, and he remembered everything. In many ways, he was better than Google.

Noland pulled up to the first empty pump, grabbed the nozzle, and pushed the PREMIUM button. He always got premium, his way of pampering the van, honoring it, the way a hunter will honor his favorite bow. The van looked like a plumber's van because it was—Noland had bought it off a retiree in Deland who had run his residential plumbing business out of it for decades. Years of daily use had given it a grungy, weathered look, with its battered sides, dented bumpers, and flecks of rust metastasizing out from the wheel wells. But that was all a sham. Noland had cleaned up the chassis and dropped in a new, fuel-injected V8 hemi under the hood. It could do a hundred and five in a pinch.

Noland didn't just honor the van; he loved it. It was a lot like himself, after all—bulky, squat, nondescript. Even in college, he hadn't been much to look at. Yes, he'd had muscles—he once bench-pressed 300 pounds for fifteen reps, to the amazement of his jock friends—but he hid them most of the time, and to most people he just looked stocky. And slow. With a build like his, people figured he had to be slow, lumbering. But like the van, he had a secret—he was *fast*. Very fast, when he needed to be. That was how he surprised so many guys on the football field. Those fleet-footed wide receivers, pigeon-toed former track stars who nailed the 40 in under five seconds. They always underestimated him. That was the special thing about him—the impossible, almost magical thing. He was five foot nine, two hundred and five pounds, and his official 40-meter split never dipped below 4.8. And yet he could catch people, even very fast people. People more talented than he was, more gifted in almost every way except that one, obscure ability—the talent for running people down.

It wasn't just something he did on the field. During his years as a cop, he had one of the best arrest records in the state. His record was so good, in fact, that he began to seriously encroach on the income of the local meth distributor, a vicious old redneck who was (Noland learned later) the sheriff's half-brother. One night, the FDLE raided Noland's home, found a half-kilo bag of powdered amphetamine under his couch, and he went straight to jail, then prison. It was not until two years later, when a new governor was elected and had the case reopened, that Noland was exonerated. The only trade-off was that Noland's father Zeb had to plead guilty to something the state attorney had him down for (legitimately, this time), and he took a four-year fall. Because of that deal, Noland got his record expunged and was able to begin a new life as a private investigator, where he could use his superpowers for profit at last.

As the gas pump chugged, he took out his phone and scrolled through the email that Faith had sent after lunch. It contained all the intel she had on Valkenburg, which wasn't much. Besides the usual stats, there were another dozen photos of him, mostly with Bisby. They must have been tight, those two. Yin and yang. Partners in crime, literally. One showed a plaid-shirted Valkenburg holding a shovel filled with yellow Florida clay. He smiled broadly—the way a crook will after he's pulled off a big score—and a bright cloth banner behind him read: EDWIN MORRIS ACUTE CARE CENTER. Noland knew the place. He had gone there to get his arm stitched up after a biker knocked him through a window. He was surprised to see Valkenburg in that context, the proud community developer, preserving the health of injured Orlandoans. As he stared at the image, Noland got a distinctly different sort of vibe than the one he'd gotten off Bisby. If Bisby was the squeaky-clean incarnation of WASP respectability, Valkenburg looked a little more down and dirty (literally, the forearms of his shirt flecked with clay). He looked like a thug who'd hit the Big Time. Become respectable. Gone legit.

Only one picture showed him with a woman, a thirty-something sylph with red hair that shone in the sun like strands of copper. Valkenburg was grinning, as usual, with his arm around the woman's waist. Cassandra Raines? No. She gripped him too closely, a look of admiration on her face. Not a wife. A girlfriend. Noland made a mental note to figure out who she was.

The pump handle went slack, and Noland walked into the station. As always, Beaumont was perched in a white wicker chair behind the register, his leathery face reflected in the glass countertop, with the rolls of purple and orange lottery tickets glittering beneath like Japanese candy. Noland dropped three twenties on the glass, then set his phone down next to them, screen up. Beaumont glanced at the screen for a tenth of a second before picking up the bills.

"Seen him around," he said. "Got a boat. Sailboat. Thirty-foot Dymon. Nice."

"For real?" Noland tried to sound impressed, but he wasn't. Valkenburg seemed the type to have a sailboat. Probably an airplane, too. "Where does he put in?"

"Not sure." He handed Noland a receipt and his change. "I think he mentioned Lake Louise. Try Ben's shop. He goes there."

"Thanks." Noland left a ten on the counter.

"You after him, Nole?"

"Could be."

Back in the van, he slipped the receipt into a green plastic accordion file that he kept under the seat. As he shoved it back into place, his knuckles grazed the rubberized butt of the Ruger he kept down there too, secured to the floor with a metal clamp. A snub-nosed, blued-metal .357, it was the perfect gun for his style of work, and he seldom left home without it. He'd paid dearly for the permits—one for the gun itself and another for concealed carry—and most days the Ruger would travel frequently between Noland's behind-the-back waist holster and its clamp under the seat. He hoped he wouldn't need the gun on this gig, but the momentary feel of its butt—its clean, dry solidity, ready for use—soothed him nonetheless.

He hit I-4 just as rush hour was starting but managed to reach the Maitland interchange before traffic locked up. He got off at the Longwood exit and drove ten minutes before he found the apartment building, an antique from the 1950s, with Spanish tile and lime-colored stucco. It was laid out in a U around a tiny little courtyard, and a deck ran along the inside of the second floor, which the residents had crowded with plants, bicycles, and barbecue grills, all shoved up against the balustrade.

Valkenburg's apartment was on the second floor at the far end of the U. Unlike the others, his doorway was bare. Noland knocked and waited. When he was certain no one was coming, he tried the knob. Locked. He touched the lock with his forefinger. Shelby. One-inch deadbolt. Piece

of shit. He could pop it in three minutes. Night was falling, but it was too early to jack the door, so he drove north
to a bar he liked in Longwood. It was called Benny's and
it served good fare: lean burgers and french fries cooked in
peanut oil. The waitresses were UCF grad students, nice-
looking and smart.

He sat at the bar and sipped a beer as Ole Miss pounded
the crap out of Vanderbilt on the big TV. For the past ten
years, he'd made a point of avoiding football, but if a game
was playing on the TV, he couldn't help but watch. Even over
a tinny, five-dollar speaker, the roar of the crowd still went
right into him, making a beeline to his heart. Inevitably, he
would find himself transported back to that last season when
his feet had seemed to spring off the coiled grass, and that
tripping, lethal sense had risen in his blood each time he
crouched back from the line of scrimmage, waiting for the
center to snap the ball. When? *When? NOW!* Then streak-
ing downfield after the wide receiver, thirty yards, forty. The
guy looking over his shoulder and Noland catching that light
in his eyes, the beam that was welded to the ball spiraling
through the air above them behind Noland's back. Somehow, Noland knew the exact instant when he should raise his
arm to swat the ball away, almost as if he could see it through
the receiver's own eyes, a kind of telepathy, as real to him as
his own breath, maybe even more so. And then the ball dropping onto the turf and the crowd chanting his name: *Twice,
Twice, Twice.*

"Who's winning?" a voice asked.

Startled, he glanced left. A woman had taken the stool
at the corner of the bar. His eyes met hers for an instant, but
she was already turning back to the hardback book she had
open on the countertop.

"Ole Miss," he said.

"You looked a million miles away. I bet you went to
Vanderbilt."

He smiled. "Maybe I went to Ole Miss."

She shook her head. "You said Ole Miss is winning. You'd look happy."

"I don't look happy?"

"No."

"How do I look, then? Sad?"

"Intense."

He laughed. As she pretended to read her book, he studied her face. Even in the dim light of the bar, the tiny wrinkles on her forehead and gathering at the corners of her mouth made faint shadows on her otherwise smooth, olive skin. The perfect symmetry of her high cheekbones suggested an improbable gene pool; both of her parents must have been very good looking.

"What are you reading?" he asked.

"A mystery."

"Any good?"

"Not yet. But I'm giving it some time."

She ran a finger around her ear. Despite her age, she had pulled her straight brown hair into two girlish ponytails that hung from her temples down either side of her head. She wasn't trying to look young, Noland thought. More of a habit. She'd probably worn it that way all her life. Simple.

"Can I buy you a drink?" he asked.

She lifted her glass. "Got one."

"How about a car?"

She looked up at last and regarded him with steady brown eyes. The way she stared at him, half surprised and half amused, let him know that she hadn't expected him to respond to her initial overture—the abortive, catch-and-release maneuver she had performed so expertly—with such good humor. Behind her eyes, the wheels were turning, and he could read her thoughts: *This lunk is a lot smarter than average.* Now she had a decision to make.

She finished her drink. "Sorry, I've got to go."

"Could I ask your name, at least?"

She smiled and slipped the book into a big purse that had been resting on an empty stool next to her. She didn't look back as she slung the purse over her shoulder and walked out.

After she was gone, Noland turned back to the TV, enjoying the afterglow of flirtation in his blood, which couldn't quite offset the hard pit of humiliation in his stomach. He had crashed and burned. Again.

He glanced at his watch. Still too early. He paid his tab and drove back down Maitland Boulevard, parking on the edge of the Sable Point Golf Course. A soft breeze blew in through the open window as twilight faded into night, stars wheeling over the empty course. He resisted the urge to call Deirdre. Early evening was when he missed her the most. That was the time she had usually come home from the V.A., moving with the weary, dogged slowness of a woman who'd been on her feet for twelve hours. Every night was the same ritual: she'd walk into the living room, kick her shoes into the corner, and peel off her scrubs. For a moment, she'd be naked except for her panties (often some bright color; his favorites were the deep yellow ones, like jasmine blossoms) until she slipped on one of the big, rock-concert T-shirts that her ex-boyfriend had given to her. Then she'd collapse on the too-small couch, made smaller by the presence of one of the dogs, or both, under her ankles.

Deirdre lived in Miami now, with her new boyfriend, a male nurse named Greg. She had begun fooling around with Greg the previous winter, but Noland had pretended not to notice. Even so, when she finally told him that she was leaving, the pain was worse than he expected. He hadn't loved Deirdre, exactly, but he sure as hell liked her. Liked the way she could crack a joke, or take an insult from one of the other E.R. staff and hurl it right back at them with a twist. He'd even liked the weird stuff about her—her pathological fear of grasshoppers, her deep loathing of mayonnaise, and her ability to break anything mechanical in a matter of minutes.

Noland couldn't blame her for leaving. As she had put it, his life was "unstable," and how could he argue with that? Still, he had toyed with the idea of paying Kiril to drive to Miami and kick the living shit out of Greg. Frugality had stopped him—Kiril wasn't cheap—and also a bit of lingering guilt. He was, indeed, "unstable," on so many levels, and not merely because of his work. Deirdre had put up with a lot of crap, much more than a woman with brains and good looks should. Still, he wished she hadn't left. Her absence left him not only lonely but a bit frightened. There was always a small but non-zero possibility that he wouldn't come home from one of his late-night missions. And the idea that morning would dawn over his empty house, with no one to miss him except Quick and Silver, filled him with dread.

Even now, sitting in the van, he was a little nervous. B&E is always a risky proposition, and he wanted to get it over with. But he forced himself to wait until after ten o'clock before cranking the engine and starting off.

He drove back to Valkenburg's place and parked across the street. The building was quiet, all the windows dark. Where was everybody? Out on the town? Dinner and drinks with like-minded yuppies? There was no time to speculate. Noland slipped on his gloves and stepped out. His eyes had already adjusted to the dark, and he didn't need a flashlight as he opened the back and got out his toolbox. Like the van, the toolbox was battered and well worn, pocked with rust. No one would guess that it contained some of the most delicate tools one could find outside of a hospital. Most were illegal, and he was careful that none bore his fingerprints. At the first sign of trouble, he could ditch the box and run away. This had actually happened on three occasions, and each time he had been lucky enough not only to evade the police but to recover the box. He hoped a similar dash wouldn't be necessary tonight.

The weight of the box registered comfortably on his shoulder as he carried it across the street and up the stairs of the apartment building. The walkway on the second floor

was dark too, and Valkenburg's door was cloaked in shadow. Noland set the toolbox down on the deck, opened it, and put on his headband flashlight. He then got out his tension wrench and tumbler rake. The rake was more valuable than everything else in the toolbox combined. He had machined it himself from a strip of titanium, honing it until it was blade-thin, and yet very stiff and strong. After years of practice, he used it with a high level of skill, able to crack almost any lock in the city. Of course, he would never be as good as Zeb. Long before Zeb had become chief deputy sheriff of Maynard County, he had been a professional locksmith, and he'd found that the skill transferred nicely into law enforcement. Noland felt the same way. He'd improved his skills dramatically since becoming a P.I. Not as good as Zeb, but good.

He knelt and inserted the wrench into the Shelby, then the rake. With an efficient but unhurried motion, he began to scrub the tumblers one by one. There were six tumblers in a standard Shelby lock, and it took him less than a minute to find the first five, wedging each one against the plug with increasing tension on the wrench. The sixth one was a bitch, though, and he had to concentrate to keep from getting flustered. *Don't get pissed off at a piece of metal*, Zeb had told him, over and over. If you get flustered, your hands will shake, and then the wrench will slip and the tumblers will fall back into place, and you'll have to start the whole damn process over again.

Noland didn't get flustered. He kept searching, the rake an extension of his hand, and after another minute the sixth tumbler clicked free. He twisted the wrench and the deadbolt slid home. Bingo.

Still kneeling, he turned the knob and pushed the door open with his fingertips. Then he waited. *The most danger-ous part of a B&E is when you step in*, Zeb had told him, over and over. *You never know what'll be waiting for you inside in the dark.*

Noland breathed in and out, slow and easy, keeping still. He listened to the void of the apartment, his heart

trip-hammering as he imagined the sound of footsteps rushing toward him. But no one came. After a full minute, he
placed the tools back into the box and closed the lid. He
stood and carried the box inside, closing the door behind.

The apartment was quiet. He could feel its emptiness like
a widow's bed. He switched off his headband and switched to
the EagleTac, sweeping its powerful little beam around the
room. The décor of the apartment was not what he expected.
Spartan. Just a few sticks of furniture and a couple of cheap
art prints on the walls. Even more surprising, it was clean.
No clutter. No dirty plates lying around. No beer bottles or
cigarette butts. The only bit of disorder was at the big bookshelf by the TV, where all the books had been pulled down
and thrown on the floor in an apparent fit of rage.

Noland looked at the pile of books for a moment, then
moved on.

A small desk stood in the corner of the living room.
Noland searched it and found nothing—no laptop, no papers
in the drawers. He emptied the trash can and found a few
shopping receipts, which he pocketed. Then, stepping into
the bedroom, he shone the EagleTac on the neatly made dou-
ble bed. Right beside the door was a bureau, and he rifled
through it, turning each drawer over and dumping the contents on the floor. Nothing. Finally, he spotted a nightstand
on the other side of the bed and walked around to it, shining
the EagleTac before him.

That's when he saw the body.

It was merely a shape at first, sprawled out on the floor.
Noland must have stopped breathing for a moment, because
when he finally inhaled, his nose caught the metallic scent
of human blood, and then, far below that, the reek of cit-
rus. It was the same cologne he'd smelled in the courthouse
that morning. With his heart pounding, Noland centered
the EagleTac's beam on the dead man's face. It was Bisby all
right, his mouth hanging open in what might have been a
look of beatific awe, if not for the eyes, which had rolled back

into his skull so that they looked white, like a shark's, with only a quarter-moon of gray iris still revealed. The carpet around him was black, an inky stain spreading out into a shape that suggested some landlocked nation on an old map.

As Noland played the EagleTac's beam over Bisby's corpse, he saw that the man had been caught off guard, his corpse left in that undignified posture of total surprise, seated on the floor with his back slumped against the wall between the nightstand and the window, his legs stretched out in a ridiculous V. On both legs, his pant cuffs were bunched at the ankles so that a stripe of pale flesh shone out.

Noland's heart knocked against the sides of his ribcage like a motor that's blown its mount. He had an overpowering urge simply to run out of the apartment, putting as much distance between himself and the corpse as possible. It was only the sound of Zeb's voice in his head that calmed him: *Whatever you see, don't lose your cool. Remember: you're just visiting.*

Noland took a breath and got down close to the body, careful not to kneel in the blood. The flashlight glinted off satin—Bisby was wearing a tuxedo, sleek and expensive looking. Noland reached down and lifted the left breast. On the white shirt beneath, a slow river of ink ran down his chest and over the starched hill of his belly.

One shot, Noland thought.

He took off a glove and pressed his fingers into Bisby's neck. Still warm. And soft, like clay.

He straightened, grabbed his toolbox, and left the apartment.

Thirty seconds later, he was back in the van, heading down I-4. He drove to an all-night diner near College Park and avoided the waitress's eyes as he ordered coffee. Then he sat in the booth, waiting for his nerves to settle. A few minutes went by. He furtively looked under the table and studied the bottoms of his shoes. Clean. No blood.

Satisfied, he got out his cell phone and called Faith.

3

"WHAT THE FUCK do you mean he's dead?"

Her voice was high-pitched, shrill, hurting his ear. Even though it was after midnight, she sounded wide awake. "Are you sure? I mean, we were just in court."

Noland laughed. "You're right. I probably misidentified the guy on the floor of Valkenburg's apartment, even though he looks just like your client. But dead."

"Fuck you, Noland."

"Fuck you too, Faith."

She sighed. "Does anyone else know?"

"I don't think so."

A long pause ensued. Noland could picture her, sitting up in bed, biting her lower lip the way she did when confronted with a thorny problem. Normally, she would come up with a good solution, but this particular problem was different. Outside her wheelhouse. Noland decided that, for once, he would have to do the thinking.

"Let me make a few observations," he said. "Your defendant was Bisby, but your real client is the firm. Right?"

More silence.

"What are they called again?"

"Selberis," she said, at last. "Selberis Constructors."

"Right. Selberis. Bisby was named in the fraud indict-ment, but no one else. Why was that?"

"The firm wasn't directly involved. He was doing con-tract work on the side."

"But Selberis was paying his bills?"

"Yeah."

"Okay. So that means that they—his partners, I mean—didn't want to see him go under. They bankrolled his defense, either because they liked him, or because they didn't want to follow him into the dock. Either way, they had to know what kind of stuff he was into. Which means that they are into it, too. I don't know what they're doing, but it must be heavier than either of us thought."

She didn't speak. But he knew he was making head-way—he could almost hear the keyboard keys clacking in her head as she ran a cost-and-benefit analysis on telling him the truth.

"Here's another guess," he said. "The money that Valkenburg took. It was a pile, wasn't it?"

He thought she would make him guess again, but she didn't.

"Fourteen million," she said.

Noland squeezed his phone.

"Shit."

"Yeah."

"Are they wiped out?"

"Not entirely. There were a couple of smaller accounts that Valkenburg didn't have access to. And the partners are all flush, personally."

Noland sighed with relief. "Good. They're gonna need it. How many partners are there?"

"Not including Valkenburg? Four. Well, three now."

"Do any of them strike you as legit?"

"No."

"You sure?"

"Yeah. They're all into it. Different levels, of course, but all in."

"Good. Call a meeting."

"What?"

"You heard me. Call the partners to a meeting."

"With you?"

"Yes."

A faint rush of air sounded on the line—she had shifted the phone to her other ear. He braced himself.

"Listen, Nole. You work for me. I meet with the clients. Not you."

"That's true. But this time you need to make an exception."

"Nuh-uh. These people are a little shady, but they're not ready for you yet. How can I ask them to sit down with a Rent-a-Thug?"

"I'm not a thug," he said. "I'm a technician."

She scoffed.

"Just do it," he said. "We're short on time."

A moment passed. He knew what the intervening silence meant—she was debating whether to simply hang up. Undoubtedly, she wanted to. But she couldn't. He was right, and she knew it.

"Okay," she said. "I'll arrange it. When do you want to meet them?"

"Now."

"*Now?* It's the middle of the night."

"Exactly. It won't be long before someone stumbles across Bisby. And when they do, OPD will be after Valkenburg. Then they'll be after Selberis. And then the whole fucking mess blows up. Any chance of finding the money will have gone straight down the tubes."

"All right, I get it. Let me call you back."

She hung up.

The diner was surprisingly full. Mostly truckers, hanging out in twos and threes in the booths. He watched them for a bit as he sipped his coffee, envying them a little. They would be moving on soon, in a few minutes or an hour at most, heading down the road, far away from any trouble.

Noland ordered another cup and a slice of pie. Then he picked up his phone again. He knew Kiril would be working the counter at the copy shop for another few hours, at least. Even so, Noland was surprised when he picked up on the first ring.

"What do you want?"

"Hey," Noland said. "What kind of a greeting is that?"

"It's late. You only call me this late if you're in trouble."

"That is not true."

Kiril waited.

"As a matter of fact, I might have some work for you."

"Might?"

"Yeah. I'm working out the details."

"When?"

"Tonight."

"What's the rate?"

"Three K. For three hours' work."

A pause followed. Kiril had his own mental spreadsheet, like Faith's. But even faster.

"Three K for three hours? It must be jacked."

"Of course it's jacked. If it weren't, I wouldn't need a big dumb Russian, would I? Are you interested or not?"

"Give me the specs."

Noland explained, in broad terms, what was required.

"Okay," Kiril said. "I'll do it. I could use an adrenaline boost. Call me when it's solid."

"Cool. But I need you to pick up a few things."

He dictated a short and very unusual shopping list, then hung up. He had just taken his first bite of pie when his phone rang again. It was Faith.

"It's arranged," she said.

"All three?"

"All three. We'll see you at the firm."

He hung up again and checked his watch. It was one AM. Five hours till dawn.

* * *

The offices of Reynolds, Adams, and Scruggs occupied a squat, four-story building off of Semoran Boulevard. It was one of those mirrored-glass affairs, International style. It looked like a solid crystal during daylight hours, shiny and impenetrable. But now, in the middle of the night, the lights from the upper-floor conference room blazed out into the gloom, as if someone had electrified the top layer of a cake.

Noland parked on the edge of the lot—this was a habit he could never shake, not even in Faith's parking lot—and walked up. Faith was sitting at the head of the conference table, dressed in jeans and a bright but wrinkled T-shirt. It was the first time he'd ever seen her without her corporate armor, and he found himself feeling a little guilty. Even her hair was in disarray, a few loose strands hanging around her face. She scowled when he walked in but kept her eyes on the other people in the room.

"Everyone, I'd like you to meet our private investigator, Noland Twice."

The three people sitting around the table were scowling too. The one closest to Faith was a big, older guy in rumpled khakis and a dress shirt—probably the same outfit he'd worn to work that day. Perched next to him was a young guy, mid-twenties, with a Van Dyke beard and a diamond stud in his right ear. Across from them was a woman in her late twenties, with long, spongy black hair. She had a pug nose and a chin like the toe of a boot, yet still managed to be good-looking, in a demented sort of way. Petite and slim, she was decked out in a black cocktail dress, as if she'd just come from a dance club.

Faith held her place at the end of the table. Noland remained standing.

"Noland," she said to him, "I'd like you to meet the part-ners of Selberis Constructors." She introduced each of them by name and title: William Redding (khakis) was Selberis's CEO; Shawn Difore (ear-stud boy) was the chief of operations; Karen Voss (dance-club girl) was VP of project management.

"We couldn't get a hold of Frank," Redding said, taking charge. His voice was appropriately gruff. "Faith implied you had some news regarding that?"

Before Noland could reply, the girl, Karen Voss, asked: "Has he been arrested?"

She looked at Noland resolutely—not frightened, but clearly dreading what he might lay on them.

"I'm afraid it's worse than that," Noland said. All their eyes snapped from Karen back to him. Even Faith's.

"Frank Bisby is dead."

Karen flinched, but only for a moment. Noland passed his eyes over the others. Shawn's mouth hung open. Redding had turned his face to the ceiling as if to implore some higher power.

"How did it happen?" Karen asked.

"He was shot. I found him in an apartment earlier this evening."

Redding cut in. "Do the police know?"

Before answering, Noland thought for a moment, getting a handle on the dynamics of the group. Redding was the leader, if only by virtue of title and seniority. But Karen was the smartest. She had pushed her lips out, thinking, calculating her next move.

"To my knowledge," Noland said, "no one knows. That's why I called you here, to talk to the surviving partners of Selberis. Well, apart from Valkenburg, of course."

Difore piped up. "But we have another partner."

"Shut up, Shawn," Redding snapped.

Noland waited a moment, amazed at how quickly a chink had appeared in their firewall of complicity.

"Oh?" he said. "And who, exactly, is this other partner?"

"He's of no concern," Redding said, gathering his bulk so that he sat straighter in the too-small chair.

Noland looked at Faith. She still refused to meet his eyes.

It was Karen who finally answered. "Our other partner is overseas. His offices are in São Paulo."

"São Paulo, huh? You do a lot of business in Brazil, do you?"

"Some," Redding said, taking control again. The anger in his eyes had turned to a dark wariness.

"I gather that this Brazilian gentleman is more of a . . . silent partner?"

At this point, Redding made a mistake of his own: he looked at Karen. She met his eyes and, very slightly, shook her head.

Redding said, "He takes no interest in our daily affairs. Nor do we in his."

"Sounds cozy."

The big man's eyes bored into him. For a brief instant, Noland could see, vividly, what Redding must have looked like as a young man—lean, big-boned, strong. Soccer player in college. But now he was just a fat, entitled guy, pushing sixty. Noland almost felt sorry for him.

Redding turned to Faith. "Why are we here, Faith?"

Faith stood up. "Ladies and gentlemen, I'm going to leave this meeting. Please direct all further questions to Noland. Believe me, he knows what he's doing."

She left the room. Noland took her seat, feeling the need to get down on the partners' level, literally.

"So?" Redding asked.

"What I want from you," Noland said, "is an agreement."

He had hoped that someone would take up this lead, at this point. Karen, perhaps. But they all stared at him, not daring to speak.

Noland went on. "I know this is frightening for you. But in a few days, Mr. Bisby's body will start to stink. Someone will call the police, and the police will discover his corpse. At that point, a murder investigation will be initiated, focusing on your missing partner, Valkenburg."

Redding said: "Val? Why him?"

"Because Bisby was killed in his apartment."

That got them. The partners breathed in unison—a sudden, communal gasp.

"Val?" Shawn asked, almost wistfully. Then he pounded the table with his fist. "That's impossible."

A vein throbbed in Redding's temple. "Shawn, will you please *shut up*?"

At this point, Karen said calmly, "Val didn't kill him."

Noland shrugged. "It's immaterial to me. I just know that the chances of finding Valkenburg—and of recovering the assets he stole from you—are diminishing by the hour. And your silent partner will no doubt become annoyed that his share of the company has gone up in smoke. Do you follow me?"

He watched as his words sank in. A look of barely suppressed terror passed between the three partners. He was sure he had almost won them over.

He was wrong.

"Why shouldn't we let the police handle this?" Karen said. "We don't even know who you are."

After she said this, she pressed her lips into a thin line and waited. She seemed impossibly formidable for such a young person. But then, by mere chance, he noticed something: her left eyelid had a slight droop—a lazy eye, as his mom used to call it. Like a curse, that eye seemed to be the locus of all the pain and sadness of what must have been an unusually hard life. Hardship had given her guts. She was tough, this Karen Voss. Noland considered the possibility that if Valkenburg hadn't shot Bisby, then perhaps she had.

"If the police get to Valkenburg first, they will arrest him on suspicion of murder. At that point, they will subpoena Selberis's records. The feds will probably get involved too."

He felt them back off collectively, as one body. But they weren't sold yet.

"What I'm trying to say," he continued, "is that the cops will be on you like flies on shit. And regarding your

question about the money, let me ask you a question first: Did
Valkenburg walk out of your bank with a suitcase full of cash?"

"He wired it," Karen answered.

"To where?"

She looked startled. "I don't know, exactly. You'd have
to ask Sabine." She pronounced it in the German style.
Suh-BEAN-uh.

It was Noland's turn to be startled. "Okay, who the fuck
is Sabine?"

Redding sighed through his pallid lips. "Sabine Werther.
Our rep at Crossland. She's out of town, unfortunately."

"Let me guess: *overseas*?"

Redding gave him a "fuck you" smile.

Noland moved on. "Okay, it doesn't matter. The money
is sitting in another account somewhere, never to be seen
again. Unless I help."

"What can you do?" Karen asked. Her tone was not accu-
satory. Rather, she seemed genuinely curious. He was taken
aback. As always, he found himself surprised by the naiveté
of otherwise worldly people. How could these well-heeled city
folk be so mixed up with dirty money and Brazilian gangsters
and who knew what else, and yet still be so clueless?

"First off, I can locate Valkenburg," he said. "And when I
do, he will give you your money back. I guarantee it."

At that point, something happened that he never would
have expected: Shawn, the kid, rose to his feet and growled:
"To hell with this. I'm done."

It was Karen who reacted, this time. "Shawn, you need
to SIT THE FUCK DOWN."

Her face was *in extremis*, wearing an expression, one of
rage mingled with crazed fear. Shawn stared at her and swallowed. When he finally sat down, he looked like a little kid
who'd gotten off at the wrong bus stop.

Karen turned back to Noland. If there had been any
doubts as to who was the real leader of this sad little crew,
they were now gone. "How much do you want?"

It was the question he'd been expecting for the past thirty minutes. Before he'd even come into the room, he'd mentally calculated how much he would need to pay off his bills and keep his business afloat for another two years. Then he doubled that value. The doubling wasn't just greed. He would be risking a lot to find Valkenburg. His license. Prison. Maybe even death. These rich folk should share the wealth.

"One hundred K now and ten percent if I succeed."

Redding said, "Ten percent of what?"

Noland laughed. "Ten percent of what I recover. Or five hundred K. Whichever is greater."

Redding shook his head. "You're insane."

Noland looked at him, then at the others. They watched him stonily. After another moment of silence, he knew that he'd overplayed his hand. A sudden shame overtook him; he was fooling himself, thinking he could work with these people. They looked down on him. Just because he was sitting across a conference table from them didn't mean he could function in their world. He had been stupid.

"Okay, I made you an honest offer." He stood up. "Sorry if I wasted your time."

He strode out of the conference room. His right hand trembled slightly on the guide rail as he walked down the stairs to the ground-floor exit. Five minutes later, he was back on 17-92, driving with the van's windows rolled down. The night air felt cool as it poured over him, drying the stress sweat that he had exuded, unknowingly, during the meeting. It felt surprisingly good. Then he thought to himself: *shit*. One and a half million bucks. He had been so close.

On the way home, he stopped at a lonely intersection and got out. The pavement was flat and dusty and made a soft crunching sound beneath his Nikes as he walked over to the corner. He felt a familiar urge, the deep, down-in-the-bone desire to get drunk, to numb himself, and somehow quiet the demons that the night had unleashed. And then, beneath this desire, was an even stronger emotion: a tremendous sense of loss. It wasn't just the money. It was the *gig*. He wanted to find Valkenburg. He had been looking forward to it. Valkenburg. That smooth piece of shit, with his raffish hair and stolen money. He needed to be taught—as Noland had been taught, long before—the true nature of things.

He was about to climb back into the van when his cell rang. It was Faith.

"You're on," she said.

"They coughed up?"

"They coughed up."

He punched the air. "Who signed?"

"Karen. Who else? The guys sat there and watched."

"Figures. She's got the most balls. Did she write two checks?"

"No. Just one. For one hundred K. Made out to Reynolds, Adams, and Scruggs. But she's putting another five hundred K in escrow tomorrow. I'll verify."

"Beautiful." He took a deep, cleansing breath and then let it out, slow. "So, the meter's running."

"Yes, it is. I assume you'll want me to cash the check for you?"

"Yeah, but I won't be able to pick it up immediately. Hold it for me, okay? I trust you."

"You shouldn't," she said and hung up.

CHAPTER

4

I T WAS TWO AM when he got to the copy shop. But even at
that hour, the parking lot was half full. Small cars, mostly.
College kids, pulling an all-nighter, scrambling to print out
their summer-term projects. It never ceased to amaze him
how steady the flow of business was, and how canny Kiril had
been to open the shop in the first place. Especially in such a
crucial location, so close to UCF.

But then, Kiril had always been smart. He even made it
to the NFL, briefly, playing for the Jags until he punched out
an assistant coach. Then, like so many big guys who find
themselves suddenly unemployed, he fell into various illicit
businesses. Debt collection was his specialty, hiring himself
out to loan sharks and bookies. But he also fancied himself as
something of a pirate. He began raiding local meth dealers.
Eventually, he got busted—on a lowly possession charge, of
all things—and spent a year in Raiford. While inside, he got
a job in the convict-run printing shop and had a revelation.
Namely, that running a copy shop was a sweet business.
Almost a scam. The markup was incredible, and once the
equipment was paid for, the only real overhead was labor,
which he could do himself, along with his younger brother,
Freddy.

So when he got out, he borrowed some money from his former loan-shark boss and scouted locations. Eventually, Kiril found a spot across the road from UCF and opened his shop—Kiril's Kopies. He never looked back. Business was good, and he and Freddy were socking away a fair amount of money. Even so, he was always open to a side hustle, so long as the downside wasn't too steep.

Noland walked across the parking lot and into the chilled air of the shop. The fluorescent lights blazed like a hospital ward, and he found himself blinking until his eyes adjusted. Most of the copiers were occupied with grubby-looking college kids, their skinny bodies vibrating from too much caffeine. At the machine closest to the counter, two girls were printing a huge stack of paper, grabbing at each page as it slithered out. Freddy was chatting them up shamelessly, but they didn't seem to mind, joking with him as they added to their stack. That was Freddy. He put out some vibe that people liked. Especially girls.

"What's up, Fred?" Noland asked.

Freddy nodded. As always, he was balancing on the two big wheels of his chair like a circus performer, one strong hand on each loop of metal. Even the slight nod of his head required a correction to one wheel, so that he seemed to acknowledge Noland's greeting with a second nod from his entire body. The chair was made of titanium and carbon fiber and had probably cost Kiril a fortune. But Freddy was worth it. Noland had never asked how his kid brother ended up in a wheelchair, but he gathered it was one of those absurd, easily avoidable mishaps that befall kids in poor countries. Hell, Noland saw it all the time, even in Florida.

He glanced across the shop to Kiril's glass-walled office. It was empty. At six foot six, Kiril was hard to miss. Noland was mystified. "Where's K?"

Freddy tilted his head toward the rear of the store. Noland walked back and found Kiril lying on the floor, belly up, digging into the guts of a Xerox machine.

"What the fuck," Noland said. "We gotta roll."

Kiril didn't reply. He was working a very small screw-driver, twisting it with Zen-like patience until his hand came out with a circuit board. He slipped the board into a static-proof bag, then rose to his feet with an ease and agility that would have surprised anyone who didn't know him better. Kiril had played center for FSU and had been one of the best O-line guys in the NCAA. Everyone expected him to have a great career. But even before he'd punched out that assistant coach, he never quite clicked in the NFL. Never found his rhythm. Noland knew it must've really pissed him off.

Kiril wiped his hands on the front of his jeans. "You got funded?"

"I'm rich."

They went to the front, and Kiril handed the circuit board to Freddy, who rolled himself to the workbench he kept along the north wall. Kiril turned to Noland. "How far is it?"

"Longwood."

Kiril got a duffel bag from his office—stuffed with the items Noland had requested earlier—and they walked out. As they left, Kiril shouted to Freddy: "Ne spat, Fyodor!"

Freddy didn't reply.

Noland drove, with Kiril riding heavily in the passenger seat, causing the van's chassis to list a few degrees. Kiril still worked out every day at Gold's, and he had a body like a retired wrestler—massive and strong, despite carrying a bit of fat. But it wasn't merely his size that made him valuable. Ever since he'd gotten out of Raiford, he had transformed into one of the most cool-headed guys around. Noland could take him into the stickiest of situations with full confidence, knowing that he wouldn't let him down—wouldn't chicken out or, even worse, go mental and start killing folks at ran-dom. That mix of cool-headed reserve and unflagging cour-age was a very rare combination. In his years as a cop and a P.I., Noland had only seen it a few times, and only once in somebody he'd care to have as a friend.

They parked in the same spot across from Valkenburg's apartment. Both of them had heavy things to carry—Noland his toolbox, and Kiril the duffel bag—but they moved swiftly and silently into the apartment building and up the stairs. At Valkenburg's door, they paused in the shadows to slip on latex gloves and medical scrubs over their shoes. Kiril had size fifteen shoes, and the scrubs stretched so thin over his Nikes that they looked like water balloons, ready to pop. Noland might have laughed, but he feared Kiril might punch him.

The door was still unlocked. Noland opened it, paused a moment, and went in. Kiril followed, closing the door silently behind him. Noland headed straight to the bedroom. He was about to shine the EagleTac on Bisby's corpse, but Kiril muttered "Fuck this," and turned on the overhead light. Noland hadn't been quite ready for this—to take in the totality of the body in full light, resting on its small island of dried blood, the left arm bent at a weird angle. A clammy feeling of nausea twisted inside his stomach.

Kiril knelt over Bisby and surveyed him for a moment.

"One shot, I think."

"Yeah."

He cocked an eye back at Noland.

"You do this?"

"Come on, now," Noland said. "You know I'm not like that."

"Nobody's like that. Until they are."

Noland swallowed. "Let's lay him down flat."

Careful not to let their knees touch the carpet, they squatted down. The blood streak on Bisby's shirt was still ruby red, an almost regal slash of color across his chest. Kiril grabbed the man's feet and pulled. Bisby's torso slid down the wall, leaving a fat brushstroke of crimson on the plaster. Noland followed the brushstroke up the wall until his eyes found the tiny hole, like a misplaced punctuation mark.

Kiril saw it, too. "Small caliber—.32, I'd guess."

"You think it went through the wall?"

Kiril unfolded a knife and dug into the plaster. "Nah, it's in the stud. You want me to dig it out?"

"No."

It was Noland's turn to get close. He stood over the body and took a tentative sniff. The smell of the cologne had dissipated, thankfully, to be replaced by the coppery smell of blood. As bad as that was, it was still preferable to the citrusy smell—the smell of wealth that had caused him to hate the guy, even in the brief moment when he'd met him. Hated the casual arrogance of him, the aura of entitlement. Of course, Noland had not wished Bisby dead, but now that he was, Noland could feel no emotion. Except for that spooked reverence one gets in the presence of recent murder.

He dug in the breast pocket of Bisby's jacket, found his cell phone, and handed it to Kiril. Kiril turned it off and dropped it into a Ziploc bag. Noland kept searching. He also found a wallet and some car keys.

"Motherfucker drives an Audi."

"Nice," Kiril said.

But it was Kiril who found the only thing of real interest. He pointed at Bisby's forearm. The man's shirtsleeves had hitched up, and the bare skin, once tan, was turning gray. Against that morbid canvas, a row of numbers had been scrawled in ball-point ink: 4586038813.

"Overseas phone number?" Noland asked.

Kiril shrugged. "Whatever it is, it must have been really important, if he felt the need to tattoo himself." He touched the first digit with his finger. The ink smeared a little.

Noland made a note of the digits, typing them into a notepad on his phone.

Dreading the next step, and looking for any excuse to stall, he turned his attention to the nightstand. It was one of those faux-mahogany numbers with a little drawer. The drawer was open, and its contents—the usual junk-drawer stuff, including a sharp letter opener and a brochure for a high-end fishing rod—looked like they'd been rifled through.

There was nothing else in the drawer but the halves of some old credit cards, sliced cleanly across the numbers.

Kiril was still looking down at Bisby. "He was shot through the heart. Just like the song."

"Yeah. A Bon Jovi fan, no doubt."

Kiril scoffed. "Whoever did it was either really good or lucky as hell."

"A pro?"

"A pro wouldn't use a .32."

Noland tried to think of anything else he should do. But there was only one thing left.

"Okay, let's move him."

Naturally, Kiril took the top half. Noland grabbed the legs.

"He's a heavy fucker," Kiril grunted.

It was true. All those lunches on the company dime. All those beers at the nineteenth hole. All that good living—it was lard on the corpse now. History encoded as lipid cells. As they muscled the body out of the bedroom, their footfalls shook the foundation of the old building. Noland cursed under his breath. They were probably waking up half the tenants. There was no avoiding it, though.

They made their way into the tiny bathroom, where they laid Bisby in the tub on his back, with his head down by the drain. It was hard to bend his legs—rigor was already turning them to cordwood—but Kiril managed it with a muffled crack. Noland reached into the duffel bag and heaved out the first bag of quicklime, forty pounds, and cut the top off with his knife. He began pouring. Kiril got the next bag and joined in. Noland did the top half of the corpse, and when he reached the dead man's face—aimed up now at the bathroom's filigreed plaster ceiling, the mouth gaping open as if waiting for the first green flies to buzz their way into it— Noland closed his eyes and kept pouring. When the bag was empty, he opened his eyes again. Thankfully, Bisby's once handsome face was buried beneath a little dune of lime.

They emptied two more bags, then stepped back from the tub. Not much of a clean-up job, surely, but the best they could do under the circumstances. On the drive over, Kiril had lobbied for wrapping the body up and carrying it out of the apartment so that they could dispose of it properly. But Noland had vetoed the idea, calculating that even if they managed to get the body out of the apartment, down the stairs, and to the van undetected—a difficult proposition, even in the middle of the night—there was no way they could effectively clean up all the blood and other evidence of the crime that would remain in the apartment. And it was the connection to Valkenburg, rather than the body itself, that they were trying to hide. No, the lime was the simplest option. Bisby's corpse would not rot—at least, not quickly— but would merely desiccate. Turn to parchment. For at least a week, there would be no smell.

Kiril had reserved a bit of lime in his bag, and he went back into the bedroom and poured it on the bloodstain. Finally, they put the empty bags into the duffel and carried it and the toolbox out of the apartment. This time, Noland slipped his rake into the keyhole and turned the wrench the opposite way so that the deadbolt slid home again. The apartment was locked.

Back at the van, they slipped off their scrubs and tossed them into a dumpster. Then they drove around the neighborhood for twenty minutes before finding the Audi, parked at a distant corner. Noland jumped out and Kiril slid into the van's driver's seat. Noland's gut tightened painfully as he beeped open the Audi's door and climbed in. He had to slide the seat forward a bit to reach the pedals. Bisby had been a tall bastard. A lot of good it did him. Noland cranked the engine, revved it, and drove off. Kiril followed, the van's headlights reflecting off the rearview mirror into Noland's eyes.

They drove across the county, thirty miles, before Noland took the car up a power line easement through some woods near 17-92. The Audi's delicate chassis shuddered dreadfully as Noland powered it over the ruts, but fortunately he didn't get stuck. He knew of a copse near the edge of this particular easement in which a tiny sinkhole was hidden, a thirty-foot depression with a perpetual pool of slime-covered water at the base. He drove the Audi to the edge and put the stick in neutral. When he got out, the cabin light pushed a weak circle of amber light into the gloom, through which mosquitos flitted in and out, momentarily visible. The crickets were in rare form, doing their harmony bit.

He closed the door, the light went out, and for a moment he was alone in the darkness with the dead man's car. Some startled bird, perhaps an owl, took flight from the treetops, dark wings whooshing overhead and then away. A shiver went up Noland's spine, bringing with it a pure, childlike terror. Was someone watching? He scanned the tree line, whipping his head left and right like a panicked child. But he saw nothing. Then he thought to himself: *How the fuck did I get here?* What chain of improbabilities had led him to this place, out in the forest in the middle of the night, about to dispose of a dead man's car?

Eventually, he got behind the Audi and put his hands flat on the trunk. The metal was cold, even through the latex gloves, as he pressed down and pushed, flexing the muscles in his back and legs. The car rolled down the side of the sinkhole and landed with a mild, unsatisfying splash, which the night seemed to swallow up.

Noland switched the EagleTac on as he walked out of the woods and back across the easement. Then he got into the van. Five minutes later, they were back on I-4, heading south toward the city. Noland found himself craving something. A treat. Handling death so intimately for three hours had unnerved him, and made him yearn for some immediate pleasure, something to remind himself that he was alive. Another piece of pie, perhaps, or a milkshake. Then he realized that what he really needed was to get laid. What better way to thumb your nose at death? He found himself fantasizing that Deirdre was still with him, at home in bed. That he might return there and catch her before work, slipping into the sheets and pressing himself against her body, warm and earthy from sleep. Remembering that she was, of course, not there made him want to weep.

"How long did that buy us?" Kiril asked.

Noland had been dreading the question. "A week. Maybe two, with luck."

Kiril clucked his tongue. "Not much time. You think you can work it?"

"If I can't work it in two weeks, it can't be worked."

Kiril didn't press him. The sun was coming up, peeking over the crystal peaks of the Orlando skyline. For anyone else, the sunrise might have been a relief, a deliverance from the night's deeds. But for Noland, it just meant that he'd never get any real sleep now. By his own estimate, he had two weeks at most before someone found Bisby's corpse and called the cops, at which point the whole affair would be over, or as good as. Two weeks was also the deadline when Faith had to go back into court, to face the wrath of Judge Abercrombie. If Noland hadn't run down Valkenburg by then, he'd be right back where he was before: broke, about to lose his house, and about to close his agency.

And, of course, there was the matter of the criminal liability he had already exposed himself to, should any of the partners rat him out.

In short, if he didn't roll up the case, and fast, he was fucked.

And he still had no idea where to find Arthur Valkenburg.

5

AFTER HE DROPPED Kiril off, he went through the drive-thru at McDonald's, then parked along the freeway so he could eat in the van. Traffic was picking up as people headed to work. Even sitting there, devouring his Egg McMuffin, he felt himself enclosed in a carapace of exhaustion. Every gesture triggered a dull ache in whichever limb he happened to be using. He was beat.

When he finished eating, he leaned back in the seat and closed his eyes for a moment, hoping for a quick nap. But the memory of Bisby's face came back to him, its grotesque rictus, that combination of awe and surprise. Noland gave up, cranked the engine, and drove away. Depeche Mode's "Personal Jesus" played on the radio.

He had left Bisby's phone at the copy shop with Freddy, who had removed the SIM card. It would take him a while to compile a list of Bisby's calls, not to mention his emails. In the meantime, Noland had his own digging to do. He busied himself going through the receipts he'd found in Valkenburg's garbage. The only suggestive one was from Target, a long list of purchases that suggested a road trip: snacks, bottled water, dry goods, painkillers. Noland pondered the list. What would he do if Valkenburg had split for real? Even if he had killed Bisby the night before, he could be halfway to the west coast by now. Or Brazil, for that matter. In that case, Noland and the partners were all screwed. Even if the cops didn't bag them, their Brazilian partner would.

Noland took out the photo Faith had given him, the one of Valkenburg and Bisby fishing. He saw again that wild look in the younger man's eyes, that roguish glint of wickedness. He remembered what Beaumont had told him, about Valkenburg having a boat. Thirty-foot Dymon, the old man had said. A very nice boat, indeed. Small enough to fit on a trailer, but big enough to live on for an extended period. And there were many quiet, out-of-the-way marinas in Florida, both freshwater and salt. Hundreds on the Atlantic Coast alone.

Noland got back in the van and drove to the south side of the city, where the corporate towers of downtown Orlando quickly gave way to the fantasy-themed hotels of International Drive. The Land of the Mouse. Traffic was heavy on I-Drive, as it always was in summer when the tourists descended. But there was no faster way to Ben's Boat Shop, which stood on the very edge of Orange County. Any self-respecting boat nut was bound to pass through Ben's, sooner or later.

Fortunately, Noland had known Ben a long time. One night, when Noland was thirteen, Zeb had come into his room and woken him. "Come on," he said. "I want you to drive somewhere with me." It was after midnight, and Noland, sleepy as he was, felt a thrill of excitement, knowing his father meant to take him on some grown-up mission. To ask what it was about was unthinkable—the very act would suggest fear. So Noland slipped on the same clothes he'd worn to school that day and followed Zeb out of the house into the pouring rain. They got into the big, unmarked Crown Vic and drove through the storm, all the way to the county jail, where his father went into the building alone. He emerged a long while later with a stocky man in tow. The man climbed into the back seat, filling the car with an overpowering scent of wet clothes and whiskey. They drove in silence across town to a clapboard house, where the man got out and went inside. On the way home, Noland watched his father's granite profile. Finally, he worked up the courage to ask who the man was.

"That's Ben Freund."

"Why was he in jail?"

"Beat up his brother."

"Why?"

"The guy stole something from him."

"Something valuable?"

"Not really."

"So why'd you get him out?"

Zeb's smile flashed in the darkness. "He's a good man. Saved my life once. When I was about your age."

Now, twenty years later, Noland pulled into the freshly paved lot in front of Ben Freund's boat shop. The lot was covered with boats of all kinds, old and new, some still covered with white plastic, straight from the factory, gleaming in the sun. The shop itself was a big, corrugated metal building, painted ocean blue. The moment Noland climbed out of the van, Ben came out of the building. They shook hands.

"Long time, Nole. You're staying fit, I see."

"Trying to, Mr. Ben."

Ben was almost bald now, with a gray fringe clinging to the back of his skull. He had to be past sixty, but his shoulders still bulged under his polo shirt. He looked as if he could lift one of the boats off its trailer all by himself.

"You in the market?"

Noland shook his head, then got out the photograph of Valkenburg. Ben took the photo and held it in his hands. They were rock steady.

"Yeah, he's got a Dymon."

"You've seen it?"

"Course I've seen it. I sold it to him. Nice rig, too." He handed back the photograph. "You looking for him?"

"Could be."

"I can tell you where he lives."

"Thanks, but I know where he lives. An apartment. He must have the boat stowed somewhere."

Ben squinted thoughtfully. "That ain't it. We delivered the boat to a house. A mansion, almost. Nearer to Lake Mary. You want the address?"

Noland forced himself to breathe evenly. Could Valkenburg have a second home somewhere—a "mansion," almost—where he might be hiding at that very moment? Could it really be this easy?

Noland followed Ben into the shop. The big hangar doors were open and men were working inside, stripping the var- nish off a metal boat with power sanders, a fountain of white sparks splashing over their shoulders. The sound was deafen- ing. Ben took him into the corner office and closed the door.

"What'd the guy do?" he asked, searching through his filing cabinet.

"Dunno. Some people want to lay hands on him. Rich people."

"Figures. I remember him. Jew-boy."

Noland winced. He could still be shocked by the casual racism of older, Southern men like Ben. But all he said was: "I didn't know that."

Ben nodded. "Real smart. Knew his boats."

"I heard he was smart."

"Too smart, sounds like."

Ben came up with an old receipt, on which the delivery address had been scrawled in ballpoint. He ran the receipt through his copier. Noland took the copy, the sheet still warm.

"Thanks, Ben. I owe you another one."

Ben shrugged, then gave him a wistful look. Noland knew exactly which memory the man was replaying in his mind—that night in the rain, long ago.

"Be careful, Nole. Dude paid cash for the Dymon." He lifted his hand into the air and waggled it. "A bit shady, if you ask me."

"I bet."

"Want a picture of her?"

"You got one?"

"I always take one. For my website."

He dug in the files again and produced a 5×7 photo, which he handed to Noland. The picture had been taken from about twenty yards away, the minimum distance to get the full length of the Dymon in the frame. Noland didn't know anything about boats, but he could tell this one was special. Even sitting on the back of a trailer, with its sails wrapped tight against the mast, it gave the impression of motion, of speed, cutting swiftly through some invisible sea. Valkenburg stood in front of it, grinning widely, a proud sea captain. Standing next to him, with one of his arms wrapped casually around her hips, was a good-looking, brown-haired woman, not grinning but looking proud nonetheless. She leaned into Valkenburg, her eyes squinting from the glare, and although the sun had caught her face at a harsh angle, Noland had no trouble recognizing her. She was a couple of years younger in the picture but had the same ponytails, the same olive skin.

Just like the night before, at Benny's.

"That's his wife," Ben said. "Pretty, huh?"

"Ex-wife," Noland said. "Now."

"I bet she dumped him."

Noland stared at the photo. On the side of the boat was a name he couldn't make out. He asked Ben.

"That's the name he picked," Ben said. "*Zigeuner.*" He pronounced it: Zee-GOY-ner.

"German?"

He nodded. "It means gypsy. At least that's what the dude said."

"Right," Noland said. "Gypsy."

*   *   *

Back on the road, he called Kiril. Freddy had downloaded the contents of Bisby's phone, and Kiril was ready to mail

him the recent calls list. Before he did so, Noland asked him
to search for a specific contact: Arthur Valkenburg.

"There's a Val," Kiril said a moment later.

"That's him. When was the last call?"

"A month ago."

"Shit. How about Cassandra Raines?"

"One sec. Yeah, there's a Cassy. Your man got a call from
her last week."

Noland clenched his jaw so hard he thought his molars
would crack.

"Shoot me her number, okay? I'm headed for her place."

"For real? You think she iced the guy?"

"Could be."

"Well, don't let her ice you too. You still owe me money."

Noland hung up.

He plugged the address into his phone and was surprised
when it led him off 17 and down an unpaved road. The road
was all broken, the van's fat tires jouncing over the deep ruts
and washouts, and he wondered how Ben had managed to
get a thirty-foot sailboat over them. Had it been in better
condition? Pine trees blocked his view, but they soon receded
into a big, open field with a two-story brick house in the
middle. A mansion? Almost. The property was at least ten
acres, protected by an impressive brick wall that gave way to
chain-link at the sides.

The gate was open. Noland drove through and parked
far away from the house, indulging his usual caution but also
because the yard was already full. SUVs mostly, all gleaming
in the sun. As soon as he got out, he caught the sounds of
shouting and clapping.

He walked around. Behind the house, the field was flat
and bare, stretching to another stand of pines, a quarter mile
away. All of it was fenced for horses. Between the house and
the pines, a dressage class was in progress, a line of girls on
horseback. Younger kids, mostly, twelve or so, each sitting
atop a horse with careless poise. On the periphery, a line of

adults—all moms—stood about thirty yards from the class. Noland slipped in among them.

They all watched as the instructor, a woman, also on horseback, shouted instructions, whereupon the girls started down the field. At some point, she turned slightly on her horse, and Noland saw, at last, that she was Cassandra Raines, erect in the saddle, her profile strong and clear against the background of blue sky. A steeplechase had been set up, made of wooden posts with PVC pipes resting on metal rungs, positioned at one-foot intervals. Today, the obstacles were set at about four feet high. Noland watched as each girl made her jump, one after another. Easy. Clearly, they were old hands at this kind of thing, despite looking like ordinary middle-school kids, as far as he could tell, each dressed in shorts and a T-shirt. Only their little blue helmets marked them as serious riders. Cassandra, in contrast, looked ready to train a pack of English barons. She wore a silk turtleneck, complete with scarf, and her riding breeches were tailored from some herringbone fabric, the puff forming a sharp crease at the top of her thighs.

The class went on for another half hour. No one paid any attention to Noland. They probably assumed he was a divorced dad, come to watch his daughter on his day off. Finally, the girls led the horses into a steel corral off to the side. Noland groaned internally—they still had to unsaddle the horses and put everything away, which would probably take another hour. But to his surprise, the whole business was done quickly, Cassandra belting out directions without ever actually shouting. She was a good coach, he saw. Strong, but not a bully. Noland knew the difference.

When it was all done, the girls filed out to their parents, who led them to the SUVs in front of the house. After five minutes, only Noland remained. He walked into the corral. The woman was lugging the saddles into the long row of cinder-block stables, which ran along the east side of the property next to a mud-spattered Dodge Ram. She had taken off her helmet, and in the sun he saw that her hair was actually a bright chestnut color. Here and there, a few strands of silver intermingled with the brown.

She barely glanced at Noland. "I'll be with you in a sec."

"No worries. I'll help."

Only then did she look at him, squinting a moment, trying to place him. She had already forgotten him, apparently, and his mouth went suddenly dry from shame, the embarrassment of realizing how much he was hoping she'd remember. But then a vague recognition flashed in her eyes. Her knuckles went white as she tightened her grip on the saddle she was holding. "What the fuck? Are you some kind of stalker? Did you follow me last night?"

"No, believe it or not, I am as surprised as you are to find us both standing here."

She stared at him a moment.

"Are you a cop?"

"P.I."

Her eyes narrowed. "Val?"

"Yeah."

She got back to work. He helped her carry some of the saddles. They were heavier than he expected (how the hell a twelve-year-old could get one onto a horse, he'd never know). Following her lead, he threw the saddles over the doors of the stalls, where a few of the horses were already settled, munching hay. She wiped her palms on a towel hanging from a hook. One of her hands had a long, red gash on it. A fresh wound, Noland was certain. She'd not had it the night before.

"Horse bite?" he said.

She looked confused, then looked at her hand. She scoffed. "No. Just rode too close to a branch. Occupational hazard."

"I bet."

She stepped forward. "I guess you already know my name."

"I do, Cassandra."

"Cassy."

"Cassy. I'm Noland Twice."

"What did Val steal this time?"

The question startled him.

"Who says he stole anything?"

"He's a thief. Val has always been a thief."

Noland waited for her to elaborate, but all she did was reach into her pocket and pull out two elastic headbands, which she used to tie her hair back into the same ponytails. As she did so, her breasts lifted slightly beneath the silk turtleneck. Noland was pierced by desire.

"I can't help you," she said, lowering her arms back to her sides. There was no malice in her tone. If anything, she sounded weary. Resigned.

"Are you sure?" he asked. "A lot of people are looking for him."

With an oddly elegant motion, she lifted her chin and looked down her nose at him. He knew what thoughts were going through her head; she was trying to figure what category of thug he fell into.

"What do you want?" she asked.

"Do you know where he is?"

"No. And I wouldn't tell you if I did."

She walked off. Noland waited a moment before following. She was messing with him, obviously. But he didn't have much choice but to go along.

"Listen," he said, catching up to her. "I don't blame you for shutting me down. But there's something you need to know."

She entered one of the stalls and began brushing down a horse, a handsome roan with eyes like wet figs.

"There's nothing you can tell me about Val that I don't already know," she said.

"Possibly. But I'll say it anyway: your ex is in deep shit. I don't know what he stole in the past, but this time it was serious money. From his partners. They want him. Bad."

She kept brushing the horse with the same steady rhythm. Still, he sensed that his words were beginning to penetrate, to

make at least a dent in the force field of her indifference. He pressed on. "Someone's going to find him. It's either going to be me, or the cops, or a third party. Of those choices, I'm his best bet."

She stopped her brushing and turned to him.

"You're wrong," she said. "He'll get away. He always does."

"Not this time."

She looked down a moment, then took a deep breath through her nose, flaring her rather patrician nostrils. "You know, I almost believe you. And I'd be lying if I said I didn't care. But I don't know where Val is. That's the truth. I haven't spoken to him in months."

Again, a note of resignation tinged her words. Noland got the impression that, despite her hauteur, she missed old Valkenburg. Her shady ex.

That figured.

He kicked at a clump of hay near his foot. "All right, Cassy. I have no choice but to believe you. But I was going to ask one more question."

She waited.

"What were you doing in Maitland last night?"

"Flirting with a man in a bar. What were you doing?"

"That's not an answer."

She put down the brush and walked off again, this time going right out of the stables and toward the house. Once more, he found himself chasing after her. She stopped on the back porch, sat in one of the expensive-looking deck chairs, and began pulling off her riding boots.

"I wanted a drink," she said. "I work in Maitland. Falco Accounting. Check it out."

"I will," he said. "You're an accountant?"

"Is that surprising?"

"You look too fit to be an accountant."

He wasn't sure why he said it—the words just came out. The truth. It always betrayed him. Fortunately, she seemed to be flattered by the statement, pursing her lips to stave off a smile. "I'm part-time now. A few nights a week. The extra money helps me run the school." She cocked her head at the stables. "Horses ain't cheap. I can either moonlight or sell a kidney."

Noland laughed, a real belly laugh, and then felt a concomitant sensation in his chest, an unexpected lightness spreading out from his solar plexus into his limbs. Finally, he recognized the feeling: he liked her. Something about the way she'd said it tickled him.

"You're an excellent instructor, by the way."

She raised her eyebrows. "You know about horses?"

"I know jocks. Those kids hung on your every word."

Her expression softened a little, her lips turning up a bit at the corners. Still not a smile yet, but getting closer.

"You got kids?" she asked.

He shook his head.

"Too bad. I'd give you a discount."

"Maybe I'll take a lesson myself."

"I don't train adults."

Noland dug a business card out of his wallet and handed it to her. She held it at arm's length and stared at it. Noland couldn't figure out what she was doing for a moment, until it dawned on him that she was far-sighted. Older than she looked.

"Ultima Fortuna Investigations," she read off the card. "Latin?"

He nodded. "It means 'Last Chance.'"

It was only then, in this last, unlikely moment, that she laughed. More of a guffaw, actually, but close enough. He wasn't even offended by it. He was thrilled.

"So what kind of cases do you handle? Besides theft, I mean."

"All kinds. But I specialize in greed and fear."

She put the card in her pocket. "Well, if I come across a matter of greed or fear, I'll call you, Noland."

"Please do. I answer my phone 24/7."

Without another word, she stood up and walked across the deck in her stockinged feet, carrying her boots into the house.

Back in the van, he bounced over the ruts again. Once he could no longer see the house in the rearview, a nauseating realization manifested in the pit of his stomach: she'd played him. He was sure of it. Months, she'd said. She hadn't spoken to Valkenburg in months. Not years. Just months. Which meant they were still friends. Why not? They still lived in the same town. They were both smart and world-weary, and they had shared years of marriage together. So what were the chances that she really had no idea what he'd been up to, or where he'd gone? What were the chances that a guy like Valkenburg hadn't drunk-dialed her, or at least texted her, even once in the past few weeks before he'd gone on the lam? Zero. Zero chance.

Noland smacked the steering wheel. She'd played him. He'd come there in desperate need, and she'd played him. He glanced at his watch. Two hours gone. Two hours closer to the inevitable moment when Bisby's corpse would be discovered, and every cop in the state would be looking for Arthur Valkenburg.

He parked on the shoulder, took out his phone, and googled Falco Accounting Maitland Florida. One listing appeared. He dialed the phone number.

The line was disconnected. He hit the website. It 404ed. After staring at the screen for a moment, he found himself laughing. Part-time, she'd said. A few nights a week. Fuck. What nerves of steel she must have, to lie to his face like that.

What else had she lied about?

Dropping the phone back into his pocket, he put the van in gear and drove on.

6

Back in the city, he texted Faith and asked her to transfer 5,000 dollars of the front money from Selberis into his business account. He could have collected the cash in person, but he didn't want to go by her office yet. Didn't want to reveal to her how badly he was tanking. No leads. No hunches. With each passing hour, the chances of his blowing the case increased by some unknown but non-zero amount, and the panic that was already galloping in his chest threatened to break loose at any moment. Talking to Faith might bring that panic even closer to the surface. He didn't want to explain to her or anyone else that all he had was some strange numbers tattooed to a dead man's arm and the name of a boat.

Fortunately, she didn't ask any questions, she just sent him the money. He collected it from a branch on Colonial and shoved the wad of cash into the pocket of his jeans. No sooner had he climbed back into the van than his phone chirruped. Faith, of course. Texting him.

—Did you get the money?
—Yeah. Thanks. I'll need more soon. In cash, tho
—How much?
—20K

—All right. I'll arrange it.
  —Cool.
—Making any progress?
  —A bit.
—Good. The clock is ticking. Our 2-week window is running
out.
      —I know. I'll call when I have some news.
—Fair enough. ttyl.

He sighed. Even though he didn't need reminding of
their time limit, her "2-weeks" statement had hit him like a
slap. Two weeks. He wasn't sure if she meant the two weeks
before Bisby's corpse began stinking, or the two weeks before
she had to answer to Judge Abercombie. Either way, it didn't
matter. She was right.

He was about to drop the phone back into his pocket,
but instead he opened up QuikNote and stared at the last
note he had made, the one with the numbers from Bisby's
arm. Of course, they could be anything. A password. A bank
account. A registration number (for a boat, perhaps?). But
whatever they were, whatever secret they unlocked, Noland
was pretty sure that Bisby had been killed for them.

He drove home. The house felt even emptier than usual,
his footfalls seeming to echo in the hall as he came in. He fed
the dogs and then worked out in his garage, lifting weights
and practicing on his Wing Chun dummy, which he'd fashioned from a section of telephone pole and some thick dowels. Today, he practiced for longer than usual, needing to hit
something, to feel the familiar solidity of the wood, polished
by the oil of his own skin after countless blocks and strikes.
It was the closest he came to meditation.

After a shower, he settled down on the couch with his
laptop, where he proceeded to look up the phone number of
every marina within a hundred-mile radius. It was a long list,
and he got started immediately, calling each one and asking if anyone had seen a thirty-foot Dymon. He had gotten

halfway down the list with no luck before he called a marina
on Lake George.

"Yeah," the guy on the line said. He sounded old, his
voice raspy from countless cigars.   "One of them Dymons
came in about a week ago."

Noland sat up, so fast that Quick, who had been snooz-
ing on the couch next to him, startled awake. "Is she still
there?"

"Yeah, she's here."

"The *Zigeuner*?"

"The what?"

Noland spelled it.

"Hold on." Papers ruffled in the background. "Nah, she's
called the *Gypsy*."

Noland thanked him and hung up.

* * *

Ten minutes later he was on the road north, driving ninety. It
wasn't until he got halfway to Lake George that he regretted
his impulsiveness; he should've called Kiril. If ever there was
a time when he needed backup, this was it. After all, Valkenburg had already killed Bisby, and Bisby had been his best
friend. As Zeb had told him, many times, there was nothing
as dangerous as a man who's killed someone close to him—a
friend, a wife, a brother. "He's already killed his feelings,"
Zeb had said. "What's he got to lose?"

So, yeah, he should've called Kiril. Even so, the closer
Noland got to the marina, the more excited he became. His
left foot bounced on the van's floor as he thought of the fortune Selberis would pay him—half a million bucks! Once he
had Valkenburg in hand, it would be easy to sweat him until
he spilled the beans, revealing whatever offshore account he
had stuffed the stolen jing into. And then he, Noland, would
get his big payday. He could pay off his mortgage, his back
taxes, and his credit cards, and still have plenty left over. The

thought of it all—everything he'd do with the money—made him smile. It would be like Christmas, every day for a year.

Of course, the question remained: what would he do with the rest of it? Sure, he could be a little more picky about his future clients with that kind of cushion, but what else? There was only one thing he really needed, at the moment. A woman. His thoughts flashed back to Cassy, sitting astride her horse like an English general. She was a few years older than he was, but so what? He was sure he could benefit from having such a woman in his life. They could join forces. They were both business people, after all. More to the point, he had come to suspect that she was the only woman he'd ever met who could keep him on his toes, match him move for move. She was whip-smart and cagey, and he was no slouch himself. She didn't suffer fools, and neither did he. She would be bored by the same things he found boring—parties and small talk and politics and religion. All that crap. What a match they would make! He and the dogs could move in with her, cohabiting in that beautiful, vast house that Valkenburg had paid for (the idea made Noland smile). He wouldn't be mooching so long as he brought some serious jing to the relationship. And with half a million bucks, he would.

He just had to find Valkenburg.

The marina was packed, a mass of white boats floating on the dark mirror of Lake George. An old man sat in the manager's hut, and from his long face and yellow teeth, Noland knew he must be the guy Noland had spoken with. Noland braced himself for a grilling, but the guy waved him in.

Noland parked on the edge of the paved lot and stepped out onto the soft asphalt. Reaching back into the van, he grabbed his old pair of police handcuffs, which he'd stolen from the Maynard County Sheriff's Department, and shoved them in his pocket. Then he got the Ruger from under the seat and tucked it into a calf-leather holster nestled into the small of his back. With his T-shirt untucked and falling past his waist, no one would see it, but he could slip the gun out in less than a second. He lingered for a moment, knowing that he should wait in the van until Valkenburg or whoever was on the boat came out. That would be the smart move—just wait for him to go for groceries or smokes or whatever. Catch him in motion, preferably at night. The problem was, since his apartment was no longer available, the boat was essentially Valkenburg's home, and there was no telling when he would emerge. Once again, Noland thought of calling Kiril. Someone should know where he was, at least. But Noland's blood was up. He was going to go for it.

The boat was easy to spot, its sailing mast an elegant spire rising above the stunted forest of electronic antennae on the yachts. The pier looked rickety, but the planks were steady and made no sound as Noland walked to the end. The *Zigeuner* rested serenely at the last berth, expertly tied with yellow nylon rope. It looked even better than in the photo, its fluid lines seeming to channel the sky around it, even as it sat perfectly still on the unruffled water. The boat's new name, *Gypsy*, was painted on the stern in sharp red lettering, vivid against the white fiberglass hull. If Valkenburg had done it himself, he was a very capable man.

Noland stopped shy of the rope. What did he do now? Normally he would knock on the door, but that wasn't an option here. There wasn't even a plank across the three-foot gap of water. Should he jump on board? Would he get shot before he landed? Eventually, he cupped a hand around his mouth and yelled: "Anybody home?"

A man's voice called from inside. "Yeah?"

"I'm looking for the owner."

"Hang on."

Noland was distinctly aware of his Ruger in its holster, the leather pressing insistently into the small of his back. His heart raced, each beat as painful and distinct as the slamming of a piano lid. After a full minute, a man emerged onto the deck, his bald head catching the sun. He hunkered under the boom and never did straighten up completely. Then Noland understood—the guy was disabled. Fucked up, somehow. Bent like a Z.

The man came over and stood on the edge of the deck. His big Hawaiian shirt billowed in the breeze like a sail. The one-inch fuzz of hair that covered his skull was silver-gray, as was his beard. His eyes were black pearls behind the lenses of his chunky Italian glasses. Not the man Noland had expected, surely. And yet he recognized him. He had the same high, broad forehead that Noland had seen in the photo of Valkenburg standing in the river. The long, swept-back hair was gone, shaved off, but the forehead was the same, as was the firm jawline, ending in the same dimpled nub of a chin. As Noland looked at the man's face, he was instantly sure, with that deep, down-in-the-bone certainty of the sort that one only experiences in moments of extreme danger or divine grace, that the person before him was Arthur Valkenburg.

"Can I help you?" the man asked, scratching his beard.

"I'm looking for Arthur Valkenburg."

"Val?" His voice sounded surprised, but it was hard to be sure because he wore thick, black-rimmed eyeglasses that made his face hard to read. "Sorry, he's not here."

"Isn't this his boat?"

"Not anymore. He sold it to me. My name's Harris."

Noland exhaled as if vastly disappointed. "Shit."

"Can I help?"

"I need to speak to him directly. Do you know where he is, Mr. Harris?"

"It's just Harris. And no, I can't tell you where he is. It's been a couple of months since I saw him. April, I guess. Why're you looking for him?"

"I need to serve him a subpoena."

"Figures. He getting sued again?"

"Something like that."

"Well, it looks like you made a trip for nothing. Want to come inside for a beer?"

As he asked the question, Valkenburg took a step closer

and winced, squinting his eyes and gritting his teeth so hard that Noland felt it in his own molars. The man really was injured—no doubt about it. And yet Noland knew he'd be risking his life to go into the cabin. Bad idea. But then another angle occurred to him—it would be a lot easier to get the cuffs on him down there in the cabin, as opposed to brutalizing him there on the dock in front of God and everyone.

"Sure," he said at last.

"Come on, then."

Noland found himself hopping across the watery gap and onto the deck. Val's silvery eyebrows —yes, even his eyebrows were dyed silver—rose above his black glasses. "You got good balance, huh? What's your name?"

"Noland Twice. People call me Nole."

They shook hands. Valkenburg's was strong and callused, in the way that comes from hard physical work. Noland followed him down the short ladder into the cabin, which took some time because Valkenburg had to pause on each step, leading with the right leg, then bringing down the left. A little groan escaped his lips on each step, but otherwise he hid it. Eventually they made it down. Noland's eyes took a moment to adjust to the dim interior, with only the two portholes letting in the sun. Then he looked around.

"Nice," he said, and meant it. He knew good carpentry when he saw it, and whoever had built the cabin was first-rate. Everything was done in blond maple, from the tiny galley to the bench wrapping around it to the numerous cabinets built at eye level, a few inches beneath the low ceiling. Unfortunately, the beauty of the cabin was tempered by clutter; Valkenburg was a slob. Empty Heineken bottles lined the back of the bench. Dirty clothes gathered in every corner. Even the air was moldy, despite the lake breeze wafting in through the hatch. But beneath the reek of the cabin itself, Noland caught a whiff of the man. He didn't stink, exactly, but had a musty smell, like old leaves.

Valkenburg popped open a Heineken and handed it to him. "What'd Val do to get sued?"

"I'm not sure. I just know he's needed."

He tilted his chin up and down, not buying it. At least that was Noland's impression. Those dorky glasses were still flummoxing him. How had the man created so simple and yet so effective a disguise? It must've taken some willpower to shave off that glossy black shock of hair that figured so prominently in all his photos.

"Well, you can leave the papers with me. I'll make sure he gets them."

"Are you expecting to see him?"

"Yep. Two weeks. He's supposed to meet me in St. Augustine. We're going to sail to St. Croix."

"You're going to St. Croix in this?"

"Sure. She's up to it. I am too, believe it or not. Sailing is better than P.T."

Despite himself, Noland laughed. In his own year of physical therapy, he and the other patients had used that same line as a refrain, a running joke to counteract anything else in their lives that they found dreadful: "Well, at least it's better than P.T."

"So you have no idea where he is?"

"Did you try his construction firm? Yeah? Then I don't have a clue."

Noland gulped the beer until it was half empty and felt the alcohol go straight to his head. He was about to pull the Ruger and urge the man down on the floor, pistol whipping him if necessary. But for some reason, he hesitated. Valkenburg was friendly at the moment, or at least pretending to be. And even though Noland knew that ninety percent of everything he said was probably bullshit, there might be a few nuggets of truth to be gleaned if he continued talking. Plus, the guy wasn't much of a threat, as it turned out. Almost crippled.

Noland decided to wait.

"If you don't mind my asking," he said, "what happened to you?"

"Old injury. Lower spine. It flared up again a couple of days ago."

Noland thought to himself: *When you killed Bisby?*

"Can you get surgery?"

"Doctor wants me to. I keep putting it off."

"Spinal fusion?"

Valkenburg gave him a crooked grin. "You've had it?"

"No. But I knew some guys who did. Linemen."

"Ahhh." A self-satisfied sound, as if Noland had just confirmed a suspicion. "I thought you looked like a ballplayer. College?"

"U.F. Until I broke my leg."

"Halfback?"

"Safety."

"You must've been pretty good."

Valkenburg was trying to flatter him, obviously, but it worked, bringing a warm flush to Noland's heart. What he had said was the truth, after all. Of all Noland's teammates in high school, he was the only one who'd been recruited by a major school. But now, with Valkenburg's compliment dangling in the air, all he said was: "Not really. I was determined."

"That'll do."

Valkenburg drained his beer and stood the empty bottle on the top of the fridge with some others. Noland studied his face. For the first time, he realized that there was something oddly familiar about his jawline. He was still trying to figure it out when Valkenburg spoke again.

"My story is not as glamorous as yours. I hurt my back by picking up something too heavy."

"What?"

He gave an upside-down grin. "Big toilet."

Noland guffawed. "The hell you say."

Valkenburg raised his hand into a Boy Scout's oath. "God's truth. A year ago last Monday."

Noland shook his head and chuckled, the way one will at another's misfortune, hoping to buck them up. Valkenburg looked down. "It's strange. The older you get, the fewer mistakes you make. But the ones you do make tend to be doozies."

Noland liked that. "Doozies, huh?"

Valkenburg popped open another beer. "Age, my friend. It's the great leveler." His face took on a wistful expression as he stared out the porthole. "The only emperor is the emperor of ice-cream."

Something caught in the middle of Noland's chest, a not-unpleasant kindling of the heart. He thought he recognized the line, though he had no idea from where.

"Emperor of ice cream, huh? Sounds like a punk band."

"It's from a poem by Wallace Stevens. About time. The way it catches up to you."

"Stevens. Right."

Noland finished his beer but found himself still thirsty. It occurred to him that he hadn't drunk any water since that morning.

"Have you got a bottle of water?"

"Sure."

Valkenburg turned his back and dug into a cabinet by the little stove. As he did so, Noland looked around the cabin some more. Like everything else, the small galley table was littered with beer bottles, but they were arranged around an open spot in the middle. There, in that clearing, a map had been spread out, its edges secured with the bottles. Strangely, the map was not nautical. Rather, it looked more like a site plan for a construction job, with blue lines graphing the outline of the buildings. He leaned over it to get a better look.

In that instant, he had one of those strange, out-of-body experiences that he had known playing football. The awareness of the ball spiraling through the air, far behind and above him. The emergent intersection of time and space, preparing to occur, when he and the receiver and the ball arrived in the same spot, thirty yards downfield.

Today, in the *Zigeuner*, he heard the whisper of footsteps rushing up behind him.

He ducked. Something thunked into the cabinet door above him. Chips of wood stung the back of his neck like rock salt. When he looked up, a bright metal J had sprouted from the cabinet, its barb sunk into the maple where Noland's head had been a moment before. Some part of his brain finally registered what the J was—a boat hook—attached to a long, leathery object—Valkenburg's arm. Attached to the arm was Valkenburg himself, grunting, trying to pull the hook out.

Noland lunged at him with both fists, aiming for the man's throat. But Valkenburg turned his body so that Noland caught him across the chest. He grunted and fell backward, taking the boat hook with him as it finally pulled free. Valkenburg hit the wall but seemed to bounce right off of it, like a cartoon character, swinging the hook into Noland's forehead. Miraculously, he got the curved side instead of the barb, but even so, something like an explosion went off inside his skull, and he felt the skin peeling back from the wound like a sliced peach. Something hot and wet flowed into his right eye, which started blinking from the salt sting.

Somehow, he found himself on the floor of the cabin, with Valkenburg kicking him. Noland grabbed the man's foot and twisted it, hard. Valkenburg fell down next to him, and they commenced grappling, with Valkenburg trying to get him into a half nelson. Noland couldn't reach the Ruger, so he concentrated on keeping Valkenburg from completing his hold. Noland found a foothold against the edge of the bench and pushed against it, driving Valkenburg under the table. He must have hit something sharp because he let out a little scream, and his hold on Noland slackened for a moment. But Valkenburg wasn't finished. He rolled over hard, carrying Noland with him, and slammed him into the floor on his other side, knocking the wind out of him. Noland jerked his arm back and elbowed Valkenburg in the face, connecting with the man's jaw.

Suddenly, he was free. He did a push-up off the floor, wondering what had happened. *Had he knocked the man out?* But then something scrabbled up the steps to the hatch—Valkenburg, making a run for it. Despite the stars that still spun in his vision, Noland got to his feet. Valkenburg's footfalls thudded across the deck above him.

Noland went up the stepladder and onto the deck. Valkenburg was already sprinting down the pier, the soles of his tennis shoes flashing white in the afternoon sun. Noland steadied himself against the boom and pulled out the Ruger. Swaying slightly, he aimed at Valkenburg, the gun as heavy as a cinderblock. Before he could pull the trigger, though, another trickle of blood ran into his eye, and as he wiped at it with his free hand, he came to his senses. He jumped down to the pier and ran.

Valkenburg had already crossed the gravel parking lot and was climbing into the cab of a white F-150 pickup. Noland raised the gun again, aiming for the truck's tires. But then he saw the old man, the manager, standing a few feet from the hut, his mouth hanging open.

"What the hell?" he said.

The truck took off, its engine roaring as it plowed over the curbstones and made for the marina's exit. Noland and the old man watched together as it left the parking lot and raced off down S.R. 70.

The old man turned back to Noland. "You look like a horror movie. You want an ambulance?"

Noland walked over to the van. Keeping one hand on the bumper, he leaned over at the waist and caught his breath. Eventually, he opened the back, found a roll of paper towels that he kept there, and used a wad to clean the blood off his face. This was difficult because his hands were still shaking terribly. Shit. Was he having a fucking heart attack?

The old man had vanished. Noland breathed in and out, real slow. A combination of fear and rage was still pumping adrenaline into his bloodstream. Another five minutes passed before he had settled down sufficiently to go back to the boat and step back down into the cabin. The boat hook was on the floor, the blunt side stained with his blood—a testament to his stupidity. It didn't take much imagination to work out what would've happened if he hadn't ducked. Valkenburg would've buried the hook in his skull. Then he would have taken his keys and driven the van out into the woods (just as Noland had done with Bisby's car the night before). Then, after nightfall, he would have fired up the *Zigeuner*'s six-horse outboard and putt-putted to the middle of the lake, where he would've tossed Noland in, with an old anchor or perhaps a cinder block chained to his ankles. It wouldn't have been the first time the old lake had received a body, enfolding it into its dark waters. There was probably a whole football team's worth of guys down there from over the years, their bones softening into pulp.

He conducted a quick search, going through the cabinets and thumbing through the few books on the small shelf. Valkenburg had left nothing of value, no wallet, checkbook, or laptop computer. He was prepared to flee at a moment's notice, which was exactly what he had done.

The only item of interest was the strange map still resting on the table, undisturbed.

Noland rolled up the map and put it under his arm. That left the matter of the boat itself. Noland didn't want Valkenburg coming back and sailing the *Zigeuner* up the St. John's. So he rummaged through the small galley and found a sack of sugar, which he took up on deck and poured into the outboard's gas tank. Then, for good measure, he took out his knife and cut every rope line he saw, and even gave the mainsail a slice or two.

As he climbed off the boat, something crunched under his foot. Valkenburg's eyeglasses. Noland picked them up. Undoubtedly, they were fake as the rest of him. A prop.

He got in the van and drove to the exit. At the hut, he rolled down the window. The old man came out.

Noland asked, "I don't suppose you got the license plate of the truck?"

The man squinted at him, then went back into the hut. Noland wondered if he was calling the cops, after all. But a moment later, he emerged with a slip of paper and handed it to him.

"I keep a record of all the plates," he said.

"Thanks. For everything."

The old man hesitated, staring at him. Clearly, he was on the verge of some momentous decision.

"You used to play for the Gators, didn't you?"

Noland nodded. Blood dribbled into his eye.

The old man smiled. "Tight end, right?"

"Safety."

He snapped his fingers. "Yeah, I remember. Twice." He held up two fingers, the way Noland's fans had done, long ago. "You were pretty good, Twice. What the hell happened to you?"

Noland got out his wallet and handed the man five twenties, along with one of his business cards. "If the dude comes back, call me."

The old man nodded. Noland took off.

Driving down I-4 with one eye was a bitch, but he managed it, making his way to a Doc-in-a-Box in Lake Mary. A young woman P.A. gave him seven stitches, a tetanus shot, and a flesh-colored bandage. At some point, she asked how he'd gotten hurt.

"On a boat," he said.

She whistled. "Took a tumble?"

"Yeah," he said. "It was a doozie."

"ANY LUCK?"

"Well, I made contact."

Kiril sighed, a slow-motion typhoon over the phone line. "You lost him, didn't you?"

"I lost him."

"Are you hurt?"

"Just a scratch. Do you still have that friend at the DMV?"

Noland read him the license plate number. Kiril said he'd get back to him and hung up.

Not knowing what else to do, Noland drove home and took a shower, careful not to wet his bandage. Afterward, he lay down on the bed and tried to sleep for a bit but was still too amped up. Angry, too, mostly at himself. If only he had brought Kiril along. Kiril would have yanked Valkenburg's ass off the boat the moment he saw him come out of the hatch. But Noland hadn't brought Kiril. Instead, he'd tried to hot-dog it. Now it was too late. Valkenburg would create a new identity. In twenty-four hours, he might look totally different. But what troubled Noland most was that he had been so good at it—the glasses, the dyed hair and beard, and, of course, the fake injury. The whole character. He was almost like an actor or a . . . Noland couldn't put his finger on it.

And then there was the fact that he'd gone to such trouble in the first place. Why would he need a disguise, out there alone on his boat? Had he known someone would come for him? Was he that smart?

Noland already knew the answer to that question: yeah, he was that smart.

Noland lay down on top of the sheets, turning the memory over and over in his head. Valkenburg had tried to kill him, which was no real shock, given the circumstances. But even so, Noland was impressed by the man's cool. He'd been quiet as a cat when he'd crossed the cabin and swung that boat hook. It took a certain kind of person to do that—to kill a stranger in cold blood. Even in Raiford, such men were a rarity.

Okay, Noland thought. The dude will off me if he gets a chance. Good to know. He was not discouraged by the revelation. If anything, it clarified matters. Valkenburg was dangerous, surely. But Noland had set his fee high enough to risk his life. Now that he knew exactly what kind of man he was up against, and the level of action required to beat him, he felt better. Relieved.

He slept.

When he woke up, he was startled to see that it was already past nine in the evening, the last glimmer of dusk long since gone. Once again, his life had been turned upside down. He got dressed and went out to the van, pondering his next step. It was pointless to go back to the *Zigeuner*. But he didn't have any better ideas, and he felt the need to do something. He got back on the road.

He had barely reached the I-4 exit when his cell rang.

"Mr. Twice?" a voice asked. A woman's voice. Whoever she was, she was half shouting into the phone, loud enough to hurt his ear. And yet, despite her shouting, he could barely hear her. Wherever she was, thunderous music was playing in the background. Some kind of dance music. Techno.

"Who the fuck is this?" Noland shouted back.

"It's Karen. Karen Voss."

Even shouting, she sounded smart. Poised. "What do you want, Karen?"

"I need your help. Someone's following me."

Normally, he would have scoffed. His clients often got paranoid a few days into a case, especially the crooked ones. He once had a guy who was convinced the FBI had bugged his toupee. But this time, something twitched in the pit of Noland's stomach—a bit of worry, and curiosity.

"Where are you?" he asked.

"At The Palace. It's off Church Street."

"I know where it is. Who followed you?"

"I don't know. Some guy. I saw him yesterday when I was at lunch. And I just saw him again. He's sitting alone near the door."

"And there's no possibility you're mistaken?"

"No."

"It could be a similar guy. Or even if it is the same guy, it could be a coincidence."

"I said no."

He remembered how direct she had been in the meeting. How smart and shrewd.

"Call the police," he said.

Her voice rose to a shriek. "Are you kidding me? No way. That's why I'm calling you."

He reached up and ran his fingers over the dingy fabric that lined the ceiling of the van, pitted like a moonscape.

"Okay, hang tight. I'll be there in a few minutes."

"Thanks. I'll be on the balcony. I'm in a red dress."

She hung up.

It was a Tuesday night, barely ten, but Church Street was slammed. He didn't bother looking for a spot nearby, just went straight to a garage three blocks away, then walked. The Palace occupied an old bank building from the 1940s, its Edwardian architecture still evident. Noland was familiar with the club from skip-tracing. If a coke dealer or a well-heeled runaway ever blew through Orlando, there was a good chance he or she would end up at The Palace.

The techno music hit him before he reached the door, the bass notes vibrating in his chest. He felt the need to enact his usual calming ritual, reaching behind his back and raking his knuckles along the Ruger's grip. In the van, he had debated whether to bring it. Even though he had a license, carrying the gun in town was risky from a legal point of view. But his brush with death on Valkenburg's boat a few hours earlier had compelled him. He needed some reassurance.

He went inside, lingering in the foyer until his damp skin adjusted to the freezing air. A smell of sweat and perfume hit his nostrils, and he braced himself before walking into the main room. Like a lot of things in Orlando, The Palace was a hybrid: a disco with the sleazy ambience of a Vegas strip club. Girls in bikinis worked the bar, doling out top-shelf booze. The bar counter itself was fashioned out of polished metal, and behind the shelves hung ten-foot mirrors outlined with red neon, which bathed the clientele in a constant, hellish glow.

The dance floor took up most of the bank's lobby, with the bar running along the right side where the tellers had once been. The original marble columns now held up the balcony, which jutted out over the dance floor and lent everything a bit of gothic menace.

Noland took a stool at the bar and ordered a G&T. Then he got out his phone and texted Karen.

—I'm downstairs. what does he look like?
—Fuzzy.

Noland took a sip from his drink and looked into the mirror, scanning the tables behind him. Sure enough, there was the guy. Coarse, unkempt beard, like bear fur, and carefully tousled, long hair sculpted with gel. This was the latest fashion, Noland knew—the Mountain Man look—recently adopted by a certain kind of young, high-tech nerd. It was a look that seemed to say: *I've got a master's degree in computer engineering, but I'm still a rugged primitive. How about it, ladies?*

Fuzzy was sipping a beer while pretending to be engrossed in his phone, whose white glow illuminated his features. He had one of those neutral, square faces that some men are cursed with. A forgettable face.

Noland texted her again:

> —Okay, I see him. go home
> —Wtf! he'll follow me
> —Exactly

Noland put away his phone. He watched the dancers in the mirror. Yuppies, mostly, not long out of college. The guys were dressed in silk shirts and slacks, and the girls in sleek, tight dresses. Then Noland's gaze wandered up, and he saw Karen. She was descending the spiral staircase, her strong legs moving gracefully beneath the fabric of her short dress. The dress was much nicer than those worn by the Barbies on the dance floor, not merely red but some improbable combination of red and gold, mixed not in the dye but in the very threads, the result being an otherworldly hue that seemed to emit its own light. Falling around her bare shoulders, the fabric looked so soft as to be almost liquid—molten. A red dress, she had said. What an understatement. Noland found himself wondering how many thousands of dollars it must have cost.

She headed for the door. Noland wondered if she would be foolish enough to glance in Fuzzy's direction—or, even worse, in Noland's own—but she did neither. She walked straight out of the club, her arms swinging leisurely, a pink purse no bigger than an eyeglass case in one hand and her phone in the other.

Noland waited. He hoped that Fuzzy would stay put. Hoped, that is, that Karen was wrong, and that Fuzzy was just another hipster who happened to frequent the same places she did. But barely five seconds had passed before the man stood up, put his phone away, and went after her. His lips were pressed together, his eyes level. A man on a mission.

Noland slid off the stool. Out front, he spotted Fuzzy already a block away, heading up Church Street. A block beyond him, on the edge of Noland's vision, Karen strode with the same confident, unhurried rhythm. Noland started after them, forming the third knot in the invisible rope they formed—Karen, Fuzzy, and himself.

He got out his phone and pretended to text in case Fuzzy gave him an over-the-shoulder. But the guy wasn't that savvy. In fact, he seemed clueless, galumphing down the sidewalk after Karen, staring at her. Definitely not a P.I., or even a cop. That was good news, but it also raised a new, more disturbing possibility: Was Fuzzy someone she knew? A spurned lover? A friend she owed money to?

Was she setting Noland up?

He followed them for two more blocks until Karen took a right into a very expensive, ground-floor parking lot. Fuzzy stopped. His mouth literally hung open as he watched her go inside.

Noland had planned on waiting for Fuzzy to go to his own car, where Noland could tackle him discreetly. But the man's total obliviousness in this critical moment was irresistible. After a quick glance up and down the street, he ran straight at Fuzzy and punched him in the gut. It was like punching a feather pillow. Fuzzy let out a soft whimper and crumpled to the small patch of grass between the garage and the sidewalk. Noland put his fist into the small of Fuzzy's back and said, "Don't move, bro."

Fuzzy clutched his middle and whimpered some more. Still squatting, Noland frisked him, extracting the obligatory leather wallet from his back pocket. The streetlamp was bright enough for him to read the driver's license: Charles Edmond Deisch.

Deisch. Noland recognized the name from the background information he'd found on Selberis Constructors.

Somebody named Deisch had been the plaintiff in a wrongful death lawsuit filed against the firm the previous year. Noland took a breath, counted to ten, and then touched the man's shoulder. "Charles, huh? I'm gonna call you Chuck. You okay, Chuck?"

"Just take the wallet," Deisch croaked, getting a bit of wind back.

"I'm not trying to rob you, Chuck. Let's get you on your feet."

He hooked his forearms under Deisch's armpits and pulled him up. Deisch didn't resist. Standing on his own now, he kept his arms crossed over his middle.

"Who the fuck are you?"

"My name's Nole. Let me buy you a beer."

Deisch blinked. "You're kidding."

"I know a place down the street. A lot nicer than that shithole you just came from. Come on."

He put his arm around Deisch's shoulder and led him down the street.

They covered the five blocks to Mulvaney's in a few minutes. After the sensory overload of The Palace, the dark cave of Mulvaney's felt soothing, almost homey. Garth Brooks warbled on the Wurlitzer, and at the pool table, a couple of beefy guys were shooting a friendly game. Noland sat Deisch down at a table in the back, then went to the bar and got two beers. When he sat down, Deisch still looked a little dazed. Noland handed him a beer.

"Go on. I know you drink because I saw you."

Deisch took a sip, then grimaced as if the cheap beer offended him. "What do you want?"

"How long you been tailing Karen Voss?"

"How long you been assaulting people?"

Noland held up his hands in surrender. "Sorry about that, Chuck. If you're really upset, call the cops. You'll probably find a couple right here in this bar."

Deisch looked down, thinking.

"Why do you care?"

"I'm paid to."

Deisch took another sip.

"I've been watching her for a couple of weeks now. Off and on. I can't do it full-time. I have a job."

"What do you do?"

"I'm a doctor."

"No shit?"

He nodded, ruefully. "I'm a specialist. Ear, nose, and throat."

Noland registered a moment of surprise. "Huh. I had you pegged as a . . ." He was about to say "web designer" but thought better of it. "Well, Dr. Deisch, you should consider your career. Criminals can't practice medicine, you know."

Deisch's smile faded. "I'm not the criminal. She is."

Noland leaned closer. He hadn't expected this answer. "What did she do?"

Deisch shook his head. "I'm not telling you anything else until you tell me something."

"Like what?"

"Who are you?"

Noland got out one of his cards and handed it to him. Deisch squinted at it.

"You're a private investigator?"

"Yeah. I'm a specialist, too."

Deisch curled his lips into a sneer. "So you work for her?"

"For her company, yeah."

Deisch tossed the card onto the table. "Well, you've done your job. You got me off her tail. Why are we here?"

"Like I said. I want to know why you were following her."

"Why would I tell you?"

Noland sat back, giving the man some room. Deisch was only a few years younger than he was, but Noland sensed that the guy was still a child in some ways. Noland would have to spell it all out, and even then Deisch might not be able to follow.

"No reason. But you should know this: just because I work for these people doesn't mean I trust them. I'd like to know your angle."

Deisch wobbled his head sideways, as if he lacked the energy to shrug.

"My angle is simple. I want her dead. I want all of them dead."

Noland caught his breath. His mind flashed back to Bisby's corpse, now shriveling in the bathtub in Longwood. Its dead eyes sinking, even now, into hollow caves beneath the lime. Noland stared into Deisch's eyes, which were blue and unusually small. Could he have done it? Was he the crack shot with the .32?

"That's a pretty harsh angle, Chuck."

Deisch blinked at him.

"By 'them,'" Noland said, "you mean Selberis? The partners?"

"Yes. All of them." He unfixed his gaze and sat back. There was an air of resignation in his posture, as if he knew all the hating in the world wasn't going to make a lick of difference. Maybe he wasn't such a child, after all. "Unfortunately, I'm not the kind of person who could actually kill anybody. I'm a doctor."

Noland laughed.

"But the next best thing," Deisch went on, "is to see them in prison. I'd settle for that."

Noland found himself suddenly irritated. Like many ex-cons, he found it gauche when normal people talked about prison. But something about Deisch's statement, with its matter-of-fact certainty, intrigued him.

"Prison, huh? So we're back to my first question. What'd she do?"

Deisch pinched the neck of his beer bottle, as if realizing that he had said too much. "It doesn't matter."

His voice lowered so much that Noland could barely hear him over the music. His expression became tinged with some inarticulate sadness. He was wallowing in fatalism. Noland felt the need to shake him up.

"They killed your brother, right?"

Deisch's face, already pasty, now turned completely white, as if someone had pulled a plug somewhere and all his blood had flowed out through the hole. He sat up straight and his chest rose and fell heavily. Noland tensed up; the ear, nose, and throat doctor was about to take a swing at him.

But the moment passed. Deisch's hand was steady as he raised the bottle to his mouth and drank some more.

"Nikki wasn't my brother. He was my cousin."

"My mistake," Noland said.

"How did you know about him?"

"I do my homework. I remembered there was a lawsuit. Deisch versus Selberis. Was that you?"

Deisch shook his head. "My uncle. Nikki's dad."

"You and Nikki were tight?"

"We grew up together." He made a sheepish, almost disgusted face, as if the cliché offended him, despite being true. "And, yeah, they killed him."

"How?"

He raised his narrow shoulders an inch, then lowered them again. "Shitty maintenance. Cutting corners. A crane malfunctioned and a cable broke. He was crushed."

Noland paused. He had to tread lightly now. Deisch might yet take a swing at him, and Mulvaney's was not the best place for this to happen.

"I understand," Noland said. "I'd want revenge, too."

"They killed my uncle, too. Indirectly. The lawsuit bankrupted him. He had a heart attack three months later."

Noland acknowledged this with a brief nod. "I'm sorry."

He scoffed. "What are you? An empathetic thug?"

Noland rapped his knuckles on the tabletop. "My dad used to say, 'Life will kick you in the ass. Sometimes you have to kick it back.'"

"Wow. That's beautiful. Thanks."

"You're welcome."

Noland's phone vibrated on his hip. It was Karen.

—Did u get him?
     —yeah. we're having a beer
—WTF?
     —I'll explain later.
—alright. I'm at my place. come by when you're done.

Noland put the phone back in his pocket, even as he considered the implications of her last instruction. An image of Karen's lovely, bare legs entered his mind, even though he had never really seen them. But then he remembered something else Zeb had told him long ago: Don't think with your dick and don't fuck with your head. It was true. He needed to keep his mind on the job. Flustered, he tried to focus on Deisch again, who was smirking.

"Your boss?"

Noland nodded. "Your would-be victim. What were you planning to do? Knock her out? Scare her into confessing?"

"I wanted to find out what she was up to."

"How did you get the idea to follow her in the first place? Why her?"

He pointed his chin at the tabletop, and his eyes took on a far-away look. "Random chance. I saw her leaving a restaurant one night. Recognized her from the trial. Without thinking, I followed her. Found out where she lives. Followed her the next night, too. And the next. She goes out a lot. Meets the others sometimes."

The hairs on the back of Noland's neck bristled. "The other partners?"

"Yes."

"Which ones?"

"All of them. Except the crazy one. Valkenburg. I haven't seen him lately. I think he bugged out."

"Where do they meet? At the office?"

He shook his head. "The fat man's place."

"Redding?"

"Yes. And they always meet late. Close to midnight. Like a coven." He sneered at his own joke.

Noland paused again. He wasn't sure how much further he could push Deisch before he fought back or, even worse, called the cops. Noland had been counting on the man's fear of self-incrimination, but that rubber band would only stretch so far. Noland decided to risk one more question. "What do you think they're up to, Chuck?"

Deisch's eyes widened as if the question startled him. His mouth hung open again, as it had outside the garage. He seemed to be making a decision of his own.

"The best I can figure is some kind of money laundering scheme. A lot of their projects are in the red, but they never go under."

"How do you know they're in the red?"

"Nikki told me."

"How the fuck did he know? He was just a construction worker, right?"

"No, he wasn't. He was smart. He had a degree. He knew that the projects were over schedule. All the guys on the crew did. The only mystery was how Selberis stayed afloat. Hell, better than afloat. They're rolling in it. All the partners. They change cars like other people change shoes."

Noland nodded, taking it all in. He wondered how much of Deisch's information he should believe.

"So you think they killed your cousin on purpose? To shut him up?"

This time, Deisch didn't react. "I wouldn't put it past them. But they don't seem brave enough for out-and-out murder. My guess is that Nicki's death was an accident. Criminal negligence, but still an accident."

"Criminal negligence, huh? But the jury ruled against you. Against your uncle, I mean."

Deisch smiled with his mouth only, his eyes remaining small and cold. "Our lawyer fucked up. Blew a cross-examination."

"Of who?"

"That kid they've got running the jobs."

"Shawn Difore?"

His snarl returned. "Right. Shawn Difore. He's a real shit. Buying cheap materials. Blowing off safety regulations. That kind of thing. Nicki was killed by a . . ." His voice trembled a little. ". . . a rusty cable. Absurd, wouldn't you say?"

Noland didn't reply. But he thought to himself: *No, I wouldn't.* Innocent people get killed all the time. It isn't absurd. It's evil. Had Nikki's death been the result of an evil act? If so, then the source of the evil in question was probably Selberis itself. One or more of the partners. His clients. Did that make him, Noland, evil as well? Probably. But then sometimes, as Zeb had told him once, all you have is a choice of evils. For the moment, Noland had chosen Selberis.

"What now?" Deisch asked.

Noland finished his beer and set the bottle down with finality. "Chuck, I'll make you a deal. We trade information. Anything I find out about your cousin's death, I'll share with you. Under the table, of course. And anything you find about Selberis's dirty deals, you let me know. I'll make it worth your while."

Deisch's eyes narrowed into slits. "That's a strange offer. Considering that you work for the other team."

"Not necessarily," Noland stood up. "Some of the partners might be dirtier than others, and I need to know that, too. But you can forget about Karen Voss. She's onto you now, and she might even call the cops. Also, I don't think she could tell you much."

"Maybe you don't know her as well as you think."

"I don't know her at all. What about my offer?"

"I'll consider it."

"Good." He picked up the card that Deisch had tossed onto the table and handed it back to him. "You have my card. I answer my phone 24/7."

Back in the van, he texted Karen.

—On my way. What's your address?

She texted it to him, a condo complex off Semoran. He headed there in a kind of daze, exhausted and overwhelmed. And wary. What did she want from him? Information? Reassurance? A casual fuck? Some of his women clients—especially the older, well-to-do ladies who often hired him to catch their cheating husbands—seemed to think that full access to his cock was an implicit part of the gig. Noland, for his part, usually went along, either out of vanity or expediency or—rarely—genuine lust. But Karen wasn't some faded flower, pissed off at her husband for cheating on her. Karen was young and sexy. She didn't need him to stud. Part of him wished she did, but an equal part just wanted the night to be over.

He checked his watch. It was almost midnight.

Day two was gone.

8

THE CONDO COMPLEX was like every other in that part of Orlando, a warren of two-story buildings sprawled over twenty acres of reclaimed swampland. The beige stucco and rounded arches over the stairwells were meant to look like something built by a Renaissance architect. The name came to Noland: Palladio. Noland had learned about him in humanities, his favorite class at U.F. Unlike most of the other star players on the team, he rarely missed class, and he felt like he was cheating himself when he did. He even dragged himself in on those Mondays after a big game when every muscle in his body felt like it had been pulverized. His humanities professor, an elderly Black woman with hair the color of cigarette ash, had been the best. Smart and shrewd. Noland had only pulled a B average on her tests, even with studying, but she ended up giving him an A. A for Attitude, he supposed. Or perhaps she had felt sorry for him. Had she seen his future?

Karen's condo was on the second floor of the last building, facing out onto a rococo fountain (more Italian bullshit). When she opened the door, Noland was surprised to see that she had traded the cocktail dress for sweatpants, a faded T-shirt, and thick purple socks.

"Slipped into something more comfortable?" he said.

"Fuck you." She stood in the doorway, her eyes hard as onyx.

Noland waited a beat. "Nice to see you, too."

"What took you so long?"

"Traffic."

She let him in. He found himself diminished under the high ceilings. Off to the right, the open-plan kitchen gleamed with shiny appliances.

"Did you find out who he is?"

"His name is Deisch."

"Deisch?" Her face went blank, then sharpened into clarity. "The guy who sued us?"

"His nephew. He's got a grudge."

Her mouth hung open. "Fuck."

"Has anyone ever told you that you say 'fuck' a lot?"

"Shut up. Do you want a drink?"

He said okay, even though accepting her offer made him feel like an enabler. Her face was already puffy from booze. She'd had enough.

"What kind?"

"Gin, if you've got it."

"I've got everything."

She padded into the kitchen. Even in sweatpants, she looked good. It must've been the dancing every night that kept her legs muscular, firm. But the rest of her looked skinny. Malnourished. No muscle tone in her arms. He got the impression that, at nearly thirty, she was still coasting on some residual level of youthful athleticism. She was one of those overachieving nerds who get straight As while never missing soccer practice, always hoping to make the first string but never quite cutting it.

She returned with two full glasses—one dark, one clear—and handed him the clear one. As she took her first sip, she pointed at his forehead. "You're hurt."

"Just a couple of stitches."

The living area was dominated by a large, postmodern coffee table, a rectangular sheet of glass resting on a chrome oval. Its cold perfection matched that of the rest of the condo, neat and futuristic. Except for the floor. One half was marble tile, while the other half was bare concrete, recently scarred and dusty.

"Sorry," she said. "I'm retiling."

"Doing it yourself?"

"It calms me down."

Noland was surprised. He didn't know many women of her age and class who would tackle a job like that. But then he realized that she was one of those people who could effortlessly master anything they put their mind to. She could probably build a house from scratch, if need be.

She clunked her tumbler down on the table, too hard, then settled back on the modish leather chair. Noland took the couch. She sat there and looked off into the middle distance, as if contemplating her fate.

"Well," she said. "I suppose I should thank you for running him off. But that's part of your job, isn't it?"

"I suppose."

She frowned into her lap. "And we're paying you extremely well. Got anything to show for it yet?"

He knew it would be a mistake to share much with her, but he was curious to see how she would react.

"I saw Valkenburg."

Her eyes flickered up to his again. "Where?"

"On his boat."

"What happened?"

He pointed to the bandage on his forehead. "He literally beat me to the punch. It won't happen again."

"He slugged you?"

"He meant to do worse."

Her eyes widened a bit and seemed to go unfocused again. "Typical."

"Oh yeah? Last night, you said he wouldn't have killed Bisby. You still think that?"

Instead of answering, she sighed. The purple bags under her eyes seemed to have grown darker in the time he'd been there.

"You know," he said eventually, "I'm not sure how this is going to play out."

"What's that supposed to mean?"

"It means that I'm trying to keep anyone from learning about Selberis's little criminal enterprise. But I might not succeed. If the cops get involved, what are you going to do?"

She looked away and wrinkled her nose.

"I'll probably kill myself."

She said it matter-of-factly, as if announcing she would go on vacation.

"Really? How?"

"Pills. I've got tons of them."

He leaned forward.

"Are you really in that deep?"

She smiled. "Like a frog in a well."

Despite himself, he laughed. "Karen, you're obviously smart. How did you get caught up in all this?"

"That's a hell of a question, coming from an ex-con."

That shut him up. How had she found out? Faith?

"Fair enough," he said.

When she met his eyes again, her expression had softened a bit.

"I heard you were a normal person, once. What happened?"

"Lots of things," he said. "Mainly, I broke my leg."

"Playing football?"

He nodded. "I was cheated by fate. Or maybe it was the system. I can't remember."

"Same here."

"I don't believe it. I bet you sailed through college without a bump."

"I didn't go to college."

Once again, he was surprised. "Really?"

"Really. My family wasn't the college-going type. I did go to secretarial school, though."

"You're kidding."

"Nope."

"So how'd you end up being a head honcho at Selberis?"

She took a sip of her drink. "I started out somewhere else. As a secretary. I found out I was good at organizing things. Jobs. Money. People. My bosses noticed. They gave me bigger roles. I made more money. I discovered I really liked money."

"And Selberis offered you more of it?"

"Yes."

"How long before you realized they were crooked?"

"Everybody's crooked."

"You think so? You think everybody has a drug lord chasing after them?"

She blinked. He knew he shouldn't ask her any more—her life story wasn't relevant to his immediate goal of keeping her and the others alive and out of jail—but he couldn't resist. "So this is what you want to be? A rich lady with a cushy job, laundering money for a crook?"

"That's a relatively small part of my job, believe it or not. And no, this was not my final goal."

"What is?"

"I want to be COO at a Fortune 500 company."

Noland found himself smiling, not because he found this funny, but because he had no doubt that she would achieve her dream, someday. If she survived.

A silence followed. He gripped his knees, not knowing what to do or say now. He had the sudden, natural impulse to simply walk around the glass table and kiss her. What would it be like? To kiss that hard, thin mouth?

"I guess I should go," he said.

But before he could rise, she spoke again. "What I meant last night was that Val wouldn't ever kill Bisby unless he had no choice. They were fast friends. Like brothers, almost."

"And brothers can't kill each other?"

She ignored his tone. "They started the company together. Way back. Bisby was the front man, and Val was the action. He took care of all the arrangements."

"Maybe Bisby pissed him off."

She shook her head. "Even if he had wanted to kill Bisby, he wouldn't have shot him. He would have . . . strangled him or something. Val is very hands-on."

Noland pointed to his forehead. "No shit."

She smiled again—a real smile this time, her eyes crinkling at the corners.

"You were a cop once, right? Before you went to prison?"

"A deputy sheriff."

"How long?"

"Six years."

She nodded as if his answer had solved some mystery. "Val was a cop, too. Did you know that?"

"Really?"

"A long time ago. In New York. Buffalo, I believe. Went up the chain. By the time he left, he was a detective. A narc."

Deep inside Noland's mind, something clicked into place. He remembered Valkenburg's disguise—the fake glasses and the limp. He clapped his hands together. "That explains a lot."

She looked startled. "Oh yeah?"

"Never mind," he said. "Why'd he quit?"

"I've no idea. I wouldn't know anything at all about it, except that Cassy told me."

Noland caught his breath. That was all it took—the mere mention of her name.

"You know her?"

"A little. We got to be friendly. Christmas parties. That kind of thing."

"You trust her?"

Instead of answering, she rose, came over, and sat next to him. Close. Her skin exuded a strong but not unpleasant mixture of perfume, sweat, and alcohol.

"You're kinda cute," she said.

"Thanks."

She put her hand on his bicep. "You've kept yourself in shape."

"It's part of my job."

She nodded, then looked into his eyes. "Wanna fool around?"

"You mean, do I want to fu—?"

She clapped her hand over his mouth. "Don't say it."

He chuckled through her fingers, then pulled her hand away. He had, of course, been expecting her question, or some version of it. But before he could reply, her eyelids closed to slits. He wondered how many other men had sat where he was now. How many guys she had used to forget the nasty corner she had painted herself into. She wanted to use him now. Another kind of sleeping pill.

He slapped his thighs. "Well, if you insist. But you have to promise me something."

She waited.

"Promise you won't kill yourself. At least, not without consulting me."

She waved him off. "I was being melodramatic."

"Sure. But even so—you promise?"

Then she gave him a third and final smile. It was sweet, this time. As if he'd just surprised her with flowers. "I promise. But you have to do your part. You have to find Val and get our money back."

"Indeed."

Then, with everything settled, he leaned over and kissed her. Softly, slowly, as if in a dream.

9

H E WOKE BEFORE dawn. She was in his arms, her slender, warm body spooned into his. She slept like a kid, mouth open, snoring slightly. He needed to pee but didn't want to wake her. She seemed helpless.

Furtively, he reached one arm to the floor and dug his phone out of his pants. There were already two emails from Kiril. The first held information on Valkenburg's truck, which was registered to a company called Rache Consulting. The second email was an image, a hi-def scan of the map that Noland had found on the *Gypsy*. The email's subject line read: "No idea."

Karen shuddered awake, lifting her head from the pillow and gasping. She seemed surprised at something, more than his presence. He dropped the phone and put his arm around her again, but she scooted away. From the other side of the bed, she turned and looked at him.

"You should go," she said.

"Okay."

He put on his pants and gathered the other articles of clothing from the trail he'd left from the living room. By the time he was dressed, she was already wrapped in a silk kimono, dotted with little pink flowers. A tight pink band cinched her coarse hair.

"You okay?" he asked.

She was not looking at him, but rather down at his phone, still on the bed where he'd dropped it. He'd left the image of the map up on the screen.

"Where'd you get that?" Her voice was nasal, stuffed up. Like half the population of Florida, she had allergies.

"Guess," he said, slipping on his shoes.

She kept looking at it.

"That's one of our projects," she said. "A site."

Noland stopped moving.

"A current site?"

She nodded. "An office park. Near St. Cloud. They started a few weeks ago."

Noland picked up the phone. He tried to keep his expression neutral as he looked at her again, but in fact he was stunned. What the hell did Valkenburg want with an office park? One they hadn't even been built yet?

"Does that help?" she asked.

"I think so, yeah," he said. "Thanks. Thanks for everything."

She smiled. In the morning light, her skin shone. She looked softer. Almost dewy.

"Call me if you think of anything else," he said. "And don't forget your promise."

"Sure."

Back in the van, he allowed himself a few moments of introspection. For a guy who'd almost gotten killed the day before, he felt surprisingly good, his muscles limber, his skin still tingly. Of course, he had Karen to thank. Her taking him to bed had been the nicest thing anyone had done for him in months. And yet, he couldn't shake the feeling that he'd made a mistake.

Once home, he took an hour off to walk the dogs, shower, and eat breakfast. Then he got back to work, starting with a Florida.gov search on his laptop, looking for Rache Consulting. He got a hit. Its first filing date had been the previous January, six months ago, the official economic activity listed, helpfully, as "any business lawful in the State of Florida."

The official address was in Colonial Town.

He got back in the van and drove west on State Road 50. Half an hour later, he reached a small, dreary office building and went inside. On the second floor, he found a plain gray door with a plastic shingle that read RACHE. Beneath that was a mail slot, the old-fashioned kind with a metal flap. He peeked through and saw a pile of mail on the floor. Then he checked the lock—Patterson. Cheap. Thirty seconds to pop. But it was too early to try. He'd wait for evening, after the people in the other offices had gone home. The time of day when no one would look twice at a workman in dungarees, shuffling upstairs with his toolbox.

That left the rest of the afternoon. He remembered the name of the construction site that Karen had told him about, the one that Valkenburg had a map of. In St. Cloud, she said. He googled it and deduced the address, which was only a few minutes away on Hazelton Road.

It took him five minutes to get there. He parked on the edge of the property, enclosed by a chain-link fence that bore a huge banner: COMING IN SPRING—ROCKLAND SPECIALTY MALL. Then, beneath this proclamation in a much smaller font: SELBERIS CONSTRUCTORS.

He hooked his fingers through the chain-link fence and peered in. No one was about. The ground had been completely razed and leveled, but not so much as a single brick or section of concrete had been laid anywhere on the grounds. A hundred yards away, on the far side of the lot, a pair of orange bulldozers sat idle. Beyond them, outside the gate, was the foreman's trailer.

Noland drove around. A lone hard-hat sat on the trailer's wooden stoop, smoking a cigarette. He squinted at Noland.

"Morning."

"Morning," Noland said. "You the foreman?"

He grinned, gray-toothed, horrible. "Do I look like management?"

"Where is he?"

"Out."

Noland looked around. Saw a Coke machine on the end of the trailer, chugging in the heat.

"You want a Jack-and-Coke?"

The man raised his eyebrows. "You're kidding?"

"Nope."

Noland fed quarters into the machine and got two Cokes, then ducked back into the van. Then, taking two airline-size bottles of Jack Daniels from the stash he kept for stakeouts, he improvised a couple of highballs by pouring a bottle into each Coke. He went back out. The hard-hat lifted his can in salute before taking a deep slurp. Noland did the same.

"So work is stopped?"

"Yeah. Crazy, huh? That's the way it is with this company. Start and stop. Ain't seen nothin' like it."

"And you still get paid?"

He scoffed. "Course not."

"That sucks."

The man nodded and took another slurp. "We had a really long stop on the last job. After that guy bought the farm."

"Somebody died?"

The man grimaced. "Bad mojo. Cable broke. Poor bastard."

Noland looked off into the distance. "Now you mention it, I do remember something about that. Young guy, wasn't he?"

"Yeah. Smart kid. And funny. Everybody liked him. Even the usual rent-a-drunks you find on a gig like this." His grin faded and his eyes narrowed conspiratorially. "Course, if you ask me, there was more to it than a broken cable."

"Oh, yeah?'

"Yeah. That kid was too smart to be on a 'struction site. Paid too much attention. Started noticing things."

"What manner of things?"

The hard-hat picked at his nose in a pensive manner. "Regulations not getting minded. Equipment listed on the worksheet that weren't really there. Shit like that. Happens all the time, but you're not supposed to notice it."

"But he did? Notice?"

"Worse than that. He complained."

Noland didn't have to feign surprise this time; he was genuinely startled.

"He complained?"

The man nodded. "Bitched and moaned. Like a union boss. Said it wasn't fair to the guys on the crew. Said we could do things better. Finish the project faster. Make more money. Man, he was a crusader!"

"Who'd he complain to? The foreman?"

"To anybody who would listen. Which was nobody, more or less. Finally, he went to the big boss. Whatsis name." He snapped his fingers.

Noland took a breath. "Bisby?"

"That's him. Bisby!" He rose from the stoop and walked over, getting so close that Noland caught the sour smell of his clothes. "You didn't hear it from me, but I think somebody decided to scare the kid. Went too far, though."

After a final, triumphant slurp, the hard-hat crumpled the Coke can and tossed it to the dirt. He looked Noland up and down for the first time.

"Thanks for the drink, bro. Who are you, exactly?"

"Name's Noland. I'm a consultant. I work for Selberis."

The man clapped his hand over his mouth. "Shit. I done said too much."

"It's okay. I'm not management. I was just curious."

"Glad to hear it. The boss ought to be back in an hour or so. If you want the official version. But don't let on that I was talking to you."

"No problem. I'll come back."

"What's your last name?"

"Twice."

The guy squinted, trying to recall where he'd heard the name before. Another lost, long-ago fan. Noland was amused for a moment, until he remembered, as usual, that he had absolutely nothing to be amused about. Somewhere between a has-been and a never-was, he was basically nothing. Just a name on the tip of people's tongues. A ghost.

He walked away.

                              *   *   *

He had lunch at a Cuban diner off I-Drive, then swung by Faith's office. A pimply intern met him in the parking lot and handed him a gym bag. Noland peeked inside, noted the dozen or so wads of cash and zipped it back up. He thanked the kid and left. Once again, he'd barely reached the van when his phone chirruped. Faith, with her uncanny timing for inconvenient texts.

—Did you get the bag?
          —Yeah, I got it. Where are you?
—In court. Where else?
          —The Bisby case?
—Nah one of my living clients
          —Oh. Cool.
—Got any news.
          —Not much
—Great. We've got 11 days left. Ur giving me a fucking heart attack
          —I know. I'm trying.
—Try harder.

He didn't reply. As soon as he got home, he stashed most of the money in his wall safe, keeping five K loose in the bag. Then he drove to the copy shop. In the manager's office, he handed Kiril the bag. Kiril raised an eyebrow and waited a beat before unzipping it. Noland was not offended when he started counting the money out on the tabletop. Eventually, Kiril looked up and pursed his lips.

"What's the extra two K for? A bonus?"

"You wish. It's an advance. For all the work you and Freddy are going to put in. Starting with you. I need you for an hour or so. Tonight."

Kiril's face sagged. "Another black op?"

"Yeah, but low-level. Should be cake."

"Oh, sure."

"I promise."

Kiril's expression was typical for him, though Noland could never decide what it meant, exactly, whether bemusement or rage. Was it a Russian thing? "Okay. But if you find another stiff, you're on your own."

Noland went into the washroom and changed into his plumber's dungarees. Then he sat in Kiril's office and surfed on his phone until five thirty, when he and Kiril left together, taking S.R. 50 back to Colonial Town. Despite rush hour, they made good time, getting all the way to Bumby before hitting traffic. They reached the drab office building by six, the sun still hot as it scoured the parking lot, empty except for a grubby little Honda. The janitor, Noland guessed. Or maybe a secretary. He parked by a retention pond in the back, then climbed out of the van as Kiril scrambled over into the driver's seat.

The familiar weight of the toolbox gave Noland a feeling of weariness as he walked around the building, headed for his second B&E in as many days. But there was no helping it. It had to be done, if he was ever going to find Valkenburg.

He had barely rounded the corner when a woman emerged from the building's glass door. She was carrying a cardboard box—white, a banker's box—the lid bulging from whatever was inside. It must have been heavy because she leaned backward as she walked, her bare arms straining. And yet she moved briskly, walking out into the blazing sun, the bounce of her ponytails unmistakable. It was Cassy.

She hadn't seen him, and he kept perfectly still as she walked into the parking lot. With a kind of mute fascination, he watched as she went to the Honda, popped the trunk, and heaved the box inside. He waited until she got into the cabin before running as fast as he could back around the building and to the van, the toolbox bouncing against his side painfully.

"What happened?" Kiril said when he jumped into the passenger seat.

"Change of plan. We're following a Honda."

Kiril cranked the engine and gunned the van fast around to the front. Cassy was already pulling onto Colonial, heading west. Fortunately, she got stuck immediately in traffic. Kiril followed her, but the traffic caught them too. Three car lengths ahead, the light changed. The Honda made it through, and the light seemed to turn yellow an instant later.

Noland said: "Go for it."

Kiril cranked the wheel to the right and drove onto the sidewalk. Three teenagers leaped to the side as he sped forward, dropping back onto the blacktop at the intersection. Kiril stuck his hand out the window to block the oncoming traffic as they bullied their way through under a hail of pissed-off honking.

"You're not paying me enough for this shit," Kiril said.

"I know."

They caught sight of the Honda as it pulled past a fried-chicken shack, slipping into the right-turn lane. Cassy was turning onto Baker. Kiril followed, getting a lucky break in the traffic. Soon they were just two car lengths back.

"Who's this chick?"

"The dude's ex-wife. She was in his office."

"You think she's meeting him?"

Noland didn't answer. The notion that he might get a second chance at Valkenburg, so soon after his initial fuck-up, seemed incredible, too good to be true. And yet it got his hopes up. He started to think about the money again, and all the problems it would solve. What was it that Karen had said? That she really liked money? Amen to that. Money was the answer to all problems. The lubricant of the gears of the world. And as he mentally enumerated all the fixes it would get him out of—his overdue mortgage, taxes, business bills, and so on—he finally came up with an idea or two of what he might do with the remainder. First, he would fix up his mom's house. A new roof, some fresh paint, a shallow ramp from the driveway to the front door, and a walk-in tub. Might even get her in-home P.T. while he was at it. Once he got her situated, he'd take a vacation. Not the usual Caribbean jaunt, but someplace cool and temperate. San Francisco, maybe. Or Seattle. And then he'd get a sports car. Something sleek and sexy and low, that he would never allow to get stuck in traffic. Something European. Porsche. The daydream wove itself like a tapestry in his head, soothing him even as he sweated in the van.

The Honda led them farther down Semoran, past the Orlando Executive Airport. Finally, it pulled into a restaurant, one of those Chinese buffet places that seemed to take up residence overnight in any vacant shop, the retail equivalent of a hermit crab. Noland and Kiril were still in traffic when Cassy got out of the car, retrieved the box from the trunk, and headed for the entrance. The restaurant had big, wrap-around windows, like an old diner, and they could see Cassy inside as she went to a booth, where a man was waiting for her.

"Is that him?"

"Just park," Noland said.

He got a pair of binoculars out of the glove box. He couldn't see the man clearly from their spot across the frontage road, but he didn't think it was Valkenburg. This guy looked too short, and he was wearing a nerdy blue cap. Then again, Valkenburg had fooled him once before.

"I can't tell," he said at last.

A waitress came by Cassy's table and stood there a good while. Cassy and the mystery man were ordering dinner. As

Noland watched, a disheartening possibility presented itself: Maybe this guy wasn't part of the story after all, but merely some random friend. But then he remembered the box; she had taken it in with her. This was a delivery. No doubt about it.

Kiril passed the time with a sword-and-sorcery game on his phone. Noland watched Cassy sit with the man, eating. The waitress came again. After a while, the man stood up. He was carrying the box as he exited the restaurant, alone. It was only when he walked across the parking lot, into the fading sun, that Noland saw the fuzzy brown beard.

"Fuck."

"Is it him?"

"No, it's another player. Let's get on him anyway."

Kiril fired up the still-hot engine as they watched Deisch get into a small, sleek BMW—a sexy little car, rather like the one Noland had been fantasizing about. Deisch pulled out onto Bumby and Kiril slid out after him. They had barely gone three blocks when the Beemer's engine roared—Noland heard it from two car lengths back. To Noland's amazement, Deisch made a ninety-degree turn in the middle of traffic, plowing over the concrete median and ignoring the stream of oncoming cars that were ready to T-bone him. For a mild-mannered ear-nose-and-throat doctor, Deisch was driving like Mario Andretti. A few pissed-off drivers laid on the horn, but Deisch kept going, completing the U-turn expertly and then speeding off in the southbound lane.

Kiril hit the gas, throwing Noland back against the seat as he positioned the van into the left lane. He prepared to jump the median, as Deisch had done, but a solid wall of cars was moving past them now, like water flowing into Deisch's wake.

Kiril smacked the steering wheel. "Blyad!"

"It's okay," Noland said. "He was onto us."

"How?"

"I don't know. Cassy may have zeroed us."

"Cassy, huh?" Noland didn't like the way he sneered her name. "She must be pretty slick. Should we get back on her?"

Noland shook his head. "She's already gone. I'd bet on it."

Kiril smacked the wheel again, but not as hard. "What, then? Back to the guy's office?"

"I have a feeling that anything useful to us was in that box. Let's cut our losses."

Kiril considered this, then scratched his chin. "Can we get something to eat?"

Noland laughed.

"Sure," he said. "Pick a place."

*　*　*

That was a mistake. They ended up at the same joint Kiril always chose, a Thai restaurant off Goldenrod with food so hot Noland broke out in a sweat even when he specifically ordered it "mild." Of course, he should have requested the "no spice" option, like the old ladies who sometimes came in, but he couldn't bring himself to do it. Kiril, for his part, always ordered his food "Thai hot," a stipulation that had once brought a sadistic grin to the waiter's face. But then, after the second or third time he'd watched Kiril dispatch a "Thai hot" entrée without apparent discomfort, the waiter nodded and understood: this big dude was Asian. A fucking Cossack.

Tonight, it took a conscious act of will for Noland to eat his food, and not merely because of the spice. He was disgusted with himself. The fantasy of capturing Valkenburg had evaporated like the steam wicking off his porcelain teacup. He had already extended himself so much on this case, committing multiple felonies, all in the hopes of a big payday. Now he was back where he started.

Almost.

The only lead he clung to was the box that Cassy had taken from Valkenburg's office, now in the possession of Charles Deisch. This unexpected twist could only mean one thing: Deisch had suckered him. Lied to him at Mulvaney's, when he had told Noland that he didn't know what Selberis was up to. If he was stealing shit from Val's office—a secret office, no less—and getting Cassy to help him, he must know a good deal. Noland could only guess at what else the man had lied about.

Thinking all this, Noland muttered to himself: "Shit."

Kiril paused his chewing. "What?"

"He fooled me."

"The dude on the boat?"

"No, the guy in the Beemer. Deisch. He may be a principal, as it turns out."

Kiril received this bit of information with a slight widening of his eyes, then continued his meal, eating in that unhurried, precise way that some big men have. Men embarrassed by their size and appetite. Ashamed of it.

"Well, I'm going to help," Kiril said.

For a moment, Noland thought he was making a feeble joke—of course he was going to help. After all, that was what Noland was paying him for. But when Noland looked closer at Kiril's stern expression, held even as the man continued chewing, he knew that his friend was making a new sort of commitment.

"Are you sure, bro?" Noland said. "You're already dirtier than usual on this one."

Kiril nodded. "That prick shouldn't have slipped me. It's a pride thing now."

He wasn't sure whether to be guilty or elated. As it turned out, he was both. He laughed.

"Cool."

Noland got the check, making sure to place the receipt in a special fold in his wallet that he reserved for business. Back in the van, he found an airline bottle of Grey Goose for Kiril and a Jack Daniels for himself. They parked near the library and watched the sun drop down beneath the crystal peaks of downtown Orlando, the sky turning a smoky lavender color. Kiril seemed preoccupied, working through his own thoughts. But then he asked the inevitable question.

"You think the dude is gone by now?"

"The main dude?"

"Yeah."

This was, of course, the question Noland had been asking himself for the past twenty-four hours, ever since Valkenburg had left him in the parking lot with a busted forehead and the shakes. If Valkenburg was smart—really smart—he would have taken the hint and buggered off to another country, someplace with no US extradition treaty where a stranger with money could disappear. Noland knew two men personally who had done exactly that—one a crooked cop, the other a crooked lawyer. They were friends now, living the good life in Jakarta, blending in seamlessly with other expats like themselves as they drew a steady trickle from numbered bank accounts in the Caymans. There were probably thousands of guys like them, sprinkled throughout the world. Valkenburg would be just another.

And yet, for some reason, Noland couldn't believe it. Valkenburg was not going to run for it.

"No," he said at last. "He's not gone. He's close."

Kiril grunted. "You think?"

"Yeah."

"Why?"

"Because he wants something."

Noland had not fully understood the truth of this statement until he heard it come out of his own mouth. But it was the only conclusion that made sense. Valkenburg wouldn't have gone to all the trouble of changing his appearance unless he intended to stay nearby. He was going back to O-Town, where someone might recognize him. And he had the site plan, of course. Something about the construction in St. Cloud involved him. But what?

As if reading his thoughts, Kiril said, "Yeah, but what does he want? Money?"

"Nah. He's got plenty of that."

Kiril wrinkled his brow. Something had occurred to him.

"What?" Noland asked.

"The name of the company he set up. The office we were at. It's called Rache Consulting."

"So?"

Kiril grinned. "Rache. It's German. It means revenge."

Though Noland didn't move, or even blink, his heart shifted silently into a higher gear. Revenge. Deisch wanted revenge. And so, apparently, did Valkenburg—or whoever set up the dummy company. The desire for revenge ran through the story of Selberis like a motif through an opera.

"Holy shit," Noland said, eventually.

Kiril's grin faded and his expression became troubled again. "But revenge for what? And on who?"

Noland couldn't even speculate. Instead, he was about to ask another question when his phone chirped in his pocket. It was Faith, texting him: —How's it going? He muted the phone and dropped it back into his pocket. What was he supposed to tell her? That he'd gotten a shot at Valkenburg and blown it? That they were dead in the water? No, thanks. He'd blunder on, hoping for a break.

They got on the road, with Noland driving this time. It was seven o'clock, and the second rush hour began as waves of people headed out to dinner or the movies. Noland did his best to avoid the worst of the traffic, jumping back onto I-4, but they still hit a snarl around the O'Rena. As they sat in gridlock once again, Kiril looked over at him.

"Speaking of revenge," he said, "you ever get mad at me?"

Noland almost laughed. It seemed an absurd question. But Kiril's eyes were locked on him, baleful.

"Mad about what?"

"You know."

Noland laughed. "Hell, I've never been mad at you, Big Guy. Why would I be?"

Kiril acknowledged this with a nod, and then a brief pursing of his lips. Good, Noland thought. Kiril was his best friend, after all. And everything he'd said to him was true. Technically.

But of course, as soon as Kiril brought the subject up, Noland's mind went back to that awful night at Doak Campbell Stadium. Gators vs. FSU, the last game of the season. Late in the third quarter, he'd gotten a pick on the Gators' twenty and took off, thinking he was clear all the way to the end zone. Then it happened—a hit out of nowhere, as if the Hand of God had swung down on some celestial hinge and smacked him. The force of the hit threw him into the air, and when he landed, his left leg touched first and took the force of his momentum. In all his years playing ball, from peewee to high school to college, he had never landed like that. He heard the bone break, a curt, clean snap like an old tree in a storm, followed by a high, thin scream that rang out over the collective gasp of the crowd.

It was his own scream.

Later, in the hospital, Coach told him that one of the FSU linemen had raced across the field and taken him out. A big Russian kid, not normally known for speed. On that one play, the kid must have been almost as fast as Noland himself. Noland understood. He admired the kid, without even knowing his name. And he kept on admiring him when they finally met, months later. They were cogs in the same machine.

What Noland never told Kiril, of course, was that sometimes, when he thought back to the night, he did get mad. Not at Kiril. Not even at himself. Rather, he was mad at his own bad luck, the caprice of chance that had contrived to put him there, in that spot at that time, the thread of his life crossing that of Kiril's for the first—and most terrible—time.

So, yeah, he was mad. Sometimes. And the only thing that could make him feel better was chasing after someone. Preferably someone crooked, with a history of beating the system.

Someone like Arthur Valkenburg.

They finished their drinks. Noland cranked the engine.

"That was the best tackle you ever made, wasn't it?" he asked.

Kiril nodded. "By far."

10

H E DROPPED KIRIL off at the shop and drove home. After a quick workout, he took a shower, the hot water burning the cut on his forehead like acid. Afterward, he changed the bandage, got dressed, and settled down on the couch with the dogs and his phone. His mission for the evening was to call the dispatcher of every tow-truck company in Orange County, giving each the make, model, and plate number of Valkenburg's Ford and offering a $100 reward for any driver who spotted it. He had used this technique before with some success, but it was always a long shot. His only other hope was Kiril's contact at the DMV, who had access to all the toll booth data in the area. If Valkenburg were dumb enough to skip a toll, the DMV would have a snapshot of his plate, as well as the time stamp and a location. Another long shot.

After he was done, he indulged himself with a glass of Maker's, hoping the booze would tamp down the pain from his cut, not to mention the panic that was already tingling incessantly in the pit of his stomach. At any moment, some handyman or bug exterminator might discover Bisby's body in Valkenburg's apartment, and the whole situation would begin to unravel. The cops would be after Valkenburg and the rest of the Selberis crew. If they managed to flip one, they could easily find their way to Noland's door.

He resolved not to think about it. At least not tonight. He had to concentrate. Everything would fall into place if he could find Valkenburg again. He kept remembering the thing Kiril had said at dinner, about the shell company: Rache. Revenge. That was the answer. Valkenburg was sticking around Orlando because he had unfinished business with a person or persons. But what? What nature of offense could motivate a man to risk his freedom? Maybe even his life? And who might the person, or persons, be?

There were two people who might know: Cassandra Raines and Charles Deisch. Clearly, both were involved in the matter, somehow, and working together. He had to find out what they were up to, and what they knew.

As to which one he should go after first, that was a no-brainer.

He climbed back into the van and drove all the way to Lake Mary, where he parked a good distance from Cassy's house. There was no moon that night, and he waited until his eyes adjusted to the dark before slipping on his backpack and walking down the long, paved road. He skulked along the edge of the property until he found a spot beneath a drooping oak tree, where he scaled the wall and dropped silently to the other side. He held still, listening. No dogs barked. No horses whinnied. Not even the far-away noise of a TV disturbed the quiet night.

He walked to the circular driveway where Cassandra's Honda was parked. There was something pleasingly incongruous about the shitty little car, parked in front of the big, fine house. He might have smiled, under different circumstances. Instead, he took off his gloves and brushed the hood with the back of his hand. The engine was cold.

He put his gloves back on, tried the driver's door, and found it unlocked. He searched the glove box. Nada. He searched the trunk. It was full of miscellaneous, horse-related items. A spare bridle. Two training helmets. A saddle brush. A tub of DMSO, the muscle liniment, whose scent Noland recognized from when his grandfather had used it on his old, arthritic joints. Noland closed the trunk gently and squatted down behind the bumper. Reaching into the backpack, he retrieved a GPS tracker, about the size of his palm and enclosed in a burnished metal case. He pulled it out of the case, activated it, and slipped it back in. The case was magnetic, and he raised it under the rear of the car until it sucked itself to the undercarriage.

Then he left, scaling the wall again. Back in the van, he opened his laptop and made sure the tracker was pinging. It was; a tiny red icon appeared on a map of Seminole County. He cranked the engine and drove straight to Benny's, where he took the same place at the bar as before. Then, preparing himself for the next, critical stage of his plan, he took a breath, got out his phone, and dialed.

"Hello?" Cassy answered.

"Hi." His voice almost cracked. He sounded like a sixteen-year-old kid. "It's me. Noland."

"Really?" she said. "Twice in two days?"

"Exactly.'"

"What do you want?"

"I happen to be at our favorite bar. I was wondering if . . ."

"Aren't you on duty or something? On the job?"

"I just wanted to talk."

"About what?"

"I'll tell you when you get here."

She paused. "Dunno."

"Come on. You can drive yourself. You'll be perfectly safe."

"Well, that's an enticement."

"Are you saying no?"

"Give me twenty minutes."

She hung up. Noland, relieved, put his phone away and ordered another beer. The gash on his forehead hurt like hell, but he was too excited to care. Would she come? His heart thumped in anticipation. Then, after a moment, he thought to himself: *you're a fool.* She wasn't his girlfriend. She was a subject in his investigation. Perhaps even a suspect. He shouldn't be so thrilled at the prospect of seeing her again.

Even so, he felt like he was floating. All his muscles and bones had vaporized into a happy, pink dream. And as he drifted inside it, it occurred to him that part of the reason he liked her so much was that he never knew what she was going to do next, which direction she'd jump. With other people, Noland usually had a good idea of what his next move was. But around her it was different. He admired that. It was fun.

When she finally appeared in the doorway (forty-five minutes later), she was dressed in old jeans and a crisp red T-shirt. She slid onto the stool next to him, her body wreathed in a scent of delicate perfume. She squinted at his forehead. "What the hell happened to you?"

He was about to make a joke of it, tell her something about wrestling an alligator or some such. But then he had another idea: he would tell her the truth. About finding Val. How would she react? Once again, he didn't know. He decided to find out.

"Your ex," he said at last.

"You found him?" Her eyes had widened.

"Yep. Lake George. On his boat."

He couldn't quite read her expression as she considered this. She looked relieved, though, when the bartender sidled up. She ordered a martini. Someone cranked up the jukebox: "Girlfriend in a Coma" by The Smiths.

"So you got him?" she asked eventually.

"Are you kidding? He nearly got me."

"That's so like him."

"Yeah."

She took a deep breath, then let it out. "What now? You grill me for information?"

"Do you have any?"

"No."

"Are you sure? You lied to me once, already."

"Did I?" One of her dark, vivid eyebrows rose quizzically, like a cat's tail.

"Yeah. When you told me about your job at the accounting firm. Falco. It's closed."

Her chin dropped a little. She looked like a kid who'd gotten caught watching TV after bedtime.

"It went under six months ago," she said. "I got screwed out of two months' pay."

"So why'd you lie?"

"Please. You can't lie to a stranger. Not really. You can only be untruthful."

"Bullshit."

She swizzled her drink with the little plastic sword that skewered the olives. Noland was helplessly fascinated, watching the mini-tornado in her cocktail glass. But then, instead of taking a sip, she put the glass back onto the bar. She was going to leave. Just like that.

Noland panicked.

"Okay, okay," he said. "I'm sorry I pressed you. It's a habit."

She sniffed. He could tell she was still readying herself to go—to write the whole evening off. To write him off, for good. But something stopped her.

"How did you become a detective?"

"It's the only thing I'm good at."

"Now who's talking bullshit?"

"No, for real. I have no skills, in the ordinary sense of the word. But I do have some useful qualities."

She waited.

"For one," he said, and began ticking off fingers, "I'm fast. Two, I'm strong. Three, I'm reasonably smart. Four, I can go a long time without sleep or food. Five, I don't scare easily. Six, I'm not unduly afraid of hitting somebody, or of being hit."

She leaned back on her stool, regarding him an expression that was no longer angry, but still remote. "Is that it? Six things?"

He ticked off a final finger. "And I can always find a parking space. It's uncanny."

Her lips tilted up at the corners. Not a smile, exactly, but maybe the possibility of a smile.

"You remind me of Val," she said.

Noland almost jumped out of his skin.

"Really?"

"Really."

"You don't seem to like him very much."

"Well, he is my ex."

"How long were you married?"

"Eight years."

"That's a long time."

"I suppose so."

"Who left who?"

Her almost-smile vanished. "Doesn't matter. I'm sorry I brought him up again."

"No problem."

He felt a complicated mixture of emotions: relief that she didn't want to talk about her ex-husband, but also annoyance that she had taken him off point once again. He decided to go along, then circle back later.

"How did you learn so much about horses?"

"My dad. His dad. Cousins. Everybody had horses. Bred them. Trained them. Raced them. The whole shebang."

"You were raised in Ocala?"

She pursed her lips, impressed. "Good guess."

"How'd you wind up as an accountant? In Orlando?"

"The usual way. College. UCF. Had to major in something. I was good at math, and so . . ." She made an out-the-window gesture with her hand. When she brought the hand back, she dug in her purse with it and found a cigarette. She lit it, took a drag, and pointed the red tip at his chest. "You were a cop, weren't you?"

Noland was startled.

"Deputy," he said. "Five years."

"I knew it!" She slapped her thigh. "Your body language. The way you sit, with your shoulders squared up, as if you're expecting someone to try and knock you over. I figured you're either a cop or an ex-con."

Noland ran a finger around the rim of his beer mug. "Well . . . I might be both."

She stared at him.

"You're kidding."

He shook his head. "Raiford. Union Correctional. Two years."

Even as he told her this, he wondered why. Why was he telling her the truth? He made his living telling lies, in large part, so why did he feel the need to be straight with her? Whatever the reason, it was too late now. He waited to see how she would react. Would this tidbit of information be enough to send her storming out? Or would she withdraw? Shut down.

In the end, she leaned closer.

"What'd you do? Take bribes? Steal dope?"

He caught himself smiling. It seemed strange, and weirdly enchanting, that she would assume that crime first: bribery.

"According to the prosecutor, I did a little of everything. Stealing. Dealing. None of which was true, incidentally."

"Isn't that what they all say?"

"That's true. Nevertheless, I was innocent. Officially. My conviction was overturned."

Her mouth parted in surprise. "How'd you manage that?"

"The governor took an interest in my plight. He was a Gator fan."

And then it happened: she laughed. A surprisingly high, girlish laugh. An intense, blissful sensation filled Noland's chest as his heart flipped over like a startled fish.

"So that's how you can have a P.I. license, right? Despite your record?"

He nodded. "My record was expunged."

She was grinning now, enjoying the fact that she had turned the tables on him. "And that's the real reason you became a P.I., isn't it? You didn't want to waste your cop skills."

"Something like that. But I would have made the jump eventually. Being a cop doesn't pay very well."

"And being a P.I. does?"

"It can," he said, "if you take the right kind of cases."

She leaned even closer to him. Her breath smelled like gin.

"That's like something my dad used to say: 'Show me an honest man and I'll show you a poor one.'"

"He sounds like a wise man."

"Val was a cop, too. In his previous life."

"So I was told. That was before you met him, right?"

She nodded. "He had a saying of his own: all the best cops either quit, go crazy, or go crooked."

Though he tried to resist it, Noland thought of his own father, Zeb. Zeb hadn't quit, or gone crazy. But he had gone crooked. Way crooked.

"Was Val a good cop?"

"He didn't brag, but I gather he was one of the best in the city. Narcotics. You can imagine what that was like."

"So he went crooked?"

"He went crazy. Then he quit. Then he went crooked."

"Well, at least he got the order right."

She squinted at him again. Puzzling over him. As if he were a math problem she was trying to figure out.

"You're still trying to beat the system, aren't you?" she said.

"Why not? It screwed me over. In all sorts of ways."

"Join the club."

The edge of bitterness in her voice shocked him—yes, even him. He decided to change the subject again.

"You still have family in Ocala?"

"Just my mom," she said. "My dad died years ago."

"Ever think about going back?"

She grimaced as if he had said something stupid. "Please. My house is here. And my business. The riding school, I mean. And anyway, I like the city."

"What about Tampa? Or Atlanta?"

She shrugged. "Are you encouraging me to move?"

He was, in fact, although he didn't realize it until she said it. He found himself mystified at his own behavior. She was his best lead—he had just bugged her car, for crap's sake. And yet he found himself hoping she'd get out of this mess somehow. The whole ball of wax that was Selberis and Arthur Valkenburg and the boys from Brazil. Noland didn't know where it ended, or how deeply she had entangled herself. But he wanted to help her. She seemed decent. She was probably nice to little kids and old people. Whatever the reason, he liked her. It would be a good thing for him, he thought, to do a good thing for her. It might even, if only for a moment, make him feel good about himself for a change.

"How come you never had kids?" he asked.

The question popped out. It was stupid and he knew it, but there it was. Fortunately, her expression remained unfazed.

"I'm sterile," she said. The statement seemed to clatter on the tabletop between them.

"You didn't want to adopt?"

"Nope. Too selfish. If I was going to go through the effort of raising a kid, it had to be my own flesh and blood. So, no kids."

She said it with such indifference that he wondered if she was faking it. But then he realized that he wanted her to be faking it. Someone that smart and pretty should want to have kids, he thought. Pass those blessings on. Doing otherwise seemed wasteful, like having a great idea but never telling anyone about it. "Did that have anything to do with you and Val splitting up?"

She rolled her eyes. "God, you can't help it, can you? Always back to Val. Maybe you should ask him out for a drink."

"You're prettier."

She scoffed but blushed a little. When she finally spoke again, her tone was all business. "No, that particular issue was not a factor in our divorce."

Noland thought of Valkenburg's photo again, that shot of him and Bisby fishing. Two gamblers.

"I gather he isn't the family type?" he said.

"Not really. And anyway, he didn't want another kid."

Every muscle in Noland's body tensed up, instantly, as if electrified.

"Another kid?"

She pursed her lips. "He has a son. From a teenage indiscretion. The kid must be grown by now."

"What's his name?"

"Val never told me. He didn't like to talk about it."

Noland felt queasy, as if he had made some rookie mistake. He didn't know why this revelation had shaken him so. The fact that Valkenburg had an adult son, somewhere, was probably irrelevant. But even so, the mystery kid represented a blank spot. One which Noland had missed.

Cassy finished her drink and set down the glass with finality.

"I have to go."

Once again, Noland panicked. But he kept his voice even as he said. "There's something I need to tell you."

She waited.

"Val," Noland said, "is in pretty deep this time. There's a good chance that he killed somebody."

She looked down. He waited for her to be startled, or intrigued, or at least interested. Instead, she waited. After a long while, she leaned forward, edging her chin out over the void of the tabletop. Then she kissed him. Deeply, parting his lips with her own. Noland was startled. And aroused. And a little embarrassed. But most of all, he was moved. Barely a day had passed since Karen had taken him to bed, and yet here he was, bowled over by a single kiss. It wasn't fair, but it was true. Cassy made him think of some greater possibility, a different life. An alternate reality that he might be able to cross into, if only he could allow himself. A life with Cassy. He felt his heart rise toward her like a flower turning to the sun. He was about to touch her cheek when she pulled away.

"Thanks for calling." She rose and slipped her purse over her shoulder. "Why don't you come over for dinner when this is over?"

"I'd like that."

She smiled, a bit sadly, then walked away. She had almost reached the door when she stopped, turned around, and came back.

"By the way," she said, digging in her purse again. She pulled out a small, metal box. Noland stared at it a full two seconds before the object resolved itself in his mind: the GPS tracker. She placed it on the bar, its burnished case glowing dully in the neon light from the Budweiser sign.

"I found it before I left," she said. "Is it yours?"

He sighed. "Yes."

"I ran it under the tap. It's probably fried."

Noland picked it up. A bit of water leaked out onto his fingers.

"Also," she said, "you're an asshole."

"Not really. I'm low on leads."

"I told you already. I don't know where he is. I couldn't lead you to him if I wanted to."

Noland tossed the tracker into a garbage can behind the bar, where it landed with a thud, startling the bartender. Noland looked back at her. "You truly don't know where he is? Or what he's up to?"

"No."

"Then why were you at his office today?"

For the first time, she flinched. With her whole body, as if he'd given her a jolt of current.

"You're watching his office?"

"No, but I saw you there."

She licked her lips.

"I do some accounting for him. For his side company, I mean."

"Okay. How does Charles Deisch fit into it?"

She flinched again. For a long while—maybe ten full seconds—she stared at him with a mixture of fear and rage. He almost withered under the force of her ire.

"Fuck you," she said.

He reached out and grabbed her wrist. Not enough to hurt her, but firm. She tried to pull away but he kept his grip. Her eyes darted in the direction of the bartender, who stood at the other end of the bar, his attention back on the TV. But she didn't call out to him.

Noland said, "Just tell me what was in the box."

"I'm not telling you shit."

"Yes, you are."

Her nostrils flared—the way a horse's might, he imagined, right before it kicks you in the ribs. Would she hit him? He thought she would. He braced himself.

"Books," she said.

A punch would have been less surprising.

"Books?"

"Books."

"What kind of books?"

"All kinds. Deisch had me collect every book in Val's office. Textbooks. Travel books. Paperback thrillers. Everything."

"Why?"

"I don't know."

Noland let go of her hand.

"Thanks."

"Go to hell, Noland."

"Call me Nole."

She left.

He finished his drink and laid a twenty down on the bar. As he walked out, he thought he heard the bartender mutter something. It sounded like, "That's too damned bad."

11

H E SLEPT FITFULLY for a few hours before a nightmare about being buried alive startled him awake. He got up, walked into his office, opened his laptop, and checked the Police Beat section on the *Sentinel's* website. Nothing. No dead bodies in Longwood.

He made himself a pot of coffee and kept working. His next web search, of public records in the states of Florida and New York, yielded no revelations. Even going back forty years, he could find no birth certificates where any "Arthur Valkenburg" was named as the father. Strike one. Next, he tried the federal sites, running a query on a database of deadbeat dads. Strike two. Finally, he switched focus to the missing son, searching for any Florida driver's licenses issued to young men named Valkenburg in the past ten years. Strike three.

He leaned back and rubbed his temples. It was rare for him to come up totally dry like this. He began to wonder if Cassy had fed him another set of lies, perhaps hoping to distract him. Maybe even put him off Valkenburg's trail.

He thought some more. Three imaginary silos formed in his mind, starting at the top of his skull and reaching all the way into the sky. Somewhere, far up in the stratosphere, each silo had a label above it, written in hundred-foot-high letters:

IMPOSSIBLE, POSSIBLE, and PROBABLE. When he weighed the notion that Cassy might have lied to him about Valkenburg's long-lost son, Noland placed its tick mark in the POSSIBLE silo, instead of the PROBABLE. The fact was that he wanted to believe her. Wanted to believe that she liked him enough to tell him the truth, for once.

Which led to the next, dreaded question: Had she killed Bisby? This tick mark he placed in the POSSIBLE silo too, even though he found it very hard to imagine her killing anyone. Hitting, yes. Killing, no. He remembered the way she had led the dressage class, perched on her horse like a Celtic queen. She was too poised, too balanced, to kill a man. Also, he couldn't see any potential motive. But then again, there was still so much of the picture missing. If he were to gather up every question he still had about Arthur Valkenburg, they would fill a 747.

His cell rang. Kiril.

"I got a lead," he said.

"Tell me."

"Your dude skipped a toll on the turnpike last night. I'll send you the details."

The email came a few minutes later. Valkenburg's F-150 had blown through a toll booth at three AM that morning, north of 417. Noland didn't have to look at a map to see where it was, because he had stopped at that very toll booth the previous day—on his way to the construction site in St. Cloud.

He got in the van and barreled down I-4, hitting early rush hour traffic as the sun was peeking over the SunTrust building. When he finally reached the construction site, he was surprised to find it awhirl with activity. The bulldozers, idle the day before, were chuffing diesel exhaust, scooping up the mountains of loose earth, and dumping them into waiting trucks. He parked by the foreman's trailer and climbed out of the van. Someone yelled at him from nearby. It was his new friend, the hard-hat, sitting high behind the wheel of a dump trunk.

"You got another drink for me?" he yelled.

Noland shielded his eyes against the sun as he looked up. "You're busy now."

"Yep."

"What changed? I thought you guys were in a holding pattern."

"Something put a fire under the boss's ass. Got everybody going again. We're supposed to lay slab in two days. Can you believe it?"

"And you have no clue as to why?"

The man pursed his lips. "My guess is, the client got pissed. Threatened to sue if they didn't see some dirt fly."

"Who's the client?"

"Bunch a fat cats in Atlanta." His eyes left Noland and looked off into the distance. "Uh-oh. Here comes the Little Boss. You can ask him."

Noland turned and saw two men coming toward him. The leader was the ear-stud boy himself, Shawn Difore, his face already drawn into a rictus of rage and mild disgust. Unfortunately, he was not alone. Three feet behind him trudged an older, larger man—the foreman, surely—in dirty jeans and a T-shirt stretched thin over his medicine-ball of a belly. The foreman huffed as he negotiated the rocks and ruts of the site, swinging big fists at his side as if for balance. Difore stopped an arm's length away and puffed out his chest. "What the fuck are you doing here, Twice?"

"I'm working. What the fuck are you doing here?"

"I'm the project manager, you idiot."

Somewhere in the back of Noland's mind, a calculation resolved itself. He knew that he was going to get nothing but grief from Shawn. And worse—he and the foreman were going to throw him off the site, which was exactly the last thing Noland needed. Considering all this, Noland decided to fight. He rose up onto the balls of his feet and turned his body to a slight angle.

"We need to talk," he said.

"Get off this lot," Shawn said. "I don't want to see your face around here agai—"

Noland punched him in the solar plexus. A solid hit, too; Noland felt a slight give in the young man's xiphoid process as he recoiled his fist and turned his attention to the foreman. The larger man reacted quickly, stepping up and swinging a haymaker at Noland's jaw. Noland ducked beneath the massive arm and stepped to the side, sliding his right foot behind him. Off balance, the foreman wobbled in place, preparing to twist back for another swing. Noland pressed down on the balls of his feet to lift it off the dirt and snapped his quad muscles, delivering a vicious kick to the foreman's groin. Even through the fabric of the foreman's blue jeans, Noland felt his shin bone crush the soft clay of the man's genitals. Noland snapped his leg back and waited. The foreman grabbed his crotch with both hands and let out a faint, gurgling scream. Then he dropped.

"SHEE-it!" someone yelled from behind. It was the hardhat, still sitting in the truck, grinning. His dental landscape had not improved in the past twenty-four hours.

Noland kept his Wing Chun stance, rotating slowly on the loose ground, where Shawn had dropped as well. None of the other crew moved toward him. The foreman had lost consciousness, with just an occasional tremor of his left arm to signal that he was still alive. Shawn, however, was awake, clutching his chest and gasping for air.

"Damn," Noland said. "Haven't you ever been suckerpunched before?"

Shawn didn't answer. Noland leaned over and lifted him up by the armpits, then stood behind him and pulled his elbows back. He then drew the young man like a bow, until Shawn's diaphragm expanded. The young man sucked air like a cracked thermos. When Noland let him go, he bent over at the waist, hands on his knees, and kept breathing, steady now. Noland had to give him credit. He knew what it was like to have your clock punched like that. Shawn wasn't trembling. In fact, he seemed calm. Composed.

Noland let him breathe another moment before asking: "Can we go inside and talk?"

Shawn straightened up. "Oh, sure. It's not like you just punched me in the chest."

They left the foreman in the dirt. Half of Shawn's suit was now stained yellow from where he'd rolled, like a pastry sugared on one side, and yet he walked with some dignity as he led Noland into the foreman's trailer. Tiny supernovas ghosted Noland's eyes until he adjusted to the shadows. A haphazard office had been set up, with a desk in each corner and corkboards lining the walls, festooned with diagrams and permits. A mini-fridge hummed in the corner. Shawn reached in and got two Cokes. He offered one to Noland.

"Thanks," he said. "Sorry about the punch."

Shawn sat down at his desk. "I guess I was asking for it, coming on that strong. What do you want?"

"Have you seen Valkenburg?"

He sneered: "You came out here to ask me that? And then you hit me?"

"You haven't seen him?"

"No."

"I don't believe you."

Shawn's sneer faded. "Why not?"

"Because he was here last night."

This statement seemed to have an even greater impact on Shawn than the punch had. His mouth dropped open. Either he was genuinely dumbfounded, or he was the best actor Noland had ever seen.

"Where?"

Noland pointed his finger at the floor. "Here, mother-fucker. At. This. Site."

"How do you know?"

"Never mind that. I just do. Why don't you tell me what he was doing here."

He gave Shawn a long while to reply. But all the man did was look down and shake his head. Not refusing to answer, but merely at a loss.

Noland went on. "Listen, bro. I'm on your side. I work for you and your partners. But you have to be straight with me. If I don't find the fourteen mil soon, before the cops get involved, I probably never will. You and your partners will end up face-down in the Everglades if your Brazilian friend gets a hold of you."

Again, Shawn seemed clueless. His face remained blank, impassive. Still, Noland sensed that the kid was close to cracking. Noland actually held his breath as Shawn finally straightened up in his chair.

"Our Brazilian friend," he said, slowly, "is named Victor Irenas."

Noland had never heard the name before, and yet it registered on him with an almost visceral thunk. Putting a name to the man, Irenas, made him real, somehow. It was a name with some weight to it. Some punch.

"Okay. What product? Coke?"

Shawn moved his shoulders up and down. "I assume. Probably lots of other things, too. His family is diversified."

"You mean his cartel?"

"No, I mean his family. Literally. His uncle is very high up in the Brazilian government."

Noland sighed. "Great. So what's your role?"

"You mean Selberis's role?"

"Yes."

"Money. We handle it for him."

"Cash?"

Shawn tilted his head pensively. "Some cash. But mostly soft money. Wired in from offshore."

"You launder it?"

"Obviously. Most of our income is from Irenas. As senior partner, he gets seventy percent back, clean and legit. We keep the rest."

"How do you handle the cash part?"

For the first time since Noland had mentioned Valken-burg, a shadow of a smile crossed Shawn's lips. "We import a lot of building material from South America. Specialty stuff. Lumber. Tile. Windows. Every shipment comes with a bun-dle of cash. And sometimes an extra shipment."

"Coke?"

"Again, I assume so."

"Who retrieves it?"

"Val. Who else? He's in charge of that side of things."

"He's very hands-on, right?"

Shawn wrinkled his eyebrows. "Huh?"

"Forget it," Noland said. "Why was Val so plugged in?"

Shawn continued. "He knows Irenas personally. Flew to São Paulo two or three times a year. They got on famously. Common heritage and all that shit."

"You're kidding. Valkenburg is Portuguese?"

Shawn's jaw dropped, as if Noland had said the stupid-est thing possible. "Not Portuguese. German. Irenas is half German. There are lots of them down in Brazil, you know. The Nazi diaspora."

Noland nodded, humbled but also appalled. Sabine Werther. Valkenburg. And now Irenas. Krauts everywhere. "Right. Who else knows him? Irenas, I mean."

"None of us. Except Bisby. He sucked up to him pretty hard. Made a few trips there, too."

"But Val did the actual work? The logistics?"

He nodded.

Noland's brain felt like it was going to explode out of his skull. He clutched his forehead and thought: *It's too much.* This whole fucking case was too much. It was going to kill him, one way or the other.

"And what about you, Shawn? What's your bit? Specifically."

"I'm just a grunt. Down in the trenches. I keep the proj-ects moving."

The next question that popped into his head was not essential, but he couldn't help himself. "Yeah, you keep it moving, I see. But as slowly as possible?"

"Keeps the payroll down. More profit for the big boss." He made a wry expression with half of his mouth, as if he knew how much of a creep he was. Noland almost felt a little bit of sympathy for him. But there was no time. He had to get all the info he could before Shawn clammed up again.

"So Val had access to the bank accounts?"

"Not that I know of."

"Then how did he clean you out?"

He pressed his lips together. This time he was stalling—Noland was certain of it. But why?

"He must have gotten the login somehow." He didn't elaborate.

Noland decided to let it go. "But he didn't take everything. Right?"

"There's another account. In the Caymans. Only Bill and Karen have access to it. I'm guessing it's still intact."

"How much is in it? Enough to satisfy this Irenas guy?"

"Not even close. If we don't get the money that Val took, we're screwed."

He sounded matter-of-fact but exhausted. Just like Karen, that night when she'd used Noland like medicine. They were all scared shitless of this Irenas dude. Even Noland began to worry; if Irenas was such a heavy hitter, he might waste them all as a precautionary measure. The thought filled him with a mixture of rage and disgust, and he found himself paraphrasing something Zeb had said to him, long ago.

"Shawn, for a smart boy, you're a fool. How did you get yourself into this?"

Uncomprehending, Shawn blinked. "I didn't know all the details, at first. It all happened . . ." He groped for the word. ". . . gradually."

"Gradually, huh? What an epitaph!" His voice had risen without his meaning it to. But Shawn's admission had softened his anger a bit. He lowered his tone. "Why is he still around? Val, I mean."

"I've no idea."

"Come on. I told you he was here last night. You expect me to believe that you have no clue?"

Shawn didn't answer, but the blank expression on his face was convincing. Noland could see that the kid really had no inkling. Then a frightening possibility occurred to Noland: maybe Shawn didn't know the reason because there was no reason. Maybe Val was simply crazed, trying to scare them. It seemed unlikely, but Noland couldn't push it out of the POSSIBLE silo.

When Shawn spoke again, his voice was almost a whisper. "You're right. He was here."

Noland caught his breath. "You saw him?"

"No. But I know someone was here last night. One of the guys came by to pick up his car. There was a truck at the gate. A guy was trying to cut the padlocks. He jumped in the truck and took off."

"That's it?"

"That's it. We checked the trailer. Nothing missing."

Then, as if the clouds had parted above him, Noland knew what to do.

"Are you going to stand guard tonight?"

"Yes, I was going to have a couple of the guys do it."

Noland shook his head. "No need. I'll stake out the place myself."

Shawn looked surprised, squinting at him. But Noland could almost see the wheels turning in the kid's head as he asked himself: *Can this Rent-a-Thug help me?*

"You think he'll come back?"

Noland stood. "How should I know? But if he does, I'll catch him."

Shawn pointed at Noland's forehead. "Looks like he caught you."

"That doesn't matter. I'll be wise to him, next time."

Shawn scoffed. "What do I do in the meantime?"

"Keep on swinging. Same as the others. If you think of anything else, call me."

"Yeah, sure," Shawn said. "I'll let you know if I get killed."

Noland wasn't sure how to take this. Was it a desperate attempt at gallows humor? Or a genuine premonition? He decided it didn't matter and walked out.

12

H E SPENT AN hour at Publix, collecting the supplies he would need for an all-night stakeout: a six-pack of Red Bull, two bottles of Gatorade, a box of Clif bars, and two bananas. The bag girl giggled when she got to the bananas—his token item of health food. In fact, the bananas were as critical as the rest of the list. Sitting in the van for hours would invariably cause his legs to cramp, and a dose of natural potassium was the best way to cure it. He didn't bother explaining this to the girl, of course. He just grinned and thanked her when she handed him his bag.

Back in the van, he called Kiril. He wasn't too happy when Noland told him the plan. For all his talk about wanting to redeem himself for the loss of Deisch in the Beemer, he sounded like a man who needed a night off, or, even better, an evening in the copy shop, working on his machines and listening to the Magic game. But Noland needed him.

"Okay," Kiril said, "but you're gonna buy me dinner first."

"I bought you dinner yesterday."

"Yeah, and you can do it again. And Freddy. I'm bringing him too."

Noland sighed. "Okay, I'll pick you up at six."

The highest tip of his sycamore tree was just nicking the setting sun as he loaded his supplies into the cooler. Strangely enough, he was in a good mood, filled with the unbidden but welcome longing to see Cassy Raines again. He kept thinking of the way she had punked him, tossing the GPS tracker onto the bar counter like a badass. Pretty fucking cool. He considered calling her now and inviting her out to dinner with him and the boys. Kiril would be impressed. But then Noland realized it was a crazy idea. He let it fall away with a private shrug of his shoulders.

When he got to the copy shop, he was surprised to find Kiril ready to go. Freddy called shotgun and pulled himself up into the van's passenger seat with his powerful arms as Kiril gently loaded his wheelchair in the back. They drove to a Japanese place—Freddy's pick—and sat at the last booth behind a white plastic screen that was supposed to look like rice paper. As they waited for their food, Noland dug into his backpack and got out a blue binder in which he carried all the clues he'd gathered so far: Valkenburg's photo, the map of the St. Cloud construction site, and a sheet of miscellaneous notes, including the ten mysterious numbers from Bisby's arm. He spread everything out on the table and stared at it.

"Any brilliant ideas?" Kiril asked.

"Give me time."

"Funny. That's the one thing you don't have."

It was true. Bisby's corpse was rotting away in Valkenburg's apartment, waiting to be discovered. And since no one knew Bisby was dead, the fraud case against Bisby was still pending, with Faith due to appear in court in just over a week. Thinking of all this, Noland wanted to cover his face with his hands and tune out the world for a moment. But he couldn't, of course. It wouldn't do to freak out in front of the boys.

Their waitress was a cute girl, and Freddy began to flirt as always. She seemed receptive, which wasn't very surprising. Freddy was a handsome little fucker, with his chiseled features and sweet smile of the sort most girls couldn't resist. Even so, Noland wondered if he had ever asked a girl out on an actual date. He suspected not. Maybe he thought that most girls wouldn't go out with a guy in a wheelchair, and he didn't want to get shot down. Or maybe he was waiting for the right one?

Noland thought of Cassy again.

When their food came, Noland hastily gathered up the papers to make room for the plates. But not before Freddy touched the page of notes.

"What's with those numbers?"

"No idea. Kiril and I found them on a dude."

"The dude in the apartment?"

Noland was startled, then angry. Freddy wasn't supposed to know that kind of detail. But Noland shrugged it off. It was only natural for Kiril to tell his brother everything, at this point. They were both on the payroll, after all.

"Yeah, the dude in the apartment."

Freddy picked up the paper and looked at it for a moment, his dark eyes moving back and forth like a chess player's, scanning a particularly interesting board. Kiril was shoving food in his face but managed to ask: "What do you think, Fred? Bank account?"

"No," Freddy said.

Kiril kept on chewing, but he was clearly anticipating Freddy's next statement. Despite himself, Noland was too.

Freddy stared at the paper a bit longer. Then, all of a sudden, he smiled. The same smile he had given to the waitress.

"It's an address."

Despite himself, Noland was taken by surprise.

"An address?"

"It's not ten digits. It's two sets of five digits. You found a map, right?"

Noland's hands actually trembled as he tore back into the folder and got out the map. In the lower-left corner was a GPS coordinate. The base coordinate of the plan.

"Nah," Noland said, looking back at the paper. "Can't be. The latitude and longitude are all wrong."

Freddy was unperturbed. "You don't understand. Your dude—he was in a hurry. He probably saw the digits somewhere. Or heard somebody saying them aloud, maybe over the phone. He had to write them down fast. He didn't bother with the degrees because he knew them already. They're the same for the whole county."

Kiril stopped chewing. "He just wrote down the decimals."

"Right."

Noland compared the two sets of numbers to the base coordinates on the map.

"Holy shit."

Within a few seconds, they were all leaning in to stare at the map, Freddy lifting himself up with his thick forearms.

"Can you pinpoint it?" Kiril asked.

Noland almost didn't hear him. Finally, he nodded. "It's there, all right. On the site."

Kiril slapped the table. "Shit! So what do we do?"

Noland thought a moment. "Same as before. But our stakeout just became a treasure hunt."

* * *

They made a quick trip to Home Depot, where they bought shovels, gloves, and other essentials, then headed for St. Cloud. By this point, there was no way they could drop Freddy off at the shop—he would raise hell if they tried—so they brought him along. At the construction site, they hung out in the van until nine, when Noland slipped out and reconnoitered. The foreman's trailer was locked, but he raked it and got inside. Kiril brought up the van and got out the two duffel bags of gear. They all went into the trailer together, with Kiril pulling Freddy up the stoop backward in his chair.

For the next two hours, they sat in the dark, with Noland peering out the trailer's sliding door, surveying the vast, empty site with a starlight scope. At just past midnight, he rose stiffly and stretched.

"Let's go," he said.

Kiril fetched the two shovels they had bought at Home Depot and handed one to Noland.

"What about Freddy?"

"He can stay here and keep watch."

"I'm coming," Freddy said.

Noland sighed, again. "Okay. But it's like a moonscape out there. Can you handle it?"

"Bite me."

Noland slid open the door and led them out. The dirt felt rougher in the dark, without the benefit of anticipation. Each step felt like he was going over a cliff. He'd barely gone ten yards before he stubbed his toe on a rock, or maybe it was a chunk of concrete, and the pain made him curse. Of course, Freddy had no trouble at all, his wheels whispering over the soft dirt. Kiril led the way, holding his phone out in front of him like a lantern, watching his GPS app.

Eventually, Noland decided to risk turning on his Eagle-Tac. In its narrow beam, he saw two mountains of dirt looming on the far edge of the lot. Noland feared that the spot they were after might be under them. Sure enough, Kiril stopped at the smaller of the two.

"Shit."

Freddy reached up and snatched the phone. "It's not very far inside," he said after a moment. "Maybe ten feet."

"Ten feet? Into that pile? We're screwed."

Noland looked around. One of the dozers was parked by the chain-link fence.

"Can you work one of those?" he asked.

Kiril stroked his chin. "It's gonna be loud."

"Do it."

It took ten minutes for Kiril to hot-wire the dozer. When he finally cranked the engine, each pop of the pistons sounded like a gunshot, echoing out over the previously silent lot. If any cops were around, maybe catching a few Zs in one of the warehouse parking lots, they were awake now. But there was no helping it; Noland had to move that dirt. The dozer's tail-light flared red as Kiril swung it around, lowering the scoop. Noland watched in a kind of awe, completely absorbed. Then he realized that Freddy was gone.

Noland spun around in the gloom, his heart pounding. Where the fuck had he gotten off to? Then he heard it—the high-pitched whine of a small generator, rising over the growl of the dozer. He was about to yell at Kiril when something exploded into light, bathing their tennis court–sized section of dirt in a white blaze. Noland froze like a startled possum as Freddy wheeled himself back from behind the generator attached to one of the big floodlights that stood on the edge of the lot.

"Thought we could use a bit of illumination."

"Freddy, you asshole!"

Freddy grinned. Not for the first time, Noland wished that the young man could somehow rise up from the chair, just for a moment, long enough for Noland to give him a light, fraternal punch in the gut. But this wish, he knew, was a lie. He could never hit Freddy, chair or no chair. Freddy was one of those holy people you could never deliberately hurt, no matter how outrageous their offense. So, once again, Noland gave up. They would have to move as quickly as possible. Kiril was already on the job, working the dozer like a pro, scooping up huge chunks of dirt and dropping it ten yards away, right in line with the fence. He was building them a little wall.

After twenty minutes, the dozer had eaten far enough into the pile that an area of flat, rocky ground was exposed. Noland motioned for Kiril to shut off the engine. They would have to dig by hand for the rest. Kiril jumped down from the seat, walked across the freshly uncovered ground, and checked his app. He then made a little X in the dirt with the toe of his boot.

Freddy said, "Maybe it's treasure."

"Gold?" Kiril asked.

Noland picked up a shovel and started digging. Kiril did the same. All the while, the big flood poured down on them, exposing their actions to God and everyone who cared to look. But at least they now had a little berm of dirt to partly hide them from the main road. This, along with Freddy's brazenness, had probably made them less suspicious-looking, ironically. Any cops that happened by would probably assume that they were a construction crew pulling an all-nighter—not an uncommon thing in the age of razor-thin margins.

"What are we looking for?" Freddy asked.

"No idea."

"I'm telling you, it's gold," Kiril said.

They measured out the next half hour in shovel scoops. Noland's knee started to hurt, an insistent little ache that gradually strengthened into fiery, shooting pain. It got so bad he shifted his stance and started digging left-handed, which helped a little. Soon they had dug a hole two feet deep and five feet wide. Nothing was there. Were they on a fool's errand? The whole treasure was predicated on Freddy's hunch—the mere guess of a twenty-five-year-old nerdski.

Something clanged under Kiril's shovel. They both dug faster, exposing the outline of a box. Noland brushed the dirt off the lid and revealed a patch of metal, army green.

"A footlocker," Freddy said, not even trying to hide the triumph in his voice.

Kiril hoisted the locker out and set it onto the flat earth. The moment he did so, the smell hit them. They reeled back in unison—even Freddy, who rolled himself backward.

Noland recognized the smell. Knew it from his days as a cop, the dreaded DOA smell. Like that of a dead junkie, five days gone in a hot car with the windows rolled up. Or a teenager, killed on a dare, his body covered with green flies at the bottom of a gully where his friends had left him, too scared to tell anyone. The fetid, rank smell of unsanctified death.

They all looked at each other.

Finally, Kiril stepped forward. "I'll do it."

Noland pressed a hand into his chest. "No, this is on me."

Holding his breath, he leaned over the metal box and then, before he had time to chicken out, unlatched the lid and threw it open. In the full beam of the floodlight, the interior seemed largely empty, the main compartment containing what appeared to be a leather ball with a burgundy satin cloth draped halfway over it. It took perhaps a hundredth of a second for the cloth and the ball to resolve themselves into what they really were: red hair, long and shiny, partly covering a severed human head.

"Blyad," Kiril said, and turned away. Noland wanted to do the same but knew that, if he did, he wouldn't have the strength to look again. And he needed to look. This was, after all, what they'd come for.

He slipped on his gloves, then reached out and touched the head with his fingertip. It felt like a pumpkin a week after Halloween. Pressing lightly, he rolled the head face up. The face was shriveled, the cheeks and jaw a moldy, russet color. The eyes were holes, boiling with blunt-nosed, colorless worms.

Freddy had rolled up next to him, leaning over in his chair to get a better look. "Was it a girl? Or a woman?" He sounded desperately afraid.

Noland didn't answer. He knew why Freddy had assumed the skull was female—the hair. Long, red hair still flowed luxuriantly down the back to the ragged stump of the neck. Noland reached out once more and swept her hair to the side. There, at the end of the stump, an inch of white bone had been exposed, cleaved by some heavy, crude blade.

He was still holding his breath, his lungs shuddering. Luckily, a light breeze picked up, and he straightened up to finally suck some air. Then he leaned down again. A metal divider separated one-third of the locker from the rest. Inside rested a slender, bright book. Noland picked it up. It was a journal, very fine, leather-bound, its cover woven in a complicated, Arabian pattern of black, white, and red tiles. He handed the book to Freddy, who took it without hesitation.

Noland stood, walked five steps away, and threw up.

"There's writing inside," Freddy called out. "Handwriting. It's in German."

Noland spat and walked back. It was his turn to look over Freddy's shoulder, peering down at the book, grateful for the floodlight now. The first ten pages of the journal were filled with flowing script, penned in bright blue ink. There was something childlike about it, the letters exaggerated, like those of a teenage girl. And Freddy was right—it was in German. Even Noland could tell that. Besides all the ders, dies, and dases, he recognized a single word: Stern. The German word for star. Noland flipped through more pages. All the rest were blank.

Using the toe of his shoe, Noland flipped the lid back down on the locker but did not pick it up. "Let's fill the hole."

"We're taking her?" Freddy asked. His voice was high. Hopeful.

"There's a big oak tree near the county line. I'll bury her there. When this is all over, I'll tip off the cops as to where she is."

He picked up a shovel. Kiril did too. It took a lot less time to fill the hole than it did to dig it. At some point, over his own labored breath, he heard Freddy weeping.

When they finished, Kiril ran the dozer over the spot a few times, dumping a couple of buckets of earth back onto it. Freddy killed the generator and the site was dark again—darker, actually, because their night vision was blown. They headed back to the trailer. Kiril started to settle down on the floor, ready to spend the rest of the night there, but Noland waved him off. "Forget it, we're heading home."

"What about the dude? He's going to come looking."

"He won't."

"How do you know?"

Noland didn't have an answer. And yet he was certain. Valkenburg had meant to find the locker, but he wouldn't try it now. He was too smart. Too careful. Noland found himself peering out into the darkness past the fence. There was a better than even chance, he knew, that Valkenburg was out there now, at that very moment, watching the whole enterprise. Or maybe he had set up a camera somewhere to keep an eye on the situation from a distance. Either way, he would know that he was too late.

Freddy piped up. "That's what he was doing here last night, huh? Looking for that girl's head?"

"For the book, more likely. The head was a message, I think."

Kiril grumbled. "Where's the rest of her?"

"God knows. With luck, we won't need to find out."

Fortunately, neither brother asked any more questions after that. They followed Noland out of the trailer and moved as quickly as they could—Kiril and Noland walking, Freddy rolling. They got silently into the van and drove off, all three of them smelling of dirt and sweat and something deeper. Ranker. The smell of grief. Pity. Even from Kiril. There it was. Unbidden, but undeniable.

"So, if our dude was coming here to find her, then who killed her?"

"I don't know. But I'm pretty sure it has to do with whatever's written in that book. Freddy, how's your German?"

But Freddy didn't answer. He had fallen asleep, his head lolled against the window. His hand was open in his lap as if waiting to receive something, a clue, a sign.

13

Two hours later, Noland was alone again, back at the wheel, I-4 twisting before him, shifting in and out of focus. The billboards' spotlights poked their beams into the predawn mist, moths flickering through them. How were moths born? From eggs, like maggots? No. From cocoons. Like butterflies.

He had buried the footlocker by the oak tree on the county line, and then headed home. A little while later, standing in the kitchen, he washed his hands with dish soap, dried them, then washed them again. Finally, he leaned over the sink and ran water over his head. His muscles hurt. He felt like he'd just played all four quarters of the Sugar Bowl and lost. Did Valkenburg's muscles hurt? He doubted it. The guy must have nerves like dead wires. How else could he creep around like that, moving from dead body to dead body? Had he killed the woman in the box? Surely not. He had come looking for her, or at least for the book. But he probably knew who had killed her. Bisby? That went into the POSSIBLE silo. But whoever had done it, Noland found himself very tired of Selberis and all its partners, with their unexpected reservoir of evil. He had bragged to Cassy that he specialized in greed and fear, and this was true. His usual clientele consisted of embezzlers, tax cheats, and the occasional drug dealer. And their wives, of course, enraged at their husbands' perfidy. But he seldom dealt with outright murderers. And when he did, they were usually a bit more refined than whoever had chopped off Sabine's head. That act, itself, suggested something exceptional—someone who had rebelled against their own humanity. But whoever it was, Noland had to find them. There was no helping it now. He was in deep.

And, of course, he needed the money.

Noland dug around in his medicine chest, found an Ambien, and swallowed it with a gulp of water straight from the tap. Then he sat down at the kitchen table and waited. Kiril had been tired, too, when Noland left him at the copy shop. They had driven there directly after leaving the construction site, the shop's clean counters and fluorescent lights lending everything an air of unreality. Freddy brewed a pot of coffee, and Noland sat in the manager's office across from Kiril, both of them sipping from disposable cups. Noland's hands trembled slightly each time he raised his cup to his lips. He took some solace in the fact that Kiril's hands were trembling too.

"What's in the book?" Kiril asked.

"No idea. Maybe a diary?"

Kiril raised a thick hand to his forehead and squeezed, as if trying to hold his brains in.

"Great. Crazy dead Germans. Just what we need."

Noland was too tired to reply. And yet his mind was racing. He was about to walk back to Freddy's cubicle and get the book so he could thumb through it. But then he realized that there was no point. Freddy was smarter than he was. If there was anything to find, Freddy would find it. Freddy was the man. Even so, Noland was pessimistic. He felt certain that they were still missing a crucial piece of the puzzle.

Kiril stared at him, his face colorless. Noland suspected he didn't look much better himself.

"We've done a night's work," he said. "Let's all go home and get some sleep."

"Da." Another sign of how exhausted they were—Kiril never lapsed into Russian except in moments of exhaustion or rage.

Noland stood. As he took a step toward the door, Kiril spoke again.

"What are we going to do?"

"We keep searching. What else?"

Kiril clenched his jaw. Noland felt his jaw muscles tense up in response. He wasn't used to being on the receiving end of Kiril's anger, and it scared him a little. It also pissed him off.

"No," Kiril said. "We should punt."

The statement seemed to land in the space between them like a lead weight. It was treacherous, and both of them knew it. But Kiril didn't back off. "Give the clients their money back. Wash our hands of it."

Noland shook his head. "We're in too deep."

"Not that deep." Kiril tapped a finger on the clean surface of his desk. "We tampered with a crime scene, but it probably won't get back to us. Not if we stop now."

"Yeah? And what if somebody talks?"

"You mean one of the clients?"

"Yeah."

"From what you say, they might be too scared to talk. Scared of this Brazilian dude."

"Exactly. If they're really scared, one of them might flip. Make a deal with the feds."

"In that case, the feds will have their hands full. They won't bother with us."

Noland sighed. For the first time in his life, he understood how a quarterback must feel—all that responsibility. All those eyes on you, all the time.

"We'll figure it out tomorrow. Get some sleep."

The corners of Kiril's mouth twisted down like sheep horns. "Okay. I'll keep Freddy working on the book."

"Thanks."

Now, Noland sat in his kitchen, waiting for the Ambien to kick in. Soon everything blurred. He walked to the bedroom, crawled onto the covers, and slept.

* * *

He woke eight hours later, feeling better. Lighter. He had slept deeply, floating in the black River of Ambien, and had not dreamed at all. No dead men in bathtubs. Nor heads in boxes. The sleep had been a blessing—a drug-induced blessing, but he would take it. Even Rent-a-Thugs need a blessing, once in a while.

He was making coffee when Kiril called.

"You alive?"

"Sort of. You?"

"Yeah." Kiril hesitated. "Sorry about what I said last night. I was a pussy."

"No, you weren't. You're my Voice of Reason."

"Fuck that."

"I mean it."

"Whatever. I'm on your side. You helped me out when I was in the Zone, and I'm sticking with you."

"Thanks, bro. I'll make it up to you." The words slid out of him, too easy. But he meant it. Kiril was his best friend, and Noland had already asked a lot of him. Serious jail time, if they were caught. And the longer they stayed enmeshed in the endless cluster-fuck that was the Selberis Affair, the better the chance the law would eventually throw a net over it all and catch them up in it.

Of course, there was still the chance they would find Valkenburg and recover Selberis's money, but that chance was diminishing by the hour. On the other hand, the stakes were rising. Valkenburg had probably killed Bisby, while someone else had probably killed the woman in the footlocker. Noland wondered, again, who she might be, what she might have done to deserve such special desecration?

Rache, he thought.

"You still there?" Kiril asked.

"Yeah, sorry. Trying to get my brain going. Has Freddy gotten anywhere?"

"A little. But you're not gonna like it."

"Thrill me."

"It's German, all right, but it's not a diary. It's a novel."

The term came at Noland so unexpectedly and out of context that he asked, "A what?"

Kiril elaborated. "It's an old book called *The Sorrows of Young Werther*. By some dude named . . . Go-thee?"

"Goethe," Noland said. He remembered from humanities class, the lady with the ash-colored hair pronouncing the name with a bemused smile: GUR-tuh. Noland felt dizzy, as if he'd been standing on his head for an hour and had just gone upright again. He put his hand on the kitchen counter to steady himself. "So, you're saying it's all bullshit?"

"Maybe," Kiril said. "What do you think?"

Before he could answer, Noland lifted the hand that he was using to steady himself and smacked the counter, hard enough to hurt his palm. The title kept echoing in his head: *The Sorrows of Young Werther*. Werther.

Sabine Werther. Selberis's banker.

"Call if you find anything else," he said at last, and hung up.

*   *   *

Even as he dialed Karen's number, he worried she wouldn't take his call. He'd only spent time with her once, and that was under extreme circumstances. Of course, this occasion didn't exactly qualify as "normal" circumstances, either. But at least he was calling during working hours. He was relieved when she finally answered.

"Hey," she said. Her tone was friendlier than he expected. "How are you?"

"I'm okay. Sorry I didn't call before."

He could almost hear her shrug. "It's all right. It's not like I expected flowers."

"You deserve flowers." Noland didn't know why he said it. But as soon as he did, he knew that he meant it.

A pause. "That's nice of you, Noland. What do you want?"

"I need to ask about your banker."

Another pause. "Sabine?"

"Yeah. Do you know where she is?"

"On a business trip, I thought. Overseas. Europe."

In an instant, his hands got sweaty, the phone almost slipping out of his fingers.

"Are you sure?"

"Last I heard she was in Munich."

"When's the last time you spoke to her?"

"I can't remember. I hardly speak to her at all, even when she's in town."

"Don't you work with her?"

"Not really. She works with Shawn, mostly. And Bill."

"Redding?"

"Yes."

"Is she Redding's girlfriend, by any chance?"

"Are you kidding? She's young, smart, and good-looking."

"Okay, I get it," he said. "It was a stupid question."

"Why did you ask? Is something up with her?"

He was about to tell her the truth but caught himself. In part, it was a lingering doubt that stopped him, the ever-narrowing possibility that the head in the footlocker belonged to someone else besides Sabine Werther. But even more important was his fear that Karen couldn't handle it. Another murder. Her mental state seemed fragile already, with all that talk of eating a bottle of pills. And anyway, what good would it do to tell her? Noland wasn't sure himself what it all meant. What the connection was.

His silence must have been revealing because Karen asked: "Something's happened to her, hasn't it?"

"How should I know? She's in Germany."

Karen didn't respond.

"Why'd she go?" he asked.

"Her bank has a branch in the city. She goes several times a year."

"She's German?"

"Half German, half Portuguese. Lots of Brazilians have that mix."

"Right. The Nazi diaspora."

"Huh?"

"Never mind. Can you tell me anything else about her?"

"Not really," Karen replied, "except that she played chess."

"Chess?"

"Yeah. Competitively. In college. She was almost a grand master." Noland nodded to himself. Chess. Yeah. That made sense.

A car horn honked in the background of wherever she was. "Listen, I have to go."

"All right. Thanks for the help. Seriously."

"Call me soon," she said.

She hung up before he could promise, and he found himself oddly relieved. He had dreaded the moment when she would ask him to come over again—perhaps that very evening. Of course, he had no right to dread this; he should want to see her again. When Karen had described Sabine as "young, smart, and sexy," she might well have been describing herself. And successful, too. She might even be trustworthy, in her own way.

But as he put his phone in his pocket and stepped out to the van, the reason for his dread became clear to him: he wanted someone else. Cassy. Since she'd met him at the bar two nights ago, he'd scarcely gone an hour without thinking of her. The merest recollection of her face caused a pleasant, involuntary expansion of his chest, a literal catching of his breath, which didn't wear off no matter how many times he replayed the film in his mind. He found himself fantasizing about running his fingers through her long brown hair. He imagined it would feel lush and soft, like seagrass.

On the way into town, he stopped by an electronics store and used a credit card to buy a new portable stereo. When he got to Kiril's shop, he picked the box up from the passenger seat and took it inside.

"Merry Christmas," he said, handing it to Freddy.

Freddy held the box in his lap, appraising it with some admiration. "Bose? Nice."

"You're welcome. Any luck with the book?"

"Actually, yes."

Kiril appeared from the back. He wore latex gloves and held the book in his hands gingerly, like something contaminated. As he approached, a chemical smell preceded him. Something vile.

"Crap," Noland said, pinching his nose. "What are you doing to it?"

"Methyl chloride," Kiril said. "Come see."

Noland followed him. Back in his office, he had set up a little chemical lab, complete with a Bunsen burner and a beaker of brown liquid. He also had a small paintbrush.

"Invisible ink," he said. "Very retro."

"You're kidding."

Kiril dipped the paintbrush in the liquid, then stroked it lightly over a blank page in the journal. Within seconds, the ghosts of letters appeared. No, not letters—numbers. Lots of them. In pairs. One number, then a dot, then another number, then a space. Unlike the elegant, flowing script of the German prose on the previous pages, the numbers were written in a blocky, almost childlike fashion.

177

3.22.1 4.17.8 17.2.1 27.8.9 1.9.22 4.9.4 8.22.1 3.7.14
8.2.21 3.4.1 5.12.3 8.22.11 4.3.14 8.9.2 8.22.4 8.11.4

Kiril passed him the journal. Noland held it in his trembling hands as he watched the numbers reveal themselves, like a Polaroid picture. Line after line of them, like data emitted from some insane computer. Finally, beneath the long list of numbers, was an IP address.

"The writing looks clunky. You think a kid wrote it?"

Kiril shook his head. "It's her. Old spy trick. You dip a matchstick in a solution, then write blind."

"What's with all the friggin' numbers?"

From behind, Freddy yelled: "It's a cipher."

"A what?"

"A code. She had a sick sense of humor."

"You mean, she wrote her notes in invisible ink . . . and in code?"

Freddy propelled himself over. "A book cipher. The number at the top is the page number."

"The page number of what?

"Of the key, dummy," Kiril said. "You use a book as the key."

Noland's mouth was suddenly dry. In awe. A strange and unsettling thought came into his mind. She's too smart for me. Sabine. The idea that she might outwit him—from beyond the grave, no less—had never seriously occurred to him until now. The feeling was rather like that dreadful, terrifying sensation he'd gotten on those rare occasions in football when he'd had to cover a guy who was better than he was. Faster.

Freddy patted him on the elbow. "Don't feel bad, Nole. If you were born in the Soviet Union, you would understand these things too."

"Bullshit. You're not that old."

"Our uncle was. He was KGB."

Kiril interrupted. "You start with a book. One that both you and the receiver have. You pick a page and you put the number of the page at the top of yours. Then, for every letter you need, you find it on the page. Then you write down the line number, the word number, and how many letters in from the left. Simple."

"But it will resist any brute-force attack," Freddy added.

Noland shook his head. After a moment, he pressed his fingertips into his temples and rubbed in a circle. "But what's it a code to?"

"To this." Freddy held up a silver disk. "We checked the IP address. It's a website. We downloaded everything. About two hundred megabytes of files. And a README.TXT. All encrypted."

"Can you crack it?"

He shook his head. "She must've used some industrial-grade crypto. We need the passcode."

"And that's what the numbers are?"

He grinned even wider. "Pretty crazy, huh?"

Noland had an overwhelming urge to reach down and yank him out of his chair. Instead, he pleaded: "Come on, Freddy. You're a fucking genius. You can crack it, right?"

Freddy shook his head, implacable as a sage. "Impossible. That's the cool thing about a book cipher. The key is bigger than the plaintext."

"The what?"

Freddy was about to explain, but Kiril gave him a look.

"We have to find the original book," Kiril said. "The actual, printed edition. We get the book, we get the passcode. We get the passcode, we decrypt the files."

Noland sat down. Internally, he was searching for something—anything—to latch on to. Some bit of dry land among the boiling rapids that Sabine Werther had dropped him into.

"What kind of book do you think it is?" he asked. "The key, I mean."

"Could be anything," Kiril said. "Normally, something commonplace. Widely available. Something she could replace if she lost the original."

Noland sneered: "You mean *The Da Vinci Code*?"

Freddy giggled.

"I was thinking the Bible. But it might be some obscure book. Something that only she—and maybe one other—had a copy of."

The brothers stopped talking after that. Noland grasped the situation. As smart as they were, they were waiting on him to make the next move. He might be a dumbass, as Kiril put it, but he was still the boss. So, what should he do?

Then, like a miracle, a thought came to him.

"Wait a minute. You said the text on the first pages was taken from a novel, right? *The Sorrows of Young Werther*?"

The brothers looked at each other, then raised their eyebrows.

"Well, shit," Kiril said. "Maybe she put the key right there in front of us."

"No," Freddy said. "Not enough pages were written down. It doesn't match."

"Well, maybe the full book," Noland said, his voice stress-breaking at the end. "The printed edition, I mean. She was giving us a clue."

The brothers considered this.

"We'll need the exact one," Kiril said. "The exact edition."

"Okay, okay, I understand. I'll find it."

Kiril closed his eyes, opened them again, and pouted. All in one fluid motion, a seamless expression of cosmic doubt.

Freddy asked, "You think the dude has it?"

"No," Noland said. For once, he was a step ahead of them. He remembered the pile of books he had seen strewn on the floor in Valkenburg's apartment. "Somebody's already been through his bookshelf and didn't find what they were looking for."

Freddy grimaced. "You really think the girl in the box did all this?"

"Yes."

"And that's why she got chopped?"

Noland didn't answer, even though he knew that this was certainly the case. Sabine had pulled some elaborate, crazy scheme of revenge. It had gotten her killed, but it was still playing out.

"Okay," he said, looking at Kiril. "Stow that disk somewhere safe."

"Will do."

Noland left. As he climbed into the van, his phone rang. Faith. Noland took a deep breath and answered it.

"Hey," she said. Instead of being angry, she sounded tired. A bit wary, as if afraid he might hang up upon hearing her voice. "How goes the hunt?"

"You know. I've got some leads."

"So we're fucked?"

"Pretty much."

"Why don't you tell me about it."

"Well, for one thing, Valkenburg didn't steal the money."

"What?"

He spent the next five minutes explaining everything. Sabine. The journal. The encoded message. The missing book. All of it. He had to stop several times to answer questions, but the more he told her the more silent she became, and soon he was monologuing. When he was finally done, he waited a moment.

"Wow," she said.

"Yeah."

"But how do you know she stole the money?"

"It's the only thing that makes sense. She had access to the accounts. And she knew how to make it look like Valkenburg did it. Anyway, if Valkenburg had all that money, he'd be long gone."

"All right, I believe you. What are your chances of finding this book?"

"I have no idea."

"Are you sure there even is a book?"

"What do you mean?"

"Well, if this Sabine was as crazy as you say, maybe there is no real book. Maybe it's just a giant, terrible joke on her part."

"No," he said. "She left the book somewhere."

"How can you be sure?"

"It's hard to explain," he said. "She wasn't a cheater."

"A cheater?"

He struggled to find a better word, but couldn't. How else could he explain to her what he had only come to sense himself in the last few hours—that Sabine was a person with a sense of fair play. A demented sense, surely, but there nonetheless. Yes, she was a crooked banker. And an embezzler. And, for all he knew, a generally nasty piece of work. But she had a twisted kind of integrity, too. She was a competitor, like Noland himself. Her game was chess, and this was her last match. They were all playing it, this final set of moves that she had concocted. She had an end game in mind. A real one, not some sputtering-off, indecisive draw. She had given them a legitimate chance. Not a good chance, but a chance.

"Lemme put it this way," he said. "If there is a book out there, I'll find it."

"Okay. What about Valkenburg?"

"Him, too."

"Well, I hope so. We've only got a week."

Noland's heart jumped. "A week?"

"Yeah. A week till I have to go back into court on the fraud case. Remember? Judge Abercrombie? A pile of evidence on Sydney Cross's desk?"

With his free hand, Noland pressed two fingers into his right temple and made a slow, circular motion. Somehow, he'd forgotten about the fraud case. He'd been so worried about Victor Irenas whacking all of the partners that he pushed *State of Florida v. Bisby Consulting* into the back of his mind.

"But he's dead," Noland reminded her.

"So? The judge doesn't know that. And anyway, if we get Valkenburg into court it will buy us some time."

"Time for what?"

"For you to get the money back. If you get the money, I can get Sydney to drop the case in return for restitution."

"Why would you want to?"

"Sydney could still go after Bisby's LLC. His estate. And anyway, settling it would prevent Sydney from subpoenaing the other partners. Or poking around Bisby's finances, which would lead back to them, too."

"You really think Sydney would go for it?"

"Sydney wants a win. That's all he's about. The easier, the better."

Noland pictured Sydney in the courthouse, in his thousand-dollar suit, looking all prim and poised and superior. Faith had pegged him accurately. He was all about the score.

"Okay, I'm working on it," Noland said.

"Right. Your great leads."

A long pause ensued. For some reason, he wished he were there with her, wherever she was at that moment. He needed some reassurance. And even though that was not her role—never had been, never would be—it was nice to think that she could calm him down, somehow.

"Did you make contact with Cassandra Raines yet?"

"Yeah."

"What do you think?"

He almost blurted out "she's great" but caught himself just in time.

"She's smart. Cagey."

"You think she knows where Valkenburg is?"

"Maybe. I'm working on it."

"I bet you are."

* * *

She hung up.

He cranked up the van and drove off. It occurred to him that he hadn't eaten since breakfast, so he stopped off at a

Korean barbecue joint he liked. He sat at the bar, which was built in the shape of a big U, and ordered a plate of bulgogi and a Miller Lite. From his stool, he had a good view of the parking lot, where he had left the van in the shade of a crepe myrtle tree. He waited in silence, staring out at the tree. His conversation with Faith had unnerved him. He had told her he could pull it off, the whole case. But could he? What were the odds that he, himself, would end up in prison by the time the whole affair was done? Then he remembered what Kiril had said—that they should punt.

Punt. Noland shook his head. Typical, he thought, for an offensive lineman to think about punting. He remembered how thrilled he'd been, back in his own playing days, whenever he and the boys on the D-line forced the other team to punt. It was a mini-victory. It meant those other guys couldn't roll with them. They were outclassed, if only for the moment. Now Kiril wanted to punt. Fuck that. Noland thought of Valkenburg's handsome face, grinning in the photograph with Bisby. Noland had promised Faith he would run Valkenburg down, and so he would. Valkenburg had probably been getting away with things his entire life. It was time someone called him on it.

And then there was the matter of Sabine's head. Whoever had put it there had done so to send a message, or perhaps as a joke, and this struck Noland as intolerably perverse. He remembered how, in Raiford, the younger convicts had a special term for things that offended them: "not proper." It had taken Noland some time to learn that the set of things deemed "not proper" contained everything from minor slights to unnecessary murder. Would they consider Sabine's dismemberment "not proper"? He bet they would. And Noland agreed. Killing somebody was one thing—he could understand the need for that. But mutilation? That was unnecessary. Barbaric. Not proper.

Vengeance is mine, he thought to himself, and I will repay.

It was the only line in the Bible that he really got.

His bulgogi and beer came. As he ate, the combination of spicy food and alcohol calmed his nerves. At some point, he looked out through the window and spotted a black-and-white OPD cruiser as it rolled lazily into the parking lot. A single dark silhouette lurked inside, which meant that it was an older officer—someone who didn't need backup. Noland was not very surprised when the cruiser stopped directly in front of the van, and the silhouette tilted its head to the side in that familiar gesture, speaking into his shoulder mic.

Noland got out his phone and texted Kiril.

> —U stash everything?

—Not yet

> —Do it now. asap

—Cops?

> —Yeah. If I don't get back to you in 2 hours call Faith

He wolfed down the rest of the food and finished his beer. Afterward, when he went to the men's room to take a leak, he spotted a fire exit. For a moment, he was tempted to duck through it, but then brushed the idea away as childish. When he was finished in the john, he returned to the bar-counter, paid his bill, and walked out.

The cop powered down his window. He had an ordinary, lived-in face that reminded Noland of old socks. "You Noland Twice?"

"That's me."

He nodded toward the passenger seat. "Get in."

"Am I under arrest?"

"That depends. Someone wants a word with you."

Noland climbed in. The cabin was very clean for a police cruiser. No candy wrappers or Chinese food coffins. No smell of puke or blood. The cop slid them out into traffic, then went full code to make a U-turn, the siren a familiar ululation blaring from the roof. The U-turn was hard, G-force shoving

Noland against the door, but he didn't complain. He'd been
summoned by the Law, and he knew better than anyone that
the Law—in the improbable form of Assistant State Attorney
Sydney Cross, with his perfect, up-styled ducktail—was not
to be kept waiting.

14

THE COP DROVE them around Lake Eola. The State Attorney's office took up the first three floors of an old office building across from the courthouse. The cop, whose name plate read PARSONS, parked on the street.

"I know where Sydney's office is," Noland said.

"I'll take you up anyway."

Parsons was tall and lanky, and he walked with a slow, loping gait. Noland had to force himself to slow down to avoid leaving the poor guy in the dust. When they finally got in, he was again confronted with a metal detector. He got the Ruger out of his back holster and handed it to Parsons, who appraised it with a gimlet eye. "Nice gun. You got a permit?"

He dug the cards out of his wallet. Parsons eyeballed them for three seconds before giving them back, keeping the gun. They rode the elevator up together, stepping off on the third floor, where the cop headed toward the rec room. Noland walked alone through the door that read ASSISTANT STATE ATTORNEY, the smell of burned coffee making his eyes water the moment he went inside. The reception area reminded him of a high school principal's office, from the wood paneling on the walls to the blocky wooden furniture. The secretary's desk was empty, so Noland walked on into Sydney's inner sanctum, which was not much bigger than a broom closet. Compared to the typical corporate digs, Sydney's was almost laughable, with the institutional green paint on the walls to the moldy plastic diffuser that covered the flickering fluorescent lights in the ceiling. The only decorations were Sydney's diplomas: U.F. B.A., U.F. Law, etc. Sydney himself was at the desk, typing on his MacBook. Eventually, he glanced up. "Thanks for coming, Nole."

"What's the emergency?"

"Funny you should ask. Last week, Faith had a missing witness. This week, she has a missing defendant."

"The hell you say."

Sydney smiled. "Bisby's wife says he hasn't been home in five days. Not answering his cell either."

"You trace his credit cards?"

"They haven't been used since he disappeared."

"Maybe he didn't like his chances with the jury. Decided to skip."

"Over a fraud indictment?"

"Maybe it's not fraud he's worried about."

Sydney's eyebrows climbed his smooth forehead. "Now that's an interesting theory. Maybe he's guilty of other crimes?"

Noland wanted to kick himself; he had walked straight into that one. He hid his dismay by scoffing. "I don't know. I only met him once. I'm after the other fella."

"Valkenburg?"

"Yeah."

"Any luck?"

"No. But I've got some leads."

"Want to share?"

"No again. But I'll let you know if I hear anything about Bisby."

"That's very considerate of you."

"Just trying to help."

Sydney shook his head and grinned a sideways grin, suggesting both admiration and disgust. "You shouldn't have left policing, Nole."

He scratched behind his ear. "Well, I didn't exactly leave by choice, did I?"

Sydney ignored the barb. Finally, he closed the laptop and sat forward. "I'm going to be straight with you. I don't believe Bisby is on the run. I think he's dead."

Noland tried to look shocked. "No shit?"

"No shit."

"What makes you say so?"

"We found his car."

This time, Noland didn't have to pretend to be shocked. He was.

"Really? Where?"

Sydney waved him off. "It's not important. Somebody pushed it into a sinkhole."

"Any evidence in the car? Blood?"

He shrugged. "Still checking it out. But it doesn't look good. I don't think he'd skip town without his car. And even if he did, why dump it in the woods?"

Noland waited a moment. He wanted to press his fingertips into his wrist and check his pulse—he was pretty sure it was off the chart—but that was not an option. "I'll need to tell Faith, of course."

"She'll be devastated, I'm sure."

"What's that supposed to mean?"

Sydney's previous grin broke now into a full-blown smile, a chorus line of perfect, white, upper-class teeth. "I meant that he was probably paying her well."

"Yeah, that's probably true. He was loaded."

"Exactly. And that's another reason I don't believe he's on the run. He's not the type to pay cash and hide out in fleabag motels."

Under different circumstances, Noland might have chuckled; this was the same conclusion he had reached about Valkenburg.

"Who do you think killed him?"

Sydney blinked. "How about your missing witness?"

"Valkenburg? No way."

"Why not?"

"He and Bisby are friends."

"Friends, huh?"

"Yeah, friends. And anyway, unless I'm very mistaken, Valkenburg's already split town himself. Maybe the country. Why would he come back? Just to shoot Bisby?"

Sydney's eyes fixed on him like pale blue lasers. "Who said Bisby was shot?"

Noland sucked on his front teeth. Another fuck-up. He was oh for two.

"I was speaking theoretically. I have no clue where either of these guys are. As for Bisby, why ask me? Surely you've got the manpower to find him, dead or alive."

Sydney turned his head. The far-away look in his eyes suggested he was measuring the weight of Noland's words, much the same way the cop outside had judged the heft of Noland's gun.

"Let me ask you something else," he said.

There was something ominous in his tone. A bead of sweat ran down Noland's back, roller-coasting over the knuckles of his spine. "Okay."

"Have you heard of an individual named Deisch? Charles Deisch."

"Rings a bell."

Sydney worked his tongue against his front teeth, as if trying to dislodge a bit of his lunch. "Allergy doctor, or some such. You might have come across him in the bio Faith gave you. His uncle sued Selberis a year ago."

"Sued them for what?"

"Negligence. Pain and suffering. Over the death of a construction worker named Nicholas Deisch. An accident, apparently, but the old man—the boy's father—sued and lost. Went bankrupt from the legal fees."

Noland shook his head. "Those blood-sucking lawyers."

"Don't be a smartass, Nole. The poor guy died a few months later."

"So, what? Are you implying that this Deisch fella had it in for Bisby?"

"Yes."

"You think Deisch offed him?"

He seemed taken aback. "I'm not sure I would go that far. No, we don't believe Deisch is like that."

"Nobody's like that," Noland said, "until they are."

"Let's put it this way: I don't think Deisch is the killer."

"Fair enough. But you think he's involved?"

"Yes."

Noland opened his hands in a gesture of surrender. "So, bring him in. Squeeze him. I would."

Sydney pointed his chin at the ceiling and laughed, too loud. "Come on, Noland. We've got to follow the law, you know."

Noland didn't reply.

"Do I have to spell it out?"

"Please do."

"We've. Got. No. Evidence."

"That never stopped you before."

Sydney clenched his jaw, muscles bunching under his ears so that he looked almost simian, despite the too-perfect haircut.

"We have no reason to legally investigate Deisch, or even to question him. However . . ."

Noland waited. In the silence that followed, Sydney did the thing he had been waiting to do—the reason he had brought Noland there in the first place. Moving very slowly, he leaned forward and placed his fist on the desk, knuckles down. A curious gesture. Noland wanted to stare at the fist, but he kept his eyes on Sydney. When the man spoke again, his voice was modulated, drained of inflection or emotion, like a robot.

"Those restrictions don't apply to you, Nole."

A shiver went down his spine. How many sins did a man have to commit before he got the ability to turn his soul off like that? Probably not so many. Noland's own tally was getting close.

"You're offering a trade?"

Cross kept his fist where it was. "Of course not. I could never suggest such a thing."

"Okay," Noland said. "If you were offering a trade, I would give Deisch a look. And in return, you would give me everything you knew about Valkenburg."

"We don't know anything about Valkenburg."

"But you might soon."

Sydney didn't move. Before Noland's eyes, the man seemed to thin out, dissipate into something ephemeral, with the illusion of depth but no actual substance. A hologram. Finally, as if triggered by some hidden timer, Sydney opened his fist and pulled his hand away from the desk. A slug of white plastic remained on the clean pine surface. A thumb drive.

"If you'll excuse me, I have to be in court." Sydney slid his chair back, stood up, and lifted his suit jacket off a hook by the window. "Good luck. Lieutenant Parsons will see you out."

He didn't look at Noland again before leaving the office, pulling the door closed behind him. Noland remained still for a full thirty seconds before he, too, stood. After a brief hesitation, he picked up the thumb drive and put it in his pocket.

In the rec room, Parsons was seated by a vending machine. "You want a Coke?"

"No, thanks. I have to get moving."

"Okay, we'll go then." He rose. "And don't worry, I'll give you back your piece."

"I wasn't worried," Noland said, and followed him into the elevator.

15

WHEN PARSONS DROPPED him off, the Korean restaurant's parking lot was bustling, filled with the dinner rush, and Noland was grateful that the van wasn't blocked. He drove straight home, parked in the driveway, and got his RF detector out of the garage. He swept the van from bumper to bumper, roof to tires, but found nothing. Of course, his inability to find anything made him even more nervous.

He went inside. After a quick shower, he made a pot of coffee and settled down at his desk. In the bottom drawer, he kept a half dozen burner phones, still in their shrink-wrapped boxes. He got one out, activated it, and called the shop. Freddy answered.

"It's me," Noland said. "Tell Kiril to break out a burner. Have him call me at this number."

He hung up. Twenty minutes later the phone chirruped.

"You in jail?" Kiril asked.

"Not yet. Did you store the goods?"

"It's taken care of. What happened?"

"I'm not sure. I think we've got a new friend."

"Oh yeah? Who?"

"The Assistant State Attorney."

"Blyad."

Noland was about to reassure him, but what could he say? He was still a little freaked out himself, replaying the scene downtown in his head, trying to figure out what was really going on. Was Sydney trying to trap him? Noland doubted it. He kept remembering the way the man had set the thumb drive onto his desk, opening his fist like a robot. Noland had found it odd, at the time, but now he understood; Sydney didn't want to leave any fingerprints.

"I've got some work to do," Noland said. "Keep the phone handy. I'll call you when I know something."

He hung up. It was barely eight o'clock, but he found himself exhausted. He stripped off his clothes and got into bed, thinking he would need to take something to settle down. But in the end, he didn't need anything. He fell instantly asleep.

The next thing he knew, it was morning. He felt better, his muscles soothed and limber. It was Saturday—Day Six— and the street in front of his house was quiet. As soon as his laptop booted, he plugged in the thumb drive and scanned it for malware. The scan didn't take long because there was only one file on the drive: a big text file, tab-delimited, filled with hundreds of rows of computer-generated data. Each row held a ream of obscure digits, but at the end was a time stamp and two sets of numbers, which Noland—after his recent adventures with Freddy and Kiril—recognized as GPS coordinates. At first, he thought the file must be a data dump from a cell carrier, continuously triangulating someone's cell phone. But after he plugged a few of the coordinates into his laptop, he saw that the motion described was not granular enough to be a person carrying a phone. Rather, it seemed more like the feed from a GPS tracker, a military-grade version of the one Noland had tried to use on Cassy's Honda.

It was a trace of someone's car.

But whose? Deisch's? Noland kept plugging in coordinates. Soon, he had a rough mental image of Individual X's invisible path through the city of Orlando and Seminole

County. One of the coordinates matched the offices of Selberis; X had gone there on the previous Thursday, at six in the morning. Another set, from the following afternoon, was near the construction site in St. Cloud. But the strangest entry was the last one—Sunday morning, way up in the northern part of the county, northwest of Wekiva Springs. Noland switched the map to satellite view. The location looked uninhabited, pine forest. But judging from the log, Deisch had stayed there—or, at least, parked there—for three hours. What was he doing? Taking a stroll in the woods? Walking a dog?

Once again, Noland wondered: Was Sydney fucking with him?

He switched back to map view and figured out his best route. Without realizing it, he moved his face close to the computer screen, until the yellow and blue lines of the highways and country roads blurred together like the intricate threading of a tapestry. He followed the yellow line of I-4 to where he would have to take the exit onto 46. A raging panic began to gallop through his bloodstream. Shit. He didn't want to go into the woods. Bad things happened there.

But then he had a thought: Maybe he didn't have to go alone. He could take Cassy! She lived on the way, and she might be up for an adventure. His heart thrilled at the thought of it.

He made himself breakfast, played with the dogs, and finally got out the burner phone. He was almost certain Cassy wouldn't answer—she was probably teaching another class—but she picked up on the second ring.

"Hello?" Her voice sounded wary.

"Hey. It's Noland."

A pause.

"I didn't recognize the number."

"Sorry. I lost my regular phone."

"That sucks."

"Yeah."

"I wasn't going to answer."

"Well, I'm glad you did."

"Me too."

A simple statement, yet it made his day. How did she manage that? How had she gained such power over him, so quickly?

"I have an errand to run," he said. "Somewhere in your neck of the woods. Thought you might like a drive."

"A drive, huh?"

"Yeah."

"Work related?"

"Yeah. Is that okay?"

"Does it involve Val?"

Noland's impulse was to lie, but he heard himself say: "Possibly."

"Possibly?"

"Will you come or not?"

He counted to ten before she finally said: "Okay."

"Great. I'll pick you up. Thirty minutes."

As it turned out, he took almost an hour, the delay due to his caution, or perhaps paranoia, which led him to drive aimlessly for five miles before doing a Crazy Ivan across the median. When he was sure he didn't have a tail, he got back on I-4 and went to her place. Now half an hour late, he dreaded the look she would give him. But no sooner had he pulled up into her driveway than she strolled out the front door smiling, dressed in appropriate attire for a Saturday drive: khaki shorts, crisp white T-shirt, and new sneakers. As she settled into the passenger seat, her thigh muscles swelled on the cushion, the hem of her shorts pressing into the flesh.

"So, what's this 'errand' about?"

"Checking out a location."

"What kind?"

Instead of answering, he cranked the engine and took off, getting back on I-4. The day was surprisingly mild, and they rode with the windows down, Cassy's hair whipping around her cheeks.

"You look nice," he said.

"Thanks."

"Are you teaching today?"

"Already did. Eight AM."

"That early? On a Saturday?"

"Earlier is better. It beats the heat. And I'm done till Monday. Most of my kids are Baptists, and Baptists all go to church."

"I'm a Baptist."

"Do you go to church?"

"Not recently."

"That's because you're wicked."

He laughed uneasily.

At the junction of 46, he headed west for twenty miles. Noland had often wondered why that part of Seminole County was so hilly, practically mountainous by Florida standards, the van zooming up and down like a roller-coaster past the cow pastures and abandoned orange groves. The groves always depressed him. They had stood fallow since the late freeze of '82, and the old trees had long since grown into tangles, their fruit drooping, unpicked. Why couldn't somebody tend them once in a while? Some government program, perhaps, to get poor people out there and pick the now-wild oranges before they got bloated and sour. What a fucking waste. But at least the groves still smelled good. Even now, he caught himself flaring his nostrils to take in the sweet odor of decay.

"I love that scent, too," Cassy said, watching him. "Even though it's kind of sad, I guess. All the old growers are gone."

"Pretty much."

She turned back to the window. "Everything comes down to money, doesn't it?"

"You know what the poet said: 'Money changes everything.'"

She raised her eyebrows. "Robert Frost?"

"Cindy Lauper."

She smiled.

"Speaking of money," he asked, "your dad went broke, right?"

"Yeah."

"What happened to him?"

"What usually happens? He made some bad investments. Bought a few horses that didn't pan out. Lost a few races he shouldn't have lost. At some point, he couldn't insure the stable. Then an outbreak of encephalitis hit, and he was done. The End."

"So you lost your inheritance?" Noland said. "Like one of those Russian princesses."

"Yeah. Exactly like that."

West of the Wekiva River, he pulled onto a one-lane road, which led through yet another grove, even more tangled and overgrown than the others. His burner phone didn't have GPS, so he parked for a moment and powered up his smartphone. He was still afraid of being triangulated, but the fear was trumped by his need to find the right path.

"I thought you lost your phone," Cassy said.

"Just found it."

They were about a mile from their destination. He kept driving until the paved road turned to dirt, leading deeper and deeper into the grove. The road was badly washed out in several places, and the van jounced over the ruts and bumps. Cassy didn't complain, placing both hands against the dashboard to brace herself, triceps flexing like steel cord. They passed several little homesteads. Mobile homes perched on blocks, weeds filling the crawlspace. Then came a long stretch of nothing, just road and orange trees. Finally, the road ended at a huge live oak and a rusty metal gate. With the engine still running, Noland got out. The gate was secured with a brass padlock. He fetched his bolt cutters and dispatched it, the heavy lock dropping to the dirt with a satisfying thunk.

Cassy watched him through the open window. "So, we're breaking and entering now?"

"What? That old lock? I think it rusted away."

She shook her head.

He opened the gate and climbed back into the cab. The boughs of the live oak screeched against the roof as he drove forward, the van's fat wheels chewing up the loose dirt. The trail threaded its way another quarter mile until they arrived at a clearing with a steel Quonset hut, like a metal garage, big enough for three cars (or maybe one F-150). The garage door was closed.

Noland parked and stepped out onto the grass. Cassy got out too, pressing her lips together in an expression of determination mixed with barely repressed rage.

"What is this place?"

"I'm not sure. But someone thinks it's important."

"Who?"

"People with juice."

Leaving her at the van, he did a quick circuit around the garage. Small windows had been cut into each side, but he couldn't see anything. One of the windows held a small air conditioning unit, with a new, green power cable snaking back to a generator ten feet out on the grass. Noland placed his hand on the generator. Cold. He thought of prying the A/C unit out and going in through the window, but it looked pretty narrow. Instead, he went back to the van and got his slim-jim.

Cassy came over and watched as he worked the slim-jim into the garage's side door. He felt the latch give way and was about to push the door open when he stopped. He couldn't quite name the feeling that came over him in that last moment, but he recognized it. The same sort of tingling, hyperaware sensation he'd used to get when running behind a wide receiver, knowing with absolute certainty that the ball was now in the air, spiraling behind him on a ballistic arc to where he and the receiver would be in 1.6 seconds.

"Change of plan," he said, putting the slim-jim away. He walked back over to the side of the garage, yanked the A/C unit from the window, and tossed it onto the grass. Cassy, who had followed him around, said. "Do you have to be so destructive?"

"Usually."

He slid the window open, poked his head inside, and looked around. A powerful smell of bleach burned his nostrils. Industrial grade. He wasn't able to see much else until his eyes adjusted to the gloom, but eventually he made out that the garage was empty except for a few austere items: a workbench, a metal chair, a few filing cabinets along the wall, some white cement-mixing buckets, and a couple of steel drums. He looked to his left, toward the front of the hut. and to the side door that he'd almost opened. Resting on the bare concrete was a car battery, with bright copper wires trailing out from the poles. He followed one of the wires to the top of the door, and the other to a ceiling brace. This second wire split off toward a pair of red jerry cans.

"Okay," he said. "I'm going in."

"Me too."

"Really?"

"Yes!" she said, blinking at him angrily. "It was your idea to bring me here. I'm not going to wait around on the grass."

"Right." He stood the A/C unit up on its end and used it as a stepping stool. Once his shoulders were inside the window, he did a clumsy handstand on the concrete and dropped through. Then Cassy crawled in, much more nimbly than he had. He helped her anyway, pressing his hands under her damp armpits and helping her to her feet. For a moment, they stood together in the near darkness. He spotted a light switch, but of course it wouldn't work without the generator. He walked over to the garage door and disconnected one of the copper wires, which ran back to the battery in the same way the others did. Cassy came over and inspected them.

"Is that what I think it is?"

"Yeah. Good thing we didn't come through the door, huh?"

She blinked. Noland knew what images were going through her mind because the same ones had gone through his a few minutes previously. The door opening. The wires making contact with the steel brace. The circuit closing. The brief squirt of electricity into the jerry cans, followed by a titanic blossom of flame, issuing forth at the speed of sound. What would it feel like as the fire peeled your skin away? Agony? Or would it feel like nothing at all, your nerve endings cauterized before they could sing pain to your brain—which would, itself, be boiled into cabbage a few seconds later.

Cassy stared at him.

"How did you know?"

"ESP."

"Bullshit."

He lifted the garage door. It slid up easily, well lubricated. Sunlight flooded in.

"This wasn't Val," she said, looking at the jerry cans again. "He wouldn't do this."

"Do what? Kill somebody? Now who's talking bullshit?"

She shook her head. "No, not like this. Val wouldn't kill somebody this way. He's more . . . direct."

Noland was about to laugh, but then considered the possibility that she might be right. After all, she knew Val better than he did.

He fetched two pairs of latex gloves from the van and handed a pair to Cassy. Then he started going through the filing cabinets. The outsides were clean, dust free. Sterilized. The first one contained medical supplies: gauze, alcohol, suture thread, and an unopened IV bag of electrolytes. The second was filled with cabin-worthy dry goods: bottled water, canned food, MREs, chocolate bars, and ground coffee. The third cabinet was the strange one. It was filled with books. All kinds. Engineering manuals. Computer coding books.

Dime novels. Fat history tomes. All of them well worn, their pages dogeared as if some grad student had been poring over them for years.

"Look familiar?" he said to Cassy, holding a book up to eye level.

"Those aren't the ones I took from Val's office."

"I believe you."

He turned his attention to the furniture. The plastic table was clean but deeply scratched, as if some intense work-shopping had been performed on its surface. The office chair seemed out of place, an expensive steel and chrome model. It, too, smelled of bleach. As he stood over it, he saw that it had been bolted to the floor. An expert job, too, the bolts set with precision. He tried to imagine the person who'd done it. Someone good with their hands. Meticulous. Probably the same asshole who'd wired up the IED.

But why the fuck would they bolt the chair to the floor?

He was still pondering this question as he became aware of Cassy's puttering around, doing her own snooping, peeking into the cabinets that Noland had rifled through.

Noland kept examining the chair. He ran his fingers over the armrests, then along the floor under the struts. His fingers touched something small and sharp. He grabbed it. When he withdrew his hand, his palm held something delicate and shiny, like a snail shell, one side gooey with a dark fluid, the color of rust. All at once, he realized what he was holding: a human fingernail, complete with the root.

At that moment, Cassy walked over to the first of the steel drums. She grabbed the lid with both hands.

"Don't!" he yelled.

It was too late. She lifted the lid and peered down. A moment went by. Then two. At some point, her entire body began to shake, so violently that for one dreadful moment, Noland thought the barrel must have been wired too, with some electrical current now conducting itself into Cassy's hand. She dropped the lid. It slammed down, so loud Noland felt it in his teeth. She stepped back, turned around, and ran. Right out of the building.

Noland rushed after her. She didn't go far—just to the van. She stopped and placed both hands on the fender. Then, bending over at the waist, she vomited copiously on the grass.

Noland rubbed her back. "It's okay. Get rid of it."

When she was done, she straightened up and wiped her mouth. "Fuck."

"Yeah. Stay here."

He went back into the garage. Even though he was pretty sure what was in the drum, he had to see it for himself. If he didn't—if he chickened out—he'd never be able to face Zeb again with any self-respect. So he lifted the lid.

The drum was filled with clear liquid, from whose surface rose a caustic odor that burned his nostrils so badly he had to hold his breath. Under the surface of the liquid, something floated languidly, a shape rather like a large, white balloon, colorless except for a dark circle at the top. It took his brain several seconds to process what he was seeing, and only when his eyes glimpsed the bloated, naked arms, and then followed them down to their hands and on to the lifeless fingers, dark-tipped, expanding like pale sausages, did everything click.

He dropped the lid, letting it slam as Cassy had. He walked out.

Still hanging on the fender, she glanced at him.

"Did you see it?"

"Yeah."

From the way she grimaced, he thought she might puke again. Instead, she gritted her teeth and squared her shoulders.

"You knew we'd find it here, didn't you?"

He was about to deny everything, but couldn't. She had seen right through him. Again.

"I thought we might find something," he said. "Something along these lines."

"Who is it?"

"Selberis's banker. Sabine Werther."

And with that, Cassy punched him in the jaw.

It was as if the mere act of his uttering Sabine's name had triggered some instantaneous reflex, a chain of causality that ended with Cassy delivering a good solid hit, straight from the shoulder, powerful enough to drive his jawbone into the jumble of nerves in the hollow beneath his ears. Nerves he never thought about until moments like this, when they exploded into supernovas of pain.

He staggered back. She came after him and threw another punch. He sidestepped her, grabbed her arm, and yanked her past him. She went flying, sprawling onto the grass like a knackered horse, landing on her elbows. Noland steadied himself against the van but kept an eye on her as she clambered to her feet. Her cheeks shone with tears, but Noland was unmoved. "Don't come at me again, Cass. I swear, I'll smack you."

After a while, she brushed the bits of grass from her shorts.

"You're telling me that thing in the barrel is Sabine Werther?"

"Yeah. Probably not identifiable, from a forensic point of view. But it's her."

"How do you know?"

"Because I found the rest of her three days ago. How many headless bodies could there be in this part of Florida?"

Cassy blinked once and her lips parted. He could tell that some part of her wanted to shriek, but some other part wouldn't let her.

"Who killed her?"

"You tell me."

She flipped him a bird.

He laughed. "She had something they wanted."

"What?"

"A book."

Her eyes widened.

"You're kidding me."

He shook his head. "Two books, actually. One is a jour-nal, written in code. They had that one already. The other is the key to the code. That's the one they wanted. So they brought her here and tortured her. But she wouldn't give it up. I don't know how, but she held out."

Cassy's eyes had left him, and he knew she was follow-ing the thread of her own thoughts. He went on. "Somebody probably got frustrated. Killed her on impulse. It must've been gratifying, for a moment or two. Then, whoever did it realized they had fucked up."

Cassy's face was still sweaty and flushed, like a kid who's come inside after a playground fight. "Mutilating her like that. It's just so . . ."

"Medieval? Yeah. But they might've had a rationale for it."

"Like what?"

"They knew she stole the firm's money. It wasn't Valkenburg at all. It was her. The whole crazy scheme was her doing. Had to be. She had access to the money. And she had a motive."

"What motive?"

"Revenge. For what, I'm not sure, but she had reasons. At any rate, they really wanted her to talk. But she wouldn't. She was too strong. And somehow, I bet, she managed to piss off the main guy. Goaded him into killing her before she might lose her resolve."

Cassy absorbed all this for several silent moments. Then, spent at last, she brought both hands to her mouth and spoke through her fingers.

"Have you got any tissues?"

"I have some paper towels."

"That'll do."

He opened the back of the van and tore a handful off the roll he kept there. She wiped her eyes and blew her nose copi-ously. When she was done, he held out his hand. "Give it to me. We can't leave any trace here. No DNA."

Her mouth hung open. "I puked all over the grass."

"I'll bleach it."

She handed him the wad of soiled towels, which he tossed into a plastic bag. He then took the rest of the roll and a spray bottle of bleach. He soaked the spot of grass where Cassy had retched, then went into the hut. It took him ten minutes to spray down everything inside that they had inspected, including the lid of the barrel. As he did so, he spotted something down on the concrete, between the barrels. He squatted down and picked it up. A crumpled cigarette pack, a brand he'd never heard of: Hollywoods. The retro-looking design on the cover made him think of something from an old movie.

He put the pack into his pocket and turned to leave. Then, almost as an afterthought, he went back in with a pair of wire cutters and disarmed the rest of the booby trap. The cops would find the hut eventually, and they didn't deserve to get incinerated. He pulled the garage door down.

They got in the van and drove back down the trail, riding in silence, Cassy's profile a study in indifference. Numbness. It wasn't until they passed Sanford that she spoke again.

"Where are you taking me?"

"I need a drink. Or six."

By the time they got to town, morning had turned into afternoon, and the lengthening shadows lent everything a hazy, desaturated tone of unreality. It was a relief to get inside the cave of Benny's bar. Even its gauntlet of blaring TVs seemed reassuring at the moment. Installing Cassy in a booth, he fetched them scotches. A half hour went by as they sat sipping.

"Are you ready to tell me about Dr. Deisch?"

If she was surprised by the question, she didn't show it. "Charles didn't kill that girl. And neither did Val."

Noland let it pass.

"How did he find you? Deisch, I mean."

She hunched her shoulders. "Dunno. He just showed up at the house one day. Asked if I would listen to his story."

"And you did."

"He said he needed my help. Finding a book. A book that someone at Selberis owned. He also said that they killed his cousin."

"What made him think the book was in Val's office?"

"I'm not sure he did think about it, really. He seemed to be grasping at straws."

"I don't suppose he told you which book he was looking for?"

As if not hearing him, she held her highball glass up to eye level and let the light from the neon signs behind the bar filter through, painting her face red and gold. A whiskey prism. When she lowered the glass again, a moment later, he noticed that the cut on the back of her hand—the one he'd noticed that first day at her stables—had almost fully healed, leaving just a faint, wine-colored mark in the shape of an arrowhead.

"Selberis is really dirty," she said. "I didn't know how bad."

"I'm shocked."

"They sometimes pay their workers in cash."

"Deisch told you this?"

"Sometimes they pay in cash for several weeks in a row. Then they'll stop all work for a month."

"Must be a loyal workforce, to put up with that crap."

She shrugged. "Guys will put up with a lot if you pay them under the table. Tax-free." She looked him in the eye. "You can relate to that, can't you, Nole?"

"What are you trying to say?"

"You're a cheater."

His cheeks were suddenly hot. He straightened up and put his elbows on the table. "Lady, you don't know a damned thing about me."

"Don't I? I've met you before, Nole. Several versions of you. Guys who have some brains and some skills but think the rules don't apply to them. That the world owes you something. Some recompense for something that happened to you once."

He scoffed. "You mean guys like me and Val?"

"Exactly. You're both prime specimens. Supreme cheaters."

She was trying to piss him off, and it was working. Even so, as he watched her sitting there, holding the drink with her elegant and unwavering hands, his anger evaporated. He felt good, despite all the rest. He laughed.

She squinted at him. "Why are you laughing?"

"You remind me of something."

"Something?"

"Yeah."

"What?"

"Disney World."

She stopped squinting and her eyebrows rose into elegant filigrees. "You are a very strange man, Noland Twice."

"We never went to Disney when I was a kid. It was just a few hours down the interstate, but my folks never took me."

She dismissed this by blowing a puff of air through her lips. "They probably never thought of it. Like people who live by the beach but never go swimming."

"No, it was deeper than that. My mom went to church. A lot. She thought Disney World was evil. Instead of Mickey Mouse ears, she saw devil horns."

"What about your dad?"

"He deferred to her. Of course, I couldn't stop thinking about it. Disney World, I mean. Every time one of my friends went, I'd go home and cry. Or kick the kid's ass. Anyway, Disney World came to represent something for me, I guess."

She hesitated a moment before asking the next, obvious question, as if afraid of the answer he would give.

"Like what?"

"Heaven."

She rolled her eyes. "Oh, for fuck's sake."

"It's true. Heaven. Or something like it. Some ultimate goodness."

She shook her head, not buying it. But she kept looking at him.

Noland asked, "What about you?"

She looked startled. "What about me?"

"What was your dream, growing up?"

"Well, my dad took me to Disney World."

"You know what I mean."

She thought for a moment. "I just wanted to be on my own. Have some land. Raise some horses. Teach kids to ride. Be my own boss."

"Sounds like you made it."

She shook her head. "I have a fatal flaw. Almost Shakespearean."

"What's that?"

"I'm attracted to the wrong sort of men."

He laughed. "Cheaters?"

"Yeah."

"Maybe one will surprise you, someday. Turn out to be better than you thought."

She didn't reply.

After a long while, she said, "I need to go home."

"Okay."

On the way back to Lake Mary, she kept her face pointed out the window. As they got closer to her house, he sank into that numb, hopeless feeling one gets after having done a really stupid thing. Why had he taken her to the grove? But then he remembered: He'd wanted something from her. The truth. Before they went into the garage, he'd been certain that she was aware, broadly, of what kind of people they were dealing with. But now, two hours later, he knew he'd been wrong. The way she'd puked on the grass—no one could fake that. Noland was an expert in fear. He had a Ph.D. in fear. He knew the real thing when he saw it.

Back at her place, he walked her to the door, fully expecting her to stride into the house without a word and even slam the door in his face. Instead, she turned under the awning and looked at him.

"Come on in," she said. "I'll make some lemonade."

He had never been in the house before, and his senses became alive with apprehension as he walked through the foyer and registered the trappings of her life. A hat rack with an old rain slicker draped over it. A brightly polished mirror, where he glimpsed his own hapless visage. A framed painting of a rugged, mustachioed man on horseback. Her father. Had to be. The last thing he noticed was a pair of pink boots resting on the tile. He was about to tease her about them when she sidled up close, put a hand on either side of his face, and kissed him. Her tongue tasted like whiskey.

"Did you ever make it to Disney World?" she asked.

"Nope. I'm still hoping, though."

She kissed him again and pulled him tight, matching her curves to his angles. With expert speed, she unbuttoned his shirt and then, without so much as a cuddle, put her mouth on his nipple and sucked it, hard. Noland winced, even though it felt good. She pulled her head off his chest and strode off toward the hallway. And Noland, ignoring the tiny voice in the back of his head screaming that all this might be one of God's awful little jokes, rushed after her, caught in her wake.

16

H E WOKE UP in her bed.

Late afternoon sun filtered weakly through the drawn blinds. Even in the gloom, he could see that the room was expensively decorated. Silk blinds fluttered in the weak, artificial breeze of the air conditioning. The intricately carved bedposts rose like African totems from each corner of the bed.

Normally, at this juncture, he would have pulled on his pants, or at least his underwear, but he couldn't find either item of clothing. He rose, reconnoitered, and walked bare-assed down the hall. He found a bathroom and went in. Like everything else in the house, it was luxurious without crossing the line into decadence. White marble sink. Trim towels. The commode was a large, vanilla-colored model of the sort advertised in housewives' magazines. As he stood over it and relieved himself, he wondered whose good taste the john should be credited to. Cassy's, or Valkenburg's? When he was finished, he paused for a moment and stretched happily—almost guiltily, still savoring the wonderful, postcoital warmth that only seemed to happen when some genuine emotion had been expressed. His body felt like a long-dry field that had just been rained upon. Awakened. His muscles were limber and strong. The overall effect was unexpected but welcome. Like a cool day in July, he savored it without questioning how it could happen in the first place.

Still naked, he toured the house. The furnishings might be new, but the house was not. Low-ceilinged and horizontal, it felt like an early Frank Lloyd Wright prairie home. Very strange for Florida. The tile floors were cold beneath his feet as he padded into the living room, centered around an impressive stone hearth. Wide, built-in bookshelves flanked the hearth, and he stood there for a while, admiring them. Someone had crafted the shelves so expertly that he wanted to touch them. He did so, running his hand along one's edge. The wood was as smooth as soap. Like the others, the shelf was jammed tight with books. Nothing else. No tchotchkes. No picture frames. No art-fair crap. Just books of all different kinds. Hardbacks and paper. Fiction, science, history. Even some philosophy.

As he walked the length of it, he came upon a single empty slot. Whatever book had resided there must have been taken recently, because it had left a faint silhouette in the thin layer of dust that had settled over the shelves since their last cleaning. Noland stopped, transfixed by the silhouette.

"Ahem," a voice said.

Cassy. Standing across the room, fully dressed in old jeans and a paint-splattered work shirt. "I like a naked man in my living room. You complete the décor."

"Glad to oblige," he said and gave her what he hoped was an insolent smile. Then, despite himself, he got aroused.

Her stare moved down. "Are you trying to point something out?"

"Actually, yes. You're missing one." He put his finger in the empty slot. As he did so, he kept his eyes on her face. She paused for a moment, her face suddenly inert, like a computer when the CPU locks up. But the pause lasted only an instant before she tilted her head quizzically. "Huh. Must have been the last time Val was here. I never noticed."

Damn, she was good.

"Not one of the books you gave Deisch?" he asked.

"Don't be stupid. I only gave him books from Val's office." Then she nodded at the shelves. "Those books are all Val's, though. From before we got married. He never bothered to come back for them."

"I don't suppose you know which one is missing?"

"Are you kidding?"

He bounced up and down on the balls of his feet.

Her mouth hardened. "You think it's the one, don't you?"

"It's possible."

"Probable, you mean."

Instead of arguing, he sighed. "Okay. Maybe it's a coincidence. Maybe he just wanted to take a book with him. Before he lit out."

She gave him a withering look. "*On the Road*, perhaps?"

He shook his head. "*Paradise Lost.*"

She smiled. "You're flattering me."

"Is it working?"

"Yes," she said. "But I haven't got time for another roll in the hay. I need to get to the actual hay. The horses. Want to help?"

"Love to."

"Good. I washed your clothes."

She went out. Noland sidled to the hall, where he found his clothes folded neatly on an armchair. He picked up his boxers and found them still warm. Even his shoes had been washed. Another man might have found this thoughtfulness touching, if a bit odd, but Noland knew better. He remembered what he told her, back at the metal shed, about leaving DNA. She had made sure that they hadn't taken any, either.

He got dressed and walked out the back door. When he came out a few minutes later, she was in the stables, carrying two plastic buckets of horse feed. She dumped each one into a different horse's trough, then handed them to him empty. "The rest is in the corner."

Noland filled the buckets from a big, black sack, whose top had been cut off in a precise, straight line. The nuggets inside were bigger than the ones he shoveled out to Quick and Silver each morning, and less pungent. Mellow. When the buckets were full, she motioned at the last two stalls, and Noland fed the horses there. One was the big roan she had ridden the first day he'd seen her. It huffed at his presence but gobbled up the food with gusto.

"What's his name?" Noland asked.

"Her name is Scaramouche. The kids call her Moosh."

"Was she ever a racehorse?"

"Yes, for a couple of years."

Noland scratched Moosh's jaw. "Did your dad give her to you?"

"Not exactly. I stole her. Last time I visited."

Before he could respond, she stepped into another stall and proceeded mucking it out with a flat, yellow shovel. She worked steadily, tossing each shovelful of manure into a wheelbarrow next to the gate. Noland liked the way she worked, liked the way she seemed not to mind the exertion or the smell. Probably been doing such chores all her life. He remembered the man in the painting, Cassy's father, with his arrogant, imperial stare. A rich guy, surely, but one who still made his favorite daughter get up at six each morning and clean the stables. A rare man, Noland imagined, equal parts wise and wicked.

A lot like Zeb.

He fed the other horses in turn. When he was done, he was surprised to feel his back throbbing. How was it possible that he, a former athlete and a guy who worked out six days a week, could be hurting from such brief labor? But then he remembered: This was real work. And real work always hurts.

Rubbing his back, he reached absently for his phone in its hip holster. It wasn't there. He caught Cassy's eye.

"In the kitchen," she said.

He went inside, looking around the kitchen for the first time. It was surprisingly spare, no fancy appliances. Obviously, neither she nor Valkenburg had cared much about food. Noland found his phone next to the coffee pot, beneath a cork bulletin board. The board was empty except for a small poster of Jesus Christ, complete with robes and locks of straight black hair.

He checked his phone. There were many missed calls, all from Kiril. Noland texted him:

—What's up?

The reply came instantly:

—Call me on the burner.

He went out to the van and got the burner from the glove box. Kiril answered on the first ring.

"Where the fuck are you?"

"I've been busy. What's the problem?"

"That nasty bit of work we covered up in Longwood last week. Remember? With the lime?"

"Yeah?"

"Well, somebody found the guy."

The pit of Noland's stomach went cold. "When?"

"Last night. It's all over the news. The pest control dude went to spray the apartment. Found the package in the tub. The bug dude almost had a heart attack."

Noland took a breath. He had hoped for a couple of weeks before Bisby's corpse was found, but he'd only gotten six days.

"What do you think?" Kiril asked. "Are we fucked?"

"Possibly. But we've got a big lead on the cops. And we know at least one thing that they don't."

"You mean about the book?"

"Bigger than that," Noland said. "We know Valkenburg didn't steal the firm's money."

"Huh?"

"I'll explain later. In the meantime, I need you to do something. Get on the internet and order every edition you can find of that book. *The Sorrows of Young Werther.*"

"German or English?"

"Both. And one more thing. Do me a favor and do a web search on Hollywood cigarettes. It's a brand."

"Never heard of them."

"Me neither. That's why they're interesting."

He hung up. He used his smartphone to google the local news. Sure enough, the story was on the *Orlando Sentinel*'s website: "Local Construction Exec Found Murdered." Noland skimmed the article, which explained how Bisby's corpse had been discovered in a Longwood apartment, and that the body's level of decomposition suggested it had lain there for a week or more. The article also named Arthur Valkenburg as the owner of the apartment, helpfully noting that his whereabouts were unknown.

After a few minutes, Noland's nerves settled enough for him to go back into the house. Cassy was in the kitchen.

"I thought you'd run off," she said.

He tried to laugh, not very convincingly.

Her eyes narrowed into slits. "What's wrong?"

"Bisby," he said. "Edward Bisby. Do you know him?"

"Of course I know him. He's still co-head of Selberis, isn't he?"

"Not anymore. The cops found his body this morning. In Val's apartment."

She blinked once, twice, and that was all. Compared to how she had reacted back in the orange grove, she seemed completely unmoved. The revelation of Bisby's death seemed to flow around her like a wave breaking on a jetty.

"How did he die?"

"Shot."

She nodded as if this didn't surprise her. Then, looking down at her boots, she asked: "Do the cops think it was Val?"

"I expect so."

As far as Noland knew, he had kept his voice even and flat. But as soon as he made this last statement, her eyes fixed on him again.

"Did you know about this?" she asked.

"That Bisby was dead? How would I?"

She said nothing for a while. Noland found himself wanting to tell her the truth—that it was he who had found Bisby and covered up the man's murder. He didn't know why he wanted to tell her. It couldn't possibly do him any good. But he wanted to, nonetheless. And the knowledge that he couldn't, that he still didn't trust her completely, pierced his heart like a sudden, silent knife. "Cass," he said. It was the second time he'd called her Cass. The first time had been earlier that day, after she'd punched him.

"You'd better go," she said. "I need to be alone for a while."

He wanted to hold her. To take the two steps across the kitchen tile and put his arms around her. But in the space of thirty seconds, she had made that impossible. Her expression went slack, and Noland felt as if she had thrown up an invisible pane of glass between them that he'd have to shatter to get to her. And even then, she might fight him off.

"Okay."

On the drive back to town, he got a text from Kiril.

—Hollywood cigarettes. They're a brand in Brazil.

Noland caught his breath.

—You're kidding.
—Nope. You know any Brazilians?

He tossed the phone onto the passenger seat. Not yet, he thought. But he would soon. Irenas. Victor Irenas. Had to be. The cigs either belonged to him or to one of his men. Either way, the man himself was on the scene. It was he who had killed Sabine. The certainty of this fact settled onto Noland's shoulders like an iron yoke. Previously, he had assumed one of the partners killed her—either Valkenburg, or perhaps Redding. Or some other, as yet unknown player. But it was Irenas. And he wouldn't stop with Sabine. He would keep killing until his money was recovered, or until every partner of Selberis was dead. Or both.

Noland drove on in a kind of daze, heading south. He barely made it to the edge of the city before a police cruiser appeared in his rearview, lights spinning. He pulled to the shoulder, and the cruiser sidled up behind him. Noland was unsurprised to see Lieutenant Parsons climb out.

Noland powered down the window. "Am I being summoned again?"

"You are."

He looked around. "I'd rather not leave my van here."

"Just follow me then."

"Okay."

17

Parsons led him to a suburb near Winter Park, where he stopped at the driveway of a heavily gabled McMansion, of the sort preferred by well-off businessmen. Could this be Sydney's house? There had long been rumors around town that he had money—family money, not entirely legit—and the engorged style of the house certainly fit the story as well as his ego.

Noland parked the van at the curb and got out. Instead of walking him to the front door, Parsons led him around to the side, where the obligatory wooden fence merged seamlessly into the neighboring McMansion, as if both properties had been extruded from the same giant nozzle. Parsons opened the gate and let Noland through. The yard was spacious and without trees. A smell of burning meat greeted them as they walked around a vast teak deck, in which an oval swimming pool rested like a huge sapphire.

"Nole!" Sydney was working an industrial-strength barbecue grill positioned between the pool and the house. His apron bore a silhouette of Texas and read: TRY THE BEST OF THE WEST!

"Hello, Syd."

"Are you hungry?"

"No, thanks."

He looked around, finally seeing another man on the far edge of the deck, facing away. The guy's shoulders bulged beneath the fabric of his T-shirt, whose bright yellow color emphasized the blackness of his skin. Football, Noland thought. College. Maybe even pro. Smoky gray hair hugged the man's skull, but he was dressed like a kid, a surfer. T-shirt. Bathing trunks. Flip-flops.

Sydney yelled again: "Tarique! Come meet Noland."

The man tossed a cigarette into the grass and walked over, moving with the inevitability of a storm cloud. His face was clean-shaven and ruggedly handsome.

"Noland, this is Tarique Bledsoe. Tarique, Noland."

The dude nodded and didn't offer to shake hands. Instead, he stood there, arms crossed, muscles popping. The dimples on his forearms looked deep enough for seabirds to nest in.

"Nole," Sydney went on, "I was wondering if you'd heard about what we found in Longwood."

"I heard."

He flipped a burger, using a stainless-steel spatula as long as a tennis racquet. "Bisby's corpse was rather ripe, despite all the calcium carbonate poured onto him." He looked up at Noland and grinned. "That was clever, don't you think? Why remove the body when you can preserve it in situ?"

"Yeah, that was fairly clever."

"How about a beer?"

"Sure."

As Sydney walked into the house, Parsons got a couple of plastic deck chairs and set them down around the glass patio table, where two other chairs had already been placed. Sydney returned a few moments later with a tray of beers and cocktail napkins. He placed a napkin at each of the four spots at the table, and then set a beer on each napkin. "Lieutenant, I took the liberty of getting you a beer as well."

"Why not?" Parsons said, sitting down. Sydney sat too, and then Bledsoe. Noland sat directly across from the big

man, who stared at him. Despite their blackness, his eyes
glittered hard and flat as zinc washers, and sent little alarm
bells ringing in Noland's head.

"So, who's your chief suspect?" Noland asked.

"Oh, I think you know the answer to that," Sydney said.

"I guess I do. Valkenburg."

"You're still looking for him, I assume?"

Noland ignored the question. "Did you find a gun?"

"No. And Valkenburg doesn't have a license for one. But
you know what that's worth."

"Yeah," Noland said. "And I think I know why you
brought me here."

"You do?"

"Sure. Information. And I'm willing to negotiate. Tit for
tat."

The tips of Sydney's eyebrows rose from three o'clock to
one o'clock. "I'm listening."

"But before we get started," Noland said, "there's one
thing that I'm not clear on."

"Such as?"

He tipped his chin up at Bledsoe. "Who's this mouth-
breathing motherfucker and how does he enter into things?"

Noland hadn't known what he was going to say until
the words flowed out of his mouth. He was simply answering the urge that had struck him the moment Bledsoe had
fixed his stare upon him, the impulse to strike the man either
physically or mentally. But the moment the deed was done
and the words were spoken, Noland marveled at the precision of his instinct, his inspired use of "mouth-breathing," a
term which would surely sting the big man even more than
"motherfucker." Bledsoe was a jock, after all, and Noland
knew better than anyone that jocks hate to be called stupid.

In the aftermath of the utterance, Noland kept his eyes
on the man and waited to see what his reaction would be.
Would he reply with some version of his own trash-talk? Or
would he simply fling the table aside and attempt to yank

Noland out of his chair? Noland held his breath. Bledsoe narrowed his eyes at him, as if Noland were some math problem that he was trying to figure out. And although Noland was careful not to show it, the man's motionless, reserved response frightened him to the core.

Sydney laughed. "Come on, Nole. This is a friendly conversation. Just four guys having a beer. Okay?"

"Sure. Okay."

"To answer your question, Tarique is a federal agent. Highly placed in an organization whose three-letter acronym I will not specify. And, like us, he is very interested in Selberis Constructors."

Noland paused the minimum amount of time to lend Sydney's statement the appropriate gravitas.

"How highly placed?"

Sydney answered for him. "High enough to help us. Or flummox us considerably."

Noland smiled and unfurled his hands in surrender. "Fair enough. Sorry about that, Agent Bledsoe. I was being a jerk."

"Forget it," Bledsoe said. His voice, fully revealed, was gentle, almost delicate, even as he added, "Motherfucker."

Noland laughed.

"So, what do the feds want with Selberis?"

Bledsoe answered this time: "A massive indictment."

"Drink your beer, Nole," Sydney broke in. "I'll fill you in as best as I can."

Noland took a swig. The beer was an import, the kind with a cap you had to pop off instead of twist. It tasted like dishwater.

"Your client," Sydney went on, "has attracted the attention of law enforcement at several levels. It seems their revenue stream is even more exotic than we had imagined."

"If you say so," Noland said. "That's not my business."

Sydney blinked like a parent indulging a sarcastic child. "Of course not. But it is my business. And Agent Bledsoe's.

In fact, it has been the focus of his job for several months. Specifically, their absentee partner."

"Victor Irenas," Bledsoe said. "Have you heard of him?"

"Is he Mexican?"

The man stifled a laugh. "Brazilian."

"No shit?"

Sydney rolled his eyes. "His uncle is the patriarch of one of the biggest cartels in South America. Victor inhabits a plane a level beneath him, but he's still a big fish, if you get my meaning."

"He likes real estate," Bledsoe added. His eyes remained baleful, but took on a new flicker of something like excitement.

"Yes, real estate," Sydney agreed, grimacing at the continued interruptions. "We can't prove it, but we believe that many of Selberis's projects have been secretly commissioned by Irenas. That is, he is both the builder and the buyer in all of these properties. Neat trick, huh?"

"It's brilliant, actually," Bledsoe said. "Any missed deadlines or cost overruns get paid back to the client. Which is Victor himself." He snapped his thick fingers. "Presto. One of the most efficient money laundering schemes we've encountered. He even gets a tax break." His voice quickened, as if whatever lingering animus he felt toward Noland had been obviated by the pleasure he now took in explaining the tapestry of deceit that Senhor Irenas had woven. "Money and equipment flow in from Brazil. Illegal laborers, too, although that's less certain. And drugs, of course. Smuggled in along with the cash. Everybody's paid under the table. But the expenses look legit."

The thrill must have been contagious because Sydney's voice ramped up too. "Everything's done through a hive of dummy corporations. A cluster of LLCs, incorporated all over three continents. But the money all flows in one direction. Back to the source."

Lieutenant Parsons piped up: "A closed loop."

Sydney's grimace deepened, more from the cop's impertinence, Noland thought, than from the conundrum at hand.

"That's the problem. A loop is something you can never break into. Can never find an end point, from a legal or even a fiscal point of view. It's impenetrable."

"Almost." Bledsoe paused theatrically. Clearly, he'd come to his big reveal. "We can trace most of the activity back to a single woman. Young bank exec. Brazilian. Her name's Werther. Sabine Werther."

It took every ounce of Noland's cool to keep his mouth from falling open. Instead, he took a surreptitious breath and let it out, slowly. Fortunately, Sydney came to his rescue.

"That's Suh-BEAN-uh," he said, gently correcting Bledsoe. "She's German."

"I thought she was Brazilian," Noland said, grateful to lapse back into his dumb redneck routine.

"She's both," Bledsoe said. "Lots of krauts in Brazil. Big community. They stick together, too."

"So, pull her in," Noland said. "Sweat her. Make her talk."

A brief look flashed between Bledsoe and Sydney. It was the latter who eventually answered. "Our case is not mature yet."

"Then ask her informally. Maybe she'll get scared. Give something up."

Sydney shook his head. "No."

"Why not?"

He looked down. "We don't know where she is."

The admission seemed to flop on the table between them, like a buckshot bird.

Noland leaned back and laughed.

"Shut up, Noland."

He stopped laughing. "Sorry, but aren't you the guys with all the toys? Satellites and radar and shit?"

Bledsoe's jaw muscles clenched. "She's vanished. Fled the country, perhaps."

"Perhaps?"

"We can't find any record of her leaving. No airline tickets. Of course, she might have driven south, via Mexico."

"But you don't think she did. Right?"

Bledsoe didn't answer. Instead, the corners of his lips turned down. He was a sore loser.

Noland continued to smile, even though a spike of hot rage suddenly poked up through his mind. He thought of Sabine's head, rotting for days under the ground in St. Cloud, and of her swollen balloon-body, thirty miles north, dissolving in the steel barrel. Someone had left pieces of the woman scattered around two counties, and these guys were dicking around. Clueless.

He leaned forward. "Okay. What are you offering?"

Bledsoe leaned forward, too. "You first, redneck."

"I'm offering this," Noland said. He reached into his pocket, pulled out the empty pack of cigarettes he'd found at the garage, and set it on the table. Sydney and Bledsoe appeared to be holding their breath, captivated by the sight of the little foil packet resting before them. It might have been the Hope Diamond.

"Brazilian cigarettes in Seminole County," Noland went on. "What are the odds?"

Both men leaned back as if blown away from the shock of this statement. Bledsoe's left eye twitched. But it was Sydney who spoke. "What exactly are you saying?"

"I'm saying that Irenas is here. In Florida. And we can get him."

"If that were true," Sydney said, "what makes you think you could locate him?"

"It's what I do." Noland paused for a moment. A thought occurred to him. A gambit. Dangerous, surely, but one he found irresistible. He took a breath and said: "Also, I've got his money."

Bledsoe's jaw dropped. Even Parsons, the old flatfoot, seemed impressed, his bushy eyebrows climbing up his deeply creased forehead.

Sydney, for his part, regarded Noland from down his long, angular nose. "What money?"

"Don't bullshit me. The pile he came here to recover. He probably needs to kick some of it back to his uncle, right? Why else would he put his freedom on the line by sneaking into the States? He must be on the hook himself. Not to mention pissed as hell."

"If you really had a hold of his money," Bledsoe said, "you'd have a sum."

"I do. Ten million."

Bledsoe's eyes widened.

"Where?"

It was Noland's turn to lean back. "Okay, I don't have the money yet. But I'm very close."

Quick as a cat, Bledsoe rose from his chair and leaned over the table, his wide torso filling the horizon. "Look who's bullshitting now. Close. My ass. You just incriminated yourself."

Noland put up his hands. "Hey, I thought this was a friendly conversation. Just four guys having a beer."

He seemed startled. His Adam's apple worked up and down like a steam valve. He looked at Sydney. Sydney stared back. He sat back down and asked, "You're telling me that you can deliver Irenas?"

"I am. And I'll even give you something in advance. A gesture of good faith."

His eyes narrowed. "Such as?"

Noland got out his phone and punched up his GPS app. He passed the phone over to Bledsoe, who clutched it with both hands like a football.

"What's this?"

"Coordinates to an orange grove. There's a Quonset hut in the back. You should check it out. But tell your boys to be careful. It's full of surprises."

Bledsoe's eyes snapped back to him. He seemed on the verge of rising again, this time for real, fully intending to grab Noland by the collar and toss him in the swimming pool. Instead, he replied, "Okay. What do you want?"

"In return for Irenas?"

"Yes."

"Immunity."

Bledsoe's left eye twitched faster. "For whom?"

"Several people. Myself, of course. And Faith. And the surviving partners of Selberis."

Bledsoe laughed. "You're ridiculous."

Sydney, who had been utterly still the whole time, placed his hands on either side of the pack of the cigarette wrapper. "The best we could offer is a plea. If the good people at Selberis agree to work with the State of Florida and Uncle Sam, they will—perhaps—be allowed to plead guilty to a lesser offense."

"Like what?"

He wobbled his head from side to side. "Tax evasion. State and federal. Something with a big penalty but not much jail time."

Noland shook his head. "Full immunity. For them, and the company itself. That's the deal."

Sydney's pale eyes scanned from one side of Noland's face to the other, as if trying to burn him with some blue-hot laser of rage. "You're an asshole. Even if we agreed not to prosecute—which is never going to happen—Selberis will be toast. Their reputation will be shot. They'll never get another contract."

Noland considered this. "Okay, you got me there. But what if you promised not to prosecute all the partners. Only go after the one most responsible for the dirty deeds?"

Sydney straightened his neck, elevating his head like a heron. "You want us to hang the whole rap on just one of them?"

"If that's the best deal I can get, yes."

Bledsoe gave a disgusted smile. "If you're suggesting Valkenburg, you're crazy. We've already got him. For murder."

"Maybe you do, maybe you don't. But I'm not talking about Valkenburg."

"Then who?"

"Isn't it obvious?" Noland asked. "Bisby."

A full five seconds passed before all three men at the table reacted simultaneously, each according to his character. Bledsoe laughed. Sydney face-palmed. Parsons whistled, then sipped his beer.

"Well, why not?" Noland continued. "He's probably guilty as hell. Moreover, he has the advantage of being dead. No cross-examination. No contradictions."

Sydney lowered his hand from his face and then ran his fingers through his thick hair, breaking up its perfect shape and tousling it considerably. A shocking gesture for him.

"That is not an advantage, Nole. We can't prosecute a dead man."

"Why not? He was the brains behind Selberis. And what if I could give you evidence that he'd committed murder too, in the not-so-distant past? It would certainly make a splash in the *Sentinel*. NBC, too. And anyway, I'm offering you the big Brazilian fish. How many perps do you want?"

Without realizing it, he had tapped his finger on the table as he made each of these points. Then, realizing he'd probably overplayed his hand again, he took a breath and waited, bracing himself for their next fusillade of objections. But it never came. Instead, Sydney merely replied, "Go on."

Noland leaned forward again. "If this plan works, you get the drug lord from Brazil. And you get Valkenburg. And you get ten million in confiscated assets. How's that for a haul?"

Sydney stroked his chin. "Of course, this is all contingent on your not being full of shit."

"Yes. But if I am full of shit, you can always go ahead with your original plan and bust everyone. Myself included."

A silence followed. Bledsoe and Sydney exchanged a brief look, then fixed their eyes back on Noland.

"Okay," Bledsoe asked. "What do you need from us?"

"For now, just one thing: Time. And no surveillance of me or the partners."

Sydney blinked. "How much time?"

"A month."

Bledsoe scoffed. "You've got three days. If you don't give us Victor by then, we drop the net over all of you."

"Deal."

Bledsoe took a celebratory sip of his beer, as did Parsons. Sydney stared at Noland's forehead, as if wishing he could put a bullet there. Noland slid the plastic chair back across the deck and stood. He didn't give Sydney or Bledsoe a second look, but he winked at Parsons, his minder. The cop downed the rest of his beer and followed Noland as they retraced their path to the gate. The St. Augustine grass felt springier than when he'd come in. Was it his imagination? Or had his mood lifted?

Noland had almost reached the van when a voice called out: "Nole?"

It was Sydney, poking his head through the gate.

"What?" Noland yelled back.

"You wouldn't try to scam us, would you?"

"Geez, dude. You know I'm not that way."

Sydney nodded solemnly. "There's one more thing you should know."

Noland waited.

"In Valkenburg's apartment. We found blood near the body."

"I'll bet."

Sydney shook his head. "Not Bisby's blood. A second individual."

Noland tried to reply but couldn't. All the saliva in his mouth had dried up, leaving his tongue stuck to the roof of his mouth as if Scotch-taped there.

"Not a lot of blood from the second person," Sydney went on. "Just a stain, really. But enough to get a grip on, forensically."

"You think it was Valkenburg?" Noland finally asked, his tongue clicking free.

Sydney shook his head again. "Wrong blood type. It's a third party. I thought you should know. Take care, Noland."

Noland nodded and got into the van.

18

HEADING WEST, HIS hands trembled on the steering wheel. He tried to ignore the red-alert alarm howling in the back of his head, but he couldn't. Blood, Sydney had said. Someone else's blood.

Noland reassured himself that neither he nor Kiril had cut themselves in Valkenburg's apartment. Not a chance. But even so, he had to reckon with the possibility that another of Selberis's partners would soon be arrested. But which one? If Valkenburg hadn't killed Bisby, then who had? Noland ran through the roster. He couldn't see any of them as a killer— not even Redding, whom he hated most of all. Once again, he was left without a clue. And yet the strangest thing was how little it all seemed to matter. He was like the stagecoach driver in one of the bad old Western movies Zeb loved so much, where the horses have bolted and the driver has to rise up on his heels and fight to keep control. Each of the partners was like a horse in the train, threatening to break free and run off in its own direction, as were Sydney and Bledsoe, who comprised a horse of their own. And yet Noland still felt he could keep hold of it all, the whipping reins burning in his sweaty hands. He just had to keep driving. He was, he knew, at least partially mad, but he needed that madness to keep him going, to see the ride through. And anyway, if he

was mad, then he was merely reflecting another's madness—
Sabine Werther's, the crazy author of the whole twisted tale.
His scheming wasn't as advanced, but he knew he might
end up like her. Dead. Dismembered. But he couldn't think
about it too long. He had to keep moving.

At some point, he got out his phone and called Karen.
She answered on the fifth ring.

"Hello?"

"Hey," he said.

They had a good connection, but she must not have recognized his voice because she asked, "Noland?"

He was wounded. How long had it been since he'd seen
her? Four days? An epoch, for someone like her. And for him,
too, under the circumstances.

"What's wrong?" she said.

"Nothing, probably. Can I come over?"

A short pause. "I have plans."

"I only need a minute," he said. "I need to look for something in your apartment. A book."

"A book?"

"Yeah. It's called *The Sorrows of Young Werther*. Sabine
gave you a copy at Christmas, right?"

Noland couldn't be sure, but he thought he heard her
gasp.

"I had forgotten."

"Do you still have it?"

"I think so. Let me check."

"Do. I'll be right over."

"Is it important?"

"Critically. I'll explain when I get there."

He bullied his way through traffic, pushing the van to
full tilt. Even so, it took him almost an hour to get there.
The moon was high and full, bathing the condos in its cold
glow. He parked near the fake Italian fountain and ran up
the stairs.

Her door was ajar.

A slit of yellow light streamed onto the landing. Noland pulled his Ruger, cocked it, and walked in. The apartment was silent. He checked the kitchen, then the bedroom. The bed was unmade. He peeked underneath. Nothing. The closet was open. Boxes had been pulled down from the upper shelves and dumped. At least one of them contained some paperbacks—romance novels, thrillers. No Goethe.

He walked back to the living room. She had finished tiling the floor, the tiles laid down with precision. Something caught his eye, and he leaned down. A few of the tiles were spotted lightly with red. He touched one of the spots. It was wet.

He left.

Not until he had reached the safety of the van, sitting inside with the doors locked, did he finally uncock the Ruger and reholster it. He cranked the van and drove ten miles in no particular direction. Finally, he called Kiril. His hands were still trembling as he held the phone.

"What's up?" Kiril asked.

"They've got Karen."

"Who's Karen?"

"One of the clients. A nicer one."

"Who's got her?"

"The opposing party."

Kiril paused. "Are you gonna call the cops?"

"Are you kidding?"

"Then what's our move?"

"I'm coming to the shop. I need to talk to Freddy. I need him to do some research for me."

"On the internet? Hacking?"

"No, in person. Book him a flight."

"Where?"

"New York."

"New York? Are you serious?"

"Yes."

"When?"

"Tonight."

*   *   *

Sunday morning was his favorite time to be outside, so he took Quick and Silver for a brief run, finding solace in the quiet streets. The sun rose over the treetops and painted the houses gold. He got back, fed the dogs, showered, and made breakfast. By the time he was done with all that, it was ten o'clock, which was the earliest he dared call Faith. She sounded groggy when she answered.

"Morning," he said. "Karen Voss has been kidnapped."

A sputtering sound followed. She had spit out her coffee. "What?"

"Karen. Kidnapped."

"By who?"

"I'm not sure."

A brief pause followed. "Valkenburg?"

"That would be the natural assumption. But I don't think so."

"Are the cops involved?"

"Not yet. With luck, they won't be."

"What do they want from her?"

"She had a book. It might be the one we're all looking for."

"The one with the code?"

"Yeah."

"So you don't think they'll hurt her?"

The question hit him like a punch to the gut. He wanted to reel from it. "I don't know. But considering what happened to Sabine, I'm guessing they might."

Faith didn't reply. He knew he'd given her some news that was potentially devastating. From her point of view—that of Reynolds, Adams, and Scruggs—the possibility that Selberis's money might be even more out of reach than they previously thought was a disaster. Not to mention the fact that another of the partners, their numbers dwindling already, might be dead soon, if she wasn't already.

"Shit," Faith said at last.

"Yeah." He closed his eyes for a moment, and was greeted with a vision of Sabine Werther's dismembered body, floating like a balloon in the clear acid. Then he remembered kissing Karen, the salty taste of her mouth. He couldn't let her end up that way. He just couldn't.

"Do we still have a chance?" Faith asked.

"At what?"

"Finding Karen. Getting the money. Saving our asses."

"Barely. I need to speak to another one of the partners. The only one I haven't grilled yet."

"Which one?"

"Redding," he said. "The CEO."

She was beyond arguing. "Hang on, I'll get his number."

"Give me his address. I'll surprise him."

*   *   *

When she read Redding's address out to him, Noland almost didn't believe it. Apparently, he lived in the heart of International Drive, somewhere among the hotels and water parks. Noland plugged the address into his phone, and it led him to the Rydell Resorts, one of the newer hotels on I-Drive. The parking lot was packed with minivans with Disney World stickers on their hatches. He had to leave the van in the fire lane, eased up against the cinder block retaining wall that separated the hotel property from a fifty-foot drop into swampland. Then he went in through the back.

The lobby was already a swirl of chaos as the Sunday morning exodus began. Preteen kids hopped up on pancakes and Cokes ran circles around their bleary-eyed parents who waited in the checkout line, wearing the same expression of sadness mixed with regret, as if only now realizing that the three thousand bucks they had dropped on this extended

weekend of cybernetic, Mouse-themed enchantment might
not have been entirely worth it. Noland got lucky and had
the elevator all to himself. He felt dizzy, not merely from the
rapid ascent but from the jarring transition, the din of the
dark lobby replaced with the silent, sterile, air-conditioned
box. A poster inside proclaimed FLORIDA WELCOMES
YOU and depicted an idealized family of affluent white people, thirty-something mom and forty-something dad with an
early teen daughter and son, all grinning ear to ear. At the
moment, Noland found the poster strangely appalling. Were
there really families like that? Bursting with happiness and
comfort and wealth? Or was it all some dream from the collective mind of Madison Avenue, the unblemished ideal of
affluent American bliss? Or, worse still, were there families
that seemed that happy on the outside, while in reality they
were a roiling mess of resentment and neglect underneath?
He reckoned it was the latter. And, thinking this, he rubbed
his eyes with his thumb and forefinger, replacing the family with bolts of lightning on the insides of his eyelids. He
was losing his mind. The elevator reached the seventh and
final floor. Redding's room was equipped with a buzzer, but
it didn't seem to work, so Noland rapped his knuckles on the
door so hard they stung. The door opened immediately to a
slit, and a pair of almond-shaped eyes stared at him.

"Can I help you?"

"My name is Noland Twice. I'm here to see Mr. Redding."

"One sec."

The door closed again, and a dull thud followed as the
safety latch was thrown. The door opened, all the way this
time, and he found himself face to face with a girl in a bikini.

"Cool name," she said. "Bill is waiting."

"He is?"

She nodded, stepping back. "Out on the balcony."

She led him through the beige-walled suite, so wide and
deep that it felt gloomy, despite the big French doors at the
back, thrown wide open to the noonday sun. Against that blaze

of light, the girl was little more than a silhouette, but Noland could tell that she was very young, beautiful but unformed, with no visible muscle tone or any other kind of armor, not even a tan. She strolled through the French doors to the balcony, which was bigger than Noland's living room. A full set of deck furniture had been arranged there—a table, four teak chairs, and two couches. She veered off to the side to where another girl, older and Black, was lounging on a deck chair. The first girl laughed about something before lying down on the chair beside her. Redding was sitting at the table with his back to the room. He looked over his shoulder and smiled.

"Hey, Noland. I thought you might swing by eventually. Come sit."

After seeing the two half-naked girls, Noland had half expected to find Redding dressed in silk pajamas, a Florida version of Hugh Hefner. But the man had accoutered himself admirably in sharp slacks and a linen shirt so airy it rippled a bit even in the desultory Florida breeze. He rose to shake Noland's hand, which required him to switch the cigar he was smoking—a slender type with the gold label still choking the neck—to his left hand for a moment. When he sat back down, he switched it back.

"Nice digs," Noland said.

Redding smiled. A complicated smile, a mixture of pride and embarrassment and something else, some amorphous dread.

"I built this place," he said, spreading his arms. "Ran the project, that is. Got the owner a sweetheart deal. In return, he agreed to let me live here for two years rent-free. It's worked out rather well, if I do say so."

"You must like hotels."

"I like things clean."

Noland couldn't help but look past his dour face at the girls again, lying there like a pair of matched Jaguars, one black and one white. Redding followed the direction of his stare and smiled wider. "Cute, huh?"

"I have to hand it to you, Mr. Redding. You got style."

He moved his shoulders up and down. "I'm a wicked man. But at least I'm honest about it."

"Good to know."

Redding leaned forward and brought his arms in, like a man playing poker in a room full of mirrors. "Now, why are you here?"

"I need information about Sabine Werther."

He brought the cigar to his mouth and sucked, the tip glowing red even in the bright sun. "Right. I had a feeling you'd be asking about her eventually."

"When's the last time you saw her?"

He moved his shoulders up and down. "Several weeks. Why?"

"She's dead."

He blinked once, then blew smoke out the corner of his mouth.

"Details?"

Noland shook his head. "They're not relevant. The salient fact is that she's dead."

Redding's eyes flickered down and he didn't speak for a few minutes. Finally, he turned halfway in this chair and called out: "Leda, why don't you and Trish go get us some coffee?"

"We're not dressed," the Black girl called back.

"Just throw on some shorts. There's cash in the desk."

She huffed out a sigh, but stood up. The other one—Trish—followed, and together they glided into the penthouse, closing the French doors behind them. Redding turned back to Noland. His smile had vanished and he now spoke through clenched teeth. "I don't give a fuck if the details are 'relevant' or not. I want them."

"Fair enough. She was murdered."

"How?"

"Somebody cut her head off. The rest of her is floating in a barrel of acid out in Seminole County."

Redding shut his mouth. He leaned back in his chair and looked off into the canopy of the loblolly pines that grew alongside this corner of the hotel, the branches barely sticking up over the balcony rail. It must feel nice, Noland thought, living up here. Like in a treehouse. But with air conditioning.

"Like I said," Noland went on, "it doesn't make any difference. All that matters is that somebody got to her before I did. And they took something from her."

"What?"

"A book."

Redding's hand trembled a moment as he flicked ash onto the deck. His previous level of shock had transformed, instantly, into genuine fear. And it wasn't merely the news of Sabine Werther's severed head that did it. Rather, it was the mention of the book.

"A book?"

"A journal. Like a diary. It contained a hidden code."

He raised the cigar halfway to his mouth again, stopped, then laid it on a big onyx ashtray on the table between them. Then he stood up.

"Wait here."

He walked into the penthouse. Noland swallowed painfully and let his hand slip behind his back, ready to pull the Ruger out in a half second. But when Redding returned, he was holding nothing but a white, letter-sized envelope. The top had already been slit, and he blew into it like a bellows, then flipped the contents onto the table. It was a few sheets of paper, photocopies. Noland picked one up. It was a copy of one of the plaintext pages from the journal, including the dark outline of the cover, and even a bit of the red ribbon that served as the bookmark.

"I got it in the mail a few weeks ago," Redding said. "Around the time Val took off with the nest egg."

Noland picked up the envelope. It was postmarked in Apopka, with a return address of St. Cloud penciled in. No name.

"Did anyone else get a letter like this?"

"Bisby did. I'm not sure about the others."

"Did you ask them?"

"No."

"Why not?"

He guffawed. "You act like we're all a big, happy family. We're more like the Borgias. Lots of little factions, joined together by greed. Nobody trusts nobody. At least, not completely."

"Okay, I'll buy that," Noland said. He laid the envelope back on the table and stretched his fingers across it, pressing it down. "The code she used. The cipher—"

"The what?"

"The key. It has something to do with another book. A novel. Did Sabine give you anything last Christmas?"

Redding looked bewildered for a moment. Then something clicked.

"Yes, she did. A book. Something strange. Written in German, I think. She said it was a collector's item."

"Do you have it?"

He thought for a moment, his jaw working like an old man's. Then his gray face went white. "Shit."

"What?"

He cocked his head in the direction of the penthouse. "Leda. The smart one. I gave it to her."

"The girl? You gave it to the girl?"

"Yeah."

"Your girlfriend reads German novels?"

"You think you're funny? She's got a master's in comparative lit."

Noland sighed. "Let's go find her."

"They'll be back in a few minutes."

"This can't wait."

"All right. Let me take a leak first."

Noland waited. When Redding emerged from the john, his movements were accelerated, like one of those antique movies, shot from an over-cranked camera. Idly, Noland wondered how much cocaine the man had just vacuumed up his nose, but he knew it probably cost a small fortune. They rode the elevator down to the lobby and wove their way through the remaining families, finally emerging into the lethal sunshine. Dodging the minivans and SUVs, they jaywalked across I-Drive and found the girls emerging from the coffee shop. Trish was dressed now, jeans and a blouse, but Leda wore nothing over her bikini except a long T-shirt, with her smooth, vivid legs tapering underneath. She looked surprised to see Redding and Noland. Trish did too.

"Wow," Leda said. "You couldn't wait?"

"Let's go inside," Redding said and reversed their momentum, leading them back into the shop. Not surprisingly, the joint was almost as crowded as the hotel, full of weary adults and sugar-crazed children. Redding managed to find them an empty booth near the kitchen door, which swung open every few seconds as a waitress flitted in or out, trailing a scent of coffee in her wake. Redding and Noland sat across from the girls, who looked bemused. Redding lifted a cup from the carrier that Leda was holding and took a sip. The caffeine's effect must have been lost in the general sway of the cocaine because he barely reacted.

"Leda, you remember that book I gave you? The German one?"

She was taken aback, her neck stretching a full inch as her head tilted away from them. "How could I forget?"

"I need it back. That is, Noland needs it."

She looked at Noland and seemed to notice him for the first time. "You like Goethe?"

"I can't even spell Goethe."

She laughed, then reached into a paper bag that Trish had been holding. It turned out to contain bagels, each pre-sliced and smeared with cream cheese. She unwrapped one and took a bite. "So why do you want it?"

"Leda—" Redding started.

"It's all right," Noland said. He leaned halfway across the table, close enough to see that the corners of her eyes were slightly pink, as if from some infection. She probably didn't eat enough vegetables. "I need the book to win a game."

She finished chewing and swallowed. "You mean, like a scavenger hunt?"

"Something like that."

Her bemused expression faded into a grimace. "Well, I'm sorry. I sold it."

The news affected him and Redding in the same manner, like a kick in the guts.

"You sold it?"

She nodded. "To a used bookstore."

"Fuck."

Trish clapped a hand over her mouth to stifle a laugh.

"Take me there," Noland said. "Right now."

"I'll get my car," Redding offered. "We can all go."

Ten minutes later, he found himself climbing into the back of Redding's Infiniti QX80, sitting across from Trish. Leda had said she would only take them if she were allowed to drive, so she got behind the wheel while Redding rode shotgun. Leda popped a stick of gum before gunning the big car into traffic, shoveling her way toward Orlando proper. She had kicked off her sandals and worked the pedals with bare feet.

"How far is it?"

"Downtown."

The bookstore, Wasserman's, occupied a corner next to a thrift shop, and Leda did an expert job of parallel parking in front. They all got out, carrying their coffees, and filed through the doors of the establishment. Leda spoke with the heavily tattooed shopgirl at the register, who led them to the foreign-languages shelf.

"Crap," Leda said. "It's not here."

Noland spoke to the shopgirl. "Do you remember anyone buying it?"

She shook her head and wandered off.

Noland put his hand over his mouth. There had only been a few occasions in his life when he had suffered total defeat, with its metallic taste in the mouth and feeling of hopelessness. The same feeling he'd get after failing to block a pass, watching the receiver from the other team hold on to the ball and turn on the speed, the bottoms of his shoes flashing white as he burned his way into the end zone for the score, leaving Noland there with his lungs burning and the breathless, lonely sensation of having been forsaken by God, by luck, by one's own supposed powers. He had the same feeling now, standing in the stupid bookstore, looking at the shelf with its stupid Auf Deutsch banner over the top.

Then something happened: he watched Leda's profile as she stared at the bookshelf. She turned slowly, looking not at him but at the shopgirl. And then, thinking no one was watching, she smiled. A rare kind of smile. One Noland recognized: A smile of triumph.

"How old are you?" he asked.

The smile vanished. "What's it to you?"

"Tell me."

"Twenty-four."

"That explains it."

She clenched her jaw. "Explains what?"

He took her by the elbow, then said to Redding. "Leda and I are going to take a short walk."

She jerked her arm away. "The fuck we are."

Redding said, "Go with him."

Her chest heaved up and down.

Noland put his hand into the small of her back and shoved her, hard, toward the door. Most people would have fallen on their face, but she just glided forward on her flip-flops. Graceful.

"Sure, why not," she said, throwing her hands up. "Let's take a walk."

They went outside. Her shadow was longer than his as he led her down toward the lake. They found a picnic table in the shade and sat down. Glowering, she tossed her head back and ran a hand through her lush tresses. How wondrous it must feel, Noland thought, to have such hair. A blessing. She must have done some good things in her previous life.

"So?" she asked.

"Who'd you give the book to?"

"I told you, asshole."

He shook his head. "That girl didn't have any memory of you, and you're not easy to forget."

"She wasn't working that day."

He shook his head again. "How fast does a copy of a German novel sell in Orlando, Florida?"

She huffed. Noland could tell she wanted to come up with something else, something clever. But she couldn't.

"Who'd you sell the book to?" he asked again.

She cocked her jaw to the side. "Some guy I didn't even know."

"Some guy? Like off the street?"

She scoffed. "I don't remember."

Noland took a breath and looked up. The sky was clear except for a few wispy, impressionistic clouds. Very odd for that time of year. A sense of vertigo overcame him as he wondered how, exactly, he had come to this place—sitting at this bench, with this girl who didn't want to be there any more than he did. He went so far as to close his eyes for a moment. When he opened them, sometime later, she was watching him.

"You about to have a seizure or something?" she asked.

"Where did you get your master's?"

"FSU."

"You must be really smart."

She shrugged. "Not really. I almost didn't finish."

"Too much work?"

She shook her head. "Couldn't take the regimen. Reading books is great when you do it on your own. But they turn it all into a job."

"What are your plans now?"

"I'm transferring to UCF. In the spring. Art history this time."

"Good for you."

She shrugged again but said, "Thanks."

He tilted his head back toward the bookstore. "What about Redding?"

"Bill? He's all right. More fun than waitressing. Have you got a cigarette?"

"Sorry."

She pouted. Noland watched her, trying to figure out which way to play it. Finally, he decided to give her a bit of the truth.

"Okay, here's the deal. I need that book. There's a lot at stake."

"Your 'scavenger hunt'?" She made air quotes with her slender fingers.

"If I don't find it, some very bad things are going to happen. To Bill and his partners. And maybe even to you. Anybody can get caught in the wind when a hurricane blows by."

Her face remained inert, an expression of existential cool mixed with terminal boredom.

"I'm a big girl."

"You sure are. But what about Trish?"

She blinked.

"What about her?"

"What happens to her when the goons drop by the penthouse? What if she's home and you're not?"

Leda took a shallow breath, then looked down.

"All right," she said. "This guy came up to me when I was out shopping. He knew I lived with Bill. He knew all about me. And about the book. He offered me five hundred bucks if I could get it. So I asked Bill if I could have it. It had been sitting on the shelf for weeks. He gave it to me, and I sold it to the guy."

"Did the guy say what he wanted with it?"

"No, but I figured it was some ego thing. A girl gave it to Bill, I think. Maybe this guy was jealous."

"Did he tell you his name?"

Without warning, she laughed. A big husky laugh, so loud that Noland was startled.

"He had a really weird name," she said. "Drent."

"Drent?"

"Yeah. That's what he wrote down on a piece of paper, next to his phone number. Has to be fake, right? Nobody's got a name like Drent. Not even a last name."

"Can you describe him?"

"About your age. Fuzzy. Glasses. Dressed like a dentist on his day off."

Noland thought to himself: fuzzy.

Drent. Dr. ENT.

Deisch.

"Do you have his number?"

She pursed her lips, then lifted her T-shirt. Just above the top hem of her bikini bottoms, a pink money belt lay flat against her smooth, impossibly taut stomach. She unzipped the belt and took out her phone.

"Here." She showed him the screen. Noland took out his phone and stored the number. Then he put his phone away and got out his wallet, which was still stuffed with cash from the gym bag. She must have eyed the bills because one of her eyebrows did an involuntary lift. Noland counted out ten twenties on the concrete tabletop, folded them once, and handed them to her.

She looked wary. "What's that for?"

"Your continuing education," he said. "And mine."

She pursed her lips, took the bills, and put them in her pouch. Then, in the congenial silence enjoyed by people who are almost friends, they walked back to Wasserman's.

19

BACK AT THE van, he called Parsons. The cop answered with typical nonchalance. "What can I do for you?"

"I need a favor. From our mutual friend. Can you arrange it?"

"I can ask. What is it?"

"A pinpoint on a cell." Noland read him the number Leda had given him. Parsons said he'd look into it and hung up.

When Noland got to the copy shop, it was more crowded than usual. But Kiril seemed to be managing okay, working the register with panache as he chatted up the students. Noland waited for a lull to ask: "How's Freddy?"

"Tired. He got to JFK at eight."

"Sorry about that. But I need him on the job first thing."

"He's on it already. He found the dude's aunt in Jamaica Plains. Had lunch with her."

"Did he get anything?"

"Just the shit we already knew. Valkenburg was a smart kid. Went to night school. Became a cop. Quit at thirty-one. Moved to Florida."

"What about his son?"

"The aunt knew he had a kid, but that's about all. Knocked up his high school sweetheart. She didn't remember the girl's name."

"Fabulous."

"Don't give up. Freddy's going downtown tomorrow."

"Where?"

"The policemen's union. He's hoping the guy listed a beneficiary on his old insurance forms."

Despite himself, Noland smiled. "Smart. But a long shot."

"Don't underestimate him."

"Never."

Kiril sat down at his computer. Noland was startled to see a hi-def scan of Sabine's journal come up on the screen, right there for God and all to see. He was about to carp about it, but Kiril cut him short. "Relax. I can do a DoD wipe in thirty seconds."

"You're assuming you'll get thirty seconds."

Kiril ignored him. "Any luck finding the key?"

"Not yet."

He pursed his lips. "Well, at least no one else has it."

"Hard to tell. They might."

"They?"

"It's not just Valkenburg. There's a crew working on this."

Kiril's eyes lit up. "The guy in the Beemer? Is he part of it?"

"No. He's on his own team."

Kiril accepted this in silence, which was a good thing because Noland didn't want to tell him the rest—that one of the surviving Selberis partners had to be in on it too. Had to be part of whatever madness was unfolding before them. Noland couldn't stop remembering what Redding had said that morning—that the partners were like the Borgias. Biting at each other, endlessly. But which one of them was a killer? Redding? He was the obvious choice. He had been closest to Bisby, Noland suspected. Close enough to know the significance of the journal and the general dimensions of Sabine's revenge scheme. But it was difficult to imagine Redding doing anything more strenuous than sitting on the deck with his girlfriends. Thinking of the girls led Noland's mind to a memory of Karen, stretched out in the bed next to him. Was she dead already? Was she hurt? He didn't know, but the thought of her being at the mercy of Irenas made him want to scream, or empty his Ruger into the sky. Neither of which would do any good, of course.

"Keep the book safe," Noland said at last. "We might still need it."

Kiril nodded. "What's our next move?"

Before Noland could reply, his cell rang. Parsons.

"Well, it took some finagling with the FBI, but we got a trace on that cell line you gave us. It's been at the same location for seven hours. You got a pen?"

Noland took down the coordinates. Then he thanked Parsons and hung up.

"Who was that?" Kiril asked.

"Our next move."

*   *   *

Kiril wanted to come along. He couldn't close the shop yet, so he asked Noland to wait until later that night before scoping out the coordinates. Noland agreed, heading home for a while. But he'd barely driven a mile from the shop before he found himself turning north on I-4.

His phone led him to Maitland Center, the sprawling office park. Noland didn't know what he'd do if the coordinates took him to one of the glittering glass-and-steel towers that dotted the park. The obligatory security guards would certainly be a problem. Luckily, he found himself driving down a service road to the back of the Center, where a small apartment complex had been tucked away, like an afterthought, near Lake Destiny. Sleek, luxury apartments, designed for consultants on long-term gigs. The landscaping was perfect in the way that only unused spaces can be, smooth sidewalks flowing over tracts of St. Augustine grass. Other than a few cars scattered through the lot, the place seemed deserted.

One of the cars, though, was Deisch's BMW. Covered with yellow pollen, half hidden under a willow tree. Noland drove by it, picked a spot far at the end of the lane, and backed in. He was about to kill the engine when the man himself appeared—Deisch—walking out from one of the units. Noland gripped the wheel. Fortunately, the doctor was intent on his phone as he shuffled down the lot, clueless as always, and Noland had the overwhelming urge to jump out and catch him mid-step once again. Instead, Noland kept still, watching as Deisch got into the Beemer and drove off.

Noland fetched his gear from the back and walked around the apartment building where Deisch had emerged. Behind the building stood a copse of pine, which hid Noland from the rest of the complex as he walked along the back. Each unit had its own little fenced yard, and Noland counted gates until he came to the right one, slipping into the small, empty yard. He popped the sliding glass door with his slim-jim and went inside, finding himself in a dark, empty living room. A brass ceiling fan spun lazily up in the vaulted ceiling, kicking up little tumbleweeds of dust in the unused fireplace. The only furniture was a bed, one of those fancy futons that fold up into a couch, placed right there in the living room. The bedding was plain white sheets and a US Navy blanket, all disheveled. As Noland stepped closer, he caught a locker-room smell of sweat and dirty linen. Deisch had been holed up there for some time.

Against the far wall, a suitcase lay open, full of Dr. ENT-style clothing: polo shirts, slacks, and silk Ts. Noland searched the suitcase. Nothing. He walked back over to the futon and ran his hand under the single, fat pillow. His hand touched metal. A big-ass gun, nine millimeter Beretta, chrome-plated and heavy as a frying pan. He checked the mag. It was full. He sniffed the barrel. No smell of cordite. He put the gun back under the pillow and moved on.

The kitchen was similarly Spartan, cupboards empty except for a few dinner plates and drinking glasses. The

microwave smelled of pizza. He went upstairs. The first bedroom was full of cardboard boxes as if someone was moving
in or out. One of the boxes was different from the others;
the banker's box Cassy had given Deisch at the restaurant.
Noland lifted the lid and went through the books inside. No
copies of *Young Werther*, but that didn't mean Deisch hadn't
found one already and taken it out.

He searched the other bedroom, which was serving as an
office, IKEA desk in the corner with a PC and two big monitors hung on aluminum trees. The PC was password-locked.
Noland tried the usual passwords—"password," "pass-
word123," etc.—but had no luck. Using a screwdriver from
his toolbox, he opened the computer case, removed the hard
drive, and put it in his backpack. Then he ran his hand under
the keyboard drawer. Something was taped to the underside,
and he pulled it out with some effort. A thick brown envelope. He knew what would be inside, but his heart still fluttered when he saw the green edges of the bills peeking out.
Franklins. Lots of them. He closed the envelope and dropped
it in his backpack.

As he rose from the chair, something caught his eye. A
picture frame, almost hidden behind the monitors. He took
it down from the wall and held it to the light. It was a photo
of a couple, smiling out of the frame as they sat at some
café. A cozy little joint on a side street of some European
city. Paris or London or—more likely—Berlin. The guy was
young, mid-twenties, strapping and square-jawed, handsome
in a rugged, outdoorsy way. The woman was older but more
striking, with her aquiline face and deep-set, intelligent eyes.
She almost blew the guy out of the frame. Still, she looked
happy, her pearly teeth gleaming in that perfect smile. A
smile he recognized.

Noland stared at the picture. It had been taken in strong
sun, and the woman's hair looked shiny and dark, a color
somewhere between black and henna-red. Noland's breathing shifted smoothly into a higher gear as he took out his

phone and scrolled through his email, eventually finding the message Faith had sent him right after their meeting at the pizza joint, when she'd first told him about Arthur Valkenburg. The woman in the picture with Valkenburg had dyed her hair a much brighter hue of red, but Noland was certain she was the same woman. For the first time, Noland knew with absolute certainty that he was gazing at the face of Sabine Werther. The mastermind. The Brazilian Fury who would torment the men and women of Selberis Constructors. A strange tingling went up Noland's spine. More than anything, he wished that Sabine were still alive, that very moment, and that he could meet her. Such people were fabulously rare.

He slipped the photo out of the frame and dropped it in his backpack.

Downstairs, he saw through the sliding glass door that the sun had begun to set beneath the pine trees. He fetched the Beretta, racked a round into the chamber, and took it and the pillow across the room. He picked a spot by the wall where he would have an oblique but uninterrupted line of sight to the front door, then dropped the pillow on the tile, sat on it, and shoved the gun under his thigh.

Night fell. The building was quiet. No TVs. No barking dogs. No lovers' quarrels. No sound at all, not even the heavy footfalls of weary I.T. consultants, schlepping it back from a long day at the tower. He became convinced that Deisch was the only resident.

After an hour, he got up and drank some water from the tap in the kitchen, then settled down again, surfing the internet on his phone. It might be hours before Deisch returned, if ever, but he was prepared to wait overnight if need be. Prison had taught him patience. He knew how to listen to the dark.

At some point, a key scratched in the lock. The front door opened and Deisch ambled in, carrying a bag of Chinese takeout and a six-pack of beer. He used his elbow to switch the hall light on, then went into the kitchen. Noland held still as a lotus flower as he registered the sounds of Deisch's sad domesticity: the fridge opening and closing, a plate being set down on the counter, hard, and a tinkling of silverware being fetched from a drawer. A familiar smell of garlic and peanut oil made its way to his nostrils even before Deisch came into the living room, carrying the full plate. He was having pad thai noodles.

When Deisch turned on the light, Noland said, "Hey, Chuck."

To his credit, Deisch didn't drop the plate.

"Noland," he said. "What the . . . hell."

"Sit down. You can eat. I don't mind."

Deisch didn't move. He still held the plate up by his chest, like a waiter preparing to set down the next course. His face had gone white.

"I'm not very hungry now," he said.

"Well, I am. Hand it over."

Deisch hesitated, then offered him the plate. Noland reached up, took it, and set it on his lap. After the first bite, he said. "It's cold, Chuck. Where did you get it? Kissimmee?"

Deisch frowned as if insulted. "Nothing's open around here. Not at night, anyway. I had to drive a while."

"Well, at least you got a decent ride. That Beemer is pretty quick. What model is it?"

Deisch shrugged.

Noland ate another forkful of noodles. "Well, whatever it is, it can push. And you know how to drive it. My partner was pretty sore when you shook us the other day."

The blood slowly returned to Deisch's face, and his lips curled into an expression of profound annoyance. "What do you want?"

"Where's Karen?"

Deisch blinked. "I don't know. Is she missing?"

"Yes."

He blinked again. "Sorry. I haven't been after her lately."

"Right. You've got bigger fish to fry."

Deisch shifted his weight from one leg to the other. Then, giving up, he sat down on the futon. "Listen—"

"You know what I found upstairs? A picture." He dug in the backpack and held up the photo. Deisch stared at it but said nothing.

"Who's the guy with her," Noland asked. "It's your cousin, isn't it? Nikki."

Deisch's Adam's apple worked up and down like a little valve beneath the taut skin of his throat.

"They were going together. For a while."

"The hotshot banker and a construction grunt? How'd that happen?"

"They met at a company picnic. Something like that. She went after him. A bit of a cougar, if you ask me."

"You think she had anything to do with his death?"

"On the contrary. She's the only person who I'm sure didn't."

Noland stopped chewing. "What makes you say so?"

"She loved him."

Noland thought he was joking—he almost laughed—but Deisch sucked in his cheeks a bit. "Nikki was cool. Everybody liked him. A lot of people loved him. That was his nature."

"If she loved him so frigging much, why didn't she go to the cops when he was killed?"

"You know the reason."

Noland sighed. "Yeah, I guess I do. She didn't want to piss off her cousin. She opted for a different kind of revenge."

"If you say so."

Noland's mind raced ahead. At last, the whole story was starting to come together in his mind, revealing itself like Sabine's invisible ink after being soaked in Kiril's potion. But so many pieces were still missing. So many gaps. Finally, he looked back at Deisch, who was staring into the distance miserably, like a kid stuck in church, waiting for the sermon to end.

"This is her apartment, right? How'd you find it? Did you follow her, too?"

Deisch didn't answer.

"I thought so," Noland said. "And you know about the book, too. How?"

Deisch still looked like a little boy, even more so as he brought a thumb up his lips and chewed on the nail. "Someone told me that all the partners had gotten a copy of a certain book. One that held secret information. But no one knew which copy was the right one."

"And you've been gathering them up ever since? Like the one you got from Leda?"

This time, Deisch registered some actual surprise—just a slight widening of his eyes. "Yeah. I bought that asshole's copy off her. Redding's. Cost me a thousand bucks."

Noland fought the urge to smile. Leda had told him she'd only gotten five hundred.

"Where is it?" Noland asked.

Deisch looked to Noland's side, up high, then fixed his eyes on Noland's again. "I threw it away."

Noland set the plate on the floor and pulled the Beretta out from under his thigh. He held the gun loosely at his side as he rose and followed the direction of Deisch's glance—the one the man hadn't been able to control when Noland asked him where the book was. A bar had been built into the room's back wall, with a sink and little cabinets for booze. Noland opened each one. The last was the jackpot—it held two books. One hardback, one paper. One German, one English.

Noland looked back at Deisch, whose eyes glittered with rage.

"You got one from Leda. Who's the other one from?"

Sitting on the short futon, Deisch had to tilt his head back to meet Noland's stare. But then he did something unexpected: He lifted his chin higher than necessary, so that, even from that diminished position, he managed to look down his nose at Noland.

"Fuck you, Noland," he said.

Then his chest imploded.

It was as if an invisible fist had punched down into the man's solar plexus, causing a momentary depression, which then rebounded a fraction of a second later, bringing with it a tiny eruption of gore and chips of pale bone. His body heaved upward with the force of the reaction, then fell back onto the futon. His torso landed at the same moment as thousands of fragments of shattered glass—the glass door had dissolved, cascading into the living room, leaving a void open to the night.

Noland rolled across the tile into the hallway, then crawled into the kitchen. He found the metal panel with the apartment's breaker switches, and he threw them all. The apartment went dark. Peaceful, almost. A light summer breeze wafted in through the aperture where the glass door had been, and from there he heard a rustling of branches. Someone was climbing down from a tree.

Still holding the Beretta, he ran out the front door and sprinted around the building, stopping when he reached the corner of the wall. The pine trees were still, and he held his breath. Then came another snap of branches, about thirty yards to his left. His eyes still hadn't fully adjusted, but he could make out a man's silhouette as it emerged from the copse and sprinted across the grass, the same strip that Noland had walked along a few hours earlier to get into the apartment. The man was getting away.

Noland lifted the Beretta and started firing. He had very strong wrists, but it was impossible to fight the gun's recoil, so he let the barrel rise as he fired, painting a line up the guy's silhouette. And on the fifth shot he hit him—the silhouette spun around and staggered to the side. Noland thought the man would go down, surely, but at the last moment he righted himself. Noland stopped shooting, and he barely heard the three curt pops, like a shoemaker's hammer, that issued from the silhouette, answered by three soft explosions on the cinderblock wall behind Noland's back, close enough to pepper his neck with shrapnel. He dropped to the grass and lay flat.

Fucker had a suppressor.

He didn't move for several moments. The Beretta's report had filled his eardrums with some dark, warm fluid, and yet he caught the sound of footfalls thudding across the grass, receding into the distance. As Noland got to his feet, a big engine revved in the parking lot, followed by a squeal of tires.

He ran back to Deisch's apartment, his chest so tight it felt like a solid membrane, pulled from all sides like a drum. No way could a human heart still beat in there. And yet he continued to function, smoothly, acting fast. He found his toolbox in the dark, along with his backpack and the two books. Then he ran outside.

All the windows in the neighboring apartments remained dark, but there were signs of life in the building down the lane, a few windows burning with soft yellow light. He could almost feel the multiple sets of eyes that must be peering out at him, from behind gingerly parted curtains. He threw everything into the van and jumped behind the wheel. Gunning the engine, he shot away without turning on his headlights, using the glow of the streetlamps to steer his way out of the complex. Pulling onto Keller Road, he flicked his lights on just as the first police cruiser sped by, heading in the opposite direction, lights spinning. As Noland sped out of Maitland Center, he could still see the cruiser's blue beams strafing the glass towers, skating around as in a hall of mirrors.

He kept an eye on the rearview all the way back to Longwood, when he finally started to breathe normally again. He pulled off his gloves and threw them out the window. Then he called Kiril.

20

WHEN HE FINALLY got home, after three AM, Quick and Silver went insane. They weren't used to him arriving in the middle of the night, and they were so hyped up that he had to take them for a short walk through the dark neighborhood, his clothes crusty with dried sweat.

It had been a long night. After he'd spoken to Kiril, he stopped off at a gas station, where he carefully checked his clothing for signs of blood. Finding none, he washed his hands and forearms thoroughly at the sink. Of course, he would never get the cordite residue out of his pores. If Parsons or one of the other boys at OPD gave him a paraffin test, he'd come up positive, sure as Sunday. But he could always claim that he'd been target shooting in the woods near his house. It was almost the truth—he practiced there often, being too cheap to go to a firing range.

Strangely, he wasn't too worried about the cops. His nerves were still too electrified with adrenaline and fear— and the sheer, elemental pleasure of knowing that he'd put at least one round into the son of a bitch who'd killed Deisch. Valkenburg. Had to be. Noland remembered the photos of him and Bisby out hunting, rifles slung over their shoulders. It must have been more than a passing hobby for Valkenburg— he was a good shot. So good, in fact, that he could've put a bullet through Noland's chest, too, a moment after he'd done for Deisch, safe from his tree perch. The fact that he hadn't might be attributable to any number of things, mere expediency being at top of the list. But whatever his reason, Noland discounted it. Valkenburg had been willing to kill him on the *Zigeuner*, and again when Noland surprised him behind Sabine's apartment, when Val had gotten off those three shots. The rules were set now. One of them was going to die.

When he was done at the gas station, he drove back into town, working the wheel in a kind of daze as he wound his way to Kiril's shop. He must have still had a crazed expression on his face because Kiril's eyes bugged out the moment he saw him.

"You having a heart attack?"

"I think so." He put the books on the desk and Kiril took them without another word, flipping through each and doing an up-and-down check against the computer screen where the scan of Sabine's journal glowered. After a few minutes, Kiril looked at him and shook his head.

A thread of hot bile rose in Noland's throat, burning like molten brass. "Are you sure? Maybe there's a twist to the code that you haven't figured out."

"If there is," Kiril said, "then we're already fucked."

Noland planted his elbows on the desk's smooth, fake wood surface and cradled his forehead in his palms. His skull hurt so badly that he imagined some tiny, overloaded blood vessel throbbing in his frontal cortex, about to burst. He almost wished it would.

He felt Kiril's eyes on him. "You gonna make it?"

"Sure."

But he was thinking back to what Karen had said, that first night in her apartment. About killing herself. Noland had talked her out of it, but he wondered now if he'd done her a disservice. Thanks to him, she was either dead or at the mercy of the same assholes who'd chopped off Sabine's head. Brilliant.

He sat up. "I got a couple more leads to run down. Have you got an old PC lying about?"

Kiril went into the storage room and returned with a dusty PC tower, which Noland took back to the van. His arms felt like tubes filled with wet cement, but he made it home without wrapping the van around a tree. After walking the dogs, he face-planted on the couch and fell instantly asleep, vaguely aware of their hot tongues mopping the back of his neck. His sweat probably tasted interesting to them. Coppery. Like fear.

He slept a few hours. A deep sleep, too, despite being face down on the couch. When he finally woke, around eleven, he felt okay. Better than usual. Maybe there was something about a gunfight, something therapeutic. He just needed someone to shoot at him every day.

His phone buzzed. Freddy.

"Where are you?" Noland asked.

"Queens. Where else?"

"Did you get anything?"

"No," Freddy said. "I got everything."

"Tell me."

"The kid's name. It's Jonathan Shawn Valkenburg."

Noland swallowed. It was the answer he had expected, more or less, and yet it struck him like a thunderbolt. Shawn. Shawn Difore. He'd changed his name. But it was him. He was Valkenburg's son.

"Great," Noland said at last. "Now get your butt home."

*   *   *

After a quick shower and shave, he packed his duffel bag with enough clothes for three days and a Readymade bin of supplies for the dogs. Then he loaded up Quick and Silver into the van and drove to Cassy's house. When he parked in the front yard, she came out to meet him.

"Hey," she said. Her expression was doubtful. "I didn't know if I'd see you again."

His heart sank. "How could you think that?"

She wiped her hands on her jeans. Her face shone with a thin film of sweat—she'd been working in the stables. She avoided his eyes, even as he gave her a hug and a kiss, which prompted the dogs to start barking furiously from inside the cab.

"Nice critters," she said.

"Thanks. I was going to ask if you could watch them. I have to go dark for a few days, and I've got no one else."

He opened the driver's door. The dogs jumped out, peed on the lawn, and began sniffing her ankles. Silver jumped up and licked her chin.

"Wow," she sputtered. "They're so . . . well behaved."

"They're not always this bad. I haven't had much time for them lately."

"Too busy out snooping?"

"Yeah."

She led the dogs into the house. He hoisted out the Readymade that he'd filled with stuff—a bag of dog food, some bowls, leashes, and toys—and carried it inside. She was in the kitchen, chopping a strip of raw bacon and tossing morsels at each dog. Quick and Silver made sure that no piece made it to the floor. She smiled absently, perhaps the first real smile he'd seen from her. When she ran out of bacon, she ducked into the fridge for a piece of leftover chicken and started chopping it, too. As she did so, Noland admired the smooth skin of her forearms and hands. His eyes fixed on the burgundy-colored arrowhead mark on the back of her right hand. Where her cut had been.

"It healed," he said.

She raised her eyebrows. "What ?"

"Your scratch. The one I thought was a horse bite. Remember?"

"Oh, yeah." She laughed and turned toward the sink. "Can't see how I managed to forget. It hurt like hell."

"I bet."

She kept her face away from him, but he was pretty sure what her expression must be at the moment. When she finally turned back to him, he saw that he was right—her mouth had hardened into a perfect, horizontal slit.

"Have you still got the gun?" he asked.

"What gun?"

"The one you shot Bisby with. The .32. I need it."

She didn't speak for a full ten seconds.

"Get out," she said, looking back into the sink. "Take your dogs too."

He shook his head. "I'm on your side, Cassy. I always have been. But I need the gun. And the truth. If you don't give them to me, both of them, I'll set the cops on you."

She faced him again, and her nostrils flared as she took a deep, enraged breath. If the .32 were to suddenly materialize in her hand at that moment, he'd be a dead man.

"You're thinking you left no evidence," he went on. "But you're wrong. The cops found blood on the carpet. Not Bisby's. I'm guessing it was from your cut."

Her eyes fluttered, and her mouth went slack. Noland rushed over and caught her as she slumped against the counter—not fainting, exactly, but a total loss of muscle control. She was spent.

"Sit down." He guided her into a chair. "Have you got any booze?"

She pointed to a cabinet above the fridge. Noland found a bottle of bourbon and poured two fingers into a dinner glass. She accepted it with a trembling hand.

"They've got no reason to suspect you," he said, lowering his voice. "They're betting on Val. Or maybe this other guy. Irenas."

She gulped the bourbon. Her hand stopped trembling, but she was still breathing fast, on the edge of hyperventilation. The dogs sensed something was wrong and began to growl. Noland shushed them.

"I have it," she said.

"Where?"

"In the barn. I kept thinking I would throw it in a lake or something. But I was afraid someone would follow me. See me."

Noland smiled. "Someone like me?"

"Yeah."

"Where in the barn?"

"In Moosh's stall. Behind a board."

Noland headed outside. The dogs followed, but the horses didn't seem to mind. Moosh didn't even huff as Noland slipped into her stall and found the loose board by the water trough. Behind was a cloth-wrapped bundle. He took it out and unwrapped the gun. It was small enough to lie flat in his palm. An antique model, 1940s, well kept, the blued metal glistening with a thin sheen of oil.

He took it with him back to the kitchen. Cassy hadn't moved.

"You got it from the nightstand, right?" he asked. "In Val's apartment?"

By this point, she'd probably gotten over being surprised by anything, so she merely nodded. "It belonged to his grandfather. Policeman's Special. Val liked to keep it close."

"Did Bisby meet you at the apartment?"

"Not intentionally. I went there to call Val. I had to talk to him. He'd left one of those throw-away phones for me in the bedroom, in case I needed to reach him. And I did. Need to."

"You had to give him Deisch's message?"

"Yeah. He wanted fifty thousand dollars for the journal. I didn't even know what that meant. He gave me some GPS coordinates and told me to give them to Val, along with the price and a bank account number. He said he'd leave the journal at that location as soon as the money was deposited. I told him I didn't know how to reach Val, but he didn't believe me."

Noland bit his tongue before saying: *I didn't either.* "So where was Bisby? Hiding in the closet?"

She winced, then nodded. "He must have been listening.
I think he wrote down the coordinates—"

"He did. On his arm."

"—and he was going to go there himself. But he made
a noise and I was startled. He jumped out and came for me.
Slammed me against the dresser. That's when I got the cut.
He picked up the phone I had used, and while he was busy
looking at the number, I got the gun. I aimed it at him. I told
him to put the phone down, but he wouldn't."

"So you shot him?"

She bit her lip. "I must've been crazy at that point. Still
am, a bit."

"Join the club."

He poured her another two fingers of whiskey. When
she looked at him again, her eyes were calmer. She looked
relieved.

"It feels good to tell someone."

"I bet."

"And now that I know what happened to Sabine . . . Do
you think Bisby did that?"

"I think he helped, yes."

She shook her head. "That asshole."

"Well, he got what was coming to him. You gave it to
him."

She considered this with a slight widening of her eyes. "I
didn't know about Sabine then. I just . . ."

"Hated the motherfucker?"

"Yeah. And feared him, too."

"They go together. Hate and fear."

She sighed exhaustedly. Noland knew what she was
feeling. The realization of discovering who you are, deep
down—what you're capable of. It's too much for most people.
But not for her, he sensed. She would get over it. It might
take a long time for her to get back to normal, but she would.
She was tough.

As if reading his thoughts, she looked at him.

"I like you, Noland."

He felt again that sudden lightness in his chest.

"Glad to hear it."

She didn't smile. "I like your heart, I mean. I like it, in spite of the rest of you."

Something caught in his throat. "The rest of me?"

"The hatred and the fear." She put her hand on his breastbone. "God played some nasty tricks on you, didn't he?"

"Deisch," he said. "Let's talk about Deisch."

She took her hand away, then nodded. "What about him?"

"He found the orange grove somehow. Must've broken in while they were out. He found the journal and took it. He found Sabine too, and he took her . . . head."

She gritted her teeth, so hard that her face took on a feral look. "He did that?"

Noland nodded. "She was already dead, I figure. They had killed her in a rage. Stealing her head was Deisch's idea of a joke. Wanted to leave it as a kind of souvenir. For Val."

She looked down at her glass. "Another asshole."

"If it makes you feel any better, he's dead too."

She paused for a moment, as a curious expression washed over her face. Shock? No. Relief.

"Deisch was blackmailing you, wasn't he?" Noland asked. "About your dad?"

Only now, at last, did her eyes widen into something like surprise. "How did you know?"

"I didn't. I was guessing. What was the issue? Something your dad was doing, not long before he died?"

She took another sip of the whiskey.

"And Deisch threatened to make that public somehow?" Noland went on. "Write it on a postcard and send it to all your friends?"

"He said he'd keep the secret so long as I helped him."

Noland got the gun out of his pocket and checked the cylinder. Bullets shining there like tiny brass buttons. Five shots left. He closed the cylinder. "Why weren't you straight with me, Cass? Why didn't you tell me he was coercing you?"

She wasn't looking at the gun. Noland didn't press her for an answer, because he already knew it: she didn't trust him. Not then, and probably not now.

"I think I got my fingerprints off," she said, after a moment.

"I'll wipe it again," he said.

"What are you going to do with it?"

Instead of answering, he rewrapped the gun in the cloth, which only now did he recognize as a tea towel.

"There's one more thing," he said.

She waited.

"It's just a hunch. But confirm it for me—your old man did some shady deals with Selberis, right? That's what the secret Deisch found was about?"

She nodded. "Dad was going bankrupt. He needed money fast."

"Who got him mixed up with Selberis? You? Or Val?"

"Does it matter?"

"It might. If the cops ever ask."

"My dad's gone. You can't put a dead man in prison. But I didn't want his . . ." She took a short, sudden breath, almost a gasp. "I didn't want his name sullied. That's all."

Noland tried to remain dispassionate as he studied her face, her steady eyes and the firm set of her jaw. He remembered the old man's portrait in the foyer—that great, old Southern tyrant who had paved her childhood with misery. And yet that same old bastard had given her his jawline. And some other qualities, too.

Absently, she ran a hand along her forehead to sweep a loose hair away. She hadn't bothered with the ponytails today. This shortcoming struck Noland as momentous. He felt sorry for her. And loved her. He wasn't sure which emotion was the stronger.

She asked, "Do you know what's in the book?"

"Money. Sabine left a trail to the bank where she stashed it. But we need the second book. Do you have it?"

"I told you I don't."

"All right."

He got out one of his business cards, flipped it over, and wrote Lieutenant Parsons's name and number on the back.

"Like I said, I'm going away for a few days. I'm asking you not to leave the house until you hear from me. Okay?"

She looked confused. "My classes. I have to teach—"

"That's fine. But don't go out alone. If anybody comes to the house that you don't know, tell them to leave. If they don't, sic the dogs on him. And call that number. He's a cop, but a sympathetic one."

She took the card and stared at it.

"What if I don't hear from you?"

He didn't answer, and she didn't ask any more questions. They walked out to the van. He was about to climb in when she stopped and put her arms around him, pressing her hands into his shoulder blades as they kissed. Once again, she had made him instantly happy and frightened at the same time. Happy that she liked him, and frightened that he might never see her again.

"I hope I do hear from you, Noland."

"Don't worry."

He got into the van and drove off. When he glanced in the rearview mirror, she was already walking back into the house.

21

HE'D BARELY REACHED I-4 when his phone rang. He didn't recognize the number.

"Mr. Twice?" a voice asked.

"Yeah?"

"I'm glad I finally got hold of you."

Even with this brief greeting, the man's accent made itself apparent. Not German. Not Spanish. Some weird combination of the two. Even so, his words were clear and crisp. There was something premeditated about his diction, precise, as if he ran each word through a lathe before uttering it.

"I'm glad, too," Noland said. "Mr. Irenas, right?"

"You know who I am? Good. That makes things simpler. It's time we met."

"Okay. Where?"

"I am staying at a house a few miles outside of town. If you would be so good as to come—"

"Let's make it somewhere public. I know a place."

Noland gave him the address of the same pizzeria where he and Faith had met a mere eight days before. The man hung up, and Noland steered downtown. He parked at a garage on the other side of Lake Eola, then walked around to the pizza joint. The lunchtime rush hadn't begun yet, and the place was still empty. A good thing. He asked the waiter to seat him at a booth in the front near the windows. He sat there for thirty minutes before an SUV rolled up. It was all black, even the windows, Darth Vader style. But a sunbeam came to Noland's aid, reflecting off the glass storefront across the street and illuminating the SUV's cabin enough for him to make out a trio of male silhouettes, two large and one average. Eventually, the driver's door opened and a big guy got out. His trim beard and crew cut looked military, but he was dressed for a vacation, blue jeans and a polo shirt, a size too small so that his muscles popped like a superhero's. He glanced in either direction before opening the rear passenger door, from which a second man emerged. This man—the average-sized one—walked toward the pizza joint, leaving the big man behind.

Noland had no doubt that this was Victor Irenas. His cheeks were tan and smooth, and his handsome face exuded a vibe of elegance and superiority—not to mention, of course, extreme wealth. His slacks held a laser-sharp crease and yet flowed gently as he walked. Walking briskly inside, he raked his black eyes around the room, spotted Noland, and walked over. He held out his hand. Noland shook with him, surprised by the strength of his grip, and by the fact that his hand was rough with calluses. A carpenter's hand.

"Hello, Mr. Twice."

"How's it hanging, Vic?"

Irenas grinned, genuinely tickled—as a king might be when the court jester has said something funny and mildly insulting. As he slipped into the booth across from Noland, he unbuttoned his sports jacket, which looked Italian, a post-modern curve to the lapels. He glanced around again. Only now, up close, did Noland detect a tinge of auburn red in the man's otherwise brown hair.

"Nice place," Irenas said. "Funky. You come here much?"

"Not really. But we're close to the courthouse, so I thought it would be appropriate."

"Ha ha. You're very funny, Noland. May I call you Noland?"

"Call me Nole."

"Thanks, Nole. Do they have good coffee here?"

"The best."

A waiter came. Irenas ordered coffee. Noland got a Bud Lite. They didn't speak again until their respective drinks arrived. Then, after a quick slurp from his cup, Irenas dabbed his mouth with his napkin and said: "You have the journal, yes?"

"Yes."

"And the novels?"

"I have two. Neither is the right one."

The corners of his handsome mouth wilted. "That's all right. For now, I just want the journal."

"How much can I get for it?"

"I'll give you a thousand dollars."

"Now who's funny?"

Irenas tightened his jaw, then adjusted himself on the slick bench, pointing his knees out of the booth. "All right. I'll throw in a bonus."

"Such as?"

He dipped a fingertip into his coffee, pulled it out, and drew a wet letter K on the table.

"You can get her back," Irenas said, "if you give us the journal. Otherwise . . ." He opened his hand as if releasing an invisible bird.

Despite himself, Noland felt the blood drain from his face.

Irenas went on, "You know what happened to the other lady?"

"Yeah."

The man smiled, revealing a line of perfect, sharp teeth. "Then you should be reminded that she—the other lady—was a relation of mine. A member of my family."

"Is that relevant?"

"Oh, yes. You see, doing what we did to her—what we were forced to do—made all of us, my associates and me, very uncomfortable. She was of our blood, after all. Not to mention one of our class. Such things should not be done to a person of her station. But this other woman." He nodded at the K, still wet on the table. "She is a stranger. And of a much lower class. An expendable class. So, you can imagine—."

"I get it."

Irenas sipped his coffee again. "So, you will sell me the journal?"

"Yes. But I want fifty grand. And the lady."

The man's eyes turned flat and bright as freshly minted pennies.

"I thought we understood each other."

"Oh, I understand all right," Noland said. "Now you understand this, fuck-face. I want fifty K. Cash. For that you get the journal and all the books I've found. Maybe you can figure something out."

His eyes stayed fixed on Noland's. After a moment they narrowed slightly.

"She is your client. Yes?"

"Selberis is my client. All the partners are."

"I am a partner too, Nole. The senior partner, in fact."

Noland nodded. "That's true. Even so, I want the fifty K."

Irenas breathed in and out, in and out for a minute or more as he turned the problem over in his head. At what point would Irenas decide it was simpler to kill him? He had no doubt the man could do it—if not him personally, then one of the gorillas outside. But then Noland reassured himself—he had a good hand to play. Irenas needed the journal. Clearly, he hadn't found the secret writing that Freddy and Kiril had revealed so easily. Noland might not have the whole puzzle, but he had the main piece.

"It seems I misjudged you, Nole. Fifty thousand is acceptable. When do you want to make the trade?"

"Tomorrow."

"Why not tonight?"

"Tomorrow."

He pursed his lips. "Where?"

Noland pointed out the window toward the lake. "See that bandshell? There's a line of benches on the other side, with a hedge behind them. At six o'clock tomorrow evening, leave the money in the hedge. Then take a walk. By the time you circle the lake, the money will be gone and the journal will be in its place."

"Ha ha. You want me to leave fifty thousand dollars in a bush?"

"It won't be there long."

His eyes went flat again.

"And the woman?"

"Release her at the same time. Tell her to give me a call. She knows my number. As soon as I hear from her, I'll leave the journal in the hedge."

He took another breath. "Very well. Do I need to tell you what will happen if you try anything?"

"Nope."

"Good."

He rose. Noland fully expected him to stick him with the tab for the coffee, but at the last moment he produced a crisp Franklin, pulling it from the air like a magician.

"Nice trick," Noland said.

"I learned a few in jail."

"Me too."

Irenas walked out. Watching him through the window, Noland saw the bearded man still standing by the car, smoking a cigarette. But he sprang into action the moment Irenas came out, rushing to open the car door. Noland waited until the SUV slid off down the road. Then he left.

*   *   *

The post–lunch hour crush jammed the streets as he headed through town toward St. Cloud. He didn't know what the construction site would be like this time—either abuzz with activity or completely dormant. Rolling up to the fence, he was relieved to find that it was the former. Everyone was busy, busting ass, and no one paid him any attention. Fortunately, he found his favorite hard-hat, grinning.

"You again?"

"Me again. I'm looking for Shawn."

"Little Boss? Ain't seen him since this morning. I think he might be at home. Maybe stuck on the shitter or something."

"Oh?"

"He looked a little pee-ked when the shift began. Stumbled around for a while, gettin' in people's way."

Noland nodded. "I don't suppose you know where he lives?"

"Matter of fact, I do. Me and a couple of guys helped him move some furniture once. He's got a nice house up on Conway and Seventh. The only yellow one on the street. You can't miss it."

Noland reached into his wallet, dug out Irenas's Franklin, and gave it to the hard-hat.

"Well, God bless you, too," the man said.

"Thanks." Then Noland walked away.

* * *

When he got to Conway, he found the yellow house tucked at the end of a cul-de-sac. It was surprisingly quaint for a young guy like Difore, with its neatly edged driveway and white trellises straining under heavy vines of bougainvillea. Noland parked in front and knocked on the door. No one answered. He walked along the side of the house, found a side door to the garage, and popped the lock with his slim-jim. Once inside, he found the door to the kitchen open. He went through.

As soon as he saw the house's interior, with velour drapes dangling little balls of yarn, he wanted to laugh. Cows grazed peacefully in the pastoral scene repeated on the wallpaper, its pattern broken only by an occasional Norman Rockwell print; he was surprised. Surely it belonged to someone other than Shawn—or had, until very recently. Some old lady, perhaps, with twenty cats. The living room had lots of shelves, all crowded with tchotchkes and framed photos. Noland paused to look at some of them. Sure enough, they showed various members of a long-lost nuclear family: balding man, stout housewife, blond daughter, and a stripling of a son (not Shawn). The few books he saw were unremarkable, mostly paperbacks. Bestsellers. Dan Brown. Stephen King. No Goethe. The only one that caught his eye was a newish-looking paperback: *The Early Poems of Wallace Stevens*. Noland thought he recognized the author's name, but couldn't be sure. He reached out to take the book down when something clicked from behind—a mechanical click.

"Don't move, Noland," a voice said. A man's voice. Measured and calm, but breathy, as if the guy had just run up a flight of stairs. Noland recognized the voice. He raised his hands, very slowly.

"I didn't figure on you being here," he said.

"I bet."

"Is it okay if I turn around?"

"Sure. Why not."

Keeping his hands up, Noland rotated slowly. Across the room, near an open hallway that almost certainly led to a den or a spare bedroom, was Valkenburg. Not the Valkenburg of the photos Noland had seen, nor the silver-bearded Harris persona he had met on the boat. Rather, this version was clean-shaven, head and face, almost like a baby. Val held a rifle, pressed into his shoulder, a small carbine with a black tube on the end of the barrel. It was pointed at Noland's head, such that Noland was compelled to look down the sight and straight into Valkenburg's right eye. Neither of them moved.

Somehow, Noland kept his voice even as he said: "I've got Sabine's journal."

"I know," Val said. Offhandedly. Noland knew he was running a risk/reward analysis on the situation, calculating whether it was better to shoot Noland right there, on the spot, or take him someplace else and then kill him. Either way, Noland's best chance was to jump sideways, now, before Val made up his mind. All his instincts told him to run for it, to count on his own body's improbable speed, once again. But no. Val was too good. He'd plug him the moment he twitched. And realizing this—realizing, that is, that he was about to die—Noland had the sickening and yet almost irresistible urge to giggle. What a fitting end for him, in a twisted sense, to die there in an old lady's house, surrounded by frilly drapes and ugly wallpaper. Killed by the very man he'd been searching for, no less, the same man he thought he'd shot, not twelve hours previous. What could be more absurd? That was the way God operated, His M.O. Always the sense of humor.

"You know," he said, "I used to be a cop. Just like you."

Val said nothing. Another moment went by. Noland's shirt cleaved to his back, soaked with sweat. He could already smell the reek of it.

"In fact," he went on, "I think you and I might have a few other things in common." As he said all this, he managed to unfix his eye from Val's and regard the rest of the man. Val was dressed differently now, blue jeans that hung baggy on his legs, and an oversized T-shirt. His skin had changed, too. Pale. Not a disguise this time—no amount of actor's makeup could achieve that particular, morbid shade. Suddenly, Noland realized: He had shot him badly. Perhaps mortally.

"How much blood have you lost?" Noland asked.

Valkenburg swallowed, his Adam's apple working up and down under his damp skin like a mechanical valve.

"Fair amount."

"Maybe we should sit down."

"I'd like to," Val answered. "But the problem is . . . The problem is . . ." He repeated it with the same intonation, like a needle on an old vinyl record skipping backward. Noland held his breath. A moment earlier, he had been prepared to jump like a jackrabbit. Now he stood paralyzed in terror and fascination. The barrel of Val's gun tracked downward from Noland's head to his chest, then to his belly, and finally to the floor. Then, as if some invisible plug had been pulled, Val keeled over and hit the tile with a grotesque thud.

Noland ran over to him, meaning to step on his rifle arm before he could raise it again. But there was no need. A red circle spread slowly from under Val's hip across the beige tiles. Noland rolled him over and lifted his shirt. A thick wad of gauze had been attached to his ribs with surgical tape, and the blood had completely soaked it, escaping freely now. Noland pressed a hand on it, hard, then used his other hand to get out his phone. He thumbed through his contacts and found the number to Ben Freund's boat shop. Ben, he knew, was the only man in Florida who could help him now.

Ben answered on the first ring.

"What do you want, Nole?"

"Another favor, Mr. Freund," he said. "A big one."

22

AN HOUR PASSED before a vehicle rolled up in the drive. It wasn't Ben's truck, but a glossy, red Italian job, so low and sleek it seemed to hover a few inches off the concrete. Noland left the window and went back to his spot on the floor next to Val before the front door was unlocked. Shawn hugged two plastic drug store bags as he came into the foyer.

"Hello, Shawn," Noland said. "You can put the bags down."

Noland watched as understanding washed over the young man's face. His eyes shifted from Noland to Val's unconscious form and then back to Noland again. His face turned white.

"Is he . . . ?"

"No, but he's close. He's lost a shit-ton of blood."

He nodded. Having overcome his shock, he moved with efficient speed into the house and set the bags on the kitchen counter. "I bought more supplies. Bandages, and an IV bag of saline."

"Good. We might need them. I called a medic."

Shawn blinked at him.

"Relax. It's someone I trust. Do you know if the bullet is still inside?"

He hunched his shoulders. "I assume so. I was going to call an ambulance, but he wouldn't let me." He sighed. "I should have done it anyway."

"Then you'd both be in jail. Do you know his blood type?"

"O-neg."

"Right. Same as yours, I bet."

Shawn froze for a moment, and then swallowed. "Yeah."

They waited in silence until a truck rumbled up. Another peek through the window confirmed that it was Ben, getting out with another man, a tall, reed-thin fellow with a fringe of gray hair. Noland let them inside. Ben scanned the room, saw Valkenburg on the floor, and gestured to his companion, who was lugging a medical bag.

"This is Clive," Ben said.

Before Noland could greet him, Clive strode around Ben and got to work. He checked Val's pulse, then took his blood pressure with a cuff from the bag.

"This man needs an ER."

"Not a chance," Noland said.

"Well, if we don't get some blood in him, he'll be dead in half an hour."

"Can you set up a direct transfusion? Arm to arm?"

"Who's the donor?"

Shawn stepped forward. "Me."

Clive's eyes shifted to him. "You're sure of the typing?"

"Yes."

"Okay. You'll need a place to sit, though."

"I can sit on the floor next to him."

Clive shook his head. "We need the blood to flow downhill."

Noland grabbed a chair from the dinner table and set it next to Val. Shawn sat down. Clive crouched between them and put one end of an IV into Val's arm and the other into Shawn's. Blood spurted from the spot where the needle went in, landing on the tile like a string of rubies.

"How will you know much has gone in?" Noland asked.

"I'm timing it," Clive said.

"Is that reliable?"

"Not really."

Noland cursed himself. The last thing he needed was to lose Shawn too. He would have to keep an eye on the guy's alertness, and the best way to do that was to get him talking. He fetched another chair and set it down nearby. "How long as he been hiding out here?"

Shawn debated with himself for a moment, then said, "He showed up last night."

"Do you know what he's been up to?"

He pushed his lips out, a bit sadly. "Same thing as when he disappeared, I suppose. Trying to undo the damage Sabine did."

"You mean recovering the money?"

"Yeah. That, and figuring out why she framed him for it."

"So you knew about that part too?"

He didn't answer.

"You could have told the others," Noland said. "That he was innocent, I mean."

Shawn scoffed: "Innocent?"

"Well, of stealing the money, I mean."

Noland watched the IV line, which was dark and solid-looking. Clive gave Shawn a wadded rag and told him to clench and unclench his fist.

"He's not really my father, you know," Shawn said, looking at Noland. "Not in any meaningful sense."

"Did you see him much as a kid?"

"Sometimes. Christmases and birthdays. He'd show up in Albany, usually with whatever girlfriend he had at the time."

"Did he ever show up with Cassy?"

"No. He'd stopped coming around by then."

"Your mom raised you alone?"

"She got married when I was ten. A good man. I took his name."

Noland sighed. He felt a subtle pull from the young man, or rather, from the child he had once been. An ineluctable demand for sympathy.

"So, you grew up and tracked him down in Orlando? Decided to move here to sponge off him?"

"All I asked for was a job."

"And he got you one. A lucrative one."

Shawn sneered. "So what? I had a degree in management. After Redding hired me, I went back to school and got another degree, in building construction. I earned my job. I was good at it. I kept the work going."

"Except when it was more profitable to slow it down."

"That wasn't my idea. For a long time, our day-to-day operations were solid. Legit. Only the funding was dirty. The back-end stuff."

"But that changed, right?"

He sniffed, philosophically. "Redding and Bisby. They started wanting more profit. Came up with the idea of the slowdowns, and the corner-cutting."

"And you just followed orders?"

"What else? I was in too deep by that point. And so was he." He nodded down at Val.

"Irenas wasn't privy to this new profit-boosting strategy?"

"Probably not. The only way he would've known was through Sabine, and not even she knew, for a while. Until Nikki told her."

This statement hit Noland like a kick in the guts. He thought to himself: *Of course.*

"Is that why they killed him?"

Shawn screwed his eyes shut. "I had nothing to do with that. Didn't even know about it."

"Who did?"

He opened his eyes. "Bisby."

"Bisby knew how to tamper with a cable?"

"Probably. Or he might have bribed a hard-hat to help. Someone to make sure Nikki was in the wrong place at the right time."

Noland kept studying Shawn's face, alert to any hint of deception, but he found none. Then again, his bullshit detector was probably impaired by the strangeness of the situation—Shawn sitting there with the IV in his arm, pumping blood down into his father.

As if reading his thoughts, Shawn said, "How did you find out I'm his son?"

"I sent a guy to New York to snoop around."

"Classic."

Noland was about to add that he, Shawn, had been an enormous pain in the ass, and that if he had come clean from the beginning Noland could have sorted everything out. Val wouldn't have gotten shot. Deisch wouldn't have died. Karen wouldn't be at the mercy of that crazy Brazilian fuck. The whole situation might be different. Better. But Shawn had kept silent. Even now, the kid just sat there, clenching and unclenching his fist.

"Who else knew?" Noland asked.

"Nobody."

"Bullshit. Sabine knew."

"No way."

"She knew. That's why she picked Val for the frame. She set him up against the others, knowing he wouldn't take off and leave you behind. And this whole rigmarole with the journal and the novels. It was her crazy scheme to get them killing each other. Like the Borgias."

"The who?"

Noland was about to explain further when a groan came from Val's closed lips. Clive took his pulse and nodded. "He's stabilizing. The bullet is in there, though. If we don't get it out, he'll continue to bleed."

"Can you do it?"

The man scratched his stubbly cheek. "I'd have to use ether. A lot. He might not wake up afterward."

"Try it."

He puffed out his cheeks and blew. Even so, Noland could tell the old guy had been expecting such a request. Steeling himself.

"Okay. We need to get him off the floor, though."

"How about the dinner table?"

Clive glanced at it. The table, which was big and hewn from oak, must've looked up to the job because he nodded. "That'll do. Let's give him a little more juice first. How are you doing, kid?"

"I'm fine," Shawn said. "Give him all he needs."

"If I did that, you'd be dead."

As if in response, Val awoke, eyes bugging out like a newborn's. He rolled his head to the side.

"Noland Twice?"

"Yessir."

"Come here."

Noland crouched down. Val blinked at him, and Noland got even closer, lowering his ear to within a foot of the man's pale lips. A sour, forgotten-closet smell of death rose off him, so strong that Noland's eyes watered.

"As soon as I met you," Val said, "I knew one of us would end up killing the other."

"I guess I got lucky."

Val rebutted this with a slight, sideways motion of his jaw. "Not luck. Karma. All the evil stuff I did in the past. It was always going to catch up with me."

"I guess it catches up with us all."

Val's eyes flickered toward Shawn, then back at Noland.

"Take care of him," Val said.

"How? You know what we're up against."

"Take care of him."

"You can help. Where's the fucking money?"

Val blinked arrhythmically, like a captive in one of those POW videos from Vietnam. Signaling something in Morse code. Or maybe he was just dying.

"Sabine's journal. You need it."

"I've got it." Then, realizing that this might be his last chance to clarify the matter, Noland asked. "You bought it off Deisch, right? Paid him fifty grand?"

Val took a deep breath before speaking again. "I meant to kill the bastard when he showed up. But he was clever. I had to pay."

"Why didn't you get the journal when you had the chance? You had two days."

His lips peeled back into a grin. "Your fault. You made me relocate. Then I was flummoxed."

"Right, the all-nighter," Noland said, remembering what Shawn had told him. But why hadn't Val told Shawn what was going on? Did he want to keep Shawn out of it?

"So," Val went on, "the little fucker bested me."

"Well, you certainly paid him off last night."

Val stared at him, clearly frustrated with his stupidity. Using his free hand, he reached over and grabbed Noland's wrist.

"The key. The book is the key."

"I know."

Again, he darted his eyes in Shawn's direction. Which was also, Noland realized, the direction of the bookcase across the room. "Take care of him. He's got everything."

"I got it, coach," Noland said, and tried to smile. "Emperor of ice cream, right?"

Val didn't answer, but Noland saw from a flicker in his eyes that he understood. He let go. His arm fell across his chest, which heaved up and down once, twice, and then stopped. The air in the room became fragile, still, like glass. Noland thought to himself: This is my doing. Another chit on my tab. Karma, Val had said. How large was Noland's own karmic debt? Big as a barn, he reckoned. Big as a storm cloud.

"Shit," Clive said, pressing his fingers once more to Val's neck.

Shawn stood up, the IV line still hanging from his arm. "Let's get him to the table. Now."

Clive kept his fingers there, hoping for a pulse. A minute went by. Then he tapped one of Val's still-open eyeballs, right on the pupil. No response. "Sorry, gentlemen. He's had it."

Shawn looked at him, then at Noland. He seemed to be waiting for someone to tell him what to do. What to feel. Finally, he pulled the IV from his arm. A drop of blood squirted onto the floor. He looked back down at Val, now a pale slab of flesh, a cooling coil of muscle and bone, never to rise or strike or surge again.

"That's so like him," Shawn said.

23

KIRIL SOUNDED PISSED when Noland called. Still angry, no doubt, about his sending Freddy to New York. He decided to smooth things over by paying Freddy a compliment.

"Hey. That info Freddy got. It was golden."

"Yeah? He'll be glad to hear it when he wakes up."

"He's still out?"

"He can't sleep too good on planes. His legs and all."

"Oh, right," Noland said. Then he thought to himself: *Fuck.*

"Well, when he wakes up, I need him to rig a wire for me. Something very special."

"How special?"

Noland gave him the specs. "The best part is, I need it by tomorrow."

"You're kidding," Kiril said. "I'm not even sure we can even find the components. We'll have to get them FedExed from fucking Taiwan or something."

"Whatever it takes." Noland hesitated a moment. "And there's one other thing."

"Blyat!"

"This is the last one. I promise. I'll text you an address."

"I don't have any lime."

"It's okay. Come when you can."

"All right. I'll be there."

"Good," Noland said. "Bring a tarp, though."

*   *   *

He dismissed Ben and Clive, giving the latter a handful of bills from the envelope he'd taken off Deisch. Shawn was in the backyard, alone with his thoughts. Noland dug around in the kitchen, looking for some kind of booze, but couldn't find any. There were two cold cans of Sprite, however, which he poured into dinner glasses and mixed with four airline bottles of vodka from the van. He carried the crude cocktails outside and handed one to Shawn.

"Drink this," he said. "Fast."

Shawn studied him. His expression was neither wary nor annoyed; merely blank. He took the glass.

"What's the next step?"

"We've got to bury your father."

He nodded. "Right."

"I've arranged to have a tarp brought to us, but I'd like to prep him a little better. Do you have a spare bed sheet?"

"Sure. Something with my monogram?"

"Very funny."

"I'll find something."

"Good."

"Where are you thinking we'll put him?"

"We can't be sentimental, I'm afraid. Given the circumstances."

"Aren't you being a little sentimental already? With the bedsheet, I mean?"

Instead of answering, Noland gulped his drink. The booze ran ice-cold down his throat and slammed into his stomach like acid. He dreaded the nausea that would ensue, but there was no helping it. They still had a lot to do that night—he and Shawn—and much of it would be very hard. He needed to borrow a little more madness from the demons in the alcohol. He was not quite insane enough.

As if understanding, Shawn took a sip of his drink and grimaced. "Anything else I should know?"

"Yeah," Noland said. "Your silent partner is in town."

He registered this with a mere raising of his eyebrows.

"Irenas? I bet he's pissed."

"He is. He's looking for a journal. Something Sabine created as a kind of weapon. Did you know about it?"

Shawn moved his chin in an indeterminate fashion. "Sabine was smart," he said. "I figured she'd do something like this, given her circumstances. Something to get back at us."

Noland found himself startled.

"You did?"

"Yeah."

"Why?"

Shawn raised an eyebrow in surprise. "You didn't know?"

"Know what?"

"She was dying."

Noland felt the air leave his lungs as if some cosmic fist had pressed down on his chest. When he finally spoke, the word that came out of his mouth sounded dry as a dead bird locked in a cellar. "Dying?"

Shawn nodded. "A friend of mine works at Shands, up in Gainesville. He saw her there. She was getting treatment. Immunotherapy. Experimental stuff. They only give it as a last resort."

"Did anybody else know?"

"I don't know. Not from me."

Noland looked up at the line of trees beyond the fence. A huge loblolly pine caught his eye, and he followed the trunk up to the fine, full crown, swaying in the summer breeze. Then his eyes moved on further, to the featureless sky, unusually clear, no rain clouds gathering. Without meaning to, he imagined the spirit of Sabine Werther, looking down at him from that blue void. Even in death, she was so much smarter than he was. Everything he'd done for the past week was a

consequence of her actions, her plan. She had wanted revenge
for her murdered lover, Nikki Deisch. But not just revenge.
Atonement, too. Penance for her sins, all the bad things she'd
done for the bank and her family. So many transgressions
that they could only be expiated by destroying the partners
of Selberis. And she might yet succeed.

He looked back at Shawn. "Listen, there's something Irenas doesn't know. Sabine wrote the book in code. No one can
read it unless we find the cipher."

Shawn scoffed. "How very South American of her. It's
like something out of Borges."

"Was he related to Goethe?"

Shawn tried to laugh, but all he managed was a twitch
of the chest. "Do you know what it is? The cipher I mean?"

"Another book. A novel called *The Sorrows of Young
Werther.* She gave a copy to each of the partners. So far, we've
found two. Neither of them is right. Now, I'm wondering—"

"I don't have it."

"Are you sure?"

"She never gave me any book. I'd remember."

Noland accepted this with another sigh. Inside, though,
he had the urge to laugh. Once again, Sabine had outsmarted
him. Always one step ahead. It was as if her mind contained
his mind, like a doll house resting on the floor of a library
inside a mansion.

He led Shawn back inside, through the frilly little
kitchen. "Whose place is this, anyway?" he asked.

"It was a repo. Went through probate. Nobody claimed
anything. I bought it as is."

Noland was appalled. "You mean some little old lady left
all this crap behind?"

"Shit happens."

Noland nodded. "It certainly does."

Shawn went down the hall for a moment and came
back with a bedsheet, a lacy pink number. Oh, well. It
would have to do. Noland was relieved to find it large and

thick. They laid it out flat next to Val. Then the dreaded moment came.

"You get his legs," Noland said.

"No," Shawn said. "I'll get his top."

For the second time in a week, Noland found himself groaning to lift a dead man's weight. But it was a lot easier this time. Val was lighter than Bisby, and Shawn was stronger than he looked. They placed Val gently on the sheet and wrapped him up. Noland didn't have a needle or thread, so he got some duct tape from the van and used it to secure the makeshift shroud. Val's body was still bleeding, but the flow had ebbed. It occurred to Noland that much of the blood seeping out now was probably Shawn's. Last in, first out.

They waited. After a time, Noland remembered the hard drive he'd taken from Deisch's apartment. He went out to the van and got the old PC Kiril had lent him. He had a keyboard and mouse but no monitor, so he hooked it up to Shawn's flat-screen TV, which was one of the few alterations Shawn had made to the décor. Shawn watched as Noland installed Deisch's hard drive into the PC and booted it up. Kiril had some hackerware installed on the main drive, and Noland was able to get past Deisch's password with a minimum of effort. Soon he was trawling through Deisch's browser history—the usual assortment of web content that one would expect a young man to have, the LASS bundle, as Noland's buddy in forensics had once described it: Ladies (porn), Autos (cars), Sports, and Stocks. Anything outside of those arenas was prima facie suspicious and, sure enough, Noland found a corporate website that Deisch had visited on only one occasion. It belonged to a bank in the Caymans. Noland found himself confronted with a login screen. The hairs on the back of his neck stood up as the little cursor blinked in the Account Number textbox. He tapped a key, and the account number auto-filled from the browser. That just left the password. He searched the rest of the hard drive and found nothing. No more documents. No password manager apps. Nothing.

He became aware of Shawn standing behind him.

"Is that what I think it is?"

Noland nodded. "All we need is the password."

"How do you know Deisch didn't already empty the account?"

"I'm guessing he didn't."

"Why?"

"Because he didn't leave town. Or the country, for that matter."

Noland turned off the PC. For the first time since he'd taken the case, he felt hopeless. In less than twenty-four hours, he would be forced to give the journal to Irenas. And what would Irenas do with it? Clearly, he suspected what it held. After all, he'd had it for a week in the orange grove as his boys tormented poor Sabine. The way Noland figured it, Irenas had lapsed into a moment of rage and killed her. His own impulsiveness must have freaked him out—even him— for a while because he left the shed unguarded while he and his crew went out to procure the barrels of acid. That was when Deisch must've snuck into the hut and stolen the journal, and Sabine's head. Right out from under Irenas's nose.

No wonder Irenas was so pissed.

He got up from the coffee table and wandered outside. He must have done so in a kind of trance because he was startled to find himself once again in the backyard, staring up at the same tree. It looked different now in the afternoon sun. Shadowy. Foreboding. Noland remembered what some famous painter had said—that the forest in the morning was not the same forest as in the afternoon. It was true.

He wished he had a cigarette. Then he had another wish: to talk with his dad.

As they drifted back into the house, he asked Shawn, "What day is it?"

"Monday."

Noland made a mental calculation. He could just make the tail end of visiting hours if he left immediately.

"Stay here," he said. "My friend Kiril is on his way. If he gets here before I get back, tell him I had an emergency."

* * *

Hanford Correctional sprawled over five acres on an unincorporated tract on the western edge of Seminole County. One might have mistaken it for just another concrete warehouse if not for the twelve-foot chain-link fence that ran around it, topped with razor wire. Inside the fence, a line of picnic tables had been placed, each with its own orange umbrella. The tables were only used on weekends, and only by cons with family visitation privileges. Noland would have to go inside.

He checked in quickly—no queue today—and wound his way through the cinder block maze. He went into the first unoccupied booth and regarded a fat con sitting on the other side of the glass. Noland picked up the phone and said: "Is Zeb around?"

The con nodded, covered the receiver with his palm, and yelled to his left. After a few moments, he got up and Noland's father, Zebulon Twice, slipped into his chair. Zeb had not changed markedly in the last three months since Noland had seen him. The same big man with the same flat face. And yet, diminished somehow. His father was getting that curved look of an old knife that has been sharpened so many times the metal has thinned out, almost gone. He picked up the phone. "What's shakin', Nole?"

"A lot," Noland said. "How about with you?"

He shrugged. "Been reading. Working my way through *The Killer Angels*."

"Very funny."

"I'm not kidding. It's a good book." He wriggled around in the too-small seat, which was the same size as the one Noland himself was perched on. Zeb gave him a vulpine look. "You fucked something up, didn't you?"

"Says who?"

"You never come on a weekday unless you fucked up."

"Bullshit." He sighed. "Yeah, I fucked up."

Zeb smiled. Not gloating, just relieved to be done with the formalities. "How bad?"

"Off the scale."

Zeb acknowledged this with a small nod. "Any way out?"

Noland had been dreading this question, in no small part because he'd been asking it of himself for the past twenty-four hours. "Yeah. I could cut my client loose. Take a loss on the case. Faith could probably keep me out of any serious legal jeopardy."

"So? Do it."

"The problem is—there's a heavy."

"How heavy?"

"The real deal. Gangster."

"Russian?"

"South American."

Zeb grimaced. "Yeah, you fucked up all right. Has he made you yet?"

"We had coffee yesterday."

"Shit."

"Yeah."

"Is that all?"

Noland hesitated. "The dude grabbed one of my clients. A woman. He's probably going to off her."

Zeb's gray eyes bored into him. "You've been with this woman?"

"Once. She's a good girl."

"Is she involved, or a bystander?"

"A little of both."

Zeb shook his head. "It's either-or. She's in or she's out."

"She's in."

The old man blinked so slowly that his eyelids seemed rusty, like gears on an old engine.

"Write her off."

"I can't."

"Can't? Or won't?"

At this point, Noland could no longer bring himself to meet his father's eyes. Instead, he looked down at the little Formica shelf that jutted out beneath the glass, where some unknown visitor had taken a ballpoint pen and engraved the word COCK into the otherwise smooth surface, along with a helpful illustration. A tiny act of revenge, surely, but Noland admired it.

"You always did have bad judgment," Zeb added, "when it came to womenfolk. Speaking of bad judgment, how's your momma?"

"She's okay. Her hip is fixed, but now her feet are acting up."

"She needs to lose weight."

"Yeah."

"You callin' her regular?"

"Every week or so. Not this week, though. Been busy."

"I can tell. Look at me."

Noland did so. It had been three years since he had seen his father without an intervening pane of glass, and yet he still found it hard to look him in the eye for too long. He still feared his father, even now, in a way that transcended the merely physical, almost as much as when he'd been a kid. He feared him as much as he loved him, the two emotions intertwining mysteriously, like perpendicular waves crossing each other on the surface of a pond, sometimes magnifying and sometimes canceling each other out. And so, when Noland met Zeb's eyes again, he couldn't hide anything. He didn't even try.

"What should I do, Dad?"

"Seems to me you've already made up your mind."

Noland nodded. The old man was right. No way was he going to let that asshole Irenas win this one. Unthinkable.

"Yeah."

And then, the instant Noland made this admission, Zeb's features seemed to sag, and his gray eyes, flat and hard as river

stones, shone wet. Noland knew what was going through his
father's mind. Zeb didn't know the details, but he knew what
Noland was up against. And although there was a lot the
old man could endure—almost anything, really—the idea
of his only son ending up behind bars again, or worse, was
intolerable. In such moments, Noland knew, the helpless-
ness of being inside could drive a con to kill himself—if not
directly, through suicide, then indirectly, through starvation
or sickness. Anything to escape that feeling of being frozen.
Limbless. Already dead, essentially, except for the sadness
and rage.

"You still hanging out with that crazy Russian kid?" Zeb
asked.

"Yeah. Him and his brother."

"The cripple?"

"Yeah."

Zeb shook his head. "Did he ever say he was sorry?"

"Kiril? Why would he? He was just playing the game."

Zeb raised his eyes to whatever ceiling lay on his side
of the glass—some beige plaster panels, Noland would bet;
prison ceilings were the same all over the country, perhaps
the world—and began to think. Unable to help himself,
Noland tried to read the old man's face. When Zeb leveled
his eyes at Noland again, they were dry and opaque.

"You know, I was there that night," he said.

For a split second, Noland didn't understand the words
his father had uttered. All he heard was a string of incoherent
sounds. But then their meaning became clear to him, like a
blurry picture snapping into focus, and he almost reeled.

"The hell you say. You were on duty that day. I remember."

Zeb shook his head. "I drove up in the squad car. Red-
lined the engine at a hundred and ten, all the way to Tally.
Badged one of the cops working the crowd that night. He let
me stand right on the fifty. I wanted to surprise you."

Noland trembled. The booth seemed to spin around
him.

"You never told me."

Zeb shrugged. "I saw you get clobbered. Didn't think you'd want to know."

Noland wasn't sure whether to laugh or scream. He thought of all the nights he'd played ball as a kid, from pee-wee to high school, when Zeb had promised to come and never had. Then, on the last game of Noland's career, he shows up. Another face in the crowd, unseen. Learning of it now, Noland felt as if the floor beneath him had disappeared and left him plummeting through space. He was in free fall. He wondered if anything would ever catch him. Silently, and despite himself, he began to cry.

"Well, I'm sorry it wasn't a very good game," he said.

"Don't be dumb. That's the way life is. Life will kick you in the ass."

"Yeah."

He was about to get up and leave, but Zeb spoke again.

"This pickle you've gotten yourself into—is there an upside?"

"A possible payday."

"How big?"

"Seven figures, potentially."

His eyes widened for an instant, then narrowed back into slits. "Well, that's something."

"It seemed worth the risk at the time. Now, I'm not so sure."

Zeb took another deep breath, then let it out slow. "You really think you'll go head-to-head with this greaser?"

"Probably."

He nodded, as if he had already known the answer. "Okay. I'm going to give you a phone number. Can you remember it?"

"Of course."

Zeb gave him a number in the 352 area code. "Guy named Simmons. Tell him I sent you. He'll help you out."

"How?"

He smiled. "Equipment."

Before Noland could reply, Zeb stood up and pressed his free hand against the glass. Noland did the same, matching him finger for finger. Noland's eyes started to water now.

"Come see me when it's over."

"I will."

As Noland wound his way back through the maze, he was certain that the guards were watching him on the security cameras. Zeroing in on him. He hoped they couldn't see his cheeks, which were still wet from tears.

He hit traffic on the way back to town. By the time he got back to Shawn's house, it was already night, without a single gloaming of dusk left on the horizon. He let himself back in and was shocked to find the house empty. He rushed into the living room. Val's body was gone.

He called Kiril's cell but got no answer. Not knowing what else to do, he sat there. An hour went by. Eventually, a car's high beams raked the front window. A minute later, Kiril and Shawn came inside.

"Where the fuck have you been?" Noland said.

Kiril shot him a bird. "Take a guess."

Noland was about to say something obscene, but his attention fell on Shawn. The kid looked hollowed out, eyes glassy, head hanging low. He had aged five years in the past five hours. Then Noland understood.

"St. Cloud?"

"Why not?" Kiril said. "In two days, they'll lay the slab. How much more buried can a man be?"

If Noland hadn't been so tired, he might've laughed. Or maybe not.

"Are you okay?" he asked Shawn.

Shawn nodded. "Better than a graveyard. At least there will always be people around."

"Right," Noland said.

24

T HE NEXT MORNING, he called the number his father had given him.

"Yeah?" a man answered.

"Is this Mr. Simmons?"

"Who's asking?"

"I'm a friend of Zebulon Twice."

"What do you want?"

"He said you could supply me with some equipment."

"What kind?"

"Heavy. As heavy as you've got."

"When?"

"Right away."

The man told him to be at Westside Park at eleven, then hung up before Noland could agree.

The park was the head of a rails-to-trails that ran all the way back to Orlando. Even on a Tuesday morning, the place was busy, old men on racing bikes and college kids walking dogs. Noland parked under a live oak and waited. Eleven o'clock came and went. At noon, three Harleys rumbled into the parking lot, their pistons shattering the general tranquility like a hail of gunfire. The bikers rode in a V formation, their leader a lank man in his thirties with a scruffy beard. No helmet, no sunglasses, nor any other kind of protection above his neck. Just sunburned skin. Noland got the feeling that he was probably handsome under the beard, but it was hard to tell.

The bikers stopped at the van. The leader had a big, hard plastic box riding pillion, secured with bungees. Something about the box's clasps and blunted corners seemed military in nature, despite a lack of insignias.

"You Zeb's friend?" the leader asked.

Noland nodded.

"I'm Simmons. You must be a really good friend."

"I'm his son," Noland said.

"He's a good man, your daddy."

"Thanks."

Simmons unhooked the bungees and grabbed the box. Lifting it, he grimaced. Noland got out of the van and opened the back doors. Simmons set the box inside, gingerly.

"I owed him a favor. Tell him we're even now."

"Okay."

Simmons hesitated. "I threw in something extra. Exploders. Two dozen. My own formula."

"Thanks."

Simmons nodded. He seemed on the verge of saying something else, but then got back on the bike. All three Harleys fired up again, and they rode off. The whole transaction had taken perhaps two minutes. Waiting until the roar of the bikes faded, Noland was tempted to open the box and look inside. But there was no time. Anyway, that was Kiril's area.

He drove to the copy shop. He had called earlier, and both Yevshenko brothers were expecting him. He lugged in the box—which was indeed very heavy; it might've contained an engine block—and set it on the floor of Kiril's office.

"What is it?" Kiril asked.

"Dunno."

Kiril crouched down and inspected the lid. When he finally got the clasps open, the underside of the lid was lined with foam bumps in an egg-carton pattern. After he stared into the box for a moment, his eyes grew wide. Then he looked at Noland.

"Holy shit. Who're we going up against? ISIS?"

"Can you use it?"

"I think so. I'll have to sight it first."

Noland shook his head. "No need. We don't care about accuracy. Just shock and awe."

Kiril shrugged. Noland knew that somehow, by nightfall, Kiril would find a way to sight the damned thing.

"This is going to be intense, huh?"

"Yeah," Noland said. "You want out?"

"Bez tsarya v golove."

"What's that mean?"

"Basically, it means: 'Don't be an asshole.'"

Noland nodded. "Did you give Freddy the specs for the other thing?"

"He's already done. You're gonna love it."

Noland braced himself. Even so, when Freddy rolled over, grinning in the same wolfish way Kiril had and holding a hair buzzer, he groaned. "No fucking way."

"A small patch." Freddy pointed to the back of his own skull. "No one will see."

"How small?"

"Very small. Just big enough for this." He held up something that looked like two wristwatch batteries positioned edge-to-edge with a tiny microchip, all connected by bright filament. One of the batteries was thicker than the other and had six small antennae sticking out like insect legs.

"What's the range?"

"A mile. Maybe two."

"Is that all?"

"Don't worry," Kiril said. "We'll be on you the whole time."

Noland knew better than to say anything more. He was entrusting the brothers with his life, and they were entrusting him with their freedom. He couldn't complain.

"Where do you want me to sit?"

"Over here." Freddy gestured at an office chair that Kiril had brought. Noland sat down.

"When's the Big Show?" Kiril asked.

"This evening. At six."

"Plenty of time."

* * *

At half past six, Noland was still waiting on the bench at Lake Eola. Other than the joggers and old people walking dogs, he'd seen no one. Had Irenas blown him off? Noland didn't think so. He remembered the precision with which the man had spoken in the coffee shop. He would be there, one way or the other. Noland simply had to wait.

In his head, he kept going over the instructions he'd given to the brothers before they'd dropped him off. "Once the shit hits the fan," he told them, "keep shooting for ten minutes. No more. After that, call the cops." He had given them Lieutenant Parsons's number. Parsons would, of course, call Sydney Cross, who would call Agent Bledsoe. At that point, Noland estimated that he would have perhaps thirty minutes total before whatever location he was currently at became aswarm with sheriff's deputies, OPD, SWAT, DEA, and maybe the damn Delta Force for all he knew. Which was fine by Noland. He and the brothers would be long gone by that point. Or dead.

The bench's backrest was uncomfortable, curved in just the right way to gouge his spine. He stuck out his legs and curled his toes inside his Nikes. The toes of his right foot touched the handle of the .32, Valkenburg's antique. Noland smiled to himself. He'd hollowed out the padding of his right shoe with an Exacto knife, and was relieved to discover that the tiny gun fit neatly inside, tucked into his arch. He could walk on it without a limp. Besides the gun and the transmitter—which he couldn't even feel anymore, taped flat to his skull under a carefully positioned lock of hair, reattached to

his scalp with actor's gum—his only other ace in the hole
was a thin plastic blade hidden in a fold of his jeans along the
back of the waistline. The blade would cut a military-grade
zip tie, and its tip was narrow enough to jimmy the lock on a
pair of handcuffs. It could also cut a man's throat. He hoped
he wouldn't need it, but he liked knowing it was there.

His phone rang, startling him. It was Faith. He started
to dismiss the call but then realized he wanted to hear her
voice.

"Hey," he said.

"Are you busy?"

"Nah, just sitting by the lake."

"Good. You deserve a rest. For a few minutes, anyway."

He tried to laugh.

"I've got some good news," she said. "Sydney called. He's
dropping the fraud case against Bisby."

Noland was surprised. Why had Sydney dropped the
case? Had he decided to make a gesture of good faith, in lieu
of his new deal with Noland? Or was he merely freeing up
his schedule for when the real case—the criminal indictment
against Selberis itself, involving money laundering and drugs
and murder and God knew what else—materialized? Noland
didn't know, and it didn't matter. "Well, that's nice of him.
Especially considering the dude is dead."

"Yeah, nice." A sound like gravel rubbing against a window pane crashed over the line. Ice, he knew, rattling in her
glass of lemon water. "I don't think Sydney has ever done a
nice thing in his life. Not willingly, at least."

"I doubt it."

"Did you get to him, somehow?"

"I made him a proposal, yeah."

Her voice grew wary. "What did you offer?"

"It's not important. I'll let you know if it firms up."

"Hmm." A smack came as she set the glass down on
her desk, too hard. "Whatever it is, it's not going to get you
killed, is it?"

"Course not."

"Or in jail?"

"Course not."

She sighed. "Well, at least you've got a big payday coming. If you can pull it off."

"Yep. It's what I live for."

"Bullshit."

This time he laughed. For real.

"Well, when this is all over," she said, "I'll buy you lunch. A nice lunch, this time."

"Do I get to pick the joint?"

"So long as it's not burgers. Or barbecue."

"You're on."

"Take care, Nole."

"You too, Faith."

He hung up, then turned off his phone.

The sun had begun to sink behind the trees when two dark-skinned men strolled along the sidewalk that girdled the lake. They chatted amiably in some foreign language, maybe Spanish, one of them laughing uproariously at the other's joke. Noland held his breath as they passed, and they didn't so much as glance in his direction. Still, Noland knew. The first one was big and broad. Another gorilla. The second was small, trim, and so badly shovel-toothed that his lips stuck out past his chin. They sauntered away. Noland was unsurprised when, five minutes later, they came back, stopping directly in front of him.

"How's it going, bro?" Shovel-Tooth said.

"That depends. You work for Mr. Irenas?"

"Where's the book?"

"Where's the money? And the girl?"

He shrugged. "Change of plan. The boss wants to renegotiate."

"Okay. But I want to see him."

Shovel-Tooth got out his cell phone and dialed. He exchanged a few words in the same language with whoever answered, then hung up. Noland finally realized that, for the first time in his life, he was hearing Portuguese. Shovel-Tooth waved him off the bench. "Come on, bro."

Noland stood and tried to pull on his backpack. The Gorilla stopped him. Shovel-Tooth took the pack, searched it, found the red journal, and smiled at his friend. "Good."

The three of them walked around the lake, the two men flanking Noland. He felt like he was being pulled in the wake of two ships, one large and one small. They arrived at a black Ford Expedition, with another gorilla behind the wheel. Shovel-Tooth and Gorilla 1 walked Noland over to the trees, where Shovel-Tooth proceeded to pat him down. It was a pretty good frisk, given the circumstances, the small man palpating Noland's waist, armpits, back, ankles, and balls in quick, perfunctory succession. Noland guessed that neither Shovel-Tooth nor Gorilla 1 expected to find a weapon on him—surely this American wasn't that dumb—but they were being thorough nonetheless. Shovel-Tooth found Noland's burner phone and pocketed it. Then they returned to the car, waved Noland into the back, and sat him in the middle. Gorilla 2 drove them out of the city, gliding along, careful not to run any stop signs. Noland watched the man's eyes in the rearview as he checked for a tail. If he saw one—that is, if he saw Kiril or Freddy—Noland was as good as dead. But the man's eyes looked untroubled. Everything was cool.

Soon, they were heading north on 417, past the edge of town.

Here we go, Noland thought to himself. And hoped the transmitter was working.

CHAPTER

25

THIRTY MINUTES LATER, they were in the country. Rural Seminole County. Noland remembered Sabine Werther's headless body, floating eerily in its barrel of acid, and he wondered what his chances were of ending up with an equally bad death. At least fifty-fifty, he reckoned, and took a big swallow, choking down the panic that was already rising in his gut. Shovel-Tooth glanced in his direction for a moment, then looked away.

Finally, they pulled onto a dirt road that led, not to an orange grove, but into a similarly unpopulated stretch of woods, the trees scraggly and thick with moss. They drove a full mile before reaching a plantation house set down in the middle of a neatly mowed pasture. At least it looked like a plantation house, with its veranda and fluted columns, a balcony up top, where the boss could presumably pace back and forth with his glass of Cutty Sark looking down on everyone. The kind of house Noland had always associated with dark, fetid evil. There were modern accoutrements, however; the lawn was partially shaded by satellite dishes listening to the sun, and a thick metal transformer station buzzed nearby, power cables snaking in and out. Someone had paid dearly to run electricity out to such a remote location, and their investment in privacy had paid off; Noland couldn't see another house in any direction.

It was almost night, but the place was lit nicely by a pair of antique streetlamps on either side of the cobblestone driveway. Two men came out to meet the car, Israeli-made machine pistols slung over their shoulders. Noland was hustled out of the car and up to the door, where one of the guards rang the bell. A few moments later, there followed a percussive sound of many deadbolts being thrown.

The door opened and a woman regarded them. Her evening dress hugged her hips attractively, and her hair was held in a complicated Japanese coif by two pink hair clips. She gave him a sheepish look.

"Hey, Nole," she said.

For one of the few times in his life, Noland was speechless. His initial shock at seeing her there, not just unharmed but obviously well kept, underwent a series of rapid transformations. From joy, to relief, to confusion, and finally to rage. But he recovered himself quickly, calming down. She was a survivor, after all. And smart. She had done what she had to do.

"Hey, Karen," he said.

She led them all into the house. The foyer was bigger than the average American living room, with a Victorian staircase and fifteen-foot ceilings and LED lights designed to look like candelabra. They walked past a big kitchen where a man was scraping raw vegetables into a pot and then moved on to the great room, complete with a stone hearth and built-in bookcases. Opposite the hearth was a seventy-inch flat-screen on which a soccer game was playing, the volume turned low. It was around this TV—and not the hearth—that all the furniture had been arranged: two leather couches and a matching set of overstuffed recliners. In the center of this arrangement, in front of the TV, a sturdy rocking chair had been placed facing the middle of the room.

Karen picked up a remote and muted the TV. She sat down on one of the couches and crossed her legs.

"Sorry about all this," she said.

"Me too. You decided to bet on the winning team, huh?"

"I wasn't given much of a choice."

"I believe you."

"You should sit. Victor will be down in a moment."

Noland didn't need to ask where to sit—he settled into the rocker. Shovel-Tooth came up behind him. "Be cool," he said, tapping Noland's shoulder. Noland put his hands behind his back and felt a pair of handcuffs close around his wrists, securing him to the rocker's splats. Then, almost before Noland could register the sensation, Shovel-Tooth's fingers ran themselves along the back of his waist, found what they were looking for, and slipped it out. When Shovel-Tooth walked back across the room, he was holding the plastic blade down at his side, absently. Without so much as a glance back at Noland, he sat on the lintel in front of the hearth, got out his phone, and started surfing.

Noland clenched his fists. Panic swept over him, from the tip of his scalp to the pit of his stomach, which felt as if it had congealed into a cold clot of some viscous fluid. He hadn't counted on his blade being found. That is, he hadn't counted on Shovel-Tooth. The guy knew a thing or two about taking prisoners. Would he find the transmitter next? Or the gun?

"Would you like a drink?" Karen asked. "I could bring a straw so you could sip it."

"No, thanks."

His scalp prickled. He couldn't be sure, but he thought he felt the transmitter there, pressed there against his skin. Was it getting hot? He imagined some kind of acid leaking out of the tiny battery and straight into his skull, like a scene from some horror movie. He remembered his father's face the day before, wearing its death mask of despair. Suddenly, he wished Zeb was with him. Not the Zeb he'd seen the previous day but the towering father of Noland's childhood, the chief deputy with his big shoulders stretching his dark green uniform and the heavy gun riding his hip. The man who could solve any problem, beat any bad guy. He would have shot all these dudes in ten seconds flat.

Noland took a deep breath, held it, and let it out slowly.

"I don't think I've ever seen you scared before," Karen said.

"You haven't known me that long."

"Well, I'm going to have a drink."

She went into the kitchen. When she returned, she was holding a martini in one hand and Sabine's red journal in the other. As if this weren't enough, she had a book tucked under her arm, a white paperback. Noland didn't need to see the cover to know what it was: *The Sorrows of Young Werther.* Sitting on the couch again, she laid the paperback to the side and began thumbing through the journal.

She laughed and held up the journal, open to one of the pages with the invisible ink revealed. "How did you make this show up?"

"Secret recipe," he said. "How'd you know it was there?"

"Used an infrared camera. But the writing wasn't clear. I was still hoping to get a better image, but you saved me that worry."

"Glad to hear it."

Instead of answering, she flipped through more pages. "You never found the right book to unlock it?"

"If I had, I wouldn't be here. Except, maybe, to rescue you."

She watched him. Her left eye—the lazy one—looked lower than usual.

"Well, let's see if I can figure this out." She turned her attention to the paperback.

"What makes you think you have the right version?"

Before she could answer, a man's voice boomed from somewhere to the left.

"Because if she doesn't, we're all in a big fix."

Irenas. Standing near the bottom of the big Victorian staircase. He was dressed for a dinner party, silk slacks and a blue T-shirt, all hanging perfectly on his trim, soccer-player physique. A gold bracelet glittered at his wrist. "I appreciate your coming peacefully, Noland. I told Jorge to kill you if you made a fuss."

Noland glanced at Shovel-Tooth, who didn't look up from his phone. Jorge.

"I'm glad I didn't make a fuss," Noland said.

Irenas chuckled. He sat on the couch next to Karen and laid a hand on her thigh. "Karen has been helping us unravel all this. As have you, Noland. Indirectly."

"Glad to help. What about my fifty grand?"

"Let's put first things first." He glanced at Karen. "Can you decipher it?"

"I think so."

Irenas turned back to Noland. "She's very smart, you know. It was she who found Sabine's journal. And the hidden writing."

"Oh yeah? And you know what that writing contains?"

Irenas sniffed. "In addition to the location of some damning financial records, it holds the login to the account where Sabine transferred the money that she stole."

Noland waited a beat before saying: "You mean the one in the Caymans?"

His eyes narrowed. "You know of it?"

"Obviously."

"How?"

"As you said, let's put first things first: Where's my money?"

Irenas gave him a real belly laugh this time, genuinely tickled. "You've got some balls, Noland. Are you seriously trying to negotiate?"

"Why wouldn't I?"

"For one thing, you're handcuffed to a chair. For another, if you keep pissing me off, I'll tell Jorge to break your leg. Your good leg. Not the one you broke in college."

Noland shuddered. His entire body vibrated, as if trying to free itself from the chair, the room, the house. After a moment, he swallowed hard and said, "That would hurt bad, I grant you. Even so, I mean to bargain."

Irenas's features hardened. "With what? We've got the journal."

"But you don't have the cipher. You won't be able to crack Sabine's code without it."

This time, Karen looked at him too, her glare matching that of Irenas's for sheer candlepower. "You're full of shit."

"Maybe. But I know one thing: you ain't gonna kill me until you get into that bank account. And I ain't gonna let you in. Not even if you break my leg or both of them or whatever. You can fuck right off."

Even as he said all this, he was aware of the nausea boiling in his belly, rising on the tide of terror and rage that consumed him. Did he mean all of it? Any of it? He hoped he did. Even so, he knew the place where brave words usually ended up. He'd learned that in Raiford.

Irenas clenched his jaw. Then he turned to Karen. "See what you can do."

She pursed her lips and rose from the couch. Carrying the journal and the paperback, she walked to an antique, rolltop desk that had been placed in a shadowy corner of the big room. Noland had a good line of sight on her, and he watched as she rolled up the top and got another two books from the little shelf inside.

He called out: "Those are the ones from Bisby and Redding, right?"

She didn't reply, just sat at the desk and started working, shifting her glance from a book to the journal and then back. She began writing notes on a legal pad.

"You won't crack it!" Noland yelled.

Irenas picked up the TV remote and turned up the volume. The soccer game must have been really good because even Jorge seemed interested now, putting away his phone and watching silently. The commentary was in English— BBC sports—but that didn't seem to matter to anyone. The first commentator sounded Scottish and was very excited: "This is the pinnacle, ladies and gentlemen. Both teams are playing their best, and you can see the amount of passion in the number of fouls we've seen. And SPEAKING OF WHICH, THERE GOES ANDRES TO THE TURF FROM A HIGH KICK BY MCLAREN."

"Who's playing?" Noland asked.

They ignored him. Furtively, he explored the back of the rocking chair, running his fingers down the splats to where they narrowed into dowels which ran into holes in the chair's saddle. It was around two of these that Jorge had handcuffed him. Noland wondered if he could lunge forward and snap the wood. Maybe. The problem was he had no leverage. And the rocker was robust, hewn from oak and designed for the buttocks of large, prosperous planters. Planters of what? Oranges? He hadn't seen any trees, but that didn't mean anything, the land could've been converted a hundred years ago. Now it was merely a great old house in the middle of nowhere, kind of like the one on that old TV show Zeb had used to like. The one about the rich oil family with the stern old man and the handsome son and the evil son. *Dallas*. That was the name. Where the fuck were Kiril and Freddy? Was the transmitter working?

Irenas turned to Karen, who was still at the desk. She looked back at him.

"Well?" he asked.

Her eyes grew wide with fear.

Irenas turned to Noland. "Cabrão."

Noland laughed—a shrill, high laugh that carried even over the blaring TV. "Cabrão. That's Portuguese, right?"

"You seem to have all this figured out, Noland."

"Hardly."

"Can you access the account?"

"No. But I'll be able to soon. I need more time."

Irenas's eyes bored into him. In the pause that followed, the Scottish commentator chattered on. "Yes, another foul by Real Madrid. Looks like Collins couldn't quite stop his kick before getting tangled up with Higuelos. They both took a bit of a tumble but it looks as if they'll both be okay." OH-keh.

"I think you know now," Irenas said.

Noland didn't answer. The paralysis that had gripped his stomach a few minutes earlier now spread across the rest of his body, bringing with it a partial numbness, as if all his skin and muscle and even the blood in his veins were turning into stone preemptively, a means of protecting itself from the harm that was coming. The worst part was that Noland knew he could forestall it. All he had to do was placate Irenas. Throw him a bone. Make friends with him. Some cowering part of him wanted to. Instead, he curled his toes against the handle of the .32. A lot of good it would do him, stuffed in his shoe. Maybe he could fire it with his foot, like one of those disabled people he'd seen on TV who learn how to drive a car and brush their hair using nothing but their feet. He imagined himself aiming the tip of his shoe at Irenas's chest and pulling the trigger with his toe.

Finally, he gritted his teeth and said: "You're a cabrão, too."

Irenas looked to Jorge, who went out of the room for a moment. He returned carrying a dark metal tool, something like an extra-thick pair of pliers, the main difference being that it had three tines instead of two. The middle one was offset from the others. Even as Noland finally realized what the tool was designed to do, a flash of admiration shot through him; like Noland, Jorge preferred to handcraft his special gear.

"I would have Jorge pull out your fingernails," Irenas said, "but I don't want to make a mess of my living room."

"Right."

Jorge didn't look at Noland as he stepped behind the rocker, but Noland felt the metal tines grab at the fingers of his clenched fist. He shouted something incoherent, but

Jorge didn't pause, prying at Noland's little finger until it was exposed and then closing the jaws of the pliers around it. The Scottish guy was still talking: "There's a shot from Sergio, ooh, deflected by Nargich easily. But you can see that Real Madrid is using their star lineup in the same way as they have all season, putting the two forwards Sergio and Collins slightly back and—OH MY GOODNESS, ANOTHER HIGH KICK FROM ANDRES. COLLINS GOES TO THE TURF."

Irenas raised his eyebrows so high they almost touched his hairline. "Last chance."

"That was really surprising," came another voice, a British one this time, Scottish man's sidekick. Noland heard the angry boos of the crowd, a vast bass-level murmur, a kind of collective roar of outrage. The last time he had heard it in person was thirteen years before, at Doak, directed at himself when he got tripped up with a wide receiver inside the ten yard line. The hairs on his neck still stood up when he remembered it, that sudden hurricane of anger, all of it indistinct except for that yell from the lowest rows: "FUCK YOU, TWICE. FUCK YOU, CHEATER."

Noland looked at Irenas. Irenas nodded at Jorge. And then came a new sound, curt and sharp, like a pencil snapping. And then the thunderhead of pain a microsecond later, obliterating all thought, all self, an agony that was both inside and outside, unendurable but inescapable. For the second time in his life, Noland heard a high, thin, disembodied scream, a tremulous wail that seemed to come out of nowhere and go into nowhere. As the scream gradually wound down, like a dust devil on a hot afternoon, he managed to end it with: "Fuck you, cabrão!"

Still sitting on the couch, Irenas looked sorry for himself. Like a man whose drunken wife has just tripped on the dance floor, landing on his boss.

"Tell me where the book is, Noland," he said. "Don't make me ask you nine more times."

"Cabrão cabrão cabrão cabrão!"

Irenas looked to Jorge again.

The metal teeth fastened onto the next of his fingers. Noland's heart raced so fast he became certain he would die, right there in the rocking chair. "Well, Collins is up on his feet at least," the British commentator said, and the crowd's boos turned to cheers. A spinning vertigo overwhelmed Noland as he remembered that this was, of course, a live broadcast, bounced off a satellite far up in space. Somewhere, in another country, on another continent, thousands of people were cheering a guy named Collins as he got up off the grass and jogged away, shrugging off his injury just as Noland and other boys had done for ages, since time immemorial. Noland wished he were there, on that faraway field.

The Scottish guy said: "Well, that's good news. It looks as if Collins is going to be fine." Fane.

"Okay," Irenas said. "Let's try again."

A fountain of bile rose up in Noland's throat. In a panic, he realized that he might choke on it, or—even worse—puke it up. He swallowed mightily, dreading the further humiliation, the final reduction to a puking, sweating hunk of meat. He feared this almost as much as the next broken finger. His poor fingers! How long would it take for Jorge to break the rest? Not long. Perhaps half an hour, depending on the amount of monologuing in which Irenas needed to indulge. That prick. That South American motherfucker. That woman-torturing, silk-pants-wearing fop. Noland wanted to kill him. He wanted to put a bullet in the middle of that smooth, tan forehead.

At some point, he became dimly aware of Karen standing at his side. She looked down at him with wet eyes.

"Please, Noland," she said. "Just tell him something."

"Indeed," Irenas said. "Tell me something."

Noland wanted to smile at her. He went so far as to work the muscles in his face, pulling his lips back in what he hoped was a smile, although he could tell from her startled reaction that it was probably some ghastly rictus. As he rounded his cheeks, drops of sweat beaded off them and ran down his chin. "Don't worry. It'll be okay."

"You think? How?"

And then, as if to answer her question, the first bullet arrived.

Normally, when one observes a gunshot striking something, the sound and the impact appear simultaneous. But Noland saw the effect of this bullet first, a micro-explosion in one of the oak columns that held up the staircase. The bullet reduced the column's shaft to a mass of pulp before traveling on, effortlessly, to the wall, where it exited leaving a silver dollar–sized hole. The entire house trembled from the shock of it—that one slug—as if the impact had penetrated the very spine of the structure. Then, at last, came the sonic boom, bursting in the room like a private thunderclap, an explosion of sound in Noland's eardrums. Before anyone could move or even shout, another sound came, a crash of water against the front of the house like some impossible rogue wave. And then came the second sonic boom. Noland thought: What the fuck? Then he understood: the second slug had taken out one of the guards on the veranda. Cavitation from the round had burst him like a melon.

Karen screamed. Noland didn't look at her. He was watching Irenas on the couch, still seated, his eyes wide with terror. For the first time, he seemed unsure of what to do, not knowing if he should run or hit the floor or start shouting orders.

Another splash of water. Another boom. Guard #2 was gone.

Another boom. The lights went out. Then the TV exploded in a volcano of broken glass, peppering the skin of Noland's arm. He lunged forward to his feet, lifting the rocker off the floor with his back, the handcuffs biting into his wrists. *You should have broken my leg*, he thought to himself as he ran backward, driving the rocker into Jorge and pinning him to the wall. He shoved the chair as hard as he could, maybe as hard as he had ever done anything in his life. A short, muffled cry issued from the spot where Jorge's head must have been, simultaneous with a sound of wood cracking. The rocker broke into pieces. Noland rotated his hips and freed himself of it, but the motion caused him to fall to the floor. Fortunately, he found Jorge already there, languishing. Noland's knee found itself pressed into the small of the man's back. He managed to get up on both knees and worked the right one up to Jorge's neck, where he put all his weight. As he did so, his hands shifted behind his back, and his broken finger conducted a white-hot filament of pain into his nervous system, so bad that he screamed. But he kept pressing down on Jorge's neck, focusing all his weight there until he heard the vertebra snap like a fresh sapling. Noland fell over again.

From nowhere, a slender hand gripped his arm.

"What the hell is happening!" It was Karen. He could smell her fear in the dark, a florid, rank smell like that of rotting Camellias.

"I need your hair clip!" he shouted.

"What?"

"Give me your fucking hair clip. Put it in my hand."

He thought he'd have to yell at her again, but a moment later something pressed into his palm. He opened the clip and felt the tip of the metal clasp. It was just the right size. And so, there in the dark, with slugs from the monstrous gun ripping through the house every few seconds, he picked the lock on the handcuffs and slipped them off. Then he nudged Karen's side.

"Stay down."

Crouching, he touched the wall and followed it, walking along until he came to the hearth. Then, steadying himself with one hand, he reached into his right shoe and found the pistol, its narrow handle vanishing into his grip like a toy. He held it out in front of him as he left the wall and made his way out into the room. His eyes had adjusted to the darkness, and he could see well enough to search for Irenas. The man wasn't on the couch, so Noland moved forward. He wasn't afraid anymore. A strange calm had settled over him. Cloaked in darkness, alone and desperate, he felt suddenly powerful. A bat in his natural element, he had the advantage now. All doubt had fallen away, replaced by a crystalline certainty. He knew what he had to do.

Another boom. Noland felt a jet of air as the slug split the air of the room, passing a few inches from his head. The house shook. Noland ignored it. He saw Irenas. The man was almost in the foyer, holding a pistol now, a big automatic up near his cheek as he watched the front door. He was correct to watch it because a moment later came the relatively curt but still deafening retort of a magnum revolver, then the snap of broken metal. Someone was shooting out the door's locks from the outside. Irenas yelled something to one of his men—Gorilla 1—who responded by spraying the door with machine-pistol fire, a glissando of dynamite pops that barely registered on Noland's already deadened ears. In the middle of that fusillade, Noland walked up behind Irenas, put the muzzle of the .32 to his head, and pulled the trigger.

Irenas dropped like a bag of sand. Noland walked on into the foyer. Gorilla 1 hadn't noticed him—he was too busy working the machine pistol. It must have been a solace to the man, at this point, to have some answer to the giant, dreadful gun that had been tearing the house apart. As he fired the pistol, the man simultaneously unleashed a stream of what Noland assumed to be Portuguese obscenities at the door, a torrent of rage and fear and—yes—defiance. Gorilla 1 had some balls. Noland admired him. He put the gun to the man's head and pulled the trigger. The man dropped. The house went quiet. Impossibly so. Nothing stirred.

"Bro?" he yelled through the door.

Someone shouted. "That you, Nole?"

"It's me, damn it!"

He unfastened the last remaining deadbolt and opened the door. Kiril was standing on the porch, pointing a gun at Noland's face. Even in the gloom, Noland recognized the gun. It was his Ruger.

"Fuck!" Noland said. "I told you to hit the road."

"It's only been five minutes. Anyway, how could I leave you alone here?"

Noland was about to yell again, but then a more troubling thought occurred to him. "Who's been working the gun?"

"Who do you think? Freddy!"

Kiril turned on a flashlight and began waving it around the foyer. Noland let him pass and stepped outside the house for a moment. Flanking the door were two large, dark splashes of what appeared to be black ink, along with a few expressionistic swirls of white bone and shiny pink fragments of internal organs. Freddy had taken out the guards with such precision that very little remained of them, the bulk of their bodies strewn somewhere in the lawn. Noland went back inside. He heard Kiril clearing the rest of the house—an occasional yell, then a retort from the Ruger. Noland made his way into the living room.

"Karen!"

"Over here!" she said.

She was crouching near the hearth. For one brief moment, Noland considered leaving her there. She had betrayed him, after all. Him and all the others. But no. He couldn't leave her, if for no other reason than that her presence in the house did not fit the narrative that he was weaving for the cops who would soon arrive. Noland pulled her up and held her.

"I think we're okay. Just stick by me."

Kiril's flashlight reappeared, waving over them.

"Are we done?" Noland asked.

"I think so. I wasted two more guys hiding in the back. And an old lady, in a bedroom." Noland couldn't see his face, but he sounded ashamed of himself.

"Did Freddy make the call to Parsons?"

"I told him to wait until I came back."

"Okay. Gimme the flashlight."

Kiril handed it over. Noland told him to take Karen outside and head for the van. Once they were out, Noland found Jorge's body, searched it, and retrieved his burner phone, which he shoved into his pocket. Then, using the hem of his shirt, he wiped the .32 clean and dropped it on the floor. Finally, with nothing left to do but escape, he lost all willpower and ran headlong out of the house. Bursts of light pierced the darkness, sparks shooting off the destroyed transformer box, filling the air with smoke and ozone. By the time he caught up to Kiril and Karen, they were across the field, almost to the point where the dirt road rounded a bend of trees. They kept running, Kiril leading them now. Finally, they reached the van. Freddy was in his chair, waiting patiently by the tree stump where, presumably, he'd set up the big gun. Noland couldn't be sure because Freddy had already broken it down and stashed it in its crate.

"I can't lift it," Freddy said.

Noland grabbed the crate, forgetting about his broken finger. He screamed again.

"You hurt?" Kiril asked.

"I'm fine." He threw the crate into the back of the van. Freddy was right behind him, already grinning as Kiril lifted him in, chair and all. Noland handed him his burner phone. "Make the call."

Karen went into the back too. Noland had barely climbed into the passenger seat when Kiril started the engine and hit the gas. They jounced over bumps and boulders all the way back to the highway, a journey of one mile that nonetheless seemed to take hours. When they finally hit the blacktop, Kiril floored the gas pedal, the engine roaring as if in triumph. They had gone perhaps twenty miles when a military helicopter thupp-thupp-thupped overhead, flying in the opposite direction.

"Here comes the cavalry," Kiril said.

"Yeah."

Noland imagined Agent Bledsoe riding in the helicopter, his muscular legs hanging out the side like a Vietnam-era gunner. As improbable as the image was, it made Noland laugh. Fuck you, cheater. He was still chuckling as he leaned his head against the window and passed out.

26

WHEN KIRIL WOKE him, they had arrived at Noland's house. Noland led them inside, and they took showers in turn (Freddy took a bath, needing some assistance getting in and out of the tub). Per Noland's instructions, each of them had brought a clean set of clothes, and Noland burned the dirties in his firepit, including their belts and shoes. Karen—who was following orders but otherwise seemed lost in a kind of daze—put on some old clothes that Deirdre had left when she moved out: lumpy sweatpants, a faded T-shirt, and a ragged pair of flip-flops.

By midnight, they had inspected themselves and the van and had found no traces of blood or other incriminating evidence. That afternoon, Noland had purchased a new set of tires—a brand he never used—and he and Kiril busied themselves swapping them out. That left the guns, the big one and also the Ruger. When Kiril took off in his car with Freddy, Noland called Faith. She answered on the fifth ring.

"It's one in the morning, Noland. What do you want?"

"Three guesses."

A long pause. "Another meeting?"

"Bingo."

"No fucking way."

"Set it up. At your office again. It's gotta happen in the next few hours."

"All of them?"

"I've already got Karen, so just Shawn and Redding. And when you call Shawn, tell him to come early. He needs to bring something from his house."

He gave her the rest of the instructions, then hung up. As he did so, he spotted Karen standing in the doorway of his office. She looked pretty good, all things considered, even in old clothes.

"You okay?" he asked.

"I've been better."

"Me too."

"What's the plan?"

"You and the other surviving members of Selberis are meeting at four AM."

"Why?"

"To settle up. Can you get access to your escrow account from my laptop?"

She nodded, even as she wrinkled her brow. "But aren't there still some matters outstanding?"

"There are. Come on. I need to take you somewhere."

"Can't we grab a couple of hours' sleep?"

He shook his head. "This has to be done now."

Her face blanched. For the second time that night, he saw fear in her eyes. But she didn't say anything. She came along as he went out to the van with his laptop under his arm.

The van was perhaps the last place on earth Noland wanted to be at the moment, and yet there he was, again, driving out into the night. About halfway to Kissimmee, he took a side road that led into the fields. Karen kept her eyes resolutely on the road as they wound their way deeper into the woods. She wanted to ask where they were going, Noland was sure, but didn't bother. In a way, she already knew.

Soon, the trees gave way to a huge expanse of darkness. Karen looked at him.

"Get out," he said.

She did so. Noland followed, his exhausted legs tense again, ready to bound after her if she made a run for it. But she didn't run, just shuffled forward in Deirdre's old flip-flops, the vinyl slapping softly on the thick, damp grass.

"A little farther," he said, and took her by the hand. In his other hand, he held the Ruger down at his side. Abruptly, they came up to the edge, where the ground dropped away into a chasm. Fifty feet below, the crescent moon was reflected in the water, smooth as freshly poured ink.

"Limestone quarry," Noland said. "My dad and I used to hunt here."

Karen looked down. She was less than four feet from the quarry's razor-sharp edge, after which the stone wall descended like the side of a bathtub.

"Water's ninety feet deep," Noland said. "At least, that's what I've been told."

She turned to him. Even in the darkness, her eyes shone brightly.

"Whatever you have in mind," she said, "let's get it over with."

"Fair enough." He took a step backward and raised the Ruger to eye level, aiming it at her forehead. She didn't flinch.

"When did you start working with Irenas?" he asked.

"As soon as he came to town. About two weeks ago."

Noland nodded. That sounded about right.

"The whole bit about you being kidnapped. That was all a farce, right? You've been with him the whole time?"

"Yes."

"And you were there in the orange grove. When he chopped up Sabine."

"Yes," she said. "Although I didn't see that coming, exactly."

"But you knew they were going to kill her."

"Yes."

Noland paused. He had expected her to be crying by this point. Or begging for her life. But her eyes remained steady. Then, to his amazement, he found that he was the frightened one. The Ruger's barrel quavered slightly in his trembling hand. Why was he so scared? Killing her should be easy by this point, given what he'd been through. One pull of the trigger and it would be over. She'd probably fall straight into the water. He wouldn't even have to touch her body.

"How did you know?" she asked.

"I knew Deisch stole the journal. Which meant he had to know where it was. And who had he been following for the last few weeks?"

She nodded in the gloom. "Of course."

"Why'd you do it?" he asked. "Why'd you let them torture your friend?"

"You know the answer."

"Tell me anyway."

"The oldest reason there is: I didn't want to be next. I wanted to live. I wanted to make something of my shitty life, before it's too late."

Despite the situation, her words struck him as crass, and yet they went straight into him. Straight into the deepest corner of his heart. He recognized the truth of them. After all, they were true for him, too. He had killed three men that night, and committed many other crimes in his past, all for the same reasons. He wanted to make something of himself, of his shitty life. Before it was too late.

"COO of a Fortune 500, right?" he asked.

She tried to smile, but couldn't quite manage it. "Anyway," she went on, "Sabine was dead the moment she stole the money. And even before that, she was dying. Did you know?"

"Yeah. Cancer."

She nodded. "And you're wrong to think that I was a total coward. I didn't tell Irenas about Val and Shawn. I bet you didn't know that Val is Shawn's father."

Noland took a breath. Despite himself, he was surprised. "I did know, actually. But I'm wondering how you did."

"Sabine told me, long ago. I don't know how she knew, but she did. And I didn't tell anyone. Not even the other partners. So, what do you say to that?"

Noland swallowed a clot of spit. It felt like a golf ball going down his throat. The Ruger trembled even more. He kept thinking of what his father would do in the same circumstances. But of course, Noland knew what old Zeb would do: He'd pull the trigger. Tie off the loose end. Kill the only living witness to what he and his friends had done.

Noland made his decision.

He twisted his hip, cocked his arm back, and threw the Ruger high into the air. He would've sworn he saw it flash in the moonlight, the dark metal catching a beam for an instant before plummeting down into the quarry. A distant splash of water marked its passing.

"Like I told you," he said. "Ninety feet deep."

She didn't move.

"Why?" she asked.

"I'm not sure, exactly. I like you, for one thing. You're smart. And tough. And brave, in your own way. But what it really comes down to is you're still my client."

He fetched the crate that held the big gun and lugged it over to the edge. It made a much bigger splash.

Karen still hadn't moved.

"You coming?" he asked as he headed back to the van.

She held still a moment longer, then followed.

* * *

They walked into Faith's conference room at straight-up four AM—another hellish hour, appropriate to the task. Once again, Faith had recused herself, while the partners were gathered at the table, sitting in the same configuration. This time, however, there was no arrogance, no trace of hauteur in their faces. They looked exhausted and scared. Even Redding's sharp blue eyes looked empty, vacant, like piss holes in the sand. The only exception was Shawn. Ironically, he still had a bit of spunk about him, sitting with his arms crossed and wearing a determined—if weary—expression. He'd grown up a lot in the last three days.

Looking at him, Noland asked: "Do you have it?"

Shawn reached under the table, pulled out a book, and handed it to Noland. *The Early Poems of Wallace Stevens.* Noland opened it to the table of contents, found the poem he wanted, and flipped to it.

Take from the dresser of deal,
Lacking the three glass knobs, that sheet
On which she embroidered fantails once
And spread it so as to cover her face.
If her horny feet protrude, they come
To show how cold she is, and dumb.
Let the lamp affix its beam.
The only emperor is the emperor of ice-cream.

Noland nodded to himself. Valkenburg said it was a poem about time, about aging. But that was only half right. It was about death. Even Noland could see that. Valkenburg had felt death approaching for a long time. Dreading its proximity. Sabine too. And, in some ways, Noland himself, although he hadn't realized it until recently.

He closed the book and set up his laptop on the table in front of Karen. He had already brought up the hi-def scans of Sabine's red journal, the encoded pages. "Here is the journal, and here is the key." He handed her the book.

Her mouth fell open. "Are you—?"

"Yes. She gave it to Val, and Val gave it to Shawn. Check it."

She got to work. As she did so, Noland stood at the head of the table, in the same spot as before. "So, this is where we're at," he announced. "Sabine Werther is dead. Arthur Valkenburg is dead. Victor Irenas is dead."

Their expressions didn't change at first. They were like dogs confronting some unusual animal, not sure how they should react. Fight, or flee? But then, once the enormity of the information had sunk in, they passed around a frightened glance. All except Karen, of course. She knew the details already.

"At this very moment," he said, "a house in the country is crawling with federal agents, who will no doubt be looking into Irenas's business affairs. Don't panic. Unless I'm very wrong, they will soon announce to the press that they have 'taken out' a major drug lord. Faith will keep you free of their clutches. You need to get on with your lives now. It's imperative that you don't try to flee or change your public profile in any way."

A long silence ensued. He wasn't sure if it signaled confusion, disbelief, or simple numbness.

Redding spoke first. "What about the money, Noland? You were supposed to find the money."

Noland looked at Karen. She nodded.

"The money is found," he said. "Assuming the amount you told me—fourteen million—is correct, you should be in good shape. Karen is going to transfer four million to a private account of your choosing. The rest has to stay in the Caymans, I'm afraid."

Shawn grimaced. "Why?"

"Isn't it obvious?"

They stared at him. Eventually, Karen said: "So the feds can recover it."

Redding's eyes bulged in their sockets, like gray mushrooms blossoming after a rain shower. "You mean . . . we're engaging in . . . actual bribery?"

Noland laughed. "You can't be angry. I mean, Irenas was going to take all of it. Not to mention kill you."

He directed Karen to the website of the bank in the Caymans. Redding rolled his chair over and gave Karen the information for another offshore account—a more traditional one, this time, in Switzerland no less. Twenty minutes later, the four million was transferred out, and the ten million left behind. Karen closed the laptop.

"I guess that's it," she said.

"I guess so." He turned to the group again. "I hope all of you will remember me the next time you need a private investigator."

One by one, they rose and filed out of the room, none of them looking in his direction. Soon, only Karen was left. She regarded him with an expression of profound ambivalence, poised somewhere between anger and gratitude. Finally, she rose too.

"Good luck, Nole. I'd rather not see you again."

"I understand. Good luck to you too, Karen."

After she was gone, he lingered for a moment. Finally, he left the room and went by Faith's office, but she was gone too. He drove home in a sort of out-of-body state, alert but numb. Back at the house, he thought he might try to sleep but knew he wouldn't be able. Not yet. Instead, he sat on his back porch and watched the sunrise over the loblolly hammock, its rays eventually reaching the edge of his empty yard.

Not long after dawn, Faith sent him a text.

—Escrow cleared. You're rich.

He stared at the message for a long time, trying to figure out how it made him feel. He decided it didn't make him feel anything at all, really.

He texted back.

—Great! Thanks for letting me know!
—What are you going to do with the $$$?
—Not sure. I could buy you lunch today.
—You're kidding.
—Nope.
—Rain check. I'm really tired. Also I have a lot of prep to do before the fallout hits.
—Okay. Rain check.

She emailed him the escrow information. He used it to transfer the money into his own shell account—in the Caymans, as fate would have it. The irony got him thinking: He needed a way to launder the dough.

He called the copy shop.

"Is it put to bed?" Kiril asked.

"Mostly. Still waiting on a call."

"Okay. Did you get paid?"

"Yeah, I'm flush. You're getting seventy-five K. Freddy's getting fifty. Also, I want to trade you. Thirty percent of the copy shop for thirty percent of Ultima Fortuna."

"Serious?"

"Serious. You're now my junior partner."

"Okay. What about Fyodor?"

"Freddy gets five percent. Hopefully, he won't feel ripped off."

"Are you kidding? He hasn't stopped smiling since last night. Smoking those goons was like therapy."

"I'm glad he found it cathartic."

His other line beeped, and he switched over. The male voice that answered was so voluminous and crazed that it made his phone speaker buzz like an amp in some acid-rock concert.

"Noland!"

"Syd! How's it going?"

"Shut up. We've got nine dead bodies at a house in Haskerville."

"Anybody I know?"

"You know exactly who we found, asshole."

"Calm down."

"This wasn't the deal, Nole. You know what I'm talking about. I wanted a LIVE FUCKING PERP!"

"Why?" Noland asked. "So you could flip him? Or spend three years bringing him to trial? No, Syd. All you really wanted was the win. Which you will have, once the newspaper articles come out. Now you can run for governor in a few years. Right?"

"Fuck you."

"No, fuck you, Syd. You were never going to take him alive. Believe me, it's better this way. I'd wager that Bledsoe has already concocted a tale of how his crack agents surrounded the house and took out the evil drug lord after a deadly firefight. All you need is for the county coroner to play ball, which I'm sure he'll do if you convince him that a continuing undercover operation is at stake. Or something along those lines. Right?"

Sydney scoffed. But his tone was a bit humbler when he finally said: "The story just went to the press."

"Excellent. So, he gets the credit for killing the bad guy. And you get the credit for recovering the money."

The anger in Syd's voice transformed instantly into hope. "You found it?"

"No, you found it. What did you get at the house?"

A full minute went by before Sydney sighed massively into the receiver, causing a different but equally tortured sound to conduct itself into Noland's ear. "We found a pistol," he said. "Small caliber. Won't get the ballistics for a few days, but I'm guessing it will match the one that killed Bisby."

"Good job."

"Shut the fuck up. We also found a book. A journal or a diary or something. Written in code. The FBI guys are working on it."

"I'm sure they'll figure it out."

"Oh, you're sure, are you?"

"I am."

In the silence that followed, Noland could almost hear the blood pulsing through Sydney's temples. He got the distinct impression that Sydney was struggling to formulate the precise words for his next statement, despite having rehearsed them mentally for hours.

"Noland, I swear. If you were at that house last night—."

"Hey," Noland said. "You like poetry?"

"What?"

"Poetry. Guy named Wallace Stevens. You should check him out. You got a pen? I'm going to give you the title of a book by him. One of my favorites. But you gotta get the exact right edition. Okay?"

* * *

Around ten o'clock, he drove to his favorite Jewish-Korean deli and bought four bagels—one for himself, one for Cassy, and one each for Quick and Silver. Then he drove to Cassy's place. Kiril had splinted his finger for him, but it still hurt like hell. Even so, Noland felt a strange lightness in his chest. He didn't recognize the feeling for a moment, until he realized that it was hope.

The Honda was still parked in the drive, but no one answered the door when he rang the bell. No barking, either. He walked around the back. The horses were grazing in the corral, unperturbed, but the big Dodge Ram was gone.

He got out his phone and called her number. When she finally answered, the signal was fuzzy, as if she were on the tenuous edge of the cell tower's range.

"Hey," he said.

"Hey."

"Where are you?"

"I'm on the road."

"Where?"

"Right now? Tennessee."

A sudden exhalation escaped his lips, as if he'd been kicked in the gut. Was she joking? She must be joking.

"Tennessee? Are you serious?"

"Yes. I've gone on a walkabout."

For one dizzying, vertiginous instant, he was at a loss for words. Had she really gone to Tennessee?

"You have the dogs?" he asked eventually.

"Yeah. I hope that's okay. They're my bodyguards."

"Well," he said. "Sure. I guess it's okay. I just didn't expect—"

"I know. It was an impulse decision. I needed to get away for a while."

A lump formed in his throat. So large that he was afraid to speak again, fearing he might actually croak the words out like an old frog. Even so, he said: "When are you coming back?"

"Not sure."

This was the answer he'd expected, of course. Dreaded. A cold panic started in his stomach and began to spread. Was she crazy? How could she leave? Now? When everything was settled? When everything was perfect?

He decided to reason with her. To change her mind.

"What about your horses? Your school?"

"My old partner is back in town. She's going to take over for a month or so."

The hiss of static got louder. He could almost feel the distance growing between them, expanding, an invisible thread stretching thinner and thinner with every moment.

"Cassy," he said at last. "I thought we might, you know, pick things up."

He waited for her next passive rebuttal. Her next excuse. But when she spoke again, her tone was sharp and matter-of-fact.

"Did you get Selberis's money?"

"Yeah, but what has that got to do—"

"You killed people, didn't you?"

It was not a question.

"What are you talking about?"

"That was the only way this could end," she said. "You had to kill somebody. Or maybe several somebodies."

At last, he registered what she was getting at. Suddenly angry, he gripped the phone. "How the fuck can you ask me a question like that. After what you've seen?"

"Did you kill Val?" she asked.

"Of course not."

"You're lying."

"No, I'm not. I don't know where he is. But I'm sure he's okay."

He felt his words sail out over the line, and he awaited the sound of their impact. More than anything, he feared she would hang up on him. What would he do then?

"I'm sorry," she said. "I don't believe you. Either way, I've had enough. Enough of lies and murder and death. I'm done. Do you understand?"

He didn't answer. Even over the static, he could hear the thrumming of the Ram's engine—a big, robust hunk of metal, which would carry her as far as she wished. To Canada, maybe. Alaska. The Arctic Circle.

"Will you call me when you get back?" he asked.

"I don't know."

He tried to think of what he would say next, what form his plea should take. But he came up empty. He stood there, the hot phone pressed to his ear, listening to the thrumming and the static. The weaker the sounds became, the more he strained to hear them. Their diminution reminded him of something from his past. From football. The sudden hush of the crowd when the QB launched the ball, and everyone watched it spinning downfield, arcing its way toward the receiver and the safety—two boys running together, motions synchronized like dancers—and everyone waiting, waiting, to see how the play would end, whether in elation or shock, triumph or failure.

And because no one knew what would happen, they all held their breath, all eighty thousand of them.

Just as Noland did now, pressing the phone to his ear. Listening to the Ram's engine, he looked out at the trees behind Cassy's empty house. And then, already dreading the day's heat, he rose up on the balls of his feet and tried to think of his next move.

ACKNOWLEDGMENTS

I WOULD LIKE TO thank the following people:
My wife Cathy and my son Connor, for listening to my ideas and putting up with my many neurotic episodes; my incredible agent Cindy Bullard of Birch Literary; my wonderful and patient editors, Terri Bischoff and Amy Ewing; the great team at Crooked Lane, especially Rebecca Nelson and Thai Fantauzzi Perez; book cover designer Nebojsa Zoric; my first readers and friends Laura Fitzpatrick, Jean Feingold, Jim Cusick, and William Cellich; my step-mother Eileen, for supporting my writing from the beginning and introducing me to many fine writers; Colin Clifton, for being such an amazing brother, not to mention my main booster and confidant; my brother-in-law Jim Campbell and his lady love Jennifer Brueser, for being such great friends, especially in troubled times; my sister Tori Gutman and her husband Kurtis Gutman for the same; my sister-in-law Joan Reisinger-Clifton for the same; and my dear friend and critique partner Margaret Luongo, the best writer I know.